KINGDOM OF
NO TOMORROW

ALSO BY FABIENNE JOSAPHAT

Dancing in the Baron's Shadow

KINGDOM OF
NO TOMORROW

a novel by

Fabienne Josaphat

ALGONQUIN BOOKS
OF CHAPEL HILL
2024

Published by
ALGONQUIN BOOKS OF CHAPEL HILL
an imprint of Workman Publishing
a division of Hachette Book Group, Inc.
1290 Avenue of the Americas,
New York, NY 10104

The Algonquin Books of Chapel Hill name and logo are registered trademarks of
Hachette Book Group, Inc.

Printed in the United States of America.
Design by Steve Godwin.

This is a work of fiction. While, as in all fiction, the literary perceptions and insights are based
on experience, all names, characters, places, and incidents either are products of the author's
imagination or are used fictitiously.

The publisher is not responsible for websites (or their content) that are not owned
by the publisher.

Library of Congress Cataloging-in-Publication Data

Names: Josaphat, Fabienne, author.
Title: The kingdom of no tomorrow / a novel by Fabienne Josaphat.
Description: First edition. | Chapel Hill, North Carolina :
Algonquin Books of Chapel Hill, 2024. |
Identifiers: LCCN 2024027918 (print) | LCCN 2024027919 (ebook) |
ISBN 9781643755885 (hardcover) | ISBN 9781643755915 (ebook)
Subjects: LCGFT: Novels.
Classification: LCC PS3610.O6656 K56 2024 (print) | LCC PS3610.O6656 (ebook) |
DDC 813/.6—dc23/eng/20240708
LC record available at https://lccn.loc.gov/2024027918
LC ebook record available at https://lccn.loc.gov/2024027919

10 9 8 7 6 5 4 3 2 1
First Edition

For my father

The blood, sweat, tears, and suffering of Black people are the foundations of the wealth and power of the United States of America. We were forced to build America, and if forced to, we will tear it down. The immediate result of this destruction will be suffering and bloodshed. But the end result will be the perpetual peace for all mankind.

—HUEY P. NEWTON, *To Die for the People*

KINGDOM OF
NO TOMORROW

BOOK ONE

Oakland, California—1968

It's crazy, all women, even the very phenomenal, want at least a promise of brighter days, bright tomorrows. I have no tomorrows at all.

— GEORGE JACKSON, LETTER TO ANGELA DAVIS,
IN *Soledad Brother: The Prison Letters*

1

NETTIE HAD GROWN accustomed to the kind of darkness the human eye couldn't recognize, the kind that stared back and engulfed a person. Sometimes she could see that darkness in a house, even in broad daylight. She could see it now as Clia's old Rambler came to a stop in front of that cul-de-sac address on Hollis Street. The house was a two-story home, commensurate with the rest of its quaint middle-class Oakland neighborhood. Yet, it was different from the other homes. It stared back at Nettie. Blank, cold, uninviting.

"Is this it?" she asked.

Clia killed the engine and gazed at the house before checking her list.

"This is it alright." She shook her head. "This ain't the projects, is it?"

Clia checked herself in the mirror quickly, patting down her natural. "Come on then!" She stepped out of the Rambler and started up the driveway, her heels clicking on the pavement. She was carrying a shoulder purse, her curves cinched in a black dress, her step, as always, determined. She never hesitated, never questioned herself, and sometimes Nettie envied that confidence. Her friend left behind a lingering spicy fragrance that she found pleasing, and Nettie breathed it in as she followed.

Something caught Nettie's eye on the front lawn. Was that trash, haphazardly scattered on the grass? Odd. None of the other homes around here were like this. In these suburbs, the homes boasted pristine lawns, large windows, and flower pots, and the California weather had been generous to the hydrangeas and the palm trees stretching along the main road. It was a change from the cramped apartments of low-income housing she and Clia were used to visiting.

Clia knocked, and Nettie shook off a piece of toilet paper stuck to the bottom of her shoe and wiped the sole of her shoe against the cement. She scrunched up her face at the smell and sight of excrement. "What on earth . . ."

Clia knocked again, and the sound drew the ire of a neighbor's dog that barked furiously, as if they'd trespassed onto his own property. Nettie hoped she hadn't ruined her platforms, and that they were clean enough to enter the house. She quickly climbed the front steps, and there, something else caught her eye: the faint outline of words that had been scribbled there on the white siding, on either side of the front door, and then erased, or scrubbed off. She looked down and noticed a bucket of soapy water, a rag floating amid the suds.

Clia saw it, too, and the two women took a step back. On the right, in large black letters, someone had washed off the word OUT. On the left, Nettie struggled to read what had been written there, at first, but she felt a prickle in her spine as she made out the remains of the word NIGGER. She saw Clia's body recoil.

"What the hell . . . ?"

They heard footsteps, and a woman's voice called out behind the door, firmly.

"Who is it?"

"Mrs. Haywood? It's Clia Brown. We're here for the sickle cell research."

The dog was still barking. Everything was quiet otherwise, no one in sight. On the other side of the house, there was nothing but a thicket of woods leading, if her sense of orientation was accurate enough, to the rushing traffic on MacArthur. The April air was crisp, with a faint fragrance of juniper and pinions.

"We agreed today was alright to come and see your son," Clia added. "Michael Haywood? Dr. Johnson sent us."

She was explaining who they were—public health students helping the doctor with his research—when finally the door opened ajar. Nettie flashed a friendly smile. She wondered what the woman would think of them standing there with their clipboards and bags, smiling back at her. Through the opening, Nettie saw darkness at first. But then two brown eyes emerged, cautiously measuring her and Clia before casting quick glances around.

"Good afternoon Mrs. Haywood," Clia said. "Remember our conversation, over the phone?"

"Yes, I remember, but listen here . . ." Mrs. Haywood's head inched out of the opening and Nettie saw more of her, a beautiful brown face with pressed, artificial curls. "I don't know if today is the right day, Sisters. Could you come back?"

"We won't even be in the way," Clia said, shaking her head. "You're last on our list today, we'll be in and out."

"Is Michael alright?" Nettie asked.

She knew the boy had sickle cell anemia, but now Nettie wondered if he had gotten sicker. Mrs. Haywood looked nervous. She opened the door and waved them in impatiently.

The drapes were all shut. Nettie's eyes adjusted to the darkness and she noticed the photographs on the walls, a small piano in the corner of the room, a living area with nicely kept furniture. The sofa was upholstered in a shiny teal fabric, and on it, Nettie saw a doll, slightly smaller than a human infant. The eyes were fixed on nothing in particular, but Nettie waited for them to move behind those heavy, unrealistic lashes. She couldn't tell if it was made of porcelain or plastic, but its brown face glimmered in the faint light of a table lamp.

"It's not a good idea to just linger on the front porch like that," Mrs. Haywood said.

"Why?" Clia narrowed her eyes. "Is everything alright, Mrs. Haywood?"

Mrs. Haywood was in her forties and had a Diahann Carroll beauty. As she spoke, she wiped her hands nervously on an apron that covered her checkered dress.

"I just . . . There's a lot I need to deal with today."

"This is for Michael," Clia said, resting a hand on her arm. "It's important, if you just let us see him. This is Antoinette, she goes to Merritt with me."

Nettie smiled, and shook Mrs. Haywood's hand. "It's just to talk to Michael," Nettie said. "Collect some data. I promise to be quick. Is he feeling up for it?"

All the other test subjects Nettie had seen were weakened by the devastating bite of sickle. Nettie still couldn't shake the image of one of the patients from a few days ago, the eyes sunken, the skin yellow and slack. Dr. Johnson's clinic saw dozens of afflicted patients on a weekly basis. It had been Nettie's idea to help him with research, to understand the growth of the disease in the community. It could be helpful as Dr. Johnson petitioned again for funding; all his efforts so far had been challenged.

"There are hundreds of other diseases and conditions out there," Dr. Johnson had mumbled, his shoulders drooping with defeat. "That's what I keep hearing, that this isn't a priority. We must prioritize ourselves."

His voice dropped and he paused, thinking about something too difficult to broach. "It's difficult to see it in the children, especially. One was too many. But two, here at my doorstep since I started practicing. Three . . . That's alarming."

Back home in Haiti, she had seen it, children with distended bellies and weakened immune systems who could not even keep their eyes open. She could write a book about it. She'd seen it when her father, a city doctor who'd retreated to the countryside, made house calls and took her along. This was how Nettie had learned about the human body, by spying on her father through door cracks when he examined patients. She'd learned about what made the body sick and what made it thrive, how to heal it not just with medicine and leaves, but also with nutrition and sunlight. Little by little, she'd move closer to the opening of the door until her father called for her. "Viens, closer. You like to watch, you might as well learn. Passe-moi le stéthoscope." She learned to hold hands with a patient, to comfort them with hope, to show compassion like her father, and now she wanted to follow in his footsteps, make him proud, and this study would be in her curriculum vitae and her applications to medical school.

Dr. Johnson had gladly accepted Nettie's proposal. This research was important work for him, but it meant a lot to her as well. This was practice for the future, and so Nettie asked Mrs. Haywood again about her son.

"Is he feeling ill? Has he been taking his medication?"

Nettie heard a set of footsteps, and a small silhouette emerged from the kitchen, a little girl. She watched her slip into the light and grab the doll from the sofa. She was probably seven at the most, with a lovely face and a large bow in the braid on top of her head. The other braids were pulled back into a bun, and there was another bow in the back, atop the nape of her neck. Something about her hairstyle was endearing. Something warm radiated in Nettie's chest. A memory, perhaps? A flash of recall of herself as a small child, once wearing bows in her hair . . . Nettie smiled at her, but the girl stared at her with empty eyes before rejoining her mother.

"Hello!" She leaned in and honeyed her voice a little. She smiled. "I'm Antoinette. My friends call me Nettie. What's your name?"

"This is Violet," Mrs. Haywood said. "Go on chile, say hello."

The little girl blinked, muttered the word. Nettie couldn't explain why, but she felt overwhelmed by a sudden sadness, the sight of this child tugging at something buried inside her years ago. Violet ran up the stairs and disappeared.

"I'm really sorry," Mrs. Haywood said.

She reached inside the pockets of her apron and pulled out a cigarette and lit it. She let herself fall against the wall and she rested there, visibly tired. She took a long drag as if seeking some elixir in it to calm her nerves. She exhaled and the smoke curled into clouds between them and it was as if a mask had fallen off her face.

"It's just . . . hell." She shook her head. "Ever since I moved here it's been one thing after another. Broken windows. Trash on my lawn. At first, I thought it was just kids, you know . . ."

She glanced at Nettie and Clia, and laughed nervously. Nettie felt a chill.

"That's what the police said, too. Just kids. But this . . ." She took another drag from her cigarette. Nettie noticed her eyes were wet, but no tears came. "Did you see what they wrote on my house?"

Nettie nodded, but she couldn't speak. What was there to say? There was a silence in the house, one that sounded louder than words.

"You know who did this?" Clia asked.

"Does it matter?" Mrs. Haywood clenched her jaw. "It doesn't matter. I don't care who did, I just want it to stop! They want to drive me out. They want me out of my home and I own this house fair and square. They can't make me leave . . . I got a sick boy on my hands!"

Nettie clutched her clipboard. This was unexpected. She'd come for one thing and suddenly found herself in an unexpected scenario. Now that they were here, it was more than just Mrs. Haywood or the house that was in danger. She was, too, and so was Clia. Whoever vandalized her home didn't want them here.

"Two weeks ago, they sat out there and pelted my house with rocks! Broke my window. I keep the curtains shut all the time. My kids can't play outside. If my husband were alive today, he would die all over again of indignation. He worked so hard for this house. And now I have to deal with this."

Nettie had heard of things like this happening in places like the South, where Dr. King was still fighting the ugliest forms of hate. This wasn't Mississippi, though. It was California. How was this possible? Clia looked around, a grave expression on her face.

"No, Mrs. Haywood, you shouldn't have to deal with this. Where is your telephone?"

Mrs. Haywood pointed to the kitchen. Clia turned to Nettie. There was a different layer of determination to her now, visible on her face as she squared her jaw.

"Why don't you go upstairs and see Michael with Mrs. Haywood? I'll make a call."

Clia and Mrs. Haywood looked at each other, and for a moment, Nettie felt left out of an exchange between them, missing the transmission of unspoken words.

"It's alright, go on," Clia said. "I'm calling for help."

MICHAEL HAYWOOD WAS in his room, sitting up in bed. He looked frail. Beyond the yellow tint in his eyes and skin, Nettie saw the glow of brown eyes, and a face that would light up any midnight sky when it wasn't contorting in pain.

"Sometimes, I feel alright," he muttered. "I do my chores, I go to school. But sometimes, I feel like I can't breathe."

"Do you feel pain sometimes?" Nettie asked. "In your extremities? Fingers? Toes?"

"Yes ma'am," the boy said. "It's how we knew I was sick."

Nettie sat on the edge of his bed. Mrs. Haywood stood by the door, watching. The room was dark, too, and Nettie was thankful for the table lamp that glowed enough to let her see what she was writing, checking off boxes. Michael had gotten screened with Dr. Johnson, who had immediately referred him to a hematologist. He was on medication, but lately, it wasn't helping. Mrs. Haywood lowered her voice as if she didn't want Michael to hear.

"Since Charles died—my husband—things just become more difficult, financially. Hematologists are expensive . . ." Nettie could feel her eyes on her, perhaps trying to read her notes. "Do you know what a blood transfusion goes for at the hospital? You seem so young."

The orange glow from the table lamp illuminated Nettie's face, and she felt her cheeks heat up. Mrs. Haywood was scrutinizing her features, judging her. Would her actual age diminish her authority here? Did this mean she couldn't work or help in any way? She was prepared to argue for herself, she supposed. She'd had to argue this with her aunt many times. Tante Mado always pleaded that a pretty girl like her should always work her charms to get what she wanted.

"You have the bone structure of a goddess," Tante Mado would say, holding her face up in the light to see her angles. "You look like your mother. You could pose for magazines, you know."

No, this would not do. This, what she was doing here, tucking her pen and clipboard away, this had more meaning. If she couldn't do this, then what point was there in even living?

"How old are you?" Mrs. Haywood asked.

Nettie looked in her eyes and smiled. "Twenty."

"That's too young to be a doctor."

Nettie explained that she wasn't yet, that this was basic practice.

Nettie and Clia visited families in housing developments, apartments, and mostly projects in the flats bearing the names of their developers in the inner arteries of Oakland. All the apartments were the more or less same in layout and in squalor. In one home, Nettie was forced to sit in a corner of the kitchen with her feet up to avoid mice from running over her. She quickly learned the price of poverty here in Oakland, and in America, by observing in each of those visits the lack of nutrition in sick patients' diets, the water that ran rust red from the tap, the small roaches crawling up the cupboards. How could people be expected to respond to treatment or heal, even, when they didn't have any real food in their refrigerator? It puzzled her that this was passing as acceptable in a country so rich and plentiful. It felt absurd, as if somehow the poor were not deserving. There was a lie here, a lie between the fabric of the two worlds. It didn't sit right.

"Still, it gives me hope that you're here. Sometimes I think about the world out there and how much it is all burning up in brimstone and fire, and sure enough, it's always the young people like you who make me believe . . ."

They walked out of Michael's room and closed the door. The hallway was quiet enough that Nettie could hear every creak of wooden planks beneath her feet. Michael needed transfusions, and it enraged her that money was what stood in the way, but she clenched her jaw. What could she do about that?

"I will talk to Dr. Johnson about it," Nettie said. "You're not alone, Mrs. Haywood."

Violet was sitting on the stairs with her doll between her legs. She was pretending to brush and comb her hair. Nettie smiled as they walked past her, but again, Violet didn't return the smile. No one in this house truly laughed, Nettie thought. It hurt to see such dreariness in children.

Clia was in the living room working on her report but put her pen down when Nettie walked in.

"How is he?" Clia asked.

"He is in pain," Nettie said. "Medicated, but he may need a transfusion."

Clia went to the window and stared out through the glass panes. The afternoon was drawing to an end, but the sky was still illuminated. There was no wind, and the palm trees were still, as if etched permanently against the sky.

"We can discuss later," Clia said, cutting her off. "Someone is here."

There was a man coming up the driveway on foot. Nettie and Mrs. Haywood had gone to the window to see who it was.

"Can I get the door, Mrs. Haywood? This is the man who came to help."

Mrs. Haywood hesitated. "Help? How do you mean?"

"Let me introduce you to him," Clia said. "You can decide for yourself if you want his help or not. I think you will."

There was a knock at the door. Nettie stood next to Mrs. Haywood, her palms clammy. She cast a glance up the stairs. Violet was still sitting there, her eyes fixed on the entrance. Clia was talking to the visitor, the door open, and they could only hear his voice, a low baritone, smooth, whispering to Clia before she whispered back. "Please come in . . ."

Clia stepped into the living room, a tall figure trailing behind her. Nettie watched him stand there in a military stance, shoulders squared, feet planted firmly on the ground. Suddenly, everything took a more distinct shape before her eyes. She understood.

The man looked at each of them in the eye. He looked to be no older than twenty-five. And what distressed her the most was how handsome he was. It wasn't something in the face, but it was in the way he carried himself. There was authority in his step and in his voice, and Nettie studied his clothes. They were impeccable. He was wearing slacks, and a buttoned-up shirt, and a black bomber jacket in black leather. His shoes were shiny, like his hair, which was thick and black, like a plume of smoke, and it served as the perfect perch for a magnificent black beret, cocked to the right.

"This here is my comrade, Melvin," Clia said. "We're in the same cadre. This is Mrs. Haywood, this is her house. And this here is my Sista Nettie."

Sista. This was what had sparked the fire between them. The word *sista* had lured Nettie into the basements of the college, and the study halls, in meetings with members of the Student Nonviolent Coordinating Committee and the Congress for Racial Equality. That word had bonded the two over class projects, visits to each other's homes, and soon Clia was helping Nettie obtain a job in the same clinic where she worked. Clia was a sista to her, but obviously to so many others who knew to show up when she called. When Melvin nodded toward her, Nettie understood that this was who Clia had called. One of those brothas. A militant. Someone who didn't come here to play games. Melvin reached out and shook Mrs. Haywood's hand.

He set something down on the sofa, a large black duffel bag Nettie hadn't noticed before. Clia explained what Mrs. Haywood told them, and then finally Mrs. Haywood cleared her throat, and went on about everything. About moving into the house two years ago, about the harassment that ensued. They were the only Black family on the block. They weren't wanted. The homeowner's association left her out of meetings and correspondence, at first, but lately, things had escalated to vandalism, threats in her mailbox.

As she talked, Melvin moved around the living room. He peeked through windows, observed where the projectile had been thrown into her window. He looked out the kitchen windows, too, ascertaining their surroundings. The more she studied him, the older he seemed to her. She noticed a mustache over his upper lip and the sideburns to match, gracefully hugging his jawline. When he moved past her to go to another window, she smelled his fragrance and it was pure soap and leather.

"I already talked to the police about this," Mrs. Haywood said, suddenly exhausted. "They said it was just kids . . ."

Melvin nodded. This time, he relaxed his stance and proceeded to remove what Nettie hadn't noticed before. Gloves. It wasn't cold out there, but she surmised he wore driving gloves, and it added a certain flair to his look.

"At first, it was always at night . . . It's always people who seem to live here, some of them are on the neighborhood association board. Now they come in larger numbers, in broad daylight, in the front of the house, in the back, throwing things into the yard, yelling things at us, like . . ."

Mrs. Haywood stumbled, looking for words. Melvin waited for her to finish, but she suddenly looked into his eyes and they stared at each other quietly until he joined his hands behind his back.

"Got tired of calling the police after a while," she said. "They don't give a damn. Don't even come when you call, and when you don't call they come and tell you to make things easier on yourself, and just move out—"

Melvin stepped away again, and this time paused by the piano, looking at the photographs on the top board. In one large frame, a veiled Mrs. Haywood clung to the arm of a handsome man with a mustache, in a white suit and bowtie, both of them cutting into a white cake. He glanced at Mrs. Haywood over his shoulder.

"You call pigs to your home and they won't come, because they're too busy throwing bricks through your window."

Mrs. Haywood froze as Melvin moved a small figurine on top of the piano, pushing it away from the edge as if to protect it from falling.

"It's just a tactic, is what that is," he said. "No different from the Klan."

"You sure know a lot about tactics . . ." Nettie was thinking the same thing as Mrs. Haywood appraised Melvin. "Where do you come from?"

"Chicago," Melvin said. "But I volunteered down in Jackson, Miss. Freedom rides."

Nettie watched Mrs. Haywood breathe in and finally surrender with a sigh.

She saw the woman's eyes go to the piano and the bench, where the glass had probably shattered and her daughter probably cried, the sharp notes breaking the peace of this house.

"Well? What do you think we should do?"

"I have to report back to headquarters," Melvin said. "Let them decide how to—"

"I already did that," Clia said. "They sent you."

"I dig it." He looked at Clia directly in the eyes, visibly unpleased with the interruption. "All the same, we have rules. We'll need backup."

"Why can't you just sit tight here yourself?" Clia shouted. "And why call for backup when we're standing right here?"

Nettie leaned in to Clia, hoping to catch her attention and remind her she didn't want to be involved. Especially if there was a potential for violence. But Clia was already balling her fists.

"I mean, you can trust a woman to handle a gun, can't you, Brother?"

The way she emphasized "Brother" made Melvin square his shoulders, squint his eyes in annoyance.

"Are you carrying?" Melvin asked.

"If I did, I wouldn't call you for backup," Clia said.

Nettie had never met a woman as bold and strong as Clia.

"I don't have time for jive." Melvin sucked his teeth and turned to Mrs. Haywood. "Where's your phone, Mrs. Haywood?"

"Why don't you give me one and see how I handle myself?" Clia said, her head bobbing defiantly. "Or are you just—"

Something crashed against the window. Mrs. Haywood let out a yelp, but it was the sharp scream of a child that jolted Nettie out of her skin. Violet was still on that step upstairs, shrieking.

Glass shattered again, the sound this time coming from the back window.

"The hell?" Clia muttered, finding Nettie's hand and squeezing it.

Mrs. Haywood ran upstairs to the children, her footsteps heavy. She was muttering something inaudible, Nettie thought a prayer. Only Melvin stood there in the shadows of the living room, unflinching. Outside, there was a revving of engines. Nettie instinctively retreated with Clia against a wall, her heart pounding. She wanted to plug her ears, make the rumble and the shouting vanish. There were voices rising now above the roar of car engines, clearly shouting intolerable obscenities.

"We told you to get out of our neighborhood! We don't want your kind around here!"

Clia cursed under her breath, and Nettie held hers. Her eyes were fixed on Melvin, his silhouette moving in slow motion toward the window. He lifted a corner of the curtain, peeked outside.

"Watch out!" Mrs. Haywood hollered. They were throwing projectiles at the house now, screaming and shouting, and Clia's nails dug into Nettie's arm, pulling her closer as if to hold her, protect her. Nettie watched Melvin come away from the window with disconcerting calm. He went to the couch and unzipped the black duffel bag, reached inside. An electrical surge ran through her as he pulled out the barrel of what she recognized, in the darkness, as a shotgun, fully assembled.

Something flew in through the window and crashed against the photographs on the piano. They fell, more glass shattering, revealing Mrs. Haywood's younger self grinning next to her husband as they sliced their wedding cake. Nettie's blood boiled as she saw a large rock dent the shiny surface of the piano. Something inside her snapped. She reached for the rock without a thought, cupped it in her own palm as she launched it like a grenade out the window, hoping to hurt whoever threw it in the first place. Still, she didn't throw it far out enough.

Melvin pumped the shotgun once. The click sent a chill down Nettie's spine, but she suddenly realized the sight of the weapon made her less afraid. Something about its presence, the assurance of its effectiveness, as well as Melvin's proximity made her hopeful. He pulled out a handgun from his jacket and walked over to them and looked at Clia, and then Nettie. Then, at Clia again.

Clia quickly took the pistol from him, inspected the chamber. It was fully loaded. She cocked it.

"You watch the back door," Melvin said. "Any motherfucker comes busting through it, you shoot 'em dead, you dig? Don't ask questions. Just kill 'em."

"Right on," Clia nodded, gleeful.

Nettie hadn't seen this look on her face before, and she wasn't sure if Clia was happy at the thought of killing or at the idea that someone, finally, had stepped up to take care of a problem. Clia inched toward the doorway to the kitchen and stood there at attention. Nettie watched Melvin again, his hand reaching for the front door handle, without hesitation. Something in the way he moved was captivating, a lack of fear as he opened the door and slid out into the shadows. Nettie went to the door. Mrs. Haywood was shouting in the background, she could hear her. "For God's sake, chile, close that door!" But she needed to see.

The sky was the color of a bruise. Purple and blue, sunlight just an after-thought as night drew in, and she watched Melvin's silhouette move down the front steps as if the hailstorm of bottles and rocks pelting in his direction were nonexistent. She mouthed for him to be careful, but he couldn't hear her. He stopped halfway down the driveway. She waited for him to say something. Anything. Instead, Melvin raised his weapon at hip level. There was no way to see very well in the dark, but that didn't matter. She knew there was no need to aim. There was a car standing in front of the gate, engine revving, and she knew what he needed to do. And he did.

The detonation was more of an explosion. It tore through the night like thunder, and Nettie's first instinct was to cover her ears. But she stood still, eyes glazed over. For a moment, she wasn't here in Mrs. Haywood's house, but in Haiti. Home. Back outside, where the dust rose and the saline smell of the surrounding marshes clung to the air, and her father's silhouette stood beside her, also pulling the trigger to demonstrate self-defense.

The screaming brought her back to the present. Voices shouted in the dark. Melvin's silhouette moved forward quickly, stealthily. He pointed the weapon at the sky this time and fired another round, and another, until all Nettie could see was the faint plumes of gunpowder smoking the air and lights shutting off at neighbors' windows. The voices that had been yelling were now shouting differently.

"Shit! Go! Go! They got guns!"

Then, there was a rendering of metal and the car took off in an awful sound, tires screeching, its blown off bumper scraping the asphalt. In the surrounding neighborhood, there was screaming, and dogs barked furiously. The neighbor's dog ran to the fence, just yards away from Melvin, growling. Melvin jumped, and on instinct, he pointed his weapon toward the dog. Not the dog! What did dogs know, other than to bark? The thing hadn't hurt anyone. She thought Melvin would shoot and she braced herself but she heard nothing. Not a sound but the barking and growling. Melvin was standing just a foot away from her now on the front steps, staring at her. Nettie dropped her hands and felt her face burn.

Melvin moved closer into the porch light. She saw a thin layer of sweat on his brow. She caught her breath as he looked in her eyes. They stood there for a brief instant, and she thought he would ask if she was okay, but he didn't. Instead, he inched even closer to her until she picked up the spicy scent of sweat on him, adrenaline rushing from his pores, and she knew he wanted to get back inside. So, she let him in, and he closed the door behind them.

2

CLIA PARKED HER car in front of the complex, and she and Nettie looked at each other. They hadn't said a single word on the road.

"I'm going to make some tea," Nettie said and sighed. The night's events were still unfolding in her mind, her pulse still racing. "Would you like some?"

"Tea? I'd like to take a look at your hand."

Nettie looked down at the small gash in her palm. She hadn't felt a thing earlier, not for a long time, until quiet fell inside Mrs. Haywood's home and Clia decided they could leave. Melvin was going to stay the night and wait for reinforcements. It wasn't until then, as Nettie and Mrs. Haywood swept up the broken glass, that she felt the wound, and she didn't know how she'd hurt herself. It was a small cut, nothing too serious. But Clia had followed Nettie to her apartment to have a closer look.

Magnolia Terraces was a simple housing block built to accommodate Merritt College's overflow enrollment, a low-income student tenement that Tante Mado frowned upon. But Nettie loved it. It was her little oasis away from the world, and away from her overbearing aunt. Clia took off her jacket, both of them moving in silence.

They'd never driven quietly like that before, except, now that Nettie thought about it, that time in April 1967, when they drove back from Stanford after Dr. King's address. They'd stayed up all night in their small motel room in Los Angeles, debating whether volunteering down South was a good idea. On the plus side, they'd be registering people to vote. But it was the Deep South, and Nettie knew it would be an uphill battle because her aunt would never approve.

"Why are you so afraid of disappointing her?" Clia had asked, sitting on the edge of her narrow bed that night. Nettie could see both their reflections in the mirror. A small fan blew hot air between them. "Everything is always about her. You don't even live under her roof. Why should she have a say?"

Nettie lowered her eyes. How could she explain to Clia the cultural weight of obligations toward her only living relative? After all, Tante Mado had saved her from death in Haiti, moved her to America, and raised her like her own. Plus, those Southern states were so far away, and the press made any place in Dixie Land sound murderous. Volunteers were disappearing, a scenario too familiar to Nettie and her aunt. After all, disappearances and pressure from an authoritarian government had driven Nettie's own father out of the capital of Haiti and into the countryside's resistance in the first place.

Clia didn't know those details. How could she feel any differently? Clia's family was scattered a little bit everywhere. Her mother had passed just like Nettie's had, but her father was wandering somewhere in Oakland or Richmond. Instead of living in the dorms, Clia lived with her cousin Theresa, and Theresa's children. Clia was her own person, free to come and go, worried about nothing and no one except her community. When they'd first met on campus, Clia was passing out flyers on behalf of the Black Student Union to protest the war, and had no problem following students down the hallways. "Did you know that Black men are disproportionately drafted to go to Vietnam, sent overseas to kill innocent people in the name of this Imperialist racist government that doesn't give a damn about them? Hell no, we won't go! Will you come with us, Sista? Will you stand with us?" A woman like that had no Tante Mado's shadow looming over her.

Clia was a woman of experience in every aspect, every facet, even in the way she now took Nettie's hand and held it over the sink to tend to it.

"It only hurts a little," Nettie whispered.

Clia made sure no glass was embedded in the cut before cleaning it, and the peroxide stung, but Nettie held her composure, just as she had when her father cleaned her scraped legs after they treaded through the sugarcane brush for house calls. She'd learned early on to tolerate the fire of doused rum over wounds. This was nothing. But she let her friend dab away before rubbing ointment against the cut. Next to Clia, Nettie felt like a girl with much to learn.

Something about her friend left Nettie feeling like she needed to work at being strong. She didn't know many people like that outside of Tante Mado, and unlike Clia, Tante Mado didn't know how to handle a handgun.

They'd kept what happened between them that night in Los Angeles a secret, the mingling of their breaths and their hands exploring each other between the sheets forever stamped on their skin, weighing heavily on their shoulders during the drive back to Oakland. Finally, Clia had broken the ice and shrugged. "What happened, last night, it doesn't bother you, right? Because it's fine . . . We don't have to make a big deal out of it."

"I'm not bothered," Nettie had said. Nettie was always standing at a crossroads. Was she gay? Did she have to write this down somewhere? She'd been with men and now a woman, and she wasn't sure that she wanted to decide. Not now, anyway. If she did, she did not know how it would be perceived or received by her aunt, or by the world, especially a world standing at the crossroads, fighting many different wars.

And anyway, in her father's folkloric practice of devotion to the ancestors and to Vaudou, there had always been room for love to flow freely between the sexes. They'd always set a table of offerings to Erzulie Dantor. In Clia, Nettie often recognized the fire of her divine mother, and she felt liberated, validated, excited even. Finally, someone who expected nothing else from her but what she was willing to give. Someone who didn't pressure her about changing herself, who didn't feel the need to turn her into a trophy, like her last boyfriend, Steve, had. If anything, that night between them had brought them closer. Nettie had doubled down in her activism alongside Clia, almost as if to prove herself. She attended meetings on campus, read more books, spent time after her night classes to chat with members of the Black Student Union. There was a palpable fire there, a need to demand respect and equal rights by doing more than just marching and protesting and sitting in, and Nettie was just as drawn to that as she was to Clia.

So nothing that had happened tonight was exactly a surprise. She knew Clia's circle was largely militant, way more reactionary than other groups. Clia had come to reject nonviolence as the months went by, and now she'd been eyeing other methods, she said, "to get to freedom."

"There," Clia said. She brought Nettie's hand to her lips and softly kissed the proximity of the wound. Her mouth was warm, slightly damp to the touch. "All better. You feel alright?"

"Thank you," Nettie said. "My head hurts. I'll put on some tea."

She pulled away gently and put the teakettle on while Clia walked out into the living room. Music blared from the other side of the wall from her neighbor Gilda's apartment. She could also smell pot burning, which meant Gilda's boyfriend, Jim, was spending the night. When she lit the stovetop, she thought she heard Gilda giggling next door.

Through the beaded curtains, she watched Clia pacing. Nettie took out the tea packets and some crackers, hoping Clia was hungry. Mrs. Haywood had wanted to feed them. But the women had to leave even as Mrs. Haywood loaded up Melvin's plate, as he offered to stay the night and keep watch.

Nettie walked through the curtain and found Clia sitting in the light of the wicker lampshade overhead, a book splayed open on her lap, the one Nettie had left on the sofa. She was reading Aimé Césaire, bit by bit. It was her favorite from the bookshelves she kept half lined with medical handbooks or textbooks.

"I don't even read French," Clia said, slowly turning the pages. She pointed to the other works on the shelves. "I guess I'm very wound up right now."

Nettie sat next to Clia, sinking into the bright yellow sofa. She removed the hairpins that held her massive braids together on both sides of her head and massaged her scalp. Her bandaged hand now throbbed with pain. Nettie let out a sigh of relief. "What a night," she said, eyes narrowed as she unbraided her hair. "I can't believe you sometimes. You've been holding out on me."

When she looked at Clia, her friend was admiring her in silence, a familiar glow in her eyes.

"Holding out?" Clia repeated.

"I didn't know you knew your way around guns."

Clia put the book down. "I don't go around saying it, but yeah, I do. I had to learn to handle myself. I always believed in self-defense. Don't you?"

Nettie nodded. Clia's free hand found hers, and she grazed Nettie's skin with a familiar affection that made Nettie nearly shiver. Clia's hair sparkled from all the sheen spray she applied before stepping out into the world. Had to maintain that "regal glow," she called it. She always said she was nicknamed after Cleopatra, who everybody knew damn well was "a Black woman," but refused to admit it. The message was drilled into them in magazines, advertisements, protest chants: *Black Is Beautiful* was now more than a slogan. It was a job that required they spend occasional weekends *working* on themselves. But it wasn't just hair and makeup; it was Nina Simone and the Four Tops, and Kathleen Cleaver on that cover of *JET,* reading about Pan-Africanism and Marxism. They loved discovering the truth together. It was more than friendship. It was sistahood. Clia showed her that she could find meaning in the political, the radical, in causes to help her own diaspora, anytime, anywhere.

"Tell me more about Melvin," Nettie said. If she closed her eyes briefly, she could still see him standing in the dark, staring into danger. "You said you two are in the same . . . cadre?"

"We are, he and I and some other brothers and sisters are organizing something new. We want to feed the children in the neighborhood before they start school. A survival program."

A fine gold chain rested against Clia's collarbone, shining against her brown skin. She exhaled and the chain shimmered, as it had that night in that hotel room, when it was just them, breathing each other in.

"Survival program?"

"Pending the revolution," Clia said. "We have to take care of our people and right now, our people have basic needs. They shouldn't want for food but they're hungry."

Which meant, Clia explained, that they could not perform in school, and could not excel, and if they could not meet expectations, they were perpetually left behind. No one was going to help, despite the studies and the research. That's where the Black Panthers were coming in with new ideas.

"Like this sickle cell research. Dr. Johnson has supported us from the beginning, to have every one of us benefit equally from this program. We have got to care for our own. We must have love for the people. No one else is going to, I promise you."

"I don't know what I can actually offer," Nettie said, pulling her hand away from Clia's. "I'm a nobody. I'm not a doctor, I'm just—maybe when I become a doctor."

Laughter from next door rolled into the living room.

"You are not a nobody!" Clia stared with that decisive, undefeated look of hers. "Don't you dare say that. You are instrumental to your people. You are looking for your purpose and I'm telling you, maybe purpose has found you. And I'm not just talking about sickle cell. I'm talking about revolution, baby. Being down for the cause."

Sure, she was down for the cause. Tante Mado didn't want to rock the boat, but Nettie wasn't going to sit by and watch people pushed into the margins. What she'd seen in Clia and in Melvin at Mrs. Haywood's was a new kind of commitment. It was as if she'd been asleep her whole life and awakened tonight to the fact that the entire country was quickly tipping over. It was becoming clear that marching and sitting in were not enough. And that was both terrifying and exciting.

"That's . . . radical," she said, thinking back to her father. "What you're demanding is to upturn everything. That kind of talk gets you hurt."

"The only acceptable change must come from radical action," Clia said. "You don't think people like Dr. King are radical? All they do is push the limits of our imagination. People down South carry guns, too, you know? It's the only way to survive in this world, Sister. You are the revolution, by default. Just look at you, your skin, your hair, the books you read . . ."

"You want me to carry a gun?" Nettie said.

"You don't have to, but why wouldn't you?"

Nettie thought about answering and what it would mean to finally open up about a past she never discussed. Clia had asked many times about her life growing up in Haiti, oceans away from here, but Nettie had painted a very broad picture: it was fine until suddenly it wasn't, and that's why she was here, and she was too young to remember much anyway.

"We all need self-defense," Clia said. "I'm not about to let anyone take my life without at least shooting back. Melvin knows. He teaches self-defense. Guns. A gun is the best tool out there to earn you safety because it doesn't require upper body strength . . . He can teach you, too."

Nettie smiled but again, said nothing. She knew how to use a gun.

"But I don't want you to have a limited idea of what we do," Clia said. "We pick up the gun because we have to defend ourselves, but we do a lot more than that. The work we do is revolution."

Nettie stirred more sugar in her cup. Outside, there were doors slammed, neighbors in motion. She heard a guitar riff and laughter became clearer. She got up and went to the window and saw Gilda step out for air. She was in one of those blouses she liked to tie up under her cleavage to let her stomach show. She stood on the patio and let her long reddish-brown hair flow down her back. Gilda liked to step out for a smoke, but Nettie thought she was really spying on others.

Nettie quickly drew the curtains shut. Gilda loved to socialize, and Nettie didn't want to be invited over tonight. She wasn't prepared for another one of those wild nights of dancing and drinking. Gilda spent long hours losing herself in a psychedelic world of acid swirls and bottomless liquor, a world that had brought Nettie nothing but trouble.

In the living room, Clia was roaming through her bag. She pulled out a folded newspaper and handed it over to Nettie. She spread it open between them, revealing a colorful illustration outlined in black of a woman carrying a rifle, her fist raised in the air. Above her, the name of the publication was typed in black letters: *The Black Panther*, Black Community News Service.

"A lot of what we do is in here," Clia said. "We educate to liberate, so start your education here in the paper."

Nettie took the paper, held it in the light. She'd seen what the media showed, seen the fear in the eyes of people who spotted them across the lawn of universities or public parks, marching in all black, proudly carrying their weapons. Unlike her aunt, Nettie wasn't afraid of them. In fact, she found them impressive in their courage to push back against the establishment and to arm themselves. Yes, they were intimidating, but there was an appeal to that. What she'd witnessed a few hours ago was that same seductive fearlessness. She liked it. A lot. She even liked the terror in others' eyes when they saw Panthers or talked about them. It gave her a thrill she couldn't explain.

"We have political education on Thursday nights. We have planning meetings down at the community center. We're testing out a breakfast program at seven."

"Seven? What about work? We start at nine."

"We'll be up cooking at six," Clia folded the paper up and set it aside. "The children are counting on it. Look, it's efficient. You'll be done right before nine and we can still make it to work. Dr. Johnson won't fault us for it."

Nettie paused, thought about what that meant. Did she even have the ability to incorporate this in her life right now, with her studying and working? And research?

Clia leaned in. "As a matter of fact, there's a rally for Brother Huey tomorrow, it's his birthday. You should come. Hear some real brothers speak. You heard of H. Rap Brown? Minister Stokely?"

Nettie quickly glanced up at Clia. Who hadn't? Nettie felt a surge of excitement and she leaned in.

"Stokely Charmichael? He's going to be there?"

"And probably Melvin, too, since you're asking about him."

Nettie chuckled nervously. There was a heat settling on her body now, burning as Clia's hand found its way to hers again, and squeezed. Clia took the newspaper from Nettie and put it aside. They sat next to each other, thigh against thigh.

"It's alright." Clia's smile was honeyed and Nettie was instantly disarmed. Clia's fingers ran down Nettie's neck, grazing her skin with the tip of her fingers, and stopping at her chest.

"You don't owe me anything," Clia whispered. "I don't own you, you like what you like. But I have to tell you . . ." Clia's lips parted in a mischievous grin. She leaned in and kissed her and the heat enveloped them both. Clia's tongue danced against her lips before she looked in her eyes. "I'm a lot prettier than Melvin."

Nettie laughed. She kissed Clia back and she let Clia push her against the sofa, finding a way to undo buckles and buttons, and clasps on her bra, and she loved feeling desired that way, even if tonight something felt different. Off balance. She didn't know what, but it felt as if the sky itself had tilted. Maybe it was the crackle of gunfire still resounding in her head. When she closed her eyes and tried to abandon herself against Clia, the night's memories scrolled by like stills from a film: that dog barking, the shattering of glass, and suddenly, the silhouette of a man with a shotgun in the dark. That last image jolted Nettie back to the real world, where Clia's mouth moved down to search for more. Nettie froze. Where had her desire from just a minute ago gone?

What had happened tonight had brought back all the despair she'd long tried to bury, six feet under, with the body of her father. Seeing Melvin in the dark with that shotgun made her think of that scar never healed, that murder gone unpunished that had changed the course of her entire life.

"What's the matter?" Clia pulled away.

Nettie shook her head, bewildered. "I . . . I don't know. I think . . ."

She suddenly wanted to weep. What was happening to her? Something was crawling up her legs and her spine, down her arms. Fear. Panic, over everything, over Clia's body pressing against hers, wanting. She thought about the events of the night and realized she still hadn't processed it all, and maybe she hadn't processed her own past either. Suddenly, she thought of Violet, young and innocent, and scarred for life.

"I'm sorry, I think . . . It's my head."

"Are you alright?" Clia raised an eyebrow, her eyes full of questions. "You want me to stay tonight? I can stay."

Nettie quickly got up and adjusted her clothes, pulling her shirt down.

"I just need to lie down and sleep."

She felt awash with guilt. She needed a minute to breathe, to think, to process this awful sense of dread wanting to overtake her. She glanced at Clia and watched her friend pat her hair down, looking into her compact mirror. She could see the disappointment and the confusion in Clia's face, although she was trying not to show it. Perhaps they should've never crossed this line. Feelings complicated everything, and sometimes she felt that, no matter how mature Clia was, no matter how many times she insisted that their trysts were just casual, there were moments when she let her guard down. Moments like tonight. And Nettie felt awful for ruining it.

"I'm sorry," she whispered. "I didn't mean to upset you."

"It's fine," Clia said, shaking her head. "Don't be sorry." She stood up and kissed Nettie tenderly. "Like I said, you don't owe me anything . . ."

Nettie suddenly felt wrecked with exhaustion. "I am a little shaken," she said. "You can't blame me for that."

"No." Clia looked at her, her eyes soft like flower petals. "I don't. And like I said, it doesn't have to be awkward between us. It's a revolution, and it's all that matters, my sister. Liberation. Let's do that."

When she walked Clia out, they kept quiet. Outside, the neighbor's music was still playing, and the city lights were on like bright yellow fireflies among the power cords overhead. The air was sweet with the scent of magnolia and gardenia blossoms. Clia paused, and turned to look at her, her face radiant. "After work tomorrow, we'll go to the auditorium," she said, beaming. "You and me. You'll see. You won't regret it."

She turned away, and then suddenly she looked like she remembered something and turned back to Nettie, her hand held out. "That'll be twenty-five cents, by the way."

"What?"

"The newspaper," Clia said. "Twenty-five cents."

Clia was not laughing. Still, Nettie chuckled, went back in for her purse, and came back out. She dropped the quarter in her friend's hand and watched her saunter down the steps, her hair catching the light on its surface. For a brief second before she disappeared in the shadows, Nettie thought she did see it burning like a bush, trapping embers in each curl.

3

NETTIE AND CLIA made their way through a thicket of bodies crowding Oakland Auditorium. Stokely Carmichael came to the podium.

"Now why is it necessary for us to talk about the survival of our people? Many of us feel . . . many of our generation feel that they're getting ready to commit genocide against us."

Dressed in a splendid African print garb, he seemed shrouded in ethereal light. Standing in its golden orb, Brother Stokely looked taller than when Nettie had seen him in newspapers and on television. Behind him, Nettie recognized H. Rap Brown seated next to another SNCC representative, James Forman, and a crew of Black Panthers in uniform. A wicker chair sat empty directly behind Stokely, Huey's chair. Everyone else had their dark glasses on, their black clothing on, and their implacable faces on.

Nettie had always been drawn to Stokely Charmichael's voice whenever she had seen him give a television interview. He commanded attention. This brother could preach. He knew the intonations and the rhythm necessary to make people listen.

"Now, many people say that's a horrible thing to say about anybody. But if it is a horrible thing to say, then we should do as brother Malcolm says: we should examine history. . . . Examine *history*."

Stokely liked to repeat the last words of his sentence two, three times, letting them bounce off his audience like an echo. His voice drowned out the whispers, the chants, the sound of women laughing. Just like that, by opening his mouth, he had organized silence. Just like that, he was taking Nettie down the road of American history, which, he said, started with genocide: the genocide of the red man, later romanticized as "cowboys and Indians." And then, the genocide of Africans, from slavery and the picking of cotton, to the genocide of Asians in Hiroshima and now in Vietnam, murdering yellow people and sending our brothers over there to do the bidding. This, Nettie understood, was about survival of all Black people, and she could see why he was such an effective orator. The entire crowd around her, all these people erupting in thunderous applause, were under his spell. Nettie was smack in the middle of body heat and rhetoric.

In the auditorium lights, everyone seemed more brilliant, more resplendent, like a gathering of gods by the hundreds, shining through their brown skin, Afros glinting like the gold of crowns. Nettie wanted to stop and admire every dress, every gravity-defying hairdo, the women's arms and ears adorned with jewelry. Mothers wrapped babies on their backs, fathers carried children on their shoulders. All of those faces were turned toward their newly minted prime minister of the Black Panther Party for Self-Defense as he talked about the White Man and his "superiority complex."

"If you do not think he's capable of wiping us out, check out the white race: wherever they have gone, they have ruled, conquered, murdered, and plagued. Whether they are the majority or the minority, they always rule!"

Nettie folded her arms on her chest to calm the thumping of her heart. She was afraid of her growing emotions around this speech, specifically because it was making sense. There was no lie there, she could not deny that, and she could see herself flying into his flame. She'd already moved a little closer to the stage.

"We have *never* spoken English correctly!" The crowd applauded this statement. "And that is because our people consciously resisted a language that did not belong to us—never did, never will. Anyhow they try to run it down our throats, we ain't going to have it! We ain't going to have it! You must understand that as a level of resistance. Anybody can speak that simple honky's language correctly. Anybody can do it. We have not done it because we have resisted . . . resisted."

His words hit Nettie somewhere inside as if someone was knocking inside her, waking her up. She'd never heard her own accent until people pointed it out and made her feel small by default of her foreignness. She remembered being scolded in Haiti for speaking the maternal language of Creole instead of French, being reminded that French was the only real, useful, and superior tongue, a shame beaten into Haitian children at a young age, the unspoken violence of colonization.

"We must begin to develop, number one—and this is the most important thing we can do as a people—we must first develop an undying love for our people. If we do not do that, we will be wiped out."

Nettie's hands joined in the clapping. She'd heard this from Clia before. Loving her people was something she was still learning to do, and Clia was teaching her this not just as a feeling, but as action. Clia knew that kind of love. She threw herself out there wholeheartedly in the community, and now she was taking Nettie along for the ride.

Stokely said the slogan should be to "put our people first." As he continued to speak, she believed it and believed him, more and more. She was part of this *our*. She was *we*. There was no more *she*, only *us*. His charisma cut into her skin, traveled deep. His words blared from the speakers hoisted up around poles of the stage, and Nettie, who was standing right underneath them, caught those words like falling rain, swallowed them like holy water. She felt them move through her body like the Holy Spirit in motion, activating a gift of light. *All power to the people.* This was a new kind of awakening, a new spiritual revival, better than scripture. This gospel was the kind to radicalize her.

"... For us, the question of community is a question of color and our people, not geography! Not land! Not land! Not land! Not geography! That is to say that we break down the concept that Black people living inside the United States are Black Americans. That's nonsense! We got brothers in Africa. We got brothers in Cuba. We got brothers in Brazil. We got brothers in Latin America. We got brothers all over the world! All over the world! All over the world! And once we begin to understand that the concept of community is simply one of our people, it don't make a difference where we are. We are with our people and, therefore, we are home."

Those last words grabbed at something beyond the heart, went to the core of her spirit. Those around her gathered, shouting, "Right on! Right on, yes!" The knocking she'd felt inside her had now stopped. A door had swung open in her mind. Now, Stokely said, it was a question of organizing our people with an African ideology.

"We're coming from a Black thing . . . from a Black thing, that's where we're coming from . . . because we can begin to pick up the threads of resistance that our ancestors laid down for us."

They'd been standing there almost an hour, and finally, Stokely was reaching the end. He read a statement by Huey P. Newton, written from behind bars. "'We are blood of the same blood and flesh of the same flesh. We do not know who is our sister, who is our brother, or where we came from. They took us from Africa, and they put thousands of miles of water between us. But they forgot: blood is thicker than water. We comin' together!'" A surge of thunder, no, applause, interrupted him. But he kept on. "'We comin' together! Blood is thicker than water. Blood is thicker than water. We are an African people with an African ideology. We are wandering in the United States. We are going to build a concept of peoplehood in this country, or there will be no country . . .'"

Nettie felt dizzy. She leaned back against a tree for balance. So, this was how it was. Everything they said and did took immeasurable passion and commitment, and if this was how Stokely spoke, then what about Huey Newton? If she cracked his brain open, what kind of food would fall out and feed the children in this new world?

She watched Stokely Charmichael wrap up by reminding them why they were here, why Huey's own mother was here: in memory of her son who still sat behind bars.

"Brother Huey P. Newton belongs to us. He is flesh of our flesh; he is blood of our blood. He may be Mrs. Newton's baby, but he's our brother. . . . We do not have to talk about what we're going to do if we're consciously preparing and consciously willing to back those who prepare. All we say: Brother Huey will be set free, *or else*."

Stokely walked off to cheers. She chimed in, applauding until he disappeared. "Or else" was cryptic, she knew it, but she had no doubt about the meaning of this threat. Or else, the revolution would consume this entire country. She knew it by his tone, and by the seriousness on all their faces. Around her, men and women were whistling and shouting. The roar of a crowd spread in waves, "Power to the People! Power to the People! Black Power!"

Nettie wandered through the crowd as if in a dream, Clia at her side. Her friend was talking, but she could barely hear a word. She couldn't wait to be alone to process what she'd heard and catch her breath. She needed to cool down from the fire she'd caught, the flames still sizzling inside. "Black is beautiful! Free Huey! Set our warrior free! Free Huey!" There was a call and response coming, at first, from a place Nettie couldn't see, but she was impressed that these men and women were keeping the beat with their hands and nothing else. They'd turned clapping into an instrument.

Nettie turned to see Clia clapping and chanting along, her eyes aglow with excitement as the Panther women marched past her. Two of them held flags and banners with leaping panthers and Free Huey slogans. The rest cradled rifles. Nettie caught her breath at the sight of these women armed to the teeth, stone-faced, dangerous. When they marched away, Nettie smiled at Clia, and Clia, with a shine in her eye, whispered, "Like I said, a beautiful thing."

The crowd had only dissipated a bit, scattering to eat, sitting in circles around drummers. The drummers kept the momentum going, playing an African beat that tugged at a chord inside Nettie. It felt like heartbreak. Each slap of the calfskin thundered in her ear like a call. She missed home, and she'd forgotten what it looked like. Here, she felt thankful for those bodies and faces that looked like hers, those distant cousins speaking a different tongue but still responding to the same conjuring.

Something Stokely said tolled in her like a bell. They took us from Africa, and they put thousands of miles of water between us, he'd said. But they forgot: blood is thicker than water. We coming together!

Later that night, driving home with Clia was a passage through a dark tunnel. She remembered little from the ride, except this new awakening, a persistent fire burning inside her. She was a wanderer in a foreign land, but blood was thicker than water, and she was drawing closer to an ancient, long-lost family that was now coming together.

EACH TIME TANTE Mado rifled through the hangers on the clothing rack, they emitted a grating sound of metal against metal that Nettie detested, recalling a memory of her aunt searching through her father's closet for clothing he could be buried in. Nettie blinked that image away. She watched her aunt pull out a slinky, silvery gown, hold it up as if to gauge its worth.

"So, tell me, how is school going? You filled out your applications for medical school?"

Nettie would have preferred a conversation over coffee, in a restaurant, but Tante Mado wasn't a big eater, and she was also very often critical of anything she didn't cook herself. Chicken breast was her biggest disappointment, as it was always poorly seasoned, and if it wasn't a Black-owned restaurant, then it was always bland, san gou. She loved shopping, however, and this department store was more of her element. Nettie's aunt liked being seen. Just walking down the sidewalks of East Oakland was a production. She lived life on an imaginary runway, modeling her stunning figure and flawless looks for the world to see, because, "You never know who's watching, you must take your chance when you can get it!" That was how she'd met her ex-husband Charles at the age of eighteen while modeling in New York City, but he'd exited her life shortly after she'd brought Nettie back with her from Haiti, unwilling to raise children, especially if they weren't his own. Tante Mado had tried hard to erase Charles from her life with a speedy divorce. *Hard.* She burned what remained of him, photos and clothes, even toiletries he'd left in her bathroom, all of it incinerated on her kitchen stove. Nettie still recalled the flames dancing in her aunt's eyes, the smell of aftershave acting as an accelerant, burning photo paper in the air, sweat beading on her aunt's forehead and arms.

"It's going fine, I guess," Nettie said, feigning interest in a black jacket with flowers printed on the shoulders, something she herself would never wear. "I'm helping Dr. Johnson with research on sickle cell. I think I can use it as part of my application."

A piano played a classical tune in the background. Nettie checked the tag on the jacket. She could barely afford a scarf or a handkerchief here, let alone an outfit. She wouldn't want to pay that kind of money for clothes anyway, she thought. Tante Mado, on the other hand, never hesitated to walk into these stores on the off chance someone would ask her out. She was divorced, she said, laughing, not dead.

Tante Mado placed the gown back on the rack and continued her search. She was always looking for a dress that would complement her skin tone and enhance her shoulders. She belonged in magazines. Nettie thought she looked like Josephine Baker, even in the way she smiled, which now happened rarely. Her teeth were bone white, brighter than city lights. Seeing her smile when she'd flown in from New York had put a young, traumatized Nettie at ease after her father's murder. That smile was still there at times, Nettie thought. If only she showed it more often. If only her aunt hadn't become hardened.

Tante Mado pulled out a pink blouse and laid it against Nettie's arm to contrast the color against her skin, all while looking in her eyes.

"Sickle cell?"

"No one's paying attention to the numbers." Nettie spoke a little louder, aware that her aunt wasn't exactly listening to those details. "Dr. Johnson's hoping our research will help change that. And he says it will look good on my application."

Tante Mado seemed to bite her tongue for a moment before adding in a hushed voice, "Tell me this isn't connected to the Black Panthers? Because Nettie, I don't want to hear about it."

Her aunt stared at her, and in her eyes, she could see the pink glow of the fabric, like small, fiery freckles. They nearly matched the rouge on her cheeks. Tante Mado placed the blouse back on the rack quietly before clearing her throat.

"I shouldn't have to explain it. We went over this, didn't we?"

Nettie's insides went cold, as if Tante Mado had dunked her into a pool full of ice water. She swallowed, fought the sensation of needles prickling through her cheeks.

"It's necessary work, the people need help. You can't tell me you want me on the sidelines because of your own . . ."

She wanted to say the word. Prejudices, or fears? But Tante Mado sucked her teeth with impatience and shot her a look to keep her voice down, but also to keep her thoughts to herself. Nettie quickly stopped herself and cast a glance around. A few shoppers were looking their way, but she was convinced they hadn't heard anything.

"It's medical work," Nettie said. "I'm not fighting, I'm helping," she added.

Nettie felt a sudden darkness cloak over her. She couldn't explain it in any other words without her aunt berating her about activism. She closed her eyes to compose herself, and when she opened them, Tante Mado had moved on to another rack.

"It's about association," Tante Mado said. "It's about fraternizing with . . . militants. Dangerous people."

"We're in a clinic, we're not dangerous people. I'm standing by this."

"Fine, do what you want." Tante Mado shrugged. "Now . . . what do you think of this?"

She held a black sequined shirt against her chest and turned to Nettie for approval.

"That's more my speed, isn't it?"

Nettie nodded while her aunt propped the dress against her arm. She felt numb. Her eyes scanned the store for an exit. Clearly, moving out of Tante Mado's hadn't been enough. Her aunt was always nitpicking every decision she made, questioning her decisions as if she were still a child. Nettie needed some air.

"Why don't you find yourself something nice? You know what you should do is come to the hair salon with me. I'm sure we can do something with that hair. Did I tell you I found a good hairdresser now, in Richmond?"

There was a lack of kindness in the way her aunt referenced her hair. Nettie paused. Her first memory of hair was arriving in America at the age of twelve and sitting between her aunt's legs as she ran a hot comb through every strand. Nettie had grown up accustomed to braids and barrettes, and her aunt had thrown all of that out the window. She'd told Nettie to hold her ears down to keep them from getting burned. "You're grown, now," she'd said. "You're a young woman, getting ready for the real world. Got to change all that hair now, become acceptable. Professional. There . . . Look in the mirror. Isn't that pretty?"

For the past couple of years, Nettie had been growing a natural, and Tante Mado looked at it as if it were a flaw. It was the hip thing to do now, all these kids being Black and proud. And Nettie did explain it to her: Black pride was not a fad. Asserting yourself in a white world was a constant struggle. But Nettie also understood her aunt's struggle. Tante Mado had been wearing wigs for years to cover her own pressed hair. She spent money to iron out every curl or undulation. It was how she fit in. She was a nurse herself, working in a hospital, and there was a code. A way of presenting oneself. Besides, how could she reasonably fit her nurse's hat on a natural?

"Every woman has a struggle with their hair," Nettie said. "I've chosen mine."

"Kisa?" Tante Mado stopped in her tracks and turned to face Nettie. "You're speaking a different language these days. Choice? Struggle? I think college is giving you too many ideas."

Tante Mado migrated to the fitting room, mumbling under her breath, something about Nettie being fresh and bold. Too bold. Nettie trailed behind with her hands buried in her pockets. She gritted her teeth. What was she, eight years old? All this time wasted accommodating her aunt's shopping and spending habits, when she could have been home studying. There were regular exams in her classes that she couldn't afford to fail. Her professor was adamant about testing the students on top of assessing their research projects, and Nettie needed those grades to mean something if she was going to even consider medical school one day.

"You have one job," Tante Mado said, squeezing into a booth with her clothes on her arm. She drew the curtain shut, and there was that sound again, metal against metal. "Study. Get your life together. I'm not saying you can't have a life. I do think a pretty girl like you should go out on a date here and there actually, but . . ."

Dates? There were dates. A few men who came and went in Nettie's life because she was looking to be distracted. She went to parties. She made more friends as she entered college, and it seemed, now that she thought about it, that men were nothing but trouble. She'd gone out to the movies with two sophomores from campus. And all these boys ever wanted to do was drive up to a dark spot and screw in the backseat. If this was dating, it was disappointing. Nettie was beginning to wonder whether something was wrong with her. Maybe she sent the wrong signals or maybe she was too naïve. And then, she met Steve.

She'd met him at one of Gilda's parties. That was her first mistake. She allowed herself a one-night stand to prove that she was in control of her body and her emotions. If she could walk away without attachments, then she could feel free. But then, she began to see Steve repeatedly. Truth be told, she liked him more than she wanted to admit. She'd never had a white lover before. He seemed genuinely interested in her and in her ideas. Maybe they could learn from each other. All the things Tante Mado tried to get her to reject, Steve seemed to embrace. At first, she extracted pleasure out of the stares when they sprawled out on the campus lawn during an anti-war concert, or a protest, as if they were defying the odds and breaking new ground. White people they spent time with called them "progressive" and "avant-garde." Black folks, on the other hand, glared until Nettie felt uncomfortable, until she wanted to crawl out of her skin. Black women snickered and whispered without restraint. And the Black men clenched their teeth, sometimes dropping comments out loud. "Ain't nothing worse than a sista sellin' out!" This sank Nettie like a ship, but she'd stuck with Steve because she genuinely liked him.

Steve talked a lot about "the man," what the man was doing to the future of this country by sending kids to war and maiming them for the sake of service to imperialism. It was impressive to watch, really, a white man rebelling against his own people's power structure. Steve, like Gilda and her boyfriend, Jim, were Students for a Democratic Society. It was nice to spend time with someone who had political concerns, until the incident occurred. One night, police cars, sirens on and lights flashing, caught up with them after leaving a party. They pulled over. Nettie's heart raced when the policeman knocked on Steve's window with his flashlight, slowly, eyes glued on her.

"License and registration, please. Step out of the vehicle, please."

It was cool outside, and she shivered when the officer proceeded to frisk her. His eyes, cold and blue, never left hers even as he rifled through her purse. Then he turned to Steve. I'm going to let you go, but not without reminding you, sir, that solicitation is a crime."

"Solicitation?" Nettie didn't understand, and she looked at Steve, but he didn't look at her. "What does that mean?"

The officer deliberately avoided looking at her and stared at Steve, urging him to clear the area, and slowly, something began to creep in her gut. A very clear, definite attempt at being shut out. Nettie was crestfallen. She had tasted shame before, but this felt different. Like a small death by humiliation. She turned to Steve, mouth ajar, waiting for him to defend her angrily. Stand up for her. There was no solicitation. She was not a prostitute. Instead, Steve grinned nervously and merely said no, it was a misunderstanding, said this was a "friend."

"You clearly took a turn into the wrong neighborhood, kid, just get out of here before we change our minds," the officer said, as if Nettie had been picked up off a seedy corner, even though they were less than two miles away from her apartment and even though she was decently dressed. He walked back to his car, and they walked back to their car, dumbstruck. Steve chuckled with relief when he started the engine. But she did not laugh. She swallowed that hard, large knot stuck in her throat.

This had been the end of them. She let him drive her home in silence, a cold silence he could not break despite his pleas and his questions. She wouldn't take his phone calls, and she refused to see him. She beat herself up over it for a long time, for deluding herself into thinking she'd been anything more than a trophy. Now that this was done, there was no time for love. There was only work, only medical school, and of course, Clia, whom she was still unsure she could fit in her life.

Her aunt was talking rapidly, throwing clothes here and there behind the curtain in the fitting room, occasionally opening the drapes for Nettie to take a peek, asking "Do you like this one?" Nettie wasn't listening anymore. Beyond the racks of clothes, something had caught her eye: a television screen playing at the register where the store clerks stood. She tried to distinguish the images playing, and she was too far to see clearly, but she could have sworn she saw the familiar face of Dr. King on there.

"There'll be plenty of time later for you to be serious about someone, have kids . . . Right?"

Nettie turned her attention to her aunt. A test. Tante Mado was always testing her without saying it, baiting to see if Nettie would bite and answer, happily, "Yes, sure, kids." She danced around her own identity that way with her aunt, who she felt was always silently scrutinizing Nettie. She never asked, never pried, but she threw little bombs in the air and waited for them to land, and maybe one day Nettie would open up, tell her about Clia.

"Oui Tantante," she said.

Her aunt's face softened. "You know what your problem is?"

Nettie could recite her aunt's next words in her head before she spoke them. She'd heard them so many times before.

"You're too much like your father. Always rebelling, doing the exact opposite of what you're told. I just want what's best for you."

Nettie watched her close the curtains and she stared, stunned. Where did this come from? They'd just curbed an argument, and now her aunt was speaking to her as if nothing had happened just a few minutes ago.

"Despite what you may believe, you matter to me. I always promised your father that I'd look after you if . . ." She caught herself. Tante Mado looked for the right words. "All I want is for you to be happy, and safe. And this means you should learn from his mistakes."

Tante Mado had always seen Antoine, Nettie's father, as someone who'd gone rogue. After all, she said, who in their right mind would trade the comforts of the city and the salary of a doctor and government official for lazy, quiet days in the countryside? He had led a comfortable and privileged urban life until Papa Doc Duvalier became president in 1957. Once Duvalier had deposed his predecessor and begun to show his teeth, Antoine had joined the opposition, a group formed of young intellectuals bent on overthrowing dictatorship. While Tante Mado made a life for herself in New York City and married, her brother and his acolytes had been sucked into a dangerous mission of taking power back by force, stocking guns for D-Day. If she couldn't save her brother, she would at least try to save that little girl of his. It was the only power she had.

Her father had treated Nettie as if she were one of his comrades and not his daughter. She'd lost her mother right after birth due to what his father said was a "placental abruption," and she had no memory of her. Of her father, there were few memories left in her mind. She could count them on the fingers of one hand. One, she carried in her like images from an old film. She wasn't sure she could see his face in it, but she could see his finger, large and brown, tracing lines in the soil, teaching the farmers potential irrigation routes for their crops. She remembered the smell of food cooking for the farmers who helped him harvest his sugarcane. The tradition of konbit always tolled in her mind, sometimes in odd, unexpected places; this collective farm work had been key, steeped in a culture of solidarity. She remembered the singing, the call and response of laborers as she circled the crops with a kanari to pour them water. She remembered her father stopping with her on top of a cliff overlooking the fields. "Konbit is the only thing that will keep us alive. They help us and we help them and we pass it on, and on. It's the way of our ancestors and we should keep it going." They took turns working each other's land, and even though he was a doctor, her father had never shied away from hard labor the way his father before him had done.

Nettie's father had also taught her about guns, how to use them in case the time came to fight again. He seemed convinced that this revolution would come sooner rather than later. She still remembered his hands on her shoulders, teaching her to square up when facing her target. Back then she was only eleven or twelve, but it became clear that there were repercussions to resistance and that the oppressor, no matter who he was, always moved to silence the oppressed.

"There are people out there who do not understand our ways," her father said. "People who want polarized power. You know what that means? Polarized power?"

These words were also engraved in her mind. Duvalier did not appreciate Antoine Boileau's ideas promoting plans for collective power, or anyone else's, for that matter. Teachers, poets, writers, thinkers, all disappeared, either murdered or incarcerated as Duvalier labeled them communists. Anyone who shared harvest and wealth on an equal footing harbored communist tendencies, and Duvalier's Tonton Macoutes enforced the elimination of those ideologues, extending their brutality throughout the countryside. Newcomers bought land, like the man who purchased property next to her father and was appointed Section Chief, parading as the overseer of the area, boasting about his power. They hated each other instantly as he began to issue threats about her father's land. It was his, he said, and he had the papers to prove it, and Nettie's father would counter with his own deed, issued by his own family. Then, the threats became more serious. Doctors, the Section Chief said, couldn't walk through these parts or those parts for home visits, they could only stay on main roads. Nettie remembered her father brushing him off. "He was sent here to intimidate us," he said. "We will not cower."

Her father taught her to hide property deeds, will and testaments, land surveys, and where to stash guns. Under the planks in the kitchen, outside in the peristyle—the house where they kept shrines and devotions to the loas and spirits—and inside the clay pots and the trunks, wrapped in Vaudou flags and bright silk scarves: guns, rifles, explosives, what her father had smuggled from friends in Cuba and the Dominican Republic to overthrow Papa Doc. All of it was hidden well, in plain sight. A day would come when they would take back the capital, her father said. He would be part of that, and they would topple the tyrant in due time.

But Duvalier's men had come for them first. Rumors said it was an anonymous tip. Others believed it started with an argument between Antoine Boileau and that Section Chief neighbor. What Nettie remembered was how, when the men came up the road, her father ordered her to hide in the sugarcane brush. This was the unfortunate memory she clung to the most, that of his hands covering her mouth.

"Don't come out, don't make a sound. Ou tande m?" She remembered her heart racing as he ushered her out the back door. "Go to our neighbor Augustine. If I don't come back for you, have her call Tante Mado in New York."

There were times at night now, in her dreams, she would revisit the green foliage in the fields swallowing her whole the way they did her ancestors, the edge of leaves cutting against her skin and her blood feeding the roots of the cane down to the earth. She squatted there and ate her pain silently while the gunshots detonated and her father drew his last breath. They dragged his body out to the front yard and left it there. She did not crawl out of the sugarcane brush until she felt her own urine trickling down her leg, hours after they were gone. This was the last memory of her father. A man of the people, lying motionless in the dirt, in a pool of his own blood. His eyes were left wide open. She saw her own reflection in them as she finally shook him. Papa! Papa! Wake up, Papa! He did not move. Nettie remembered that sudden violent vacuum of aloneness. She remembered running. Running through the bush.

Augustine, the only neighbor her father had trusted, was the one who took her in, kept her hidden in her house. She called Tante Mado in New York. Tante Mado arrived three days later, breathless and beautiful, alarmed. Tante Mado, the sister who had always warned her brother against repercussions, who had always doted on her only niece, now became Nettie's mother, her guardian, only living relative. Ever since, her aunt prioritized their survival above all.

What would she say then, if she knew Nettie had, just the day before, stood in a crowd full of revolutionary ideologues, chanting Black Power, fists to the sky? All her aunt wanted was to keep her locked up in a box, and yet that one rally in the auditorium had instantly done the opposite. Unlocked her shackles and freed her to go out and *do*.

"I worry about you all the time," Tante Mado said. "When I think of what would have happened to you if I hadn't come for you . . . Do you remember?"

She looked at Nettie, searched in her eyes for recognition of a memory.

"I do," she continued. "I remember that day, you were so scared. You didn't speak for days."

Nettie felt hot, all of a sudden, uneasy in her skin. She looked down at her shoes. She couldn't do this, revisit this memory with her aunt, and she found it cruel. This was Tante Mado's way of reminding her, all the time, what she owed her.

"I just don't want to lose you," Tante Mado said. "I swear sometimes when I think about this, it gives me an ulcer."

Nettie didn't answer. What was there to say?

Nettie rested the clothes on a rack behind the fitting room door and told her aunt she was stepping outside. She needed some fresh air now, and before Tante Mado could protest, she made her way through the endless racks of clothing. She didn't remember the store being that big, as if it was deliberately stretching and extending itself to keep her from leaving. Just when she found the exit door, someone shouted something outside the dressing room.

"Dear God! No, not Dr. King!"

Nettie turned around. What was it? The television screen was now barely visible, obstructed by the number of customers suddenly gathered in front of it, transfixed. The clerk behind the counter shook her head in dismay. Nettie ran to the television, but she already knew that something horrific had happened judging by the clear and distinct sound of gunfire, and the screaming on the television screen. She covered her mouth to muffle the sound of her own terror as the gray images unfurled before her eyes. A man was on the ground, and others rushed to his side. Other men in suits stood pointing at the building across from them, perhaps at a person vanished into the shadows after having gunned down the reverend.

4

NETTIE WAS ALREADY familiar with the Bottoms, but this was her first time stepping foot inside their community center. Children filed through the side door, some accompanied by their parents. They all wore school attire, uniforms, and were carrying books and bags, their jackets nicely buttoned up. Nettie studied the place, looking for a familiar face, but recognized no one. Clia was nowhere in sight, odd because she'd consoled Nettie over the phone for an hour, helping her move from grief to rage. There was going to be blood in the streets. The country was going to burn. Riots were already breaking out in Detroit, in Washington, DC, in Chicago, Baltimore, Louisville, state after state erupting, burning and looting. During a televised press conference the day after the Reverend died, Stokely Charmichael had warned of repercussions. "There no longer needs to be intellectual discussions, Black people know that they have to get guns." What were they supposed to do now?

The months that followed the death of Dr. King seemed to fuel an anger that could only be staved by action. Nettie saw more and more young people flocking to Clia, flocking to the Panthers, and arming themselves. The air was charged with a new kind of empowerment and Nettie tried to find her place in it, continuing her slow research with Dr. Johnson and with Clia until January rushed in, and Clia called her on the phone with a request.

"We're going to take care of *us*," Clia had said. "You'll come to our breakfast program?"

It was an act of service to others. It was what Dr. King preached about. And Nettie, still feeling empty and grief stricken, said yes. She would come.

The sun had just come up overhead, the sky a faded blue. It was still early. Could she catch the bus back if she needed to? Then her eyes landed on a flier on the back door, where some children had gone running in. It was large enough to stand out. From just a few feet away, she recognized the familiar black panther leaping out. As she approached, she caught the smell of eggs frying. Voices clamored loudly inside. People were shouting directions, and children, lots of children, were laughing and chattering. She paused in front of the flier and read it:

FREE BREAKFAST FOR CHILDREN
SERVED HERE, EVERY SCHOOL MORNING
MONDAY THROUGH FRIDAY
FROM 7 A.M. TO 9 A.M.

Nettie stood in the doorway, taking it all in. The dining hall was rather small, but every table as far as her eye could see was occupied. Little girls and boys ran past her, promptly removing their jackets upon arrival, as a woman at the entrance greeted them with a clipboard.

"Good morning, welcome, Little Sister, Little Brother, what's your name? Are you hungry? Go ahead and get yourself a seat."

Nettie watched them scramble to find empty seats around. The room buzzed with energy, small voices shouting and laughing, their spoons clanking against the rims of bowls and plates. The adults in the room were serving them. A group of men walked out of the kitchen carrying hot plates.

"We have eggs and toast here and hot cakes from the kitchen! Who wants hot cakes?"

"Me! Me! I want hot cakes!"

"No shoving, everybody gets fed! Here you go, little man. Grow big and strong on that!"

So this was it, Nettie thought. The revolution in action. All these children were on their way to school. This free breakfast was helping support families who could not feed these children in the morning, and the more Nettie thought about it, the more she felt her heart swell. Service to others. Those words tolled in her head and she held on to her bag. She stood there, unsure of what to do.

Maybe she should ask someone about Clia? She studied the comings and goings of the workers, until suddenly, a voice jolted her out of her reverie.

"Good morning, Sister! Here to volunteer?"

Nettie turned around. She looked up into those deep brown eyes, and she recognized the fullness of those eyebrows and that square, military stance that had cut through the dark of night: the man with the shotgun.

"Hi," she managed. "Yeah, I think so."

"You think so?" Melvin looked at her from head to toe, and she stiffened. "You really need to be here at six thirty. That's when volunteers report to the kitchen."

"Clia said seven. I didn't know . . . Is she . . . ?"

She lost her words. Did she ever really have them? She felt her face and ears grow hot as Melvin relaxed his stance. He was wearing jeans, she noticed, and a buttoned-up shirt that opened up at his throat. He was wearing an apron over all of it, and he wiped his hands against the canvas. She began to ask him if he remembered her from Mrs. Haywood, her heart racing a little, but he cut her off.

"I don't know where our comrade is, but I could use a hand feeding these kids. We have double the number of kids this morning, we can barely keep up. Are you down? Or are you just going to stand there and watch?"

The way he said it was almost full of reproach.

"Yeah, I'm down," she said. She could do it. This was no different than a konbit. "What do I do?"

Melvin nodded for her to follow. "Right," he said. "Come this way."

He glided through the room with so much assurance it unnerved her. He knew what he was doing, and she didn't, and now he was in charge of her for the next few hours. He swiftly walked into the kitchen, pointed out rows of plated food. There were more men in the kitchen, standing by the stove, cooking and plating, moving in an organized assembly line. All she needed to do, he said, was take the plates out to the kids and make sure they ate.

"We keep it simple," he said. "If they are still hungry and ask for seconds, give them more. Plenty to go around for everyone. No one walks out of here to sit on a school bench hungry, you dig?"

Nettie nodded, and took the plates off the counter. The food smelled delicious.

Melvin led her out into the dining hall, expertly balancing plates on his forearms. She tried to keep up with him, but when she had a moment to pause and take in the small faces of the children gleefully emptying their plates, her eyes followed Melvin through the room. She was baffled by the stark contrast of him, six feet tall and serving little children breakfast as if this was his home, as if he was the host. She could hear his chatter with the kids. "What's happening, my man? What's in that backpack? Why is it so heavy? You got homework in there?" Occasionally, he would lean in and talk to them, and they looked at him with interest. What a far cry from the armed soldier who had held down the fort at Mrs. Haywood's that night! There was something drastically disarming about it, seeing a strong man like him move about the room with both authority and kindness.

The other volunteers talked to the children about their health, encouraging them to eat and learn, and sometimes one of the women would start a cheering session as she clapped her hands.

"All power to the people! Black is beautiful!"

The children came and went. When one group left, another arrived. There was a constant flow, and in the middle of the chanting and cheering, Nettie almost forgot about Clia. There was still no sign of her when the last wave of children cleared the room and the volunteers began to clean up. It was twenty-five minutes past eight, and she looked around nervously. Not showing up was out of character for Clia.

If Nettie caught the bus now, she could make it to work in time, she supposed. If the bus came on time. She was scrambling to find her purse when she finally took note of Clia storming in, haggard. She put down her bags and wiped her brow, taking in the scene around her. Nettie waved. Clia barely smiled, and Nettie knew immediately that something was wrong. She could sense it, or see it, hanging over her friend's face like a shadow.

"Where were you?" Nettie asked. "You said to meet you here at seven. Thank God Melvin was here to—"

"I'm sorry," Clia said, breathless. "I tried to be on time. Something came up and I . . . I'm sorry."

"Everything okay?"

Clia nodded, said she was held up and then offered to help clean up.

"Won't we be late for work?" Nettie asked.

"Don't worry. Dr. Johnson knows where we are, it'll be fine."

Something about Clia still wasn't quite right, but Nettie couldn't explain what. Her friend rolled up her sleeves and quickly helped to wash dishes, put away the kitchen utensils. There were discussions in the dining area. Nettie watched Melvin sit in a circle with the other volunteers, exchanging ideas about menus and donations. What businesses and community members would offer donations? How would they collect? They were taking notes, but Clia and Nettie had to go to work.

They drove in Clia's car. The cool spring air carried with it the scent of green trees and magnolias, and Nettie took a deep breath through her open window. Clia stopped at a traffic light and pulled out a cigarette, and Nettie looked at her arms in the sunlight. She was wearing large wooden bangles stacked in different shades and designs, a trick she'd confessed she used to conceal old tracks on her arm, scars from a past life marred by needles and dope. She lit her cigarette.

"What did you think?" Clia asked. "Did it go well?"

Nettie shrugged. She could only report on the hiccups she'd observed, mainly having to do with the flow of volunteers in and out of the kitchen, bumps and awkward moments where the service needed to speed up a little.

"Yeah, but that's alright," Clia said, cigarette stuck between her lips. "That's why we do this, we run tests until we smooth out all the kinks."

Until it was all good, she explained. Then, they would feed an entire nation.

"Melvin said you're a natural," Clia said.

"Did he?"

Melvin. He'd disappeared as soon as they were done. Nettie didn't have a chance to ask him about Mrs. Haywood, what happened after she and Clia left, to ask him about himself at all.

"It was interesting to work with him," Nettie said. "He's very . . . orderly. Military, almost."

"I hear being a GI will do that do you."

"Oh . . . So, he is military?"

Clia blew her cigarette smoke out the window and nodded, a twinkle in her eye. She looked amused. Nettie looked away.

"I should have known," Nettie said. "He's interesting."

"Interesting?" Clia stepped on the gas, maneuvered around traffic. There was an air to her now, as if she was stopping herself from saying something more.

"I mean, I thought what he did back at Mrs. Haywood's was impressive," Nettie said. "But seeing him like this, it's just . . . He's like a different person."

Clia nodded quietly. After a moment, she looked at Nettie.

"It's a beautiful thing, brothers cooking, feeding children. It's got an appeal to it, doesn't it? It certainly changes your perception of things, of how things should be. Women love brothers who step up like that, I guess. . . . But there's a lot more to Melvin than what you see."

"Oh? What do you mean?"

"I mean . . ." Clia thought for a moment, then shrugged. "Nothing. Melvin is what you said . . . Interesting."

Nettie burned with questions. This was so cryptic, Nettie thought, but maybe she shouldn't show too much interest. She'd noticed Clia's silence more than anything, noticed what Clia left unsaid, and so Nettie didn't say any more.

5

CLAYTON YOUNG WAS a captain in Clia's cadre. He was in his early twenties, with a bushy goatee and stunning hazel eyes. Nettie had squeezed his hand and noticed right away that he spoke with a distinct Baton Rouge drawl.

"Martin Luther King Jr. is dead. Medgar Evers is dead. Anyone who says nonviolence is the solution is a fool and a jackass."

His political education classes, which occurred every Tuesday evening in his apartment, were an opportunity to learn about the rights of citizens, electoral power, legal rights. Clayton was incredibly effective in discussing readings: Fanon's *The Wretched of the Earth*, *The Autobiography of Malcolm X*, as well as the organization's newspaper, *The Black Panther*, which Nettie had read cover to cover. That was how she'd learned about the death of seventeen-year-old Bobby Hutton, days after Martin Luther King Jr., and about international groups struggling for freedom like the Zimbabwe Guerilla Fighters. But what drew Nettie in, and everybody else in the room, was his breakdown of the Ten-Point Program.

"You can read and analyze all the texts and dissertations amongst yourself, but *this* platform, this basic list of demands? That's got to be in your consciousness, you got to memorize that, and it's simple enough for all of us to recite. Basic. What do we want?"

Clayton knew it by heart. "We want freedom. We want power to determine the needs of our community. Full employment for our people. We want an end to the robbery by the capitalists of our Black community."

He could cite all ten points and elaborate on them without looking at the plan, and now Nettie found herself muttering under her breath trying to engrave them in her mind as well. She wiped her brow, aware of the heat in Clayton's living room. She was one of at least fifteen people sitting on couches, chairs, and floor pillows, absorbed in his lecture. Some of them, Clia had whispered in her ear, were here for good. They kept returning, committed to learning more, showing interest in belonging and taking action. Others were here for the first time, or the second. But Clia said there were people there she could tell weren't going to last. A lot of them came in angry and disappointed that they weren't actively going out to engage in a war, guns drawn. Nettie took time to watch faces, to see if she could also tell, but it was difficult for her to draw conclusions so soon. She wasn't as experienced as Clia, and besides, she was more interested in the conversation. When Clayton had started to speak, he looked in their direction. She brushed it off and tried to absorb the words. Ever since the rally, Nettie felt she was carrying words inside her, turning them over like stones with every step, trying to remember who said them and when. Because Clayton Young knew. And he was preoccupied with turning words into action.

"That's what that Ten-Point Program is about, it's applying those principles!" he said, nearly shouting into his audience. "Just like number seven: we want an immediate end to police brutality and the murder of Black people. How did we do that? We picked up our guns and told the pigs to back off, and they sure got the message. We're gonna go down that list and keep applying. We want free healthcare, those sisters over there are doing the work."

He pointed to Nettie and Clia. Nettie realized Clia had already told him, obviously. She remembered how Clia had whispered in his ear before he started, and he'd looked in Nettie's direction and nodded.

"They got a sickle cell program going on, and then we're gonna offer that free healthcare for all Black and oppressed people."

After the meeting, Nettie watched Clia encouraging those leaving to buy a newspaper. "Read the truth," she said, collecting their money. "Mainstream media shapes derogatory images of us and of Brother Huey, but we tell you what it is, what is happening in our community. Educate yourself, sistas. Twenty-five cents."

They were among the few stragglers who stayed in the living room. Clia handed Nettie a drink, whispering, "Commitment." Her purple lips were wet with root beer. She had picked out her natural and let her hair out that day. Large earrings dangled from her ears, four circles joined together in an adinkra symbol. She'd sat through the lecture quietly, showed no emotion, not even a nod or a response, and Nettie supposed it was because she'd heard it a million times before.

Every member who committed to the Party, Nettie learned, had stacks of the *Black Panther*, read it avidly, and sold it. The paper was like a portal, reporting who in the community had been imprisoned, whose death went uninvestigated, whose bail needed to be posted, and who needed legal assistance. She knew about Black American soldiers dying in Vietnam, about Cuba, and even Haiti. Her heart skipped a beat when she saw Papa Doc's name mentioned, the atrocities committed by the Tonton Macoutes in his name. Everything was written by Panthers, from a Panther revolutionary standpoint. Nettie combed through it carefully for announcements, updates on programs and demonstrations, and for letters from Huey Newton. It was the only way she could hear his voice as he addressed the world from behind bars.

When Clia turned to her, Nettie smiled. "I don't think I can sell the paper like you do, it's just not what I'm good at. At all. I don't have it in me the way you do."

"I simply don't accept that, nor do I believe it." Clayton's voice startled them both. He'd approached stealthily, his footsteps muted by his own brown shag carpeting.

"Check this out, Sister . . ." He asked for her name again, and he repeated it a few times. Then, he said, "Sister Nettie, selling the newspaper isn't the goal. Education is the goal. Therefore, focus on that. What did you recently learn in the paper by reading it? Share that with the people, teach them what you know and show them where you got that education from. Circulate to educate, you dig?"

He assessed her, examined her from her toes to the top of her head, and for a brief moment she felt uneasy. "Besides, selling newspapers will not be a problem at all for you, I can tell. Not with a face like yours."

Nettie felt her face tingle. She smiled awkwardly, looked to Clia.

"All you have to do is smile like that, and that's a paper sold," he said.

Clia shook her head, rolled her eyes. She didn't smile, which Nettie registered. Instead, she folded her arms on her chest and clenched her jaw.

Nettie could feel awkwardness growing between the three of them. Or maybe it was between just the two of them, the way Clia talked firmly while still avoiding Clayton's gaze. Instead, she was counting the money she'd made from her newspaper.

"We're going to be at the clinic this weekend, in the Panther office." Clia emphasized that last part. "Dr. Johnson needs help organizing. I think Nettie will be of great help."

"Right on," Clayton said, staring at Nettie. "I do believe so myself."

He finally turned to Clia and with one quick motion, he gestured for her to follow. He excused himself, and Clia glanced at Nettie.

"I'll be just a minute."

They disappeared into a hallway, leaving Nettie alone. She took a breath, hoping her friend would return quickly. She walked around the living room, slowly, examining the spines of books on the shelves. Clayton Young had tons of those, many on Marxism and on the Cuban Revolution. But other than books, and a few records, there wasn't much else to see.

After a few minutes of standing around waiting, she went to find Clia. They were going to walk home together, that was the plan. She turned down the hallway and froze. Clia's back was against the wall, and Clayton was very close to her, his hand pressed against the wall, forming some kind of barricade with his arm. His free hand gripped Clia's sleeve and she yanked it away. Nettie's jaw clenched. Clia finally tore herself away from him and walked down the hallway to rejoin her friend. They quietly grabbed their bags and headed out of the apartment. They walked at a fast pace, leaving the neighborhood behind, and for a while they didn't say a word. They passed rows of apartment buildings all resembling each other and rows of telephone poles aligned downhill with their wires suspended overhead.

Finally, Clia sighed and looked in her direction. "So, what do you think of it all?"

Nettie shrugged, noticing that Clia wasn't addressing what had just happened. "He's interesting," she said, careful with her words. "Has a way with words. But then again, who doesn't? Feels like the brothers can be persuasive, with guns or with words."

"Yeah, well . . ." Clia dropped her voice, almost mumbling. "He is a man. Men are predictable. You learn to work around it."

They continued walking, their heels clicking on the sidewalk. In the streets, vehicles honked and pulled to a full stop.

"All men are predictable? You think so?"

"Do I think so?" Clia glanced at her. "Shit, have you met men? Look, it's like this: these men I roll with, this organization I am in, it's full of real men. I mean, brothas who want to love the people, that's a real man to me. But, some of these brothers come in here hungry for other things, like power over things they never had power over before. Brothers like these barely last three months," Clia said. "That's how you know who's a true Panther and who isn't. And that kind of weeding out is necessary."

Overnight, Clia said, things were changing. The pigs, under the command of higher authorities, were cracking down on the Party, and this made it incredibly difficult to know who to trust. "Because of that, it's hard to be with someone who's not one of us. Relationships are even more difficult, because we can only trust each other."

Nettie shook her head as they stepped off the curb and crossed the street. A warm heat now settled over the city. Dusk was closing in. Clia rolled back the sleeves to her shirt, above her elbows, and waved at a pedestrian on the other side of the street, someone she knew. It seemed she always knew people in her neighborhood.

"So what's the story between you and Clayton?"

Clia stared back in surprise, but Nettie had to ask. They couldn't ignore what Nettie had just witnessed. There was no telling what the two were discussing. Nettie had the feeling that her friend was slipping from her fingers, and she felt silly for it because Clia did not belong to her and, as far as she knew, they weren't in a relationship.

"Is there something going on between the two of you?"

Clia looked away from her and shook her head, and Nettie knew immediately she'd made a mistake.

"There's nothing going on between Clayton and me."

Nettie nodded. She wasn't sure this was true, but she said, "Okay."

"Nothing."

Clia went quiet, as if processing information in her mind. A soft breeze blew the aroma of food cooking on stoves, floating through open windows of apartments. Nettie waited for her to gather her thoughts and speak.

"Clayton is a good brother," Clia finally said. "He's a good leader, and I . . ." She hesitated, shook her head, as if she couldn't find the right words. "I owe him."

Clia stopped and looked in Nettie's eyes as if waiting for the words to sink in. Nettie hoped to catch their meaning. She didn't want to press her. If Clia wanted to talk about her past, she had full license.

"If it wasn't for him," Clia added, picking up her pace as they came upon Lake Merritt, "I'd be dead. Just another piece of trash in these gutters. Clayton was patient with me. He helped me get clean, and he did it all through the Party. Got me involved so I cared about people outside of myself. He got me to see the truth. This Party is my family."

The lake was now dark blue, capturing the color of the night sky. She looked toward it and paused. "It's my life," Clia said. "Where I belong. I'll stay in it as long as I can. I'm no good to anyone without it."

Nettie cocked her head. "You? No good? I don't believe that, nor do I accept it."

It took Clia a minute to chuckle along and soon, Nettie felt their hands touch. She hooked her pinky finger around Nettie's and kept walking, in the dark. A white bird flew overhead, and Nettie saw it glide toward a cluster of trees, losing itself in a thicket of branches and leaves. Some kind of owl, a great horned, at that. Seeing it stirred something in her, a long-lost memory of her father grabbing her hand in his as she pointed to an owl in the night sky. She couldn't remember much these days, not even his face. But she remembered the bird disappearing in the fronds of palm trees, and her father urging her to keep quiet. Bad luck, he said, to point out an owl and call it out. Owls were a bad omen, here to announce death. She averted her eyes and kept walking, ignoring the sudden icy chill in her chest.

THE BLACK PANTHER Party's satellite office in East Oakland operated out of a rental house off the edge of a small suburb. Nettie got off the bus directly across the street and stared at the two-story classic Victorian with green hedges lining the walkway all the way to the front steps. The large banner hanging from the second-floor balcony confirmed that she was in the right place, a roaring black panther swaying in the breeze.

It wasn't fear or nervousness she felt crawling in her stomach. Somehow, she had managed to inoculate herself against fear after her father died. Nettie had accepted that death would come for her one way or another. She'd cheated it once before in that cane field waiting for the Tonton Macoutes to leave after they murdered her father. She wasn't sure she could continue cheating it much longer. What she felt climbing the front steps, rather, was guilt for defying Tante Mado's wishes for her to stay in her place, to not make any trouble. How could Nettie make her see? There was no point in trying to be someone she was not.

As soon as she made eye contact with the armed guard at the entrance, Nettie relaxed. "I'm here to meet Dr. Johnson," she said. "At the clinic. Is this the right place?"

He gestured toward a poster affixed on the door. It bore the name of the office, and a short list of services offered. "There's a separate clinic entrance around back," he said. "But since you're here, might as well come through. Officer of the day will direct you. Watch your step."

He certainly looked intimidating, dressed in black with a bandolier across his chest, ammunition at the ready, shotgun held tightly against his shoulder. Nettie pushed against the heavy door with both hands. It was two inches thick, made of metal, and painted black. She'd never seen one like it.

The officer was at a desk on her left with a notepad, stacks of newspapers and pamphlets, and a telephone. He was about her age, maybe older by a year or two. "I'm Reggie Hicks. Dr. Johnson is in the clinic. Just follow the hall down the right over there. Our comrade will show you."

His comrade was a young woman on watch duty by the window. The light pouring in revealed not only her features but also the holes in the glass window. Small, round holes that cracked through the pane. Gunshot holes, dozens of them. Where curtains would have hung, there were flaps secured in place, to enable the Panthers to look through and even fire their weapons through if needed. Nettie followed the young woman halfway down a dark corridor, wondering how many patients came and went this way, past the sand bags stacked along the wall to soften the blow of bullets.

Nettie walked past a staircase and heard clicking coming from the second floor, and ringing phones. She passed what she thought must have been a dining room, now turned into more office spaces. There were men and women there, sitting at desks, talking on the telephone or pounding away at typewriters that clacked and dinged as she walked by. A sister was speaking into a phone receiver. "As soon as we can, we'll send someone down there!" Another brother was on the phone, taking notes. "And how many people are attending?" he asked, scratching his natural with the tip of his pencil. "We can put together a delegation, but we need to pass this on to our deputy minister of education at headquarters."

On every wall, Nettie saw the immortalized faces of revolutionary figures on the wall: Che Guevara, in black and white; Malcolm X; Eldridge Cleaver, frozen in mid-speech. And there were posters demanding, as always, that Huey be released. Smaller flyers depicted local politicians announcing their run for mayor, city council, state representative.

She came to a large room devoid of furniture except for a long table littered with different boxes of ammunition and a closet in the back. A man was standing in the middle of the room, hunched over the table, talking to a teenage boy in a volunteer shirt that spelled out the word MOVE. Nettie decided this was definitely not the clinic, and then she recognized this man in uniform, that stance, those large athletic shoulders. Melvin. He looked up and saw her and pointed in the direction of another door further down. Nettie spun on her heels. The clinic was exactly there.

Dr. Johnson was alone, opening boxes and pulling out items. That room, too, had walls lined with sandbags, which made it look smaller, and feel warmer. The windows there were barred as well. There was no furniture, and Nettie wondered where they'd put their patients.

"Ah, you're here!" Dr. Johnson seemed relieved to see her. "Help me unload those boxes, will you? Clia can't come today. We have very little time before patients start coming in."

She'd come in right in the middle of the office's reconfiguration. The Panthers were relocating their newspaper staff upstairs and sending the clinic downstairs. Dr. Johnson looked more relaxed than he did in his office. Nettie guessed he was in his late forties, with a few gray hairs. She always saw him in his formal clothes at work where he exchanged his jacket for a doctor's coat. Today, he was wearing jeans. The sleeves of his long, flowing dashiki were rolled up.

They set up a small front table as a desk, flanking it with their file cabinets. Two volunteers came downstairs with beds, and Nettie took over unloading the boxes of supplies to store them in a closet. She followed them upstairs to get more boxes down. After two trips they seemed to grow larger and heavier, obstructing her view from the stairs. She proceeded slowly until one of the boxes felt like it was flying out of her hands. Nettie gasped, worried she'd dropped it.

"Give it here, Sister." Melvin cradled the box against his chest. "I got it!"

Nettie whispered, "Thank you," but Melvin had already walked away.

They took a few more trips up and down the stairs, passing each other in the hall, then again inside the clinic, and he said nothing. How odd, she thought. They'd served breakfast together, been in Mrs. Haywood's house together, and he still treated her like a stranger. Or not quite a stranger, but someone he didn't have time to rap with. Nettie wasn't sure whether to be annoyed or upset by it, but she let it roll off her shoulders. The clock was ticking, and there were supplies to organize.

"We've just received new kits," Dr. Johnson said. His eyes were shining like a schoolboy's as he pulled drawers open. "Can you sort these?"

Nettie got down on the floor, unboxing and taking inventory.

"Where do you want these?"

Melvin startled her as he entered the room with two small boxes, one under each arm. She pointed him to a desk in the corner before thanking him.

"What's all this stuff anyway?" Melvin asked, stacking the boxes with care so they didn't fall off.

"Saline bags," she said. "For blood transfusions."

Nettie watched him reach in his back pocket. He produced a knife, the blade rather wide and long. He tore into the tape and Nettie cringed.

"Careful." She was afraid he'd tear into the bags and cause leakage. Melvin folded the blade back and pulled out a saline bag. It was intact, and he examined it, held it up in the light.

"You done all this before?" he asked.

Nettie looked at him. "What do you mean? Set up an office? Yes, I have."

"I mean blood transfusions, Sister."

"I'm not a nurse," Nettie said. "So no."

"It's . . . life-saving," he said. "It can be, anyway. I've seen it done."

Melvin's mind seemed to drift again and she waited for him to finish his thought, but he didn't. Nettie looked at him quizzically.

"Where?" she asked.

Melvin blinked and looked at her.

"Where have you seen it done before?" Nettie repeated.

Melvin drew his breath and tossed the saline bag back into the box. "Khe Sanh."

Nettie stared back, unsure of what he'd said.

"'Nam," he added.

"Oh."

She didn't want to push it, but now he had her attention. Of course. She'd never to her knowledge met anyone who'd been in Vietnam. All this talk about the war, all these protests and people who came and went around her, and now here was a man fallen out of it right in front of her. Questions began to coalesce in her mind, but now was not the time to ask them.

"How are you going to fit all that in here?" he finally asked.

"You tell me," she said, resuming her task. "Clearly, we'll need more space than this. Can you give us at least one more room?"

"That's not my department," Melvin said.

"What is your department then?" Nettie asked, flustered. "Oh right. I forgot. Weaponry?" She got off her knees, stood tall, and gestured toward the room across the hall. "I saw you in there when I came in, handling all that ammo."

Plus, he did come to Mrs. Haywood bearing guns. Melvin stared at her, a hand on his hip, and she felt self-conscious looking back at him, the curve of his nose and his nostrils, his shoulders that seemed chiseled by an old athletic life.

"Security, that's my department, yes!" Melvin said. "And that over there is our armory." He folded his arms on his chest. "Want to see it?"

Melvin motioned for her to follow, and he crossed the hall. Nettie repressed a chuckle and shook her head in exasperation. Sure, why not? He was the kind of man who probably needed to show off his toys, and maybe he wanted to impress her and expected her to cheer and clap. She decided to be polite. She could tell Melvin was the serious type, who probably never joked or laughed much. Besides, she welcomed the break. Her arms and shoulders were still achy from carrying boxes.

There was a table in the middle of the armory, covered with a towel, on which several gun parts were laid out next to brushes, cleaning rods, and an oil container. The young volunteer with the MOVE shirt was there wearing gloves, and cleaning and oiling every piece and part of weaponry. She couldn't tell how many weapons there were, but she guessed about fifteen to twenty.

"That's a lot of fire power."

"Those are the weapons we recently fired." He walked toward a large closet in the back of the room. "*This* is the actual armory."

He opened the door. The closet was methodically organized, all the rifles, snipers, and shotguns standing next to each other in double rows on the top shelf. Every other shelf held handguns and boxes upon boxes of ammunition. There was material there to start a small war.

"The rest of it I can't really show you," Melvin said.

There was more? She looked beneath her feet, looking for a trap door. He gestured toward the young volunteer, who nodded and said hello politely.

"Lewis's job is to clean the weapons, and to take inventory," Melvin said, his deep voice resounding against the walls. "Nothing leaves this room without me knowing. I say this because if you're going to be working here, you need to know you cannot come in here without one of us being present."

"Right." She nodded. "Well, if we ever need to hold patients at gunpoint and force them to take their meds, I'll be sure to call you."

She smiled at her own joke, but Melvin didn't smile back. In the corner of her eye, Lewis lowered his head. Did Melvin ever laugh? She tried to picture it, and she couldn't. Outside, the phone rang a couple of times, and she heard footsteps in the office. Without saying a word, Melvin closed the closet door as if he'd decided the show was over. Nettie's eyes went to Lewis, still wiping parts and then quickly reassembling the guns. He was possibly sixteen, she figured, no more, and handsome. A thin dark mustache was starting to arch over his upper lip.

"You know how to put all these together?" she asked.

Lewis looked up at Nettie and nodded. He came from a family of hunters, he said, and then his parents had signed a release for him to learn.

"I go to the range on Sundays." He grinned. "Comrade Melvin teaches technical education. He can teach you, too."

Lewis threw a quick glance toward Melvin and then stopped himself, as if he'd said too much, or spoken out of turn. Melvin gave him a hard stare, and he lowered his eyes, returning to this task.

"That's alright, I don't need teaching," Nettie said.

Melvin fixed his eyes on her, and right when he opened his mouth to answer, Dr. Johnson poked his head in and interrupted them. They had patients.

NETTIE CLIMBED THE stairs to her apartment in the dark. The outdoor lights in the staircase were out again, but she wasn't going to bother the superintendent about it. She'd learned to live with minor inconveniences, like the leaks in her bathroom that took forever to be repaired or the washer's broken coin slots in the laundry room. No, someone else could call these lights in. Yet she nearly tripped, almost falling back in the dark. She caught herself in time and gasped. There was a woman sitting there in the staircase, pale legs exposed under the moonlight. Gilda was smoking. She giggled.

"Watch out, or you'll break your neck in the dark."

Nettie was immediately irritated. She wanted to yell at her to move before she tripped someone else, but what was the point? Gilda lived in her own world like that, oblivious, like when she had dumped her boxes in the hallway on move-in day. It was how they'd met, arguing over walking space on the sidewalk. Later, they bickered over her music playing next door, always too loud, and always, Gilda seemed to take it in stride with a wide grin on her face.

"Don't worry, it's not your fault," Gilda said, flashing her carton of cigarettes. "I just yelled at the super, these lights have been out a week now. I can't wait to move out. We all should. Smoke? Oh wait, right, you don't smoke."

This was what happened when she slipped out of her neighborly role, Nettie thought, and tried to be friends. She had allowed herself to let loose and partied with her once. Once. Ever since then, Gilda expected her to join in the fun every time she threw a party and now treated her like an actual friend, as if they had anything in common other than their address.

Nettie guessed she was about to chain-smoke for a while. It was how Gilda reflected on things. She was always outside the apartment with a cigarette or a drink, staring at the moon. That's how Nettie knew she was alone. When her boyfriend, Jim, was there, she was indoors.

"Good night," Nettie muttered.

"I saw you the other day, you know."

"I'm sorry?" Nettie paused in the staircase, turned to look at her.

"You were at that rally on the tenth, at the auditorium. The Black Panthers?"

Nettie squinted, watched Gilda stand and stretch her long, slender body. Her hair fell down her back like a cascade of fire. How had she not seen Gilda? And why would she have been there?

"We went down to see Eldridge, show some solidarity. He lectured at Berkeley, Jim's taken me to see him before. We really support what you're doing." At the look of Nettie's confusion, Gilda carried on. "The resistance against racism and imperialism is needed, you know. We all have that same common enemy . . ."

She was rambling now, and Nettie began to step back slowly, to end this conversation. But before she could reach her apartment door, Gilda was already climbing the stairs after her, catching up. "Hey, wait, Nettie . . . Wait."

Nettie sighed and scoured her purse for her keys. She didn't want to talk anymore. But Gilda didn't get the hint. Or rather, she did, but she ignored it.

"Listen, I know . . . I know what happened between you and Steve has sort of changed things. You haven't been over since. It's not my business, so I'm not asking you to talk about it unless you feel comfortable. But I want you to know, I think of you as a friend. I think we could learn a lot from each other."

Nettie looked at her as she buried one hand in her pocket, her other hand still holding on to her cigarette. The tip of it burned red as she took another drag, then blew the smoke away from them. Learning from each other was what she'd tried with Steve, and the consequences still hurt.

Gilda inched closer. "I think we want the same things," she said. "You, and the Panthers, and me and Jim, and SDS . . . We should have a meeting! We could have it at my place. Come over, have some drinks, talk about how we can ally ourselves to your cause?"

Nettie shook her head. "All I do is volunteer there," Nettie said. "I'm not an official member of the Black Panthers."

Gilda nodded as if she didn't quite believe her. She took another drag off of her cigarette, and then to Nettie's horror, she tapped the ashes in the dirt of a potted plant right outside her door.

"Will you think about it?" Gilda asked. "I really think it could be beneficial."

"You're talking to the wrong person," Nettie said. "You should talk to some-one in the higher ranks. I really need to get to bed now, Gilda, I'm sorry. I'm tired."

"Ah sure, okay. Talk to you soon!"

Nettie shut her door, locked it. She was glad to be inside, away from the world. She wondered if there was any value in ever attempting to go out again. Now she was feeling even more pressure living there, with Gilda stalking her.

She braided her hair in large chunks that night, wrapped it, and then changed into her nightgown. On her vanity, next to her bottles of perfume, she lay her earrings down next to a black-and-white photograph of her father and her when she was five. Or was it six? His eyes smiled more than his lips did. He was in a suit, the fabric crisp. His hand was resting on Nettie's shoulder, pulling her close, either to proudly display her to the world or to remind her who she was, and who and where she came from.

6

CLAYTON YOUNG'S POLITICAL education classes filled up every week with newly recruited members who came to hear him. His oratory skill was a gift, not something learned, a tool he used to shape the minds of the people. Nettie often thought he could be a university professor.

But Nettie also noticed that he was especially and increasingly obsessed with Clia. Very often, he would single her out after classes, pull her away from Nettie and demand she stay longer in his office. He fell into the habit of reassigning her from her usual duties to other, more menial tasks that began to feel like punishment. It was like watching a cat corner a mouse. When she asked to join the women in security, he instead reassigned her to distribute newspapers on the street corners. As a consequence, Clia began to shut down.

At the People's Clinic, Clia barely said a word. She focused on her work and lost her ability to crack jokes and giggle the way she always had with Nettie.

"Are you going to tell me what's wrong?" Nettie asked.

Clia glanced toward the door and shrugged. She clutched a stack of folders against her chest, none of them labeled.

"What's all this?" Nettie asked.

Clia shook her head. There was no light in her beautiful brown eyes. Slowly, Nettie began to understand.

"I have to stay and file. You're going to have to figure out a ride home."

"Okay . . . Do you want me to wait for you? I can help—"

"No! Jesus Nettie, just go home, I can't be your chauffeur all the time."

Nettie blinked, stung by those words. This was not the woman she knew.

"Okay," she said, swallowing back the hurt. "Understood."

Outside, there was barely any sound. The men and women on duty were in the kitchen. Reggie had made cornbread, collard greens, and smoked turkey, and the group of Panthers on duty that day gathered around the stove to talk.

Clia stole another quick glance toward the door and then looked at Nettie, her tone softening. "I'm sorry. I didn't mean to . . . I'll try to stop by your place later tonight. I asked for someone to take you home. Reggie will send a ride your way as soon as they're ready."

"I'll ride the bus, thanks."

"Don't be mad. I said I was sorry."

Nettie took a breath and smiled. No big deal. She could take a bus, even though it was Sunday and transportation ran slow. It would take her longer to get home but she'd make it. "I'll see you later."

Nettie watched Clia make her way to the door. She couldn't shake a feeling of dread washing over her, as if there was something unsaid left clinging in the air. Yet, she knew it was unwise to force things. If Clia wanted to talk, she would talk. Plus, Clia always said she could handle herself. Besides, there was a certain freedom in taking the bus; she might as well enjoy the peace and quiet on the way home.

She quickly began to organize gloves, tongue depressors, alcohol, cotton and gauze, Band-Aids, and thermometers inside glass jars, lining them up by the small sink.

"Afternoon, Sister."

Nettie jumped, fumbled with the jar in her hands. Melvin was standing a few feet away from her, adjusting his driving gloves.

"I didn't mean to scare you. Heard you needed a ride home?"

He was wearing a button-down shirt, off-white. His leather jacket was thrown over his arm as he now adjusted his sleeves. He wasn't wearing a beret today.

"I have to ride out on a mission," he said. "Pick-up job in Vallejo. Would you like to come with me?"

Nettie's heart beat a little faster as Melvin looked at her, sucking up all the air in the room with his stature. Something in the air smelled new, something that hadn't been there before.

"Vallejo?" Nettie had never been out there before. That sounded more exciting than riding the bus.

"It's only a half hour out," Melvin said. "I'll bring you back home before you know it. Unless you have a curfew or something."

"No!" Nettie laughed nervously. "I don't have a curfew."

"Alright then," he said and walked out of the room.

She gathered her bag and jacket quickly, turned the lights off, and followed in his footsteps. She had no idea where they were going exactly, what "a pick-up job" meant, but she was going anyway, riding in a car with a Black Panther, her heart racing a little faster now, and Lord, if Tante Mado could see her now.

THEY DROVE DOWN I-80 East basking in the salt mist of Big Sur. The ocean glittered under the sun, at first blinding Nettie before lulling her into a state of semi-sleep. On the radio, the announcer ushered in Marvin Gaye, and then music broke through the silence. *Stand by you like a tree, dare anybody to try and move me.* Melvin drove with one hand on the wheel, and his other arm outside the window.

He drove a dark blue Bonneville, incredibly immaculate on the inside. No books, no clothes on the back seat, no trash on the floor. It even smelled clean, as if he'd just stripped it that very morning and waxed the leather. On the dashboard, there was a box that resembled some kind of radio, with four buttons and a microphone. It emitted a static sound as they drove, followed by scrambled voices. Melvin turned it off.

"So what's this pick-up job?"

Melvin shot her a glance, leaned in, and turned the music down a little, but Marvin was still crooning in there. Nettie got another whiff of that spicy tobacco scent on him.

"An old friend of mine is making a donation to the party." Melvin's other hand pulled out a pack of menthols. He caught a cigarette between his lips and held it there a while. She studied the shape of his sideburns, the geography of his interconnected beard and mustache, the fine trim, the way the cigarette clung to his lips when he lit it. The outline of hair was sharp, precise, and his brown skin was almost lit from the inside, splendid, like smoked quartz. She looked away, worried he might catch her staring too hard.

The afternoon sun glowed a shapeless gold, and the seagulls glided over-head. Nettie thought there was nothing more beautiful than the sight of the ocean. She tried to remember the sea back home, its waves claiming the shores, its conch shells pink and shiny under the sun, and the sailboats. Music cleaved through the cool air. *You're all, you're all I need to get by.* On her right, Nettie allowed her eyes to hug the curve of hills and mountains. California's landscape evolved into small deserts, suddenly, as if they were entering another country, but then soon again, there were signs of city life. Off the side of the road, a large palm tree sign swayed in the wind above an arrow, calling motorists into the Seabreeze Motel.

"You do that often?" Nettie asked. "Pick up donations?"

"I do," Melvin said. "I do what is requested and needed for the party. Most of my assignments are for defense and security."

"You mean . . ." Nettie shot him a look. "Guns?"

"We stay armed and ready," Melvin said. "Last time pigs raided our office, they confiscated what we had, and I don't like feeling at a disadvantage."

He was driving at a reasonable pace, ignoring the honks of a Cadillac that swerved around them. Armed and ready. Sounded like her father, locking his pistol away and mumbling under his breath as if he knew his death was imminent. Nettie blinked the memory away as Melvin glanced in her direction. Say something, she thought.

"I see."

"Why? Is that a problem?"

"It's not exactly how I normally spend my Sundays," she said. "Riding in a car with guns, that sounds dangerous."

He drove straight down the road while Nettie ran scenarios in her mind. What if the mission went wrong and there was a shootout? What if they got pulled over by the police? How would she put this into words for her aunt, that she was behind bars because she had been on the road with a Black Panther and some guns in the car?

"When you roll with Panthers, you have to expect these things. We already have guns in this car as we speak."

Nettie tried to remain calm. She was hoping he was joking, but this was

Melvin. He was not. At least, he didn't seem to be. He was very seriously looking at her. It was fine, she decided. It was what her father had done.

"You're not scared, are you? You want me to let you off at the next stop?"

"I'm not scared."

"You sure? Because you look a little—"

"This isn't new to me. I'm just . . ." How could she say this? She took a breath and let it out. "Concerned, you know, that we might get stopped. Aren't you?"

"We get stopped all the time, guns or no guns. Why should I be any more concerned?" Melvin repeated the question as if befuddled by it and now she felt silly for speaking at all. Had she offended him? He was judging her, she was sure of it.

"What I mean is—"

"I know what you mean," he said. "People see the Black Panthers as violent because we carry guns. I dig it. And yet white people exert violence on us every day, and no one asks them about perpetuating that stereotype. They force us into the ghetto, take away our rights to an education, to food, to vote or own property, our right to live, and then they unleash the pigs on us. All of that is violence, isn't it?"

Nettie bit her lip. Why did she open that can of worms? She was beginning to wonder if she should have caught the bus. But she knew in her heart she'd rather be here, despite her aunt's voice in the back of her mind.

"Until the pigs decide to put their guns down, until they stop brutalizing our people, I have no reason to put mine down. If anything, I feel more secure with protection in the car."

Melvin sounded exactly like every other Panther she'd heard speak so far. Even in political education, they professed self-defense. Get a gun, arm yourself, the revolution demanded it. Nettie looked out her window. If she could just keep her mouth shut and enjoy this landscape, this change of scenery, and only speak when spoken to, she could make it through the rest of this day without incident.

"When I met you at the Haywoods' house, you think I should have gone out in the night and found a peaceful, nonviolent resolution to those racist honkytonks harassing that family? How do you think that would've turned out?"

She decided to not offer any answers, but Melvin was still talking.

"They haven't bothered them since, by the way," Melvin said. "You got to demand respect from racists. Self-defense is intelligence. That is my gospel, Sister, take it or leave it."

Nettie looked at him, but his eyes were now on the road.

"I should have shot them all, if you ask me," Melvin said. "All of them, one by one. Even that goddam dog."

"You don't like dogs?" Nettie asked.

Melvin slowed down a little. He glanced at Nettie and scowled, and she immediately regretted asking the question. Didn't she just convince herself to be quiet? Yes, but . . . dogs? Nettie threw caution out the window. If all her conversations with Melvin were going to be tense, she wasn't going to show him any fear.

"They're really good, loyal animals," Nettie said, looking out the window. "That dog was just doing his job."

She took note of his disbelief, and suddenly, she regretted the entire day. She should have taken the bus. She really couldn't wrap her brain around this man. At times, talking to him was like an exercise in maintaining civility. They could not be friends, she felt, without arguing.

"So, you're a dog person, then?" Melvin sucked on his cigarette.

She didn't mind dogs. She vaguely remembered a dog in her past. Her father kept one for a while on their property in Port-au-Prince, a black dog. She remembered it disappearing, and a rumor circulating that Duvalier wanted all black dogs eliminated. Odd that this memory was returning to her now.

"You know, before I got drafted, I had it in my mind to go down South."

Nettie watched him blow out a plume of smoke. Ever since he'd mentioned his tour in Vietnam, everything made sense: the way he carried himself, the authority in his voice, the way Party members looked at him and looked up to him.

"I was seventeen, I went down to Mississippi to volunteer with Snick."

"Snick? You were SNCC?"

"I used to believe in nonviolent struggle. Even went down in the picket line once or twice. You ever been down South at all? To Mississippi? Alabama? Georgia?"

Nettie shook her head no, but she had considered it. She'd only been in California since she'd emigrated to the United States.

Melvin nodded, checked the rearview mirror. "I thought I could make a difference. Take everything you think you know about Freedom Summer, and multiply that by ten."

Nettie had heard stories, but she'd never met anyone who'd been there.

"My cadre focused on voter education." He glanced at Nettie. "When they started to board buses to go downtown and register . . ." Melvin paused. "Folks lost their jobs for that," he said. "Lost their lives. Got lynched for it. The sheriff, the plantation owners, the clerk of courts, White Citizens' Councils, all of them conspired to keep that right from us. Those who fought for that right, you know what happened to them? They had fire hoses turned on them and dogs sicced on them."

Nettie stiffened in her seat, uneasy, ill at the thought of dogs mauling bodies.

"Big dogs," Melvin said. "German shepherds, hellhounds. Tore up this man's pants and ate up his arms. I can't shake that image out of my mind, no matter how hard I try."

Melvin fell quiet for a moment, and she wanted to press him again, but now the light seemed to have gone from his eyes. He smoked without a word. The engine rumbled as he stepped on the gas. The Bonneville picked up speed. A chorus of male voices was now singing *I know, to you, it might sound strange, but I wish it would rain.*

"I don't have any room in my heart for dogs," Melvin said finally. "They're an extension of their masters. Too easily corrupted."

She couldn't argue against that.

"My concern is the people," he said. "Always the people. And we must develop an undying love for the people—"

"Or we will be wiped out, I know."

"Oh, you know, huh?"

Melvin and Nettie locked eyes, and for a moment, they finally were speaking the same language. She knew how to finish that sentence. She'd studied it in the material they passed around in political education classes. She even heard it from Prime Minister Carmichael. There was a magnificent light in his eyes as he looked into hers, as if he was seeing her for the first time.

For a while, they drove in silence, the road stretching before them for infinity. Every now and then, the music cut to a commercial break, an advertisement for Riunite on ice and Colgate. When the music returned, Melvin turned the volume down again.

"What else do you know?" he asked. "I've been doing all the talking, now it's your turn. Tell me more about yourself."

He wanted to know more about what she was studying, what she wanted to do with her degree, what books she was reading. Most of the exciting reads for her were the instructional texts that came with her life-saving skills courses. Applying a tourniquet or giving mouth-to-mouth resuscitation gave her the impression of actually being of help, of exercising the power to save lives the way she remembered her father doing, stopping in on villagers in their hometown with his satchel, hovering over patients in bed, spoon-feeding them quinine for those nights their bones burned of malarial fever. Even when he poured that potent, bitter neem tea with salt in a child's mouth and made them drink it, her father was using his knowledge to heal. She loved to read those books, too, she told Melvin, on botany and herbal medicine, but she often had to get those on her own at the library. Here, in America, they believed less in the power of leaves and more in a Western kind of science, and she was willing to embrace that, too.

"I'm afraid it's not very revolutionary reading," she said. "Not too exciting."

"But saving lives *is* revolutionary," Melvin said. "There are many ways to join a revolution. As long as you're reading for knowledge. It seems your father knew that. . . . Where is he now?"

Nettie was briefly caught off guard. She realized he didn't know, and she didn't want to go on about what really happened.

"He died. A long time ago."

Melvin seemed to nod in acknowledgement of what she said, and she quickly added to change the topic, "Yes, he knew that. He loved books."

Melvin had read a little bit of everything, he said. Marx and Engels, Chairman Mao's *Little Red Book*, Fanon, lots of Fanon, and Robert F. Williams's *Negroes with Guns*, and Hailey's *Autobiography of Malcolm X*, which, according to him, was one of the most important books ever written. Of course, he'd read literature, he said. He knew Baldwin, and Richard Wright, and Ellison. But he also knew Quincy Troupe, someone Nettie hadn't come across before.

"Have you read any books by women?" Nettie asked.

"I can't recall," he said. "Why? What are you, one of those feminists? You're going to scold me for not reading women's books?"

"I'm not asking you about women's books. I'm asking you about books by women, which isn't the same thing."

Outside her window, a sign announced they were entering Vallejo. She felt relieved, but also disappointed. Being with Melvin was both unnerving and nourishing. She didn't want the conversation to end.

"Why do I feel like you're judging me right now?" Melvin asked as the Bonneville switched lanes, following signs to Lofas Lakeside.

"I'm not judging you," she said. "But I feel like the answer is no."

When she glanced at Melvin, she saw something she'd never seen before. To her surprise, Melvin was smiling. Not a full grin, but a smirk, as if he was amused by her and her refusal to be honest.

"I think you're jiving," Melvin said.

Nettie smiled and looked away. They turned into a quiet, quaint suburban area that almost resembled Berkeley Hills, where Tante Mado had lived when she was still married. They drove into a private residential community on the outskirts of a lake, and she knew they'd arrived when he started to slow down, looking for a house number. The homes all boasted manicured lawns. There was a uniformity to American landscapes that left Nettie unsettled, and she was thankful for little places where homes kept their individuality.

Melvin stopped in front of a house with large cypress trees in the front. He parked next to a station wagon and extinguished his cigarette in the ashtray. Just when she was about to offer to wait in the car, he rolled his window up and asked her to come in with him.

"Are you sure?" she said. "I was going to wait. I don't want to be in the way."

"Don't worry about it," he said, pulling his beret out of the glove compartment. "It's really not a big deal."

He led her to the front door. He kept his gloves on, adjusted his beret before knocking. She took notice of his handgun in the waist of his pants, which quickly disappeared in the folds of his jacket. He knocked with confidence and waited, hands clasped behind him. She heard footsteps and wondered if she should have stayed put. She might ruin it if she said the wrong thing. The door opened and a woman, a tall and stunning beauty, stood at the threshold.

"Melvin!"

She flashed a smile. Her skin was resplendent in the afternoon light, as if she'd just oiled it. She wore a flowing floral gown that swept the floor. Nettie watched her throw her arms around him and hug him while he said her name. Blue? What kind of name was Blue? That's when the woman seemed to finally notice Nettie, over Melvin's shoulder. Her smile instantly vanished.

"Oh, who is this?"

Melvin introduced her as a "comrade," Sister Nettie, along to pick up the package. Nettie felt her face burn with something she could only identify as fury, and she couldn't understand why, in part because she was too busy being polite. She realized now that she'd expected to walk into a den full of men, swaggering and posturing with ammunition, armed to the teeth. Why wouldn't it have been a woman? But also, why would Melvin not tell Nettie? Clearly this woman had expectations of this visit, none of which included the presence of a female road-trip companion.

The way Blue clung to Melvin, Nettie knew she had no place here. She felt manipulated, and stupid, standing there while Blue sized up her boots and dress that suddenly felt juvenile compared to her seductive robe.

"You didn't say you were bringing company," Blue said.

"I can wait outside," Nettie said.

"Blue doesn't mind," Melvin said. "Come on in."

The house was a small museum of collectibles, mainly in music. The walls were adorned with framed vinyl discs, small statues and prizes, posters of a trio of women at a microphone in form-hugging gowns. Nettie studied them as they passed, one by one, as Melvin and Blue talked. She could feel Blue's glacial glances, but Nettie didn't care anymore. After all, she hadn't asked to be brought here.

The foyer led to a living room adorned with more portraits, and there was a piano in the corner. Sitting on the rectangular frame, a photo flashed white smiles from a couple at a wedding. Nettie recognized Blue, looking fresh and dainty in a white gown and elaborate veil of flowers scattered everywhere, this time with a uniformed serviceman at her arm. In another photo, a group of soldiers gathered under a canopy of bamboo, all in their military fatigues. Four of them were lined up shoulder to shoulder, the other two squatting in the front, and she inched closer as she recognized a young soldier who looked very much familiar. Melvin? She squinted for a better look. Yes, it was Melvin, hand locked in a dap with another man who, now that she compared the photographs, Nettie thought was probably the same serviceman next to Blue in the wedding picture.

"Can I get you anything?"

"I'm fine," Nettie said, startled. She pointed at the photograph of Blue at the microphone between the other women. Her lips were forming an "ooh," and she was loving someone from a distance, you could tell. Longing.

"Is this you?"

Blue acquiesced, nodding her head slowly before she muttered, "Yes." In the corner of her eye, Nettie saw Melvin remove his gloves and study the place. How long had it been since they'd seen each other, Blue asked? Archie was still alive then, wasn't he? Nettie captured the name but didn't ask questions.

"We don't have much time," he said. "I have to head back to Oakland and make another stop with our sister here."

There was an awkward silence, and Nettie wished she could knock her heels three times and vanish home like that Dorothy girl. Blue's pretty face drooped with disappointment. "Don't you at least want a drink?"

Nettie felt a tingling under her armpits, and down her spine. She felt she'd stumbled upon a pile of broken expectations, and even though the tension was palpable, she was now too curious to look away. This was like watching a train derailing. Her eyes went to a minibar across the room. She wanted to ask for a drink, actually. She felt thirsty, and the bar was begging to be used. She noticed fresh ice in the crystal bowl with a set of golden tongs. Glasses were out. Two.

"I don't drink," Melvin said.

"Oh, right . . . I forgot. How could I forget? How about water?"

"I'll take water," Nettie quickly said.

She registered the thinly veiled anger on Blue's face as she poured her a glass of water. Nettie thanked her politely, drank immediately to quench her thirst. She stared down at her toes, then turned away to avoid seeing the disaster of a woman's dreams shattering, Blue's arms falling at her sides, dejected. Behind Melvin, there was a shelf with a picture of that same serviceman. This was Archie, she was sure of it. Then, slowly, she began to understand. Her eye shifted to the folded American flag encased in glass next to the photograph. She registered the silence of the house. No one else was coming out. It was just the three of them here.

"I'm fine, though," Blue said icily after a while. "Thank you for asking."

"I know," Melvin replied, his eyes scrolling her up and down before staring back in her eyes. "I can see that."

Nettie saw Blue's entire body thaw under the compliment. Melvin had game. It was smooth to the ear and she surprised herself by nearly laughing. She held it in. This shit was better than the theater. Free entertainment, except there was the strange sensation that she was being forced into a voyeuristic role.

"Time was always good to you," Melvin said. Then, nonchalantly, he skipped over the pleasantries. "So, where are you keeping this donation?"

"Of course," Blue said. "You've always had your priorities straight."

Blue's eyes went from Nettie to Melvin, and to Nettie again. Then, she excused herself and walked away. As soon as she left the room, Nettie stared in Melvin's eyes, looking for remorse. But she saw none. Melvin turned away from her. Unbelievable, she thought. This was more than awkward. It was unjust. This woman was practically tap-dancing to get him to connect and he was, but he was also pushing her away. That was art, and it unnerved Nettie. Men like that weren't idiots. They were deliberate about what they did and what they said.

"Why did you bring me here?" Nettie whispered.

Melvin turned to look at her, then turned his gaze away.

"It's cool," he said. "Be cool."

Nettie was exasperated, but she couldn't get into an argument now. It wouldn't be appropriate. She took more steps around the room, studying some of Blue's recordings on the walls, some photos on stage with other women from a band. Her eyelashes were as voluminous and fanned out as bird wings. She flashed the same dazzling smile in every photograph. Nettie had questions, but she was afraid to break the silence and make things worse.

Blue returned a few minutes after, dragging along a case against the soft pink carpeting. Melvin took it from her. He laid the suitcase flat onto the sofa and popped the small locks. Weapons and boxes of ammunition were thrown haphazardly inside. At least twenty to thirty combined weapons. How? Nettie's mind raced. Nothing made sense. Why did this woman own so many guns? Where did they come from, and why was she just giving them away?

Melvin inspected the weapons slowly. Blue walked to the bar and poured herself something, a whiskey of sorts. Nettie couldn't tell for sure. Blue didn't use any ice. She took a sip while Melvin aimed a pistol at the floor, inspected the chambers, tested the trigger. He swung his head, left and right, slightly. Maybe. Yes. He didn't dislike them, it seemed. Nettie was reading his body language, but he wasn't saying much.

"Is this all of it?" he asked.

"How much do you think they're worth?" Blue asked, her eyes on her drink.

She was swirling the amber liquid in the glass. Nettie saw Melvin flinch, and he turned a sour face to Blue.

"You said this was a donation," Melvin said. "Did I misunderstand?"

"No, I just want to know." Blue's eyes went to Nettie, then back to Melvin. "They got any value?"

"They do to the Party!" Melvin tossed the pistol back in the suitcase. It made a heavy metal sound when it fell against the other guns. Barrel thumping against barrel. "But I'm no arms dealer so I don't know what they go for. I can leave them behind if that's what you want."

"It's not what I want," Blue said. "When I called and asked you to come, I was hoping we could talk. Catch up. You won't even make conversation."

She sipped more of her drink, nearly emptying the glass.

"Conversation?" Melvin's voice could have snapped bones. He quickly pulled his gloves out of his pocket and began to slide his gloves back on. The room was ice cold now, and Melvin took a breath. "I'm very busy, Blue, you know I am, otherwise I would stay. You want me to take the guns or not?"

"Busy?" Blue laughed, but it sounded hollow. "I don't give a damn about no guns, right now, Melvin. You're always so . . . cool and smooth about everything, but you won't talk to me. Ever since Archie—"

"I don't want to talk about Archie!"

Nettie said she would step outside, but they didn't seem to hear her.

"You could have stayed the night of the funeral," Blue said, her voice breaking. "Why didn't you stay?"

"I think you should ease down on the sauce, Sister," Melvin said.

Nettie felt like a child caught between screaming parents. Melvin snapped his fingers and Nettie understood his command before he spoke the words. He gestured toward the door. They hadn't made it down the hallway when they heard Blue's voice.

"Wait!"

Nettie froze. Melvin kept walking and had just made it to the door when Blue hurried in her gown, breasts bouncing, her drink swirling faster, carrying the case. She stopped by the curtain. The afternoon light came bursting through slits, casting shadows against her lovely face, her troubled eyes wet with invisible tears.

"Melvin," she said. "Just take them. I can't bear to even look at them."

She was out of breath. She was a beautiful, pitiful sight, and Nettie wondered, if she hadn't been there, what Melvin would have done. Would he have stayed? Melvin stared at her.

"I'm fine." Her lashes fluttered just a bit. "I just don't want these around anymore. And . . . I know Archie would want you to have them. So, they're yours."

Melvin took the case, and when he walked past Blue, he stopped. Nettie waited by the door, watched him lean in and mutter something, and watched her listen, nodding in response. She couldn't hear what they were saying, but something he said got her to be still. She looked up at him. He leaned in and kissed her forehead, and walked away.

When they pulled out of the driveway, Blue was at her window. She never smiled at Nettie. She didn't even wave.

Back on I-80 West, Nettie allowed herself to look at Melvin's hands on the steering wheel, at his profile, his face as he stared straight ahead. She tried to keep her eyes on the road, too, but she could feel the weight of this new silence between them. Nettie wanted to lash out at Melvin. But she decided to keep calm, let the music spilling out of the radio fill the silence. Cars rushed past them, and the Pacific looked like a vast stretch of gold flakes flashing in the sunlight. Suddenly, he turned the radio off.

"I'm going to get off here," he said, turning his blinker on. "Won't be long. I want to go try these out."

It took her a minute to realize he was referring to the guns. Nettie started to shake her head. She didn't like this plan. She wanted to be home.

"You said you didn't have a curfew. We won't be but a minute." Melvin cast her a side glance. "Unless of course, you were jiving when you said you didn't need teaching."

He veered left, off the road into a service driveway off the main interstate, and soon she saw a sign for a state park and shooting range. She could almost hear the off-beat thrashing of her heart. Once again, she didn't know what to expect, but suddenly it dawned on her that they were once again headed into the unknown, just the two of them, and that anything could happen out there in the California desert, the Bonneville leaving nothing in its trail but a thick cloud of ochre-colored dust. She looked in the mirror, plagued by the sudden self-awareness that she was a woman, and he was a man, a Panther, no less, driving into possible danger. Yes, anything could happen, and no one would know.

7

MELVIN STOOD NEXT to Nettie, towering over her. She wondered, for a brief moment, whether this made any sense. She was a volunteer sickle cell researcher. What was she doing here with guns? The brightness of this day, the sun licking her skin, and this presence behind her reminded her of what that was like, years back, when her father held her hands together around a pistol. She'd come full circle and it was eerie.

"I bet these haven't been cleaned in quite some time," Melvin said. "If it jams, put it down and try another one."

His voice was smooth now that he was standing so close. He'd taken off his jacket, rested it in the corner, and spread out the contents of the bag on the table. Melvin had clearly been here before. She could tell by the way they greeted him as they walked in and registered. No one stopped him coming in with his own ammunition. They let them through the back door to the outdoor portion of the range.

Melvin kept the two top buttons on his shirt open, and she resented the distraction. She quickly pulled her eyes away from his chest and rested them on his weapon of choice pulled from the bag. A carbine. She took a step back, watched him rest the butt of the rifle against his shoulder before taking aim. For an eternal minute, he looked through the sight and stayed there, in full concentration on his target, a black silhouette far in the distance. He cocked the weapon, and she remembered his military training. He looked at ease, and before she could form another thought, Melvin pulled the trigger. Her eardrums vibrated. Melvin was still aiming. The weapon detonated each time with a sonic *boom, boom, boom!* Nettie heard nothing for a while except a whistle. Then, silence.

She dropped her hands but her heart was pounding. Melvin held a button down to call the target back. He'd hit it right in the face, and in the chest, near the heart. Melvin examined it and then turned to her.

"You alright?"

"I'm fine!" she said, her voice trembling. She cleared her throat.

"You look scared."

"I'm not scared!"

Melvin looked on with a flicker in his eyes, and she felt a strange fire build up in the muscles of her arms, her legs. She was not afraid. She would show him, she had to, now. It was a question of pride. She was not going to make a fool of herself, not with a defense captain of the Panther Party egging her on like this or, should she say, showing off to her.

"Show me what you got, then."

Men were all the same in the same childish ways, she thought. A man playing with guns was no different than a boy playing with toys. And she didn't have to play along. She knew that. But he'd rattled something in her.

"You need some help?" Melvin offered. Then, he caught himself. "Oh right, I forgot, you don't need teaching."

Nettie took a shotgun off the table, and then balanced it in her hands before gripping the barrel. Melvin rested a hand on her shoulder, and she held her breath.

"Try it from the hip," he said. "Those rifles have a hell of a kickback. You'll hurt your shoulder."

The air smelled of leaves of grass, dust, the thickets of aster spreading around in the distance, and gunpowder.

"I'm not that delicate," she said.

She rested the rifle against her shoulder again. Just like her father had shown her. Cocked her head far into it so she could see what it was the barrel should be seeing: the target was still. She wrapped her finger around the trigger, and she was once again with her father, and she was about to tear into the sanctity of nature with a bullet just like that first time. Her father's voice, a whisper in the wind. *Feu!*

She felt the breeze blow softly and she let it, waited until it shifted. She swallowed and felt her throat itch with thirst. When she finally pulled the trigger, the kickback sent the butt of the gun hard against her clavicle. Her shoulder bounced back hard with the explosion, and her ears rang again despite the ear muffs. It happened quickly, and when she looked into the scope, it took her a minute before noticing the faint dust settling in the air. She'd grazed the target, but it was still there in its place.

She could feel Melvin behind her, probably smirking, but when she turned around he wasn't smiling, not even with his eyes. He was serious.

"This here is a shotgun," Melvin said, watching her rub her shoulder. "You don't need to worry about aiming. You're dispersing bullets, so you're bound to hit your enemy somewhere. This time around, don't be so stubborn. Try it like I said. From the hip."

Her head was spinning, but she felt her nostrils flare. She hated that he was right. But she moved it to her hip and pulled the trigger again and again. On the second shot, she hit the target and saw it flinch. She could feel Melvin looking at her, this time in silence. Overhead, a large-winged bird circled and swooped down toward the trees.

Melvin nodded. "That's pretty good," he said. "I think it's because you're angry. Anger makes you a better shot."

"I'm not angry." She felt her ears burn from embarrassment.

"Sure, you are," Melvin said, now loading bullets into a rifle. "You ain't said a word since we left Blue's house. You got something on your mind, you should say it."

Nettie watched him test another gun. Her blood ran cold. So, he knew. . . . He was right, once more, about her anger, and she decided she might as well tell him. What else was there to do?

"I don't like how you treated her," Nettie said. "She didn't deserve that."

Melvin fired his weapon again, and this time the target came closer and closer, featuring a large hole in the face and in the heart. His accuracy was disconcerting.

"She clearly has feelings for you," Nettie said, exasperated. She had to make

herself heard over the sound of gunfire, and the ear protectors muffled everything but the sound of bullets and her heart thumping in her chest.

"Really? You know that from those few minutes we were in and out of her
place?"

"You can't tell me you don't see it. She dressed up for you. Wanted you to
stay for drinks. You knew this, and you brought me along. That's why you asked
me to come, wasn't it? You used me to humiliate her. Or were you just hoping to
humiliate me? Because you did both."

Nettie realized how quiet it was around them. Suddenly, she took notice of
the fact that the other shooters had stopped shooting and were now glancing
over to their booth. She'd been too loud, way after Melvin had stopped firing.
Melvin stood before her, one hand draped over his weapon and the other on his
hip, watching her. She looked away.

"I'm sorry. . . . I don't appreciate being caught between you and your girl-
friends like that."

"Are you finished?"

She swallowed, disarmed by his question. Behind his protective glasses, his
eyes were full of fire.

"I don't appreciate being judged or lectured about what I do," he said. "I
serve the Party. End of story."

Melvin shook his head and picked up another rifle, semi-automatic. He fired
a few rounds, and the sound nearly stopped Nettie's heart. She watched him,
observed his stance, legs apart, shoulders wide, head cocked. When he finally
put the weapon down and turned to face Nettie, his skin was dewy with sweat.

"Blue is not my girlfriend," he said. This time, he sounded calm. "I can't help
it if she has feelings, I don't lead women on, especially if they're already taken.
Archie and I, we were Bloods. I wouldn't do that to a brother. I didn't come
here to play games with women. I don't have time for that, you dig? The Party
comes first."

Nettie lowered her eyes. She regretted having said anything now, she should
have kept to herself. Someone down the other end of the range fired a few
rounds, and by now the sound was becoming background noise for Nettie.

"Right," Nettie nodded. "No women, no feelings. I dig it."

He seemed very serious about it, and Nettie felt disappointed by this admission. Why was she disappointed? She shook her head to chase away that feeling of unease. In a way, wasn't he just like her, not looking to attach himself to anyone, just focused on his purpose?

Melvin made room for her to step up and test one more, a pistol that felt slightly too large for her hands. When she assumed position, he leaned in a little closer to check her stance, and he rested his fingers on both her shoulders.

"Relax your shoulders, breathe, and hold those arms up higher. Breathe, Sister."

His touch made her shiver. She felt clumsy, suddenly unable to fire a decent shot, even though he complimented her on her form, telling her she was much better now after she went another round and finished her ammunition. Somehow, she could still feel his hands on her skin. She could still smell him.

"You sure are mouthy for a sister your size," he said.

"Excuse me?"

"Pay attention," he ordered. "You waverin' all over the place."

Nettie clenched her jaw. Mouthy? She fired the weapon angrily, determined to tell him off. He was too good at getting under her skin, she decided. When the target came back, she'd struck it right in the chest. Melvin whistled as he gauged it.

"Like I said, you're a much better shot when you're angry."

Melvin lit another cigarette, and now the smoke from it mixed with the haze of gunpowder floating in the air. Nettie looked at him in disbelief. He'd called her mouthy on purpose, teased her, provoked her, riled her up to get results. She didn't know whether to hate him or like him.

"Look here," he said, removing his muffs. "If I ever decide to let my feelings for somebody show, I'll make sure it's with someone committed to the cause," Melvin said. "Someone from the Party, a revolutionary willing to fight till the end, you dig?"

His words trickled and fell somewhere in her and stopped, stuck, unable to dissolve.

Nettie swallowed. "That's very romantic, in a very morbid way," she said.

Melvin looked at her, snickered. "Alright then. I just leaned in and told you something personal. I expect you to keep that shit to yourself. I expect you can do that just fine?"

She nodded. Sure. He gathered their weapons and placed them back in the bags, one after the other. Nettie put in her gun, too, as he held the bag open.

"I still think it was unfair of you to bring me," she said.

"And deny myself the pleasure of an open road with a beautiful sister by my side?"

It took her minute to realize he was speaking of her. Nettie felt her cheeks burn. She tried to hide it but she knew he was looking at her while he talked.

"I had to bring you along," he said. "I knew a sister like you would keep me in check. I get in, get the job done, I get out. Now come on, let's head on out before it gets dark."

She was glad they were leaving, but she also wasn't. Something about the gunfire had ignited a fire in her, a need to continue pulling that trigger. She followed Melvin back to the car, watching him from behind, and she liked how he swaggered, how he carried himself, and how smooth the brother was with words in the most unexpected moments. Nettie felt an odd thrill coursing through her.

She hadn't held a gun since she was a girl. When her father had taught her, the process had left her in constant fear. But with Melvin, it was . . . fun. Once she admitted this to herself, she felt relieved, and as they got back on the road, she felt a little sad that the day was coming to an end. When they got back on the freeway, the sun had started its slow and magnificent descent into the horizon. It was five thirty. They'd been out longer than she anticipated, and now it was almost night.

Melvin turned the radio on, and a song was already playing: *Reach out, I'll be there*. Nettie kept her eyes on the sky as it began to blush in a vivid orange. She remembered sunsets nearly like these. She could conjure up the sky from back home sometimes at sunset. When it was blue, almost indigo, pure, she could hear the flutter of wings overhead as the birds zipped through, the way it was when they came for her father. As she remembered that sky, she remembered her father lying face down in a pool of blood in the front yard. She'd fallen so deeply into that memory that she almost didn't hear Melvin's voice, until he reached out and touched her arm.

"Hey, you awake?"

She turned to him, startled. "Yes!"

He let go of her arm. His hand was warm, and his grip strong enough that she wanted it to stay there.

"Are you hungry?" he asked. "Because we're coming up on Oakland. I know a place where we can eat once we get to town. If you want to."

"Yes . . . I could eat."

Melvin nodded, and they fell back into an easy silence, the wind rushing by like a dream.

THE DINER WHERE Melvin took her was Black-owned. The majority of patrons there were Black, too. It was on the north end of Lake Merritt, in downtown Oakland, a part of the city Nettie had never ventured in, brimming with community schools and grocery stores, and near a mosque with a crescent moon atop its minarets. They sat across from each other and ordered the fried chicken that Melvin vouched for. She'd caught a few female glances thrown his way the moment they entered the restaurant. Some of the men they saw greeted Melvin with a nod, one of them embracing him with an "As-salamu alaykum."

It was difficult to look at him, she realized, since the shooting range. Something had shifted, and she was convinced she was the only one to feel it, but now his very glance and touch made her lower her eyes. She wrapped her fingers around the cool glass of 7 Up she ordered.

"How do you know so many people here?" she finally asked.

Melvin removed his jacket again, setting it next to him. "I used to be on CAP duty in this area a lot when I started." He looked at her and she raised her eyebrow. "Community Alert Patrol," Melvin added. "I was assigned to this area many times. We'd be on alert for pigs. When they showed up with their guns to harass the community, we'd show up with our guns and police the police."

That's what the police scanner in his car was for.

"One time, this one pig wet his pants and fell right on the sidewalk when he saw us. He was alone." There was a shine in Melvin's eye as he conjured up these memories. "He wasn't partnered up, and that was his mistake, because usually they're not alone. They travel in packs. I never saw a honky get paler than a sheet before. I mean, he was transparent, he was so scared."

Nettie would have missed the fact that he chuckled softly, had she not been paying attention.

"Do you hate them all?" she asked. "The police, I mean." She repressed a shudder. Melvin looked at her and nodded, hardly missing a beat.

"Pigs are the lowest form of animal, and that's what we're dealing with," Melvin said. "Their only function is to enforce white supremacy by keeping you in the ghetto. I grew up with pigs harassing Black kids in the neighborhood. They corner you, accuse you of stealing, killing, raping, anything to lock you up and put you away out of sight. Anything to remind you that you ain't shit and you ain't never gonna be shit."

Melvin paused for a second, as if measuring his own anger. Then, he smoothed down his mustache with his fingers.

"Only thing worse than a pig is a brother who joins the ranks of the pig. You can't turn against your people," Melvin said. "And you can't help your people by joining the oppressor."

The waiter slid plates of fried chicken between them. Nettie's mouth watered. She hadn't realized how hungry she was, and the chicken was delicious. They both tore into it, teeth sinking into the meat as they held drumsticks and wings between their fingers. When they made eye contact again, they both laughed. She'd never let her guard down like this before with any man, her lips all greasy.

"Anyway," he said, "you asked. Before us, people lived in terror of them. Not anymore. Now, we police the pig. Make them sweat as hard as they make us sweat. Fuck 'em!" He caught himself and looked Nettie in the eye, and said, "Excuse my language."

She smiled, noting how his language had changed throughout the day.

"Anyway, I don't patrol anymore," Melvin said. "Huey felt I needed to be in control of defense, so he had me reassigned."

"Huey . . . Newton?"

How did they know each other personally? Had he visited Huey in jail? By the time they ordered more drinks, Melvin was already talking about Huey and that fateful night involving the death of Officer John Frey.

"We should build a church to Huey Newton," Melvin said.

Nettie watched him eat. Melvin's conviction was almost infectious. And there was also the unsaid. Huey was every Black man tracked and harassed by the police. Melvin could have been the one in prison right now.

"Aren't you ever scared?" Nettie asked. "Of anything? Of dying?"

Melvin paused, considered the question as if he'd never thought of it before.

"No. I've seen people around me die in the field, just blown to pieces, gutted . . ." His eyes darkened as he seemed to remember this. "For what? Because the white man decides everyone should fall in line with imperialism. Because the white man decides who is expendable in the fields or in the ghetto. That's not living. That's already death. So, in a sense, I know death. I been dead. And I know lots of folks in the ghettos, they feel dead."

He lowered his voice, so that only they could hear each other speak. There was a fire inside Melvin now rising and setting her ablaze.

"The Black Panther Party offers us a chance to wake up and live. To fight and die a true death, one with dignity attached to it. We're feeding children, educating them in liberation schools, providing them with better healthcare."

He put down his utensils, leaned in closer, and tapped his temple as he spoke.

"This is the genius of Huey P. Newton, to know that guns alone won't help us win, but that we should face all of these problems and address them with simple solutions, solutions that work for us and that are not ideated by this racist establishment. We can't wait for others. We do this ourselves. If others want to support us, then fine, but we do this ourselves."

Nettie remembered Gilda and leaned in, too.

"My neighbor is SDS," Nettie said. "She says SDS and the Panthers have the same goals. She asked me to arrange a meeting, and I don't know anything about that stuff."

"Why would she ask you that?" Melvin squinted, staring right into her, and Nettie felt immediately embarrassed. "Let her leadership figure it out," he said. "Anyone who wants to work for the Panthers can go through the channels."

"Your turn now," he said. "Tell me something about you," Melvin said. "Make it a fair exchange. Who taught you about guns?"

Nettie swallowed her food quickly. She laughed nervously, shook her head.

"My father," Nettie said. There was a brief silence, and she realized Melvin needed details. "He taught me about guns. He was a doctor with daring revolutionary ideas, I guess you could say."

Melvin raised an eyebrow but waited for her to continue, the flame in his eyes still dancing. "A doctor with a gun, that's some Wild Wild West shit."

"He taught me to shoot, he felt it was important. He knew there would be a . . . a day coming and I'd need to be prepared, just in case."

"In case what?"

She shrugged, too nervous to look at Melvin at all. But Melvin leaned in, his interest suddenly sharpened. She'd never told this story to anyone, and yet now she felt safe enough to share. There was no real danger in revealing this much. Not to him.

"My father was a member of a political organization opposing Duvalier. Papa Doc."

Melvin nodded. He knew. Her eyes held on to Melvin's, and she felt a rush, something crawling under her skin, or something breathing onto her skin, and she wondered if her father's ghost was here with them. So she talked about her father's gun smuggling, the hiding places. She talked about his argument with the neighbor, the Tonton Macoute who pegged her father a communist. She mentioned the day he came with guns, the memory now rattling her so much she skipped details, went straight to her aunt taking her in. Melvin listened, his finger running across his mustache.

Finally, he looked at her. "I knew it," Melvin said. "I knew you had the fire in you, Sister. Your daddy was a revolutionary."

"He's dead," Nettie snapped. She saw Melvin stare back, quizzical. "Being a revolutionary didn't pay off. He still got killed. That's where I fail to see the point of it all. He died out there like a dog. He never stood a chance."

There. She'd said it. All these years she'd wanted to say this, a small truth that was in fact too large, too heavy for a child to carry. Nettie stared down into her drink, thinking of the blood and her father's helplessness. He was one man, taken by surprise, and that had cost him his life. Her heart felt cracked now, as if bursting under the weight of a grief nurtured too long. She needed to set it down.

"He shouldn't have sent me to hide," she said, eyes stinging. "I could have done something. I could have handled a gun on my own. It's all just so stupid . . ."

"You were a child," Melvin said. "What were you going to do, take on Tonton Macoutes with your small child arms? On your own? Sounds to me like he was protecting you like any good father. Giving you a chance at escaping, hiding, surviving. That's called protecting the people you love. Love is not stupid. Foolish, maybe, but not stupid."

Nettie took a sip of her drink. Something in her chest hurt, a thing called grief buried deep through the years, resurfacing tonight. Don't cry Nettie, she thought. Just don't.

They stayed silent long enough for her to swallow the hurt, blink the tears away so she didn't look too weak.

"I got an uncle back in Chicago, but I'm pretty much an orphan," Melvin said. "My daddy drank himself to death when he came back from the war. I can't say as much for him giving me a shot at life, but I made it. I try not to be sentimental about it. So I feel in that way, you and I are very much alike. Raised by aunts and uncles. Orphaned from our parents. Fighting the revolution."

It felt as if they were rediscovering each other, after having been lost for a lifetime. His uncle, he said, had been a Deacon for Defense and Justice in Louisiana. His frame of mind was right in line with Melvin's, in that they both agreed on self-defense against the viciousness of white supremacy.

Nettie drank in Melvin's stories through her pores. She'd never really heard of a league of deacons pushing back against the Ku Klux Klan and providing defense to organizers like Dr. King. The more Melvin talked, the larger he seemed. There were chunks of history she didn't know a lot about, specific to men like his uncle, Melvin said, men who would not make the history textbooks.

Melvin lit a cigarette and blew the smoke in the air. He talked about how socialism disrupted the corruption of imperialism and how it could put collective power and responsibility in the hands of the people. He talked about education and how a newspaper's role in educating the people could free them from the mental slavery of imperialist forces. If the people were educated, then they would make better decisions about how to select their leaders and improve their quality of life. Duvalier, he said, was not a true revolutionary. And Nettie's heart skipped a beat when he said this.

"He started out as a revolutionary," Melvin said. "But you can't turn around and become the oppressor to your own people. You can't make a militia that turns around and brutalizes and terrorizes your people."

Then, Melvin leaned in and rested his hand on hers. She held her breath and felt an electric current run up her arm.

"If your father hadn't saved you from death, you wouldn't be here. It's meaningful that you're here, doing this," he said.

His hand was warm, and he squeezed her fingers gently, driving his point into her very marrow.

"The ancestors blew you into the path of the Panthers. They knew exactly where you needed to be. That's what matters. That you are here, working for the people." In the light overhead, she saw his mustache, freshly trimmed, black like his eyebrows, like his hair, and she pictured herself running a finger through it. "You are going to change this world, one sick patient at a time, you are going to do for our people what no one else has done. You're going to apply to medical school. You're going to be that one we all have been waiting for."

Nettie wasn't sure if she should pull her hand away first or if he would let go. Her free hand wrapped around her drinking glass, held it tighter. She felt alive, feeling the ice-cold condensation on her palms and the warmth of the light overhead, and the gaze of this man who had just spoken life into her.

"Thanks for resting your burden on me," Melvin said. "I know it's hard. Now I guess we're even, huh?"

Outside the window, darkness swallowed the city, leaving the structure of buildings standing under streetlights. Melvin kept his eyes on her, and she suddenly felt afraid that he'd seen too much. There was a wind inside her and now it was becoming imperative that she calm it, before it was too late.

8

BUT PERHAPS IT was already too late. The entire two weeks that followed, Nettie invented ways to see Melvin again, or created diversions for herself to stop thinking about Melvin, and his hands on her wrist, his grip on her shoulders and waist at the shooting range.

In the morning, she looked at herself in the mirror and wondered how it was possible that a man she so often sparred with had found a way to crawl under her skin like that. She brushed him off every strand of hair and braided the sections with a kind of rage directed at her own self. In the evenings, when the sun went down and she sat in her biology class, she would begin by focusing, writing notes during the professor's lecture. She'd done well so far in her survey and research methods course, shown she was not so bad at the mathematical side of it all. She was on track, and working with Dr. Johnson, and being able to interact with clients like Mrs. Haywood, was a great help. And yet now, her mind would drift halfway through the lecture, drown out the professor's voice and bring her closer to Melvin's, the deep velvet of his voice strumming her inner chords. "You're going to be the one we all have been waiting for." She was losing her grip, and only when class was over would she realize she'd been daydreaming.

The night he drove her home, after their excursion to Vallejo, Melvin didn't open the car door for her. He sat there and waited for her to say goodnight, and he said goodnight, too, and she scrambled out of the Bonneville like an idiot. She wasn't sure what she wanted, but she was disappointed that he hadn't leaned in to kiss her. She showered angrily that night, cursing herself for expecting more. He had been very clear earlier that day. He couldn't make space for love stories.

Still, she'd started waking up earlier and going to the community center to serve at the Panthers' breakfast program. When she was done, she headed to Dr. Johnson's clinic for work, until the late afternoon. Three evenings out of the week, she went to her classes on campus. Life had started to feel like a fast ride that left her little time to herself at home, little time to cook or entertain herself, let alone time for Tante Mado, who had started to complain.

"I barely see you these days," she said over the phone. "Are you feeding yourself? I made some good poul nan sòs yesterday, saved you some."

The gesture was kind, considering that Tante Mado had never believed much in manje dòmi, leftovers that sat there in the refrigerator, turning. Food had to be freshly made and eaten in her house. She must have been concerned enough about Nettie.

"You're already small as it is," Tante Mado said. "Make sure you eat. Good food. You should come get it, spend the night."

"Thank you Tantante," Nettie said. "I'm finishing my application packages. I'll be there as soon as I can."

But between exams, classes, application letters for medical school, work, and volunteering with the organization, Nettie was preoccupied. And now there was the constant dialogue in her mind with Melvin. About revolution. If she wanted to step up and out, if she wanted to be more than a spectator, then what better way was there? She no longer saw Melvin at the breakfast program. She also didn't see him at the Panther office in the evenings. It was as if he'd suddenly vanished, and she now was concerned that he'd gone or maybe been reassigned without her knowledge. She wanted to ask about him, but she stopped herself.

Then, one evening as she was walking to the Panther office, she saw a few men gathered in front of the entrance gate, talking with animus as a black town car pulled up. Melvin walked out of the office and got into the car with the other men. She held her breath, afraid to move or call attention to herself. He was in his most impeccable uniform, dressed in black from head to toe, his jacket shining in the streetlamps already lit in the dusk. The car took off, and just like that, he was gone.

Inside the office, she ran across Lewis, who was leaving the gunroom. Nettie asked what the car out front was about, carefully leaving Melvin out of her inquiry.

"Do you know what's going on?" she asked.

"Some of the comrades are off to Alameda County," he said.

She looked at Lewis, stunned. "You mean . . ."

"They're visiting Huey," Lewis said with enthusiasm. "If Huey called and asked for me by name . . ." He smiled. "I'd come running."

The innocence and the fire that burned in Lewis were almost familiar. His eyes were a lot like her father's when he practiced placing a gun in her hands. *The world only matters if you can participate in its revolution*, she remembered he'd said. What did this mean for Melvin, that he would see Huey tonight? It was a sobering reminder that Melvin belonged to something greater. He would be discussing important matters. He wouldn't be at the breakfast program the next morning, either. Perhaps the intimacy and attraction she'd felt that evening after Vallejo was all imagined.

When she went into the clinic and opened her desk drawer, however, Nettie found a book. *Black Feeling, Black Talk*, by a young poet, a Black woman named Nikki Giovanni. She didn't know whose book it was, but her heart sauntered in her chest as she thought of her discussion of books with Melvin. Maybe this was from him. No one seemed to know for sure, and there was no note. Who else could it be from?

She took it home with her that night. She read the poems with voracity, hoping with her entire might that this was Melvin's secret language, his way of sharing with her even when he was away. And every day, she looked for him to thank him. But there was no sign of Melvin.

Instead, she ran into Clia, and as happy as she was to see her friend, something in their dynamic had changed. There was a spark missing. Something dulled, as if it had been polished out of her.

"You said you'd come by and see me," Nettie said. "I'm worried about you."

Clia's schedule had been very busy. There was lots of work, lots of newspapers, and meetings to attend.

"Were you? I'm sorry, I just don't have a lot of time left on my hands for tea and crackers, you dig?"

Those words hit Nettie hard again, like a cold shower. She remembered how curt Clia had been with her the last time they spoke. "Okay," she said. "I dig it, I guess. I didn't realize this was all our time together meant to you, just hours spent drinking tea. I thought we were friends."

"Friends don't ditch each other like you ditch me these days," Clia said. "You think I don't know?"

"Know what?"

"You've changed!" Clia looked in her eyes. Nettie saw a flash of bitterness there. "Something about you is different now."

"I don't know what you mean but you know, Clia, it's fine. Forget I asked, I was genuinely concerned for you. My mistake."

"I don't really know whether you mean that, whether you really are worried about me, whether you care."

Nettie's face was growing hot. She stopped walking, eager to settle this increasing agitation. Arguing with Clia in a public place felt awkward. In a way, it did feel like they were involved in some lovers' spat and stuck in it, not going anywhere. Like fish swimming in a half-empty barrel, thrashing and circling around in circles.

"Do you care, Antoinette?" Clia steadied her voice, careful not to raise it so the words stayed between them. "Let's be real—the whole time we've known each other, I don't think you ever came over to my neck of the woods. Not once. You don't even know where I live."

"What's that got to do with anything?" Nettie asked.

"If you want to call yourself my friend, you should at least know where I live."

"If you want me over your house, then invite me!"

"Invite you? What, you think I live at the Sheraton?"

This was the invitation, Nettie realized. Clia ranted on about how her friends didn't need invitations, but Nettie understood that she wanted to feel like she mattered, like she was sought after, and why not give her that? After all, she was right. Clia was the one always coming over to her place. Never the other way around.

"Alright," Nettie nodded. "Fine, I'll come over. Tonight."

"Fine!"

CLIA'S HAIR WAS a burning bush in Nettie's hands. She brushed the section in her hand endlessly before squeezing it between her palms, gathering it the way she braided her own hair, in two parts, and wrapped it around her head. It was what Clia had requested.

"You don't have to be so gentle," Clia said, glancing at their reflection in the mirror. She was sitting on the floor between Nettie's legs. Nettie, who herself was sitting on the edge of the bed, met her eyes in the mirror. "I'm not that tender-headed."

Nettie had never braided another woman's hair. She had learned by watching the hired help in her father's house braid their own hair, and also her own, sometimes pulling and untangling with force. She remembered vaguely how one of the women preserved her shed hair from malevolent spells, burned it and mixed it in Nettie's hair pomade to help it regrow.

Sly and the Family Stone played on the turntable. It set the mood, but what they really wanted was to cover the music and sounds outside. In the living room, Clia's two nephews were roughhousing, and her cousin Theresa, with whom she shared the apartment, was frying fish. The incense stick burning on the nightstand was intended to keep that smell from seeping underneath her door.

Three strands of Clia's hair formed a magnificent braid, close to her scalp. Nettie pulled a little harder to make the hair tighter. Clia sighed. "I'm thinking about going down to Florida for a while," she finally said. "I need to get away from here."

Nettie looked in the mirror, sought her face.

"I know someone down there who's got an orange grove," Clia said. "In Clearwater. She writes me letters about it. Nothing but orange trees and sunshine, and when you step out and smell that Florida air, she says you smell nothing but the sweet fragrance of orange blossoms…" Clia was drifting in thought now, a faint smile on her lips. "I don't even know what that smells like, but I imagine I do. Have you ever smelled those before?"

Nettie shook her head. No, she'd never been to an orange grove before. "Maybe orange blossoms smelled like oranges?"

"I don't think so," Clia said. "I mean, I don't know, maybe. I hear they smell really sweet, like … open fields. Like freedom."

She chuckled softly. The fragrance of incense was interfering with Nettie's ability to imagine. What did sweetness or freedom smell like right now but patchouli?

"Sounds like that *friend* is making a convincing argument," Nettie said. She hesitated before asking. "Who is it?"

Clia looked in the mirror and grinned as she looked in Nettie's eyes. "Why do you ask?"

Nettie didn't know why she was asking, but she was curious about this new dream, these orange groves, this person who sounded like she was taking her friend away. And if Clia went away, who would be here for her? Suddenly the thought of Clia leaving was overwhelmingly frightening.

"Would you come with me?" Clia asked.

Nettie paused. Her fingers forgot to braid. She leaned in, cradling Clia's head.

"To an orange grove?" Nettie smiled. "What would someone like me do down there in an orange grove?"

"Grow oranges," Clia said. "Harvest them, sell them. Be with me. Be free."

"I don't understand," Nettie said. "What about everything you have here? What about the Party? I thought that was your life."

What did Clia know about oranges anyway? She couldn't mean that. Nettie waited for her to say something, but Clia sucked her teeth.

"Forget it. I shouldn't have asked. . . . Of course, you wouldn't come."

"You're serious about this? Clia, what is going on? Is it Clayton? What happened?"

Clia's eyes shifted in the mirror and found Nettie's. The two sat silently, staring at each other's reflection. Outside, they heard a thud as if someone hit a wall, and Theresa called after the boys to simmer down. Nettie thought about the times Clayton had cornered Clia after meetings, argued with her, reassigned her to other tasks she did not need to be doing. It was all clear now. This wasn't about oranges, not necessarily. This was about escape.

Nettie continued to braid, but her hand trembled.

"You don't have to put up with it, whatever it is," Nettie said, pulling the hair tighter between her fingers. "You are not a thing God made to satisfy a man's hunger. You're more than that. You said it yourself, you are a revolutionary." She didn't know where those words came from, but something deep in her chest burned like coals on hot fire. "Just because you think you owe him—"

"I do though," Clia said. "A great debt, and according to him, if I don't pay it, then I'm counterrevolutionary. He won't stop until he breaks me, until I give in."

"Counterrevolutionary?" Nettie said. "This is bullshit. Don't let him make you feel that way. That's wrong, Clia, you know that."

She bit her lip. What was the suitable word for this situation other than *sexism*, in its lowliest, dirtiest form? Who would do such a thing but a chauvinistic male who felt entitled to women's bodies?

"We should report him. Isn't there a way to report him to . . . headquarters?"

"No!" Clia's eyes widened and she shook her head, vehemently. "Talk some sense, Sister. Shit like this just makes a brother angrier."

She finally turned from her seat on the floor. Her beautiful eyes stared into Nettie's through thick, damp eyelashes.

"I've thought about it, though, about giving in, just to get my peace of mind. Just so he'd leave me alone. I'm just tired. I just want him to understand. I want to be left alone. I don't want this. Not with him . . . or any man."

For a moment, they said nothing, and Clia started to play with her own hair, wrapping the tight coils around her finger. Perhaps she was walking around the orange grove, learning how to pick them, how to pollinate and crossbreed different varieties.

"There's got to be something that can be done," Nettie said. "Just because he's your section leader doesn't mean he has the right."

Clia found her breath and suddenly, she snapped out of her dream state. She looked at Nettie in the mirror, the incense smoke rising above her in thick white curls.

"Men are all the same in the end," she muttered.

Nettie wanted to agree, but then she thought of Melvin. She felt slightly hypocritical, rationalizing with Clia that she didn't have to fall for Clayton's trap. Because on the other hand, she was falling for one herself. Melvin. Was he the same as Clayton Young? No. She was certain he wasn't.

"You told me this organization is made of good men, and good women, that want change," Nettie said. "Right? Clayton is not a reflection of the Party, is he? I'd like to think some of them can be decent."

Clia's eyes narrowed in the mirror. Her light brown hair framed her head like a lion's mane. Nettie continued to braid furiously, letting her fingers do the work, forcing herself to not look at her friend for fear of betraying emotion. But Clia was already reading her.

"You mean like Melvin? I hear the two of you have been spending time together..."

"It was just a mission," Nettie corrected. "He seems alright, I don't know."

"Alright? Is that all? Because I know what the women out there see in the brother. He's what women say they want in a man, isn't he? A warrior. A Black Panther. He enters a room and women want to drop their panties."

Nettie cocked her head and stared at Clia in the mirror, her face now burning. "That is *not* me, you know that. But also, what if I was attracted to him, let's suppose I was. Then what?" Her heart was racing, but she looked to Clia, hopeful. "Is that a problem?"

"You need to be serious about the revolution. You're letting Melvin distract you."

"Oh, so you and me, that's not a distraction? But Melvin is?"

Clia's face darkened. Nettie knew she'd hit a nerve.

"See, when I said you changed? This is what I meant!"

Nettie blinked in the mirror but Clia didn't budge. They'd stung each other enough and now they stared at their bruised reflections, Clia breathing hard like a wounded feline.

"That's not called changing," Nettie said. "This is always who I am."

"If you say so."

They fell into an uncomfortable silence, and Nettie wondered if she should continue working on Clia's hair. You don't braid a sista's hair when you're angry. She wanted to let go, but Clia cleared her throat.

"Look, I always said I don't care what you do with yourself. Be who you are. You're grown, you do what you want. But I thought we were in this for the revolution and now, every time he turns up, I feel like I lose you some."

Nettie's heart was swelling with regret. She could still feel Clia's eyes on her in the mirror, studying her movements, and she tried not to flinch, not to give away her uneasiness at those words. She was a fool all along, hoping or thinking that Melvin would ever see anything more in her than a comrade, someone volunteering her time.

"Melvin's a good brother," Clia said. "He's invested in the revolution and he means business, I know that. He's serious. But at the end of the day, he still has a dick. And guess what dick does?"

Nettie's arms dropped. If she could run out of this apartment right now, she'd leave Clia with her hair half braided, half bush, and they would never speak again. But this was where they were. Now Nettie had to be forced to think of Melvin in that way, think of him as a man, with a dick in his pants, and it made her sweat a little.

"You sleep with him yet?"

"It was only one mission," Nettie said. "We just talked. Nothing wrong with talking, is there?"

Nettie was growing uncomfortable, not just with admitting that she was interested in Melvin, but with the feeling that this was not quite what Clia wanted to hear, even if she was asking questions and seemed genuinely interested.

"Talking leads to fucking!" Clia's lips stretched into a faint smile of pity. "And Melvin is good at talking. You are so naïve."

The fragrance of incense started to dwindle, and Clia reached for another. Nettie watched her light it as she tackled the final sections of hair between her hands, braiding them into an organized, tame row. She tried to concentrate, but now Clia's voice was coming back against the music.

"I don't want to talk about Melvin anymore," Nettie said impatiently, cutting her off. "What are we going to do about Clayton?"

Clia's eyes sparkled. "We?" Nettie felt her warm breath through the fabric of her pants and the hair on her arms stood. "This is *my* problem," Clia whispered. "Not yours."

Clia's voice was firm. She looked away, at a distant corner of the room, and Nettie felt her evaporate. She mumbled some words, but none of them came out clearly. Nettie continued to braid in silence. When Nettie was done, Clia looked at her whole self in the mirror and Nettie smiled at how beautiful she was with her hair pulled back. Now she could see aspects of her face that didn't immediately stand out under her Afro. Her jawline, her forehead, even her eyes seemed accentuated differently.

"Right on," Clia whispered. "I dig it."

Their eyes met in the mirror and Clia offered half a smile. "Don't worry about me, I got this. Some brothers just need more convincing, I can handle it."

She turned to Nettie and thanked her, and then said she had a lot of other things to do. Nettie's blood turned cold. This was Clia's way of letting her know she wanted to be alone. That was that.

"Is that it?" Nettie said.

"What else did you want to talk about?"

Nettie stared, bewildered, infuriated that Clia was distancing her on purpose. It made her feel rotten. She grabbed her jacket off the bed.

"Alright," Nettie said. "I'll go."

She made her way to the bedroom door, fuming, but Clia grabbed hold of her arm, pulling her into her embrace. Clia kissed Nettie, gently at first, and then with more intensity. This time, this kiss was peppered with a disconcerting hint of desperation. Although Clia's mouth was warm, even though there was a safety in the way she held her, Nettie's heart was pounding at the thought that, here, they were not alone. Not like last time. Nettie held her breath and felt her friend's heart racing. Finally, Clia let go, and looked at her with fire in her eyes.

"Just promise me that you won't talk about this. About me, about anything I told you. Especially about Clayton. You hear me? Stay out of it."

Clia's breath was warmer now as she exhaled. She tightened her grip around Nettie's waist and held her firmly. Nettie suddenly felt overwhelmed with sadness. She wasn't sure why. But she nodded.

Clia finally released her and opened the door for her to leave. Nettie walked out into the dark hallway and smelled the fish frying as if Theresa had set up the stove right outside. When she turned to look over her shoulder, Clia had already shut the door.

9

MELVIN WAS BACK. Nettie could hear him outside the clinic, speaking in hushed tones. She was standing in the hallway when she caught a glimpse of him with about five other brothers in the armory around the table. The men in the armory room must be high-ranking officers, given their demeanor and the authority in their voices.

Her assumptions had been right after all. Melvin had too much on his plate with the Party to have time for her. He was meeting with Huey and going on missions. This was not a man who would ask her out on a date. *Get real, Nettie!* she told herself.

As she prepared the patients' paperwork, she felt stupid for expecting more of him. He was in a meeting, after all. Not only had he barely acknowledged her when their eyes met, but he had continued to talk as if she wasn't even there. Fine, she thought. It was fine. She didn't need to talk to him. Besides, this wasn't why she was here. Don't be distracted, that's what Clia had said. She was here to heal people like her father had done. Ensure collective well-being. That afternoon, Michael Haywood returned to the clinic for a blood transfusion and lay on the table, and Nettie could see he was now a much different child, his face fuller. Which meant the transfusions were working.

"Look at you, son, you're not even scared of those needles," Dr. Johnson said to the boy, securing the syringe in his arm with medical tape. "After all you've been through, this is nothing. Right?"

"I'm not scared of a sting, Doc."

Mrs. Haywood sat in the room, watchful. She didn't offer a full smile, but her eyes glowed with gratitude.

Nettie could administer first aid, but she wasn't allowed to perform this kind of procedure yet. Still, she handed the instruments over with gloved hands to Dr. Johnson when he asked. Prepping and drawing blood really fell under Clia's job description, but Clia was calling in sick so much that her absence was becoming a problem.

"Has she said anything to you at all?" Dr. Johnson finally asked, opening the clamp on the line and waiting for a drip. Nettie's eyes followed the blood as it traveled all the way through.

"No," Nettie said. "I don't talk to her much these days."

She didn't like lying to Dr. Johnson or anyone, for that matter, but she had sworn silence to Clia. Dr. Johnson nodded and connected the line to Michael's port and let the blood do its work, checking on his comfort level.

"We'll be back shortly," Dr. Johnson said to Michael. "In the meantime, you can rest."

He asked Nettie to follow him to his office.

"It's unfortunate you don't have a nursing license," Dr. Johnson said. "You could be doing Clia's job. I think we can safely assume she may not be returning. It's not very professional to make me wait like that. I have patients. I need to hire someone."

Nettie felt her stomach churn. This would mean Clia losing her livelihood. What could she do? It wasn't her place to say anything.

"But instead of hiring you, I'm writing you letters of recommendation to actual medical school. Which is what you want anyway, isn't it? Here . . ." He nodded, smoothing his mustache, and motioned for her to come to his desk. "I finished them this morning," he said. "Four in total. Care to read them? Tell me your thoughts?"

Nettie couldn't contain her smile as her eyes ran down the lines of praise. Even in this awkward, heart-wrenching moment, she dared to feel happy. A diligent assistant, curious about the medical world, but mostly, as he so eloquently said, "always eager to help change what others will not." He mentioned her hours of dedication to the free clinic, mentioned how her dedication to the sickle cell survey was instrumental in providing care.

"Thank you," she said, her cheeks hot.

"I notice you're applying all in-state," he said. "Don't you want more options? Howard's got scholarships down in DC, I can get you details."

Nettie's palms prickled. Washington, DC was so far away from California, she thought. She'd never even seen leaves change colors and fall off trees, never even seen snow. The merest drop in temperature in California sent her bones into shock. She would be completely alone there, without Tante Mado. She would be leaving it all with no anchor to cling to, adrift like a balloon wandering into vast places.

"I'll give it some thought," Nettie said.

Later that evening, after the Haywoods left, Dr. Johnson cleaned up his desk and put on his jacket. Then, he called out to her. "I know you'd be a good doctor, you have what it takes. Plus, a sister as a doctor in a field overrun by men, healing, that's powerful."

He reached for the doorknob and said, "Just don't get in your own way," he said. "Stay the course." He closed the door behind him.

Washington. Maybe. Why not? She tried to catch her breath, dread lurking in the back of her mind. She couldn't do Washington, what was there to think about? If she stayed in California, would that not be staying the course? What did that mean?

"How did you like the book?"

She did not hear Melvin come in, and she should have felt him there, but she was too busy panicking over the idea of Howard University. And then she took another breath. Melvin. Finally.

"The book? You mean the poetry book?"

Her heart beat a little faster as Melvin nodded. He'd found the small, privately pressed volume in the City Lights bookstore after they last talked, he said. He thought she'd appreciate it.

"I like it," she said. In fact, she liked it a lot. But she had to feign indifference for the sake of her own dignity. She proceeded to file the last patient records of the day.

"You're mad at me, aren't you?" Melvin folded his arms over his chest. "I can tell when you're mad at me. You have that look."

"What look?"

Melvin leaned in, resting his hands on her desk. "You clench your jaw like that, and your nostrils flare . . . You're mad because I was gone a while. Why don't you just say it?"

She shook her head and wedged the last folder into the filing cabinet. She shrugged.

"You don't owe me an explanation about your life," she said. "You have things to do. I have things to do."

"Do you have things to do tonight?"

She looked at him. Was he asking her out? He was. She liked spending time with him and wanted to get to know him more, but she was also ready to turn him down, because she really was busy. She still had reading to finish for class tomorrow.

"Can we go out? You and me? Watch a movie and eat?"

She saw that he was very serious about his request. He stood there against the desk, in a military camouflage jacket, unsmiling, and there was no sufficient reason to say no. She nodded, and opened her mouth to say okay, but her reply was covered by another voice, shouting down the halls. "To the clinic! Take him to the clinic! Shut the door!"

The commotion grew louder before two men barged in, carrying a third. It took Nettie a moment to realize what was happening. The one they carried was wounded, badly. Blood stained his shirt around the abdominal area and spread out through the fabric. They set him down as he moaned in pain on one of the two hospital beds. Nettie's heart raced as uneasiness began to settle in. This voice . . . Her blood ran cold at the chilling recognition of this body. This face. She covered her mouth to stifle a gasp. Lewis!

"Help me," he whined. "Please. My Momma. I want my Momma."

Under the bright yellow light, she saw Lewis's childlike face, contorted in a grimace. He was too young to be here, bleeding like that in the body of an almost man. Nettie reached for his shirt.

"Pigs got him just two blocks away," the men said. "Shot him. They're still after him."

Someone shouted down the hallway. "Hey! Pigs lining up outside! Pigs are vamping on us!" Melvin was already scrambling out of the room, his hand on his holster. Nettie heard the sound of feet rushing through the building, covering the sound of her own heartbeat in her ears. She used both hands to tear Lewis's shirt open. Blood oozed out of the gunshot wound. Her body felt numb, nearly paralyzed, and she felt alarm bells ringing all at once in his ears.

"Sister, can you do anything?" The Panthers were staring at her with concern. "We can't call Dr. Johnson back. Pigs got us surrounded!"

Outside, there was a scramble as fellow Panthers ran in and out of the armory. She heard Melvin's voice down the hallway, shouting orders. The two brothers stepped away from Lewis, drew their weapons, and left the room.

"Miss Nettie?" Lewis's lips were trembling. She quickly regained possession over her own thoughts as he began to ramble. "I don't want to die. I don't want to die like this. Don't let me die."

She felt her legs again. Quickly, her brain dictated what to do. She ran to the closet and searched, her eyes running through boxes until she found what she needed. Towels here on the shelves, and in another drawer, two rolls of gauze. Those would have to do. She reached for them, she noticed her hands had already smeared blood onto the fabric.

When she returned, she looked in his eyes.

"I didn't do it," Lewis mumbled, his lips moving faster than the words could come out. "They said . . . freeze. I didn't—"

"Hush." Nettie showed him the towel, her lips trembling. "Don't talk. I have to stop the bleeding. I'm going to apply some pressure."

She'd never seen so much fear in someone's eyes, and the weight of the responsibility crushed her. What if he died, like her father? Because this was what would come next, she knew, if he didn't get the proper care. When she applied the towel to the wound, he caught both of her hands and guided her. He closed his eyes and grimaced as she pressed down.

Melvin returned, outfitted with a bandolier of shells and a rifle. As if this was war, and for all she knew, now, it was. She was caught in the middle of it. Melvin studied Lewis.

"Pillows," she shouted. "Over there, grab me more pillows!"

Melvin's look was one of puzzlement, so she yelled again. "Please! Pillows!" She elevated Lewis's head as high as he could bear it. "He needs a hospital," Nettie said to Melvin. The words were heavy in her mouth, rolling about like stones, but she managed to be coherent. "He'll need surgery."

Melvin glanced at Nettie. "We on lockdown right now," he said. "They want us to turn him over, and I'm not letting them in here without no warrant. Lewis ain't going nowhere, so you're it right now."

"What? What do you mean I'm *it?*"

He started out of the room, but Nettie ran after him. "Wait!" She caught his arm. "Melvin, if we don't get him to a real doctor, he's going to die."

Her voice cracked. She was sure he heard a tremor in it. But surely, he could see for himself how bad it was. They both turned to look at Lewis, his body barely visible under the white sheets. Melvin's jaw clenched. "Well then, don't let him!"

He pulled out a handgun from his holster, a large semi-automatic. A .357 Magnum. It was his own personal gun, the one he let her use at the gun range. The barrel was shiny, longer than she remembered. He popped out the chamber to show her it was loaded.

"Keep them pigs out! You dig?"

She nodded. Yes. It was déjà vu from Mrs. Haywood's all over again. No, it went back further than that. Fifth memory. Last one. Her father lying there, a rivulet of blood crossing his forehead and feeding the earth. Except Lewis was alive, still. He wasn't dead.

Melvin's eyes were full of questions, and she had to let him know she was as serious as he was, too. She had to protect Lewis. She couldn't let them take him. He wasn't going to die that way.

THERE WERE AT least five police cars outside, blocking the street. The officers were shielded behind their car doors, weapons drawn and aimed at the building, but no one was shooting yet. All Nettie could hear was shouting. "Turn in the suspect!"

She watched from the window as people from adjacent buildings poured out onto the sidewalks, as if all here for a spectacle. In the corner of her eye,

Nettie saw two vehicles from the media park a few blocks down. Customers from the record stores, barber shops, and dry cleaners around the block quickly ran out at attention, yelling at the police. "Leave them alone! They work for the community!"

A police officer's voice resounded on a bullhorn.

"These are orders from the Oakland Police. You are harboring a suspect."

Nettie stepped away from the window and returned to help Lewis apply more pressure on his wound. He looked paler now. Nettie felt a knot in her throat now, her anxiety building into a kind of anger she could not suppress. There was only so long a man could last before he bled out. She couldn't tell who was speaking, at first, but she could hear the upstairs staff descending. Women, all speaking as they readied their own weapons. On the bullhorn, the police continued shouting that Lewis was reported to have stolen something from a pawn shop.

"This is your last warning!" The officer barked, his anger cleaving through the airwaves. "You turn him in, or we shoot our way in!"

"Do it!" Nettie recognized Melvin's voice. "Go ahead!"

There was a cold silence throughout the building. Not even a whisper. Just palpable hesitation from the pigs as they stared at the building, waiting for orders. Waiting for someone to open fire. Nettie went back to the window, saw nothing outside but pedestrians and police cars. Finally, Melvin spoke up.

"What do you want with him, pig?"

Nettie felt for Melvin's gun in her back pocket. Lewis whispered something she couldn't hear. She came back to him.

"I'm right here," she whispered.

She clasped his wrist where he still felt warm, and pressed two fingers against his artery, running quick math in her head. Ninety beats per minute. The rapid pulse gave her a chill. She folded Lewis' hands over the towel and pressed down. "Keep the pressure, I'll be right back."

Nettie went to the clinic door and opened it just slightly enough to peer into the hallway. She couldn't see anything from that vantage point except the dark shadows and the faint light at the end filtering through the sandbagged wall. She crept down the hallway quickly, her heart pounding in her chest so loudly, she imagined everyone else could hear it. At the end of the hall, she peeked her head out to see the Panthers standing by the entrance. Men, but also women, mostly women, all armed to the teeth, positioned at the windows, waiting, finger on the trigger, their faces mean as if they were all Lewis's mother.

She couldn't see Melvin, at first, but when he spoke again, she saw that he was among three Panthers looking through a slit in the wall she hadn't noticed before. A response followed through the bullhorn.

"We have a witness from a robbery, saying he was down at Duveil's Pawn Shop on Telegraph!"

"Bullshit!" One of the women shouted through an opening in the window. "Prove it!"

"Where's the witness?" Melvin yelled.

There was a hesitation, and then the police responded with the same threats. Melvin sucked his teeth.

"You got no witness, and you sure as hell ain't coming in here to get nobody. That kid needs medical attention because you shot him! We called for an ambulance and now you're gonna sit there and block the way. We know what this is."

One of the Panthers pumped a shotgun and yelled through the slit. "You're gonna die today, pig!" Then Reggie's voice came through and said they had to be smart and calculated, not impulsive. They should avoid a shootout. Those were their orders. The women in the room were even harder than the men. "We ain't turning nobody in!" they said, squaring their jaws, ready for a fight.

"Excuse me?" Nettie heard her own voice rise in the dark and, suddenly, every pair of eyes in the room turned to her. She knew Melvin was looking at her.

"Lewis will bleed out if we don't do something now."

A figure quickly emerged from among the faces. Melvin looked angry. "Didn't I tell you to stay back there?" he said.

"I'm not going to watch him die back there alone," Nettie snapped. "He needs medical attention. Time is of the essence."

"Who's watching that back door while you're here giving us orders?"

"I'm not giving you orders. I'm just—"

"Get back in that room and do your goddamn job!"

Nettie recoiled. "Don't talk to me that way!"

"Hey, hey, hey, look here!" Reggie stepped in between them, his arms up in surrender. "We don't have time for that right now, we got pigs at our door. Don't be foolish."

Nettie trembled from head to toe. She wanted to look at Reggie, but her eyes were throwing daggers at Melvin, her nostrils flared. How dare he? She gritted her teeth and spun on her heel, eyes wet with tears. Who did he think he was, yelling at her this way?

Lewis was still breathing, but he was calmer now. She brought him some water from the sink, held his head up for quick sips. What would Dr. Johnson do if he were here? What would any good doctor do, really, if they weren't able to operate? She couldn't heal the cause of his suffering. It would take a surgeon to extract that bullet that was slowly killing him. She hoped it hadn't hit a major artery.

She heard a commotion outside. She went to the window just in time to see that the people had now stepped further back and looked increasingly concerned. The police were still in position, shielding behind their car doors in wait. But the one holding the bullhorn now stepped closer toward the entrance. What was happening?

Suddenly, she saw a silhouette emerge in the walkway. Melvin. She watched as he advanced toward the officer with the bullhorn, and the officer suddenly took one small step back. She watched him walk with assurance, before stopping a few feet away. They were now throwing a few words at each other, and the officer's fingers twitched nervously. There were at least twenty Panthers in the house aiming back at him through the boards and slats of this house, from the small newspaper operation upstairs to the clinic and the kitchen downstairs. They would pump him with lead.

Nettie's hands grew cold. Melvin was done talking but he was staring the officer down, and then the officer shook his head. It wasn't a no, but not a nod either. He simply shook it to mean, Nettie surmised, he was unhappily considering the situation. Melvin was stone. Still. Nettie instinctively brought her gun up and pointed it out there, as a reflex for defense if something went wrong.

The officer finally took a step back and Nettie thought she could see right through his paleness. The news crew stationed on the side also stood back, and then the people started to move out of focus for Nettie, as if they were slowly disappearing. They were instinctively flinching, too, seeking an exit. The officer raised his hand in the air to signal to the others and Nettie thought she heard him say, "Stand down," and there was a hesitation from the officers to comply. They kept their weapons up until the officer in charge stepped away.

Melvin watched the officer walk out to the sidewalk, off the property, before backing up to the house. He was not turning his back to them until he reached the doorway and that was all she could see of him now.

Lewis was breathing still when she returned to his bedside. "Stay? Don't leave me, please." He was weakening and now she realized, maybe he was asking if he was dying. It was unnerving watching life slip out of a body, horrific to watch someone actively die and stand there, powerless. That hadn't been covered in any of her public health courses. Every class she'd ever taken, all of it felt meaningless. Lewis could not be helped with any of that.

Someone was approaching. She could hear footsteps, and she gripped the gun again, holding it with both hands. She aimed it right when the door flew open. Melvin walked in and froze. For a moment, there was silence between them as she adjusted her eyes and brain to the fact it was just him. No one else.

"It's okay," Melvin said, eyes on Lewis. Then, he turned to Nettie. "We got an ambulance on the way. You can go now if you want."

Nettie glanced at Lewis, his hands still laid over the towel and the blood. She shook her head.

"I'll stay," she said. "He asked me to stay."

Fifth memory. Her father cold to the touch when she reached for him and shook him. The painful stretching of the hours as she called for him. Papa! The dreadful memory of silence had returned, Lewis drifting in and out of consciousness. How could she do right by him? How could she have kept her father alive? She reached for Lewis's hand and clasped his fingers but he did not grip hers back. Melvin was still there, staring at her, but she barely saw him through the veil clouding her vision.

"I can hear sirens." Melvin's voice broke the silence, even as he managed to soften his tone.

Nettie blinked. How much time had passed? But she heard them, too, now in the distance, faintly, like an already broken promise.

Minutes later when the siren blared outside the building, it sounded like something heard in a dream. She tightened her grip on his hand to let him know she was still here. But she wasn't sure he could feel it. His eyes were closing.

10

THE BONNEVILLE PULLED up at the curb in front of Nettie's apartment. It must have been ten, she thought. Maybe eleven. She'd lost track of time. Overhead, the sky was moonless, a draping of tight, dark clouds swirling and colliding into each other. Grief had stolen their words, rendered them mute.

Lewis had been in surgery for several hours, and the bullet had been successfully removed, but there was some organ damage and he was left comatose. They did not seem confident. The Panthers who had followed the ambulance all waited in the hallways of the hospital along with Nettie, softly speaking just to keep their own hope alive. And just where were the pigs now? They had vanished a few minutes after the ambulance got on the road. Melvin had sat silent in his corner of the waiting room when the final word came, and was just as silent now in the car.

When she thought about Lewis, Nettie felt her brain short-circuit, like a bad electrical current running through. She kept seeing his parents, the fear on their faces, his mother's tears in the hallway as the doctors pronounced him gone. Nettie had run into the bathroom and thrown up. What was worse than listening to a mother mourn a child in that way? It sounded awful, like a dying animal. *My boy! They took my boy!* It was still pulsing in her bones as if she knew that pain. As if this pain already knew her.

Thunder rolled through the night sky, right above them. With the windows down, she smelled rain clinging oppressively to the air, the scent the earth gives before it is drenched in downpour. How did they even get here, she and Melvin?

She had no recollection of the trip itself. He'd said nothing to her. All he did was smoke.

Melvin killed the engine. "Are you going to be alright?"

Nettie did not know how to get out of the car. Her eyes were swollen with tears. She knew she probably would not sleep tonight, not with the sound of Lewis still pleading in her mind.

"He didn't deserve this," she said. "He shouldn't have died. Kids are not supposed to die." Something clung to her throat. "We should have acted faster."

"We did what we could," Melvin said coldly, his eyes fixed on her.

"We should have gotten him to a hospital sooner."

"Don't you think I know that?" Melvin snapped.

Nettie jumped. Her eyes went to Melvin, and he was shaking his head, jaw set.

"He decided to join the Party, he graduated to manhood when he signed on. So let's call him a man. Childhood is a luxury we as a people cannot afford."

Nettie's blood curdled at Melvin's tone, searing with anger. He licked his lips and went on, each word flying at her like daggers.

"In the pig's mind, Lewis was not even a human being. He was a target and that's how they disengage. That's the reality. Lewis chose this path and we should honor that."

"So, it's his fault? You're saying he shouldn't have signed up?"

"He signed with his parents' consent because it was dangerous, and he knew it, it's not a game! He took a risk. We can't deny that."

"But you make it sound like it's his fault," she said.

"It's not about fault. It's about responsibility. Don't put words in my mouth. What is wrong with you?"

"What's wrong with me?" Nettie raised her eyebrow, furious. "What is wrong with *you*, Melvin? Why do you always do this?"

"Do what?" He turned his body to Nettie and faced her. "What do I do?"

"You get enraged, and you talk down to me. You're condescending."

"What the hell are you talking about?"

"That!" She pointed the finger in his face. "You think you can just talk to me any way you want. The way you yelled at me in front of everyone was humiliating and you know it."

"With the pigs aiming their guns at us? You wanted me to be polite?"

"I didn't deserve that. I get that you're pissed off, but you don't have to be an asshole. I'm not the enemy!"

"An asshole?" Melvin raised his eyebrows and his face changed. "You had an order! All you had to do was follow my instructions, and you walked out of the room. I'm not the one who did that. *You* did that. You're mouthy and unruly, and disrespectful, too, right about now."

Nettie felt herself spiral down into a pit. Disrespectful? Her? Why was she doing this to herself? She didn't have to volunteer anymore, not when the prospect of being of service meant people unjustly dying. She unbuckled her seatbelt, her tongue loosening to let out an expletive she very seldom used. "You know what? Fuck you!"

"Fuck me?"

Nettie grabbed the door handle and stormed out of the vehicle and slammed the door with force, hoping the violence would shatter the window. But it didn't. She walked away without another look, through the vestibule and up the stairs. She didn't turn around when she heard him call her name. She didn't know if he'd left or not, but she knew as she climbed the stairs that he hadn't started the car yet, that he was still there, probably boiling in his seat. How had they gotten here?

Gilda was having another party. She could hear the music blaring, and laughter, the smell of pot suffusing the air. Overhead in the skylight, she could have sworn she'd missed a crack of lightning. Everything was briefly illuminated in a silver blue light before returning to normal.

Nettie went in and shut the door behind her. She was safe now. She could be fully angry and devastated at the same time. She could shower, drink tea, let her braids down. She could do anything. And yet, when she ran the water and washed off the blood, she was still trembling. She knew there would be no sleep tonight. She was not going back to any of this. It was a mistake. Dr. Johnson would understand if she explained. Tante Mado was right, this was nothing but trouble for her. The heartache and danger that came with this kind of commitment were too much to handle at once. Perhaps the revolution was not for her after all. Perhaps all she should and could do was focus on the good. Her job, helping people heal, and her studies, those things were good. Good enough.

She wrapped herself in a robe, still damp from her shower. Outside, rain began to pour. At first, softly, barely audible. Then, the rain became a downpour, a loud shower over the city that sounded like a rumble in her head. She knew she was wrong about leaving the Panthers over Melvin. But she couldn't face Melvin anymore. She was tired.

Raindrops banged against the windows like small stones more than they splattered. Even the sky was mourning. At first she didn't hear the knocking at the door as it mixed in with the thunder, and when she did, it frightened her. It was loud, insistent, and authoritative. She thought for a brief moment that it might be the police. The second round of knocks came soon after. The clock read nearly midnight. Who was at her door so late? Maybe it was Gilda, who quite frankly needed to grow the fuck up. Nettie was not in the mood for her oblivious joy.

Thunder clapped as Nettie swung the door open.

"You?" She took a breath, her heart thumping wildly in her chest. "What do you want?"

Melvin was standing there, his collar propped to protect his neck from the rain.

"I shouldn't have said what I said," he said. "Can we talk? You and me?"

He was soaked, his hair and skin gleaming as the wind picked up the sheet of rain behind him, breathing fast. He must've run from the street and up the stairs to beat the rain. He didn't sound angry. He had cooled off enough, perhaps. She shrugged, and he took this as an invitation. He brushed past her, touching her with his wet sleeve. She closed the door. He'd never been inside her place before and she could tell his eyes were taking a quick inventory of the place: the curtain, the bedroom door, the stove. He turned around and faced her.

"I don't have anything to say to you," she said.

"That's fine! But I have something to say, and I need you to listen."

"Oh, you're going to lecture me in my own home?"

Melvin chuckled, his teeth bone-white, gums purple, lip curled into amusement. She saw the exasperation in his eyes. He wiped his hands on his pants, wiped his brow. Nettie kept her eyes on him and moved her concerns about her wet carpet to the back of her mind. It could wait. Still, she handed him a kitchen towel to wipe the rain off. He dabbed himself for a minute. They stared at each other briefly. She folded her arms over her chest and waited.

Melvin shifted his gaze to the carpet. "I shouldn't have talked to you that way, you're right. But the thing is, you talk like you got me figured out, and you don't."

She raised her eyebrow. This wasn't how she would start a peaceful conversation, she thought. He ran his hand against his chin and jaw, where thick, black hair curled against the hours of the night. He looked at her, his eyes like pieces of coal, dark and then fiery. She felt a small shudder as the rainwater dripped down his eyebrows and rolled onto his skin.

"You don't know anything about me," he said, wiping his sleeves dry as if the towel could clean his anger off his skin. "You don't know my shit, what I've been through. Yet, you keep coming at me. I don't like that."

She had no idea what he meant by that, but her heart seemed to know, because it was now galloping in her chest.

"I keep coming at you? How so?"

"You like to challenge me. You're hard-headed. You don't listen."

"Oh. Sure, I see, I'm the problem. Okay."

"I know I'm not perfect. I'm angry about a lot of shit, and yeah, I may be a little quick to snap. I try to be better. But when you've seen what I've seen, you would think you've earned the right to speak your mind how you see fit without being challenged, you know. But you challenge me and it just—"

"I don't understand what you're getting at."

"If you could just let me finish, woman . . . Goddamn."

Nettie's heart sank. The more Melvin talked, the more she could see through his frustration.

"I'm not angry with you," Melvin said. "You didn't cause what happened tonight. *We* didn't do this. We didn't pull the trigger on that boy. I shouldn't have been so hard on you today. I know you think I don't give you the respect you deserve, but I do respect you."

He paused and shook his head. She could tell he was tripping against his own thoughts by the way he sucked his teeth. No, this was perhaps not what he wanted to say. Maybe it was coming out wrong. He lifted his gaze and looked at her again.

"I don't need you to challenge me when we're in a situation like this. You could get hurt. I've seen it happen, people just . . . Wars are bloody. Just listen to me, and let me keep you alive so we don't have any more deaths on our hands."

"We're not in Vietnam, Melvin. This is Oakland."

"I know that!" Melvin's voice was suddenly grave. "I don't need you telling me what time it is. It's a revolution happening right now, and we're all caught up in it. It's a war out here, too. That makes you a soldier, Nettie, whether you like it or not. I saw you today, I watched you, and yeah, I yelled at you, but what you did today was . . ."

He squinted and took a step closer to her. "The way you committed. You were all in with us, and that makes you a soldier in my book. Makes you my responsibility. My job. To protect you. Not let anything happen to you."

There. Now that he said it, now that it came out of his mouth, her heart felt mechanically unsound, like gears shifting backward. She rested against the kitchen counter and tried to catch her breath.

"I don't need you to do that," she muttered.

"I don't care," he said. "I'm still in charge of your safety when you're around. And that's got me all fucked up," he added, stepping even closer. "All I've done since meeting you is think about you. I just want you out of my head sometimes."

He chuckled softly, without really smiling, and it was like watching a black flower burst open, blossoming under moonlight with the dark purple folds of his lips and gums.

"I'm sorry I'm such a burden to you," she said.

Something pounded against the wall next door. They heard laughter and the beat of some song drowning under the current of voices. Melvin's eyes were piercing now. She felt impaled in place, unable to move.

She wanted to push him to say more. But a man like Melvin wasn't going to, she decided. She wanted to say something clever or smart, or hurtful even, but looking in Melvin's eyes was like falling off the edge of a cliff.

"I told you before that I didn't join this organization for *this* . . ." He gestured softly so she knew what he meant when he said it. This thing between them. She let out her breath.

"And yet here I am . . ." Melvin said. "Falling for you and shit."

Nettie looked up at him and then down at her toes. What could she say?

"I don't know what to say."

She saw drops of rain roll off his perfectly smooth skin and wanted to wipe them off. Her eyes remained fixed on that bare patch above the button of his shirt, glistening with sweat and rain. Melvin threw the towel on the table. For a moment time felt suspended between them.

"You can ask me to stay," he said. His voice ran through to her like a stream finding its way. "Because truth be told, all I want to do tonight is take you to bed."

Melvin was always so direct and disarming, and now she had no ammunition left. She was not running from him this time, not looking away.

"If you don't want that, of course, then I'll leave."

"No," she said, undone. "Don't go . . . Stay."

As if he'd expected this, he peeled off his jacket, threw it on the chair near him, and stepped even closer to her. Close enough she could smell the rain on him and the cigarette he'd been smoking. She badly wanted a taste of all of those things off his skin. His hands gripped her hips just as her hand found the belt of her robe, and she yanked it, gently, just to get him started. His eyes went to her bare flesh and she could see him breathe deeply, placating himself. "Come here," he whispered.

Their mouths finally found each other and Melvin's tongue found hers, took hers, tied her up in velvet and cigarettes and kept her, hungrily asking for more. His teeth bit into her lip. There was a soft prickle of his mustache against her lips that she liked, and a desperation and clumsiness to how he groped her, how her own hands struggled to unbutton his shirt, how he lifted her off the ground and carried her, bumping into kitchen chairs and then the table itself. They held on, bruising and scratching skin as they explored the maps of their bodies for the first time.

They held the minutes of the night in their hands, kissing each other, finding old wounds. Nettie found constellations of scars left by shrapnel across Melvin's back and caressed them. This was different, she felt. This was grown-folk lovemaking. This was far from the rehearsed gestures and feigned climaxes with the boys she'd been with before. The kind of man Melvin was, she could study and find a whole history for just in the way he entered her body, brutal yet kind, gazing into her eyes as if looking for himself, for some kind of home to stumble into, navigating with her. It was he who said how the ancestors blew the wind in their sails so that one day they would find each other. Something like that, beautiful and true, painful and yet delicious, good enough to wrap her legs around and keep close. This was what she wanted, this was where she belonged, in the arms of someone who knew her before the world did, who knew her skin, her hair, her mouth, her dreams, someone who beneath the sheets would take her to freedom. This, she thought as he moved his hips deeper into her, was a step closer to God, like a pilgrimage to a promised land, a coming home.

MRS. WASHINGTON WORE a black mantilla over her hat, and kept her head down, but Nettie could hear her sobbing from a distance. She saw her gloved hands squeeze her husband's as she cried from somewhere deep within.

Behind her, relatives wiped their eyes and blew their noses. Behind them, a sea of people, community and church members, friends from Lewis's school, and teachers. And then, around the church, Panthers everywhere. Panthers in every row, every corner, Panthers at the door, Panthers in the pews. Panthers wearing identical and distinctive clothing, their black leather jackets buttoned or zipped up over powder blue shirts. They all wore berets, some of them adorned with revolutionary pins, and small white carnations pinned on their lapels. They stood at attention, lining the walls of the parish, their faces stoic as the pastor spoke on. They were a wall themselves, Black sentinels all beautiful to watch, each one a testament to true power.

Nettie had only been to her father's funeral. She didn't know how to feel at a funeral, except profound emptiness. She thought that, maybe, she should cry. Perhaps that was the real demonstration of pain. And God knows, she felt pain. But she hadn't wept at her father's funeral, either, perhaps from shock at having lost everything and being so suddenly and violently alone. She didn't really cry until Tante Mado announced they were leaving for America. That had been the trigger, this abrupt uprooting from the place she called home, her land, her house.

Up by the casket where Lewis lay sleeping, she saw baskets of flowers on easels, and then, as close to his mother as possible, a large photo of Lewis himself. He hadn't even grown a full mustache yet. All she saw was his face, begging her not to leave his side, as if she held his life in her hands, and she had, until they were stained with his blood. A Panther flag rested on the bottom half of the coffin, and she stared at that black cat leaping out at them.

Someone in the choir began a hymn. She didn't know the song. And now, listening to that spiritual spill out of a woman's bosom and throat, overflowing into the pews like a cascade of fresh and holy water, Nettie's heart swelled until it grew hard like a jagged rock. There was a heaviness in her chest, and she closed her eyes to stave off the pain. For a while, retreating inside her own mind was effective. But then she opened her eyes abruptly, aware that she'd had them closed too long, and somehow sensing that someone in the crowd was staring. She couldn't tell who, even when she scanned the room. There were too many people, and most of them faced forward. Most of them wore dark glasses. She looked for Melvin, but she couldn't see him until the service ended and the sea of people poured outside of the church to load the casket into the hearse. He stood in the ranks with the other men who would be Lewis's pallbearers.

The cars were already revving their engines, ready to depart for the cemetery. In the shade of an old magnolia tree, she found some comfort away from the wailing and grieving of Lewis's mother, and from his relatives who came to mourn. As they loaded the casket in, children gathered around the church, even climbed trees and walls for a better view.

"Nettie! Over here!"

She turned around, startled, and almost squealed Clia's name. Clia immediately raised a finger to her lips to keep her quiet. Nettie shook her head, incredulous. She hadn't seen Clia since their last meeting and now here she was, in the flesh, barely recognizable. She was dressed in a modest black dress down to her knees and glasses, a style that seemed almost borrowed from an older relative's closet. A jacket over the dress, sheer stockings, platforms. She wore a hat that concealed half her face. Nettie stepped closer to make sure she was seeing right.

"My God, Clia? Where have you been?" Nettie hissed, trying to keep quiet. "I haven't seen you in weeks."

"I know." She kept her voice low, too. "I just . . . had to come. For Lewis."

Clia wore no makeup, Nettie noticed. No jewelry, either. She could easily disappear in a crowd and wouldn't stand out. Her hair, usually worn out, was now concealed.

"Is that a wig?"

"You don't like it? Do I look stupid?" Clia smiled, the corners of her mouth twitching nervously. The wig came with curtain bangs, which covered her forehead, and suddenly, Clia looked like a stranger.

"It's . . . different." Nettie swallowed.

"You hate it!"

"No, I don't, I don't hate it at all. It's just not . . . I've never seen you in a wig. You, of all women. I don't hate it though."

"I hate it." Clia smiled, but she kept the wig on, and with the tip of her nails, she reached in to scratch her scalp. Nettie wondered if she could reach it at all as the wig shifted a little. "It's itchy and I guess I should be thankful that it keeps my head warm a little, but it's . . ."

"Not you."

They looked at each other and Clia's hands clasped around her small purse. She adjusted her glasses. She was not happy. Nettie could see it right away. Her face, usually smooth as a river pebble, looked dull. Nettie could almost reach out and touch the sadness in her.

"What changed so suddenly? Did I miss that issue of *Ebony*? It's the one with Diana Ross on it, isn't it?"

Clia looked at her and Nettie knew she would not laugh back. Humor, also gone.

"Coming here was hard," Clia said.

"Yes, I know, I—"

"No, I mean, it was hard to leave my house. To get out of bed. I'm not feeling great but it's not that I'm sick, don't worry." She reached for Nettie's arm and squeezed, but Nettie knew what she really wanted was to be closer, to hold her, to speak to her as if no one else was present to overhear. "I don't know what hurts. I just . . . it's something I can't describe to you, but it's not . . . I need to get better."

Nettie felt her heart race. Was it drugs? She quickly realized she'd overlooked that possibility. After all, her friend's behavior had changed. She'd withdrawn a lot more, and then disappeared. She had begun to dress differently. Could it be? As if reading her thoughts, Clia shook her head.

"I'll be fine," Clia said. "It's something I need to do, but I'm . . ."

"What?" Nettie knew what she was going to say before she said it, and a knot was lodging in her throat. "What do you need to do?"

Clia paused, and then she started to roam through her purse. She pulled out a card and handed it to her. Nettie saw Clia's handwriting, beautiful but rushed. An address to a place down in Clearwater. Nettie looked up, dismayed.

"Florida?"

"I'm going."

Clia mumbled something under her breath, but Nettie didn't want to hear it. Her eyes were stinging. There was a panic in her head, a fear about being abandoned by the only woman she loved as a sister. Her only friend.

"Just like that? You're just leaving like that? Is this about—"

She caught herself just as Clia urged her to keep her voice down, finger on her lips. Nettie clenched her jaw.

"You've made up your mind? You're just going to let him run you off without—"

"Antoinette, I'm tired. I don't know anyone who can help me right now—"

"I don't know what to do, but I can try if you let me."

"You can't. Besides, you don't need to beg me to stay. I go where I want to go, you don't have to follow me. You've already chosen who you want to follow anyway."

"What does that mean?" Nettie frowned, searching Clia's eyes for answers. She could tell by the way her friend was squaring her shoulders that she was going to get into this.

"Do you even feel anything for me at all?" Clia asked. "Because I know how I feel about you, and all I want is for you to to tell me I mean something to you. I want you to come with me but I know you won't because you're . . ."

"I'm what?"

"You've made your choice. I saw you with Melvin."

Clia lowered her voice as people walked downhill in their direction and passed them, grazing shoulders, chatting. Both women looked at the floor until the group was gone. Engines rumbled in the distance. She felt certain she was tussling with an unfamiliar monster now. Jealousy. Clia's jealousy. And she wanted to argue against it, argue that it shouldn't be a source of worry, but wasn't it?

"I saw you that night, after the shooting. The night Lewis died. . . . I came to see you at your place after I heard, but I didn't go further up the stairs." Clia paused, a crack in her voice. "I saw him go up and knock in the rain, and you let him in. And I waited, a little bit, to see if he would come out. But he didn't."

Nettie stilled herself. Why did she feel caught? Because she'd tried to convince Clia, a while ago, that there was nothing between her and Melvin, and she hadn't lied. But things had changed now. At least in Nettie's mind, they had. She hoped he felt the same way. He'd spent the night with her, in her bed, and she'd even made him breakfast in the morning, a privilege she'd denied Clia. And now Nettie felt awful, so much so she wanted to weep for having been so blind.

"I can explain," she said. "Melvin and I, we . . ." She fumbled and tried to make sense, but maybe it was impossible to say it.

"You let him spend the night," Clia said. "You chose. Him."

"You're blowing this out of proportion," Nettie said, lowering her voice. Her mind raced. "Besides, you said you didn't own me, that I could do what I wanted. Isn't that what you said?"

"Yes, and so you did." Clia smiled, but a sad smile. The sun met her face with a pale glow and she swept her synthetic bangs out of the way.

"Why can't I love both of you?" Nettie said, breathless. Her body was on fire and she needed to defend herself, she felt strongly about that. "I don't understand why I have to choose. I don't know what you want from me."

"Nothing," Clia said. "If you don't know, it doesn't matter. It doesn't. It's better for me and all of us if I just leave. Just accept it. It's better."

Nettie swallowed, already feeling the weight of her friend's absence. Already, there was a void. Nettie took a breath, knowing she could not stop her.

"If you want to stay in touch, write to me," Clia continued. "I know you'll have your hands full."

Nettie cocked her head. "Are you going to be alright?"

"None of this is your fault, Nettie." Clia shook her head. "It's how it needs to be. I am alone as it is, in a world full of wolves. I don't want you turning against me."

Nettie looked over her shoulder. They were closing the hearse now. She saw the men step away from the vehicle and scatter to greet other people and chat. She had to go back out there to Melvin. They would drive together to the cemetery.

When she turned around again, Clia wrapped her arms around Nettie and squeezed. For a moment, Nettie couldn't move, baffled by the strength in Clia's shoulders and arms. She finally managed to hug back before Clia planted a kiss on her cheek.

"This revolution is not a game," Clia whispered before pulling away. "Be strong, and trust your instincts. Always."

She took off on foot, moving through the parking lot before disappearing around the corner. Nettie tried to follow but stopped after she lost sight of Clia, who vanished among the cars all parked under the hot sun, their rooftops radiant with heat. Nettie swallowed back that double edge of grief. Clia didn't want to be followed. Didn't want to be found. And even though Nettie knew where she was headed, watching her run away was too bitter to process.

11

"ARE YOU GOING to look out the window all day, or are you coming back to bed?"

When Nettie turned around, Melvin was still wrapped in bedsheets. The end of his cigarette was bright red, plumes of smoke hanging in the amber light of her table lamp. The light danced magnificently on his skin. He was still naked. Knowing he was comfortable in her apartment aroused her.

"Are you expecting somebody?"

"No," she answered. "I'm just nervous."

She stepped away from the window and climbed back next to him, curling against his warm, hard body. The funeral had taken a toll on both of them. All they'd wanted in the following days was love and the silence after it. Melvin's heartbeat was steady and comforting. She rested her head on his chest and listened. In the background, Otis Redding was singing *I've been loving you too long, I don't want to stop now.* Nettie blinked away memories of Clia, but inside, there was still a gaping wound. She missed her. Now that she was gone, Nettie wanted her back, selfishly needing her companionship. She wanted to say to Clia that their relationship meant more, that sleeping with her that night in Los Angeles was not just an experiment. But it also frightened Nettie, and now that she couldn't articulate this to anyone, she had no other choice but to write her friend letters and postcards.

Melvin's hand traveled up and down her thigh and hip. Her body caught fire. How could she even have a conversation with him when he touched her that way? She almost gave in, almost said she was thinking of Clia, and it was true, she was. But she didn't know how to mention Clia's name without falling into a rabbit hole of questions.

"I think after what happened with Lewis, all those raids happening in the news . . . I get scared."

She did find herself always glancing out the window now, living in perhaps an irrational fear that the police would have the place surrounded, or that they'd come barging in. The last incidents at the office had been traumatic enough. She'd also seen what the police could do to the Panthers up in Los Angeles, or back east in New York. She was haunted by images she'd seen of them in the news, always handcuffed, which meant the police were deathly afraid of them. She saw them against the wall, lined up half naked as the police searched them. She hated those images in the newspapers, hated seeing what they did to these men.

After the police raid on Eldridge Cleaver's home in January, Huey had issued a mandate that all Panthers were to keep at least two weapons in their home and protect themselves. And somehow, she feared this level of harassment would spread to the two of them. She didn't have a plan for what to do if it did, and perhaps that frightened her even more.

"I know losing Lewis was hard on you," Melvin said. "I just don't want you to lose sight of your life because of that, though."

"I'm sad, too, because I think of Clia." She looked at Melvin. She'd almost said too much, but all the others knew was that Clia had gone missing. "Not knowing where she is bothers me."

"She's a grown woman, she can take care of herself, trust me." He leaned in and kissed her bare shoulder. Outside, Nettie heard children's voices playing. They were kicking a ball around on the courtyard. "She clearly doesn't want to be found."

It was lonely now, life without her friend. Dr. Johnson had moved on and hired another nurse. There was a gaping hole inside Nettie, a cold draft blowing through it when she closed her eyes and thought of Clia's mouth, her skin. But mostly, there was remorse, a wave of guilt consuming Nettie for not fighting harder to keep Clia. There was no denying now that Clia had been right. She'd made her choice.

"I don't like knowing that you're scared," Melvin said. "You shouldn't be. And if I'm with you, you should know I can protect you."

"No, I know you can," Nettie looked in his eyes. "But what if you're not around?" Melvin looked at her. "Is it true? You're leaving again?"

She'd heard the conversations on the phone, and recently, once again, Melvin had disappeared for two days. The last time he did this, he'd been ordered to visit Huey in prison, and he'd left town completely.

"How did you know about that?" Melvin squeezed her shoulder. "I was going to tell you myself."

She felt part of herself dwindle and become small. She didn't want him to go, of course, but she knew better than to ask him to stay. He was not an average date, nor an average man. He was a Panther, serving a paramilitary structure that demanded him to obey. She was never going to go on dates with him the way other women did, see a movie, grab dinner, receive flowers. That was not who they were or would ever be. Instead, they spent time reading, helping with organizing, distributing newspapers, and going to meetings, when they weren't at the gun range.

Nettie told herself she had to be satisfied with that. Even if, deep down, she wanted more. Steven had made her feel close to that, but it had ended so abruptly and traumatically that she had cast that emotion in the back of her mind, in a drawer with occasional past memories. She had tried to kill that emotion.

And now that she was falling in deep over the edge with Melvin, it was almost frightening. She was afraid of that precipice, the darkness of it, what it whispered in her ear when she and Melvin made love, or when Melvin's fingers entered the forest of her hair without hesitation, gripping at her insides as if he already knew her. The darkness told her this was love. And she was terrified of the power it commanded over her and her time, restraining her so much that she no longer wanted to study. All the chapters in her anatomy and biology books were suddenly written in some ancient cryptic tongue and her mind wandered from the priorities of her job. Dr. Johnson's patients had to sometimes repeat instructions or information for her to process what they were asking.

Nettie had already been struggling to meet with Tante Mado and cook meals together the Haitian way. But she now found herself completely consumed with her new schedule. Any time there was a Panther activity, and anytime Melvin was part of it, she wanted to be there, to the point where she now wondered how much the two were the same in her mind. She knew this was dangerous territory, but how could she turn back now? For the first time, she belonged to a family of brothers and sisters outside of her aunt's orbit, to people who looked in and through her and saw her usefulness and her potential, people who were making their voices heard, channeling rage and passion, wielding Black power, wanting solidarity and equality by any means necessary. She had become drunk on the promise of the revolution, quenched her thirst at the lips of Melvin, and now when Tante Mado popped in with precooked American meals, she ran out of things to say.

Just three days ago, after Tante Mado had surprised her with a slice of pineapple cake, her aunt berated her.

"You're either avoiding me or you're seeing someone," Tante Mado said. "Which one is it?"

Nettie was at a loss for words. Which was safest to admit to? "What do you mean?"

But she could feel her aunt boring a hole through her. Tante Mado looked at the cake, the way her niece dug into it and filled her mouth, a tactic to stall conversation.

"You've been going on about the Black Student Union since I walked in that door," she said. "I asked about school and that was the first thing out of your mouth. Is that what it is, then? Is it the unions? The revolution? Are you avoiding me because of that?"

Nettie could tell already that Tante Mado was not pleased. The lines around her mouth told Nettie of bitterness.

"Tell me you're seeing someone, then," she said. "A fling. Romance to pass the time until you get to medical school. A boy, I can take. But I—"

"A man." Nettie heard the words fall out of her mouth and she couldn't catch them. They were laid out for Tante Mado to pick apart. And now that it was out, Nettie felt she needed to regain control. "I'm seeing a man."

What ensued next was silence, followed by a smirk, her aunt's eyes burning like coals in the fire. A man. Okay. The layers of her response unfolded between the two, one at the sink and the other still seated, dismayed. Nettie was not a girl anymore. She was a woman. She was reminding her aunt of this.

"That's really all I can say for now," Nettie said as she got up from her seat. She collected the plate, the cake, the forks, took her time just to avoid eye contact. "There's not much else to add."

"That's all?"

Only the fragrance of Tante Mado's cigarette lingered in the air as Nettie washed the dishes, and then she saw her aunt's reflection in the window, crushing her cigarette butt into a cup of coffee, drowning her ashes, watching them sink before they floated.

"Well, I sure hope he's nice," she said. "I hope he's ambitious. I hope he is not like your father."

Those words stung. There was always a strange mix of love and bitterness in Tante Mado's tone when she spoke of Nettie's father.

"He believes in revolution, too, if that's what you mean," Nettie snapped. "He is a revolutionary. That's what I love about him, in case you're wondering."

"Oh." Tante Mado raised an eyebrow, and Nettie could read the disappointment as it settled in her aunt. She offered a slow nod. "Well . . . History repeats itself, it seems."

The hot water nearly burned Nettie's hands but she let it run anyway. She scrubbed harder. Her father would not disapprove of Melvin. He would be proud of Nettie's choices. She was sure of that. Her aunt sighed, and didn't add any other thoughts. But when Tante Mado left, Nettie headed to Gilda's for a drink, then two, because she barely kept alcohol in her house. She couldn't tell Tante Mado more about Melvin, didn't explain exactly what kind of revolutionary fighter he was, but she'd come close. She wanted to. Maybe she needed to, just to set the record straight once and for all.

What Nettie didn't know was whether Melvin felt that he belonged to her. They were just pieces involved in a greater machine, revolving around each other but always parting, Melvin off to revolutionary missions. She had no right to claim him for herself. She knew many people in the Party did not abide by traditional relationship rules, but rather advocated for no attachments, no interferences. The only goal was to serve the people.

Yet now in the bedroom, as she let herself melt against him, she hoped to remind him he, too, could belong to her.

"I heard . . . Where to, this time?"

She knew the answer before he said it. Yes, Chicago. Again. She couldn't help feeling a strange sort of jealousy toward that city, as if the place had the power to take him away from her. Quickly, Melvin sat up in bed so that he could put his cigarette out in the teacup she'd started leaving on her bedside table for this purpose.

"When do you leave?" she asked.

"Monday," he said.

"Monday? Next week?" Nettie frowned. "When were you going to tell me? And what's in Chicago anyway?" she asked.

Melvin took a breath. She imagined he had to think about whether he should give her details about his orders. But he didn't mind.

"There's a new chapter forming there," Melvin said. "They requested permission from Huey and the chairman to be official. Huey wants me to go, seeing that I know the city. My old stomping grounds. I know people there."

"How long will you be gone?" she asked.

He was escorting the field secretary to Illinois, he said. "I'm to help them set up the chapter, get organized, so they have the structure in place to operate, carry the Panthers' name the proper way."

"That could take weeks," she said.

He grabbed her by the hips and pulled her close. She never wanted him to leave, but she also loved that Melvin was in such high demand.

"Tell me what it's like, visiting Huey in jail?" she asked.

Melvin looked grave. He took a breath, looking for the words to describe it. Finally, he shook his head. "Jail is jail," he said. "I can't describe it because it's counter nature. Most of the brothers who end up there are treated like animals. That's what it is. A place to hole up animals."

She'd seen Huey on television during interviews, once or twice. She'd seen pictures of him in the newspaper. Always, every time, behind bars, with cameras and microphones and recorders up in his face. He was always consistent in his message, that he didn't deserve to be in jail, that he was a political prisoner, that the government held him there due to their own racism, and that the revolution was going to come whether they liked it or not. Melvin was confident that Huey would get out. He had a good lawyer, and justice was on his side.

"Besides, Huey's a genius. He's knowledgeable of the law. He'll get out, and then the revolution will spread like fire, and we'll burn down the whole fucking world to the very ground, start it all over again, you'll see." His eyes sparkled and Nettie smiled. "Start a new world, where our people are truly free, and can have their land, and food, and education. And where those prisons built to shackle our brothers and sisters are abolished. Pigs won't know what to do with themselves. A world where we truly off the pig!"

She nestled her face in the crook of his neck, breathed him in until her lungs were full. He cracked a smile through the veil of smoke. The room was hazy with tobacco smoke.

"That's the kind of freedom I want," he said. His fingers curled around her ear and traced the outline of her face. "A world where you won't have to be afraid of a damn thing ever, whether I'm around or not. You can be the queen of your own kingdom, with your own castle. I wouldn't mind being in that castle, too, now and again."

She giggled. Love put Melvin in a good mood. He let his guard down with her, shared dreams with her.

"Maybe not a castle, but a big house!" Melvin thought for a minute. "A big ol' house with Adinkra symbols all around it, so we know it's real African and shit." Their bodies rocked softly against each other when they chuckled. "And that house sits on acres and acres of land, at least forty. And it's got all this grass all around it, wild grass that sways in the wind, and when you sit on the stoop you can hear the sound of little children's feet running in it, stepping in it, crushing it under them heels, nobody yelling at them to get off. Swish, swish, swish for acres all around. Freedom, know what I mean?"

Nettie's smile had vanished. Her heart felt like it was cracking. Why did she have to go fall in love with this man? She nodded to say yes, she could see freedom there. She could also see a future imagined, a dream with children in it, something she didn't know Melvin carried with him. That was easier to imagine and want than an orange grove, she supposed. Suddenly, Melvin looked at her as if he was remembering something or discovering something amusing. His eyes shined.

"What?" she asked.

He moved her aside and rolled over to reach for something on the floor. He found his jacket and began to search through it, in the inner pockets. He pulled something out to show her and held it up before her eyes.

"This . . ." He turned it on its side. A very small black snub-nosed revolver that barely weighed the anticipated weight. He popped the cylinder open. The chambers were empty. He handed it to her. "This is yours."

They locked eyes and she smiled. A gift. A very Melvin kind of gift. No flowers, no chocolates or jewelry. It would either be books or guns. And she found this, as much as she tried to deny it, profoundly romantic.

"It's small, but it'll send a motherfucker to the grave. And that's all that matters. Good at close-range but works long-range if you can stop wavering so much and just make each of them rounds count."

She sat up on the bed and held it in her hand. It was so small, she could probably fit it under her clothes or carry it in a purse. She pointed it at her reflection in the mirror, at the other side of the room. Melvin straightened the crook in her elbow as they both looked in the mirror.

"Bang!" he whispered in her ear. "Right between the ribs."

She'd never had a gun of her own before, and with Melvin's hands now on her hips, she also felt a thrill. Safety, for herself and by herself. There was a newfound power in her own grip. She knew Melvin felt it, too, as their eyes met in the mirror and her arm fell at her side.

"You keep going like you're going, no wavering, and you're gonna be a defense captain."

His breath warmed her skin like a hot island wind. It drove her out-of-her-skin crazy. He wrapped his arms around her, pulled her close. Held her. Told her he would be there to stop her from falling or stumbling. He was breathing power into her. Keeping her safe in the wilderness, rebuilding the walls of this divided kingdom. In Melvin's arms, the jumbled world could briefly reassemble itself piece by piece, take shape, and rebuild itself anew.

12

JUNE 21, 1968

The Black Panther Party for Self-Defense, in light of the vicious and racist propaganda dropped into the Black community by the fascist pigs, issues the following decree as approved by our section leader, Clayton Young. As of June 20, 1968, the following individuals have been purged from the Black Panther Party and are no longer considered members:

1. Lucinda Hall
2. Vernon "Little Man" Duhay
3. Coleen "Clia" Brown

These individuals are considered agents with counterrevolutionary intentions, due to separate malicious actions of spying and reporting to the honky and his racist institution. They are against the revolutionary struggle. Should these members show their face in any part of the communities of East and West Oakland, they shall and will be dealt with. All power to the people!

Nettie folded the Black Panther newspaper and tried to swallow the knot lodged in her throat. She hurried down the sidewalk, rehearsing in her head what she was going to say as she cursed out Clayton Young. That good-for-nothing dickless motherfucker! Those would be Clia's exact words. How could he accuse Clia of such things? What malicious actions? This was just a man retaliating against rejected advances. That motherfucker ought to grow up. She was going to tell him all about his lack of manhood, that's what he needed to hear.

She turned the corner and paused. This could mean the end of her as well. Nothing about what was happening was normal. It'd been almost two months since Clia had been gone, and six weeks or so of not seeing Melvin, of aching for him, of not knowing where they stood anymore. Melvin would telephone her late at night just to hear her voice. He was always at someone's house and unable to talk too long. Was she supposed to wait until he returned every time he went away for that long?

Clia hadn't even called to say she was doing alright in Florida. Nettie missed talking to her, and even with their own history, she wished she could ask her for advice right now. A cool breeze blew as Nettie caught her breath. She'd walked from the bus stop to the office, and she felt exhausted. There was an odd sensation of heartburn that kept returning. Sometimes she even woke up with that sourness on her stomach. It had to be the anguish over Melvin, she thought, and Clia, and Lewis's death.

Dusk was closing in when she arrived, cloaking the city in a shade of violet. But there were people gathered outside, talking amongst themselves, crowding the sidewalk. Nettie approached the office, puzzled, cutting through the crowd.

When the guard let her in, she gasped. Several Panthers were gathered in the front room, picking up overturned furniture. There was paper everywhere, sheets and sheets covering the floor, here and there, as if a storm had blown through the walls and knocked everything over. Nettie's blood turned cold. She saw Reggie walk past the wall of sandbags, toward the armory.

"What happened?" she called, running after him.

"What do you think?" His tone was icy. "Pigs vamped on us, that's what."

In the armory, Reggie and Nettie stood there, absorbing the chaos around them. The police had taken everything. All the guns in the closet were gone. They'd brought some type of warrant, citing a search for illegal weapons. It was an easy ploy for the pig, Reggie said, to go for the guns. Black people arming themselves was always a terrifying prospect for the oppressor, even when the oppressor himself was armed and perpetuating the violence. The police said they'd release any gun that was legal and registered. But in the process, of course, why not kick the hornet's nest?

Nettie bolted out of the room. The clinic! Maybe they hadn't completely ransacked everything.

Down the hall, she found the door to the clinic unhinged. The two hospital beds in the corner had been overturned. The drawers had been pulled open and thrown onto the floor. All the medical equipment had been piled up in the center of the room, file cabinets pulled away from the walls. Cabinet doors stood open to reveal complete disarray. Nettie felt something crunch under her foot and she bent over to take a closer look and then clenched her teeth, horrified. They had thrown all her needles and transfusion kits in the trash can and burned them, leaving nothing but blackened and melted plastic wrapping.

"No." Her voice came out hoarse, as if belonging to someone else. Nettie felt a roiling in her throat now, something hot and boiling within that she could not contain. "Why?"

Her eye was on the wall behind her desk, where children's drawings to thank the Panthers had been torn down the middle. Nettie felt her nails dig into the flesh of her palm as she gritted her teeth. Her eyes filled with tears.

"Pigs!" The word came out like a grumble, her mouth filled with spit. She understood now. "Fucking pigs!"

A hot tear rolled down her cheek and she wiped her nose. There was throbbing pain at the base of her throat now, rage hacking through her like a saw.

She untacked a drawing from the wall and stared at the rainbow painted over tall buildings. She felt a hand on her shoulder. Dr. Johnson was behind her. He stood there, taking in the scene. Nettie could hear noises outside, furniture being dragged back into place. She shook her head, threw the drawing onto the desk. She wanted to say, "Look at what they did! Was this really necessary?" But the words wouldn't come out.

Why would they need to do this? She knew why. The same evil that took her father's last breath by portraying him as a communist was now attempting to annihilate what the Panthers were doing. This evil, which the same everywhere, knew that part of crushing resistance involved turning the narrative around and falsely painting the opposition as evil. Labeling the Panthers as the enemy was devastatingly effective, and it hurt.

Dr. Johnson let out a big sigh, put down his bag. Without a word, he began to pick up, pushing the beds back, picking up the mattresses, sorting through the trash can. She watched him work and tried to control the sour tide still rising in her. Yet, there was a quiet resolve in Dr. Johnson, despite his own shock, to keep going. And she felt stupid standing there, stewing in her own anger, drained from energy before she even started. What was the point of crying over spilled milk? There was no time to waste.

AS NETTIE BROWNED chicken with onions and tomato paste at home later that evening, she felt her stomach turn upside down. She couldn't lie to herself any longer. She placed a lid tightly on the pot to seal in the aroma, and took a bite of her salted crackers. The salt was the only relief she could get these days. She stood over the sink and chewed slowly, fighting back tears. She didn't want to acknowledge it yet because if she did, then it would be real.

She felt increasingly sapped of energy in the past month. At first, she thought she was just overworked. But then came the difficulty of navigating the smells of breakfast, mornings when she was unable to keep her stomach contents down. Even the fragrance of her own perfume made her ill. Nettie had thrown out every bar of soap in the house and replaced them with others she still couldn't stand to smell.

She knew something in her was different with the absence of a period in June and now July. But the most telling thing was the sharp pain in her womb. She had been organizing patient files for Dr. Johnson and thankfully was alone when it first came. The pain nearly brought her to her knees, as if someone was driving a needle through her uterus. She knew it, that instant, that someone was claiming space in her.

She couldn't just blame Melvin for this. Worried she might lose him between Oakland and Chicago, she'd taken liberties lately. Maybe the way she'd wrapped herself around him in bed was on purpose, an attempt to hold on to a piece of him before he left. And that piece of him was in her, already knocking her stomach around and upside down. How was she going to explain this to Tante Mado? To Melvin? When was he coming back, anyway? Was he coming back? His absence and his silence drove her to the brink of despair. On the few phone calls they'd exchanged, he could barely answer himself. I don't know, he'd said. I can't say yet, just a little while longer. Nettie was beginning to doubt herself and him and everything in between.

A knock at the door startled her. She went to open it.

"Mailman screwed up again," Gilda said. "They gave me your mail. Something from Florida."

Her neighbor was standing in her doorway, holding out an envelope. She was wearing a long dress covering her knees, and her long, fiery hair was swept to the side of her pale face. She flashed a grin and kept talking as if she'd been wound up mechanically before knocking.

"I have family friends down there, around Boca Raton. Worst sunburn I ever had but the resorts make decent drinks. Have you been?"

Nettie recognized her name on the envelope, but there was no return address. At least she knew it wasn't from one of the medical schools she'd applied to; the last one that she'd received had been from UC–Berkeley and she'd opened it and read it with excitement and apprehension, and she knew right by the first line what their decision was. *Dear Ms. Boileau, we regret to inform you . . .* She had stopped reading after the obligatory politeness. The rejection was brutal, even when she tried to take it in stride. There were other schools to hear from, however. Plus, it was still early.

Besides, how could she think of school now that she was convinced she was pregnant? How was this going to work? She couldn't see herself giving birth and going to school at the same time. It all felt like too much, like a big mountain that she couldn't push away. It wasn't fair, she thought, opening the envelope.

Inside, she found a postcard with large, bold letters that indeed spelled the word FLORIDA. Inside each letter were illustrations of pelicans and orange blossoms, and white people smiling on a beach. She turned it over and breathed a sigh of relief. Clia! She read the quick message scribbled on the back and almost burst into tears.

Greetings from Clearwater, my sister, what's good? I found my orange grove. I wish I could package that fragrance and send it to you Nettie, that sweet sweet fragrance that somehow reminds me of you. This being the South, though, feels like I came here chasing a myth. Some things don't change. But here in the orange grove, I can keep time very still just by thinking of you.

Love always, Clia.

Nettie ran her finger against the grain of the card and stared at it longingly. She brought it closer to her nose, as if looking for the scent of orange blossoms. Clia's scent, maybe? Oils, incense, sugar? Nothing. She'd forgotten that the door was still open. She felt her stomach churn.

"Are you alright?" Gilda asked. "You look awful."

Gilda reached in her pocket and pulled out a pack of cigarettes. Nettie immediately stopped her.

"Please," Nettie said. "Don't."

Gilda stared back, in awe at first. Then she pushed the door open, forcing Nettie to step back.

"Sit down, honey. You need some tea. Have you got chamomile?"

Nettie took a breath. The afternoon air outside had followed Gilda in and lingered for a bit, still warm before September ushered in. On Friday nights like these, Melvin would come over, carrying new books for them to read, a record to listen to, and be sitting at her table to eat. But there was a void inside her, now that he was away, and it hurt, as if someone had torn a piece of her off and cast it out.

"I think I'm a little sick," Nettie said. "I have a headache. Maybe a flu."

Gilda had found something. Mint. She readied a cup, and had lifted the lid on the pot curiously and now the kitchen smelled of onions and mint tea. It was too much. Nettie rushed to the sink to save herself from vomiting on the floor. Gilda stepped back and watched in horror. Nettie felt the world come out of her, and it took her a minute to realize the humiliating position she was in, throwing up in front of her neighbor. Nettie waited for the wave of nausea to pass, now that her stomach felt empty. She ran the water and splashed her face, washing everything away, even her tears. Then, she turned the heat off the chicken and moved the pot to the back of the stove.

"Please go," she begged, eyes burning with tears.

"Oh, sweetie."

Nettie poured herself a glass of water and drank. She opened the kitchen window and took deep breaths, and then she felt Gilda's eyes on her as she gulped down the coolness. Silence deafened them both for a minute. Gilda was now looking at her curiously, with a hint of a smile on her lips.

"How far along are you?"

Nettie's hands went cold. Her eyes locked with Gilda's and Gilda stared back, seemingly unimpressed. Nettie wanted to cry. Everything was falling apart, and she was going to lose it here? In front of Gilda, of all people? Clia couldn't have stuck around for this?

"I'm not judging you," Gilda said. "I just know what this is, I can tell. That, and the soda crackers you left out on the counter, say it all."

"Two months I think." Nettie said and blinked the tears away. "My aunt is going to kill me."

"She's not," Gilda said. She went to Nettie and put an arm around her. "They say that, but they don't mean it."

Nettie eyed Gilda and wanted to tell her, you don't know Tante Mado. It's not that she'll literally murder me. She will kill herself out of shame and leave me no choice but to kill myself out of honor. Was that an exaggeration? Nettie hung her head. Fuck! Melvin, where was Melvin?

"What about your boyfriend? I don't think I've seen him come up here in a little while."

Nettie averted her eyes. She burned with shame. Gilda looked like she understood something and nodded quietly, and suddenly Nettie hated her. She felt her heart wrenching, and she needed privacy to mourn this loss she was certain she was experiencing. Melvin wasn't here. Melvin had left her; that was probably the truth, and she just had to accept that.

"Can your doctor help you at all?" Gilda asked. "There are options. Your doctor should be able to discuss them with you and . . . Hey . . . Don't you work in a doctor's office?"

Nettie's eyes shifted toward Gilda. She stared at her and saw not a flower child but a weed. It had invaded the garden and wanted to grow, and Nettie knew it was time to pull it.

"Are you . . . gonna keep it?"

"Excuse me?" Nettie felt her stomach burn again. "How is this any of your business?"

"I'm sorry," Gilda said, shaking her head. "I shouldn't. I always do this. You're right. It's none of my business. I just wanted to offer advice. From one woman to another. You and I are both in college. We want a future, a career. We want the freedom to do so many things. I imagine you have to make quick decisions when you're pregnant, but if I were you, I'd think about my future."

Nettie stared at her, stunned at this young woman's audacity. She was making sense for her own world. Gilda did not know her, understand her, appreciate her circumstances. She wasn't even a real friend. Was she suggesting what she thought she was suggesting? Out of what? Mercy? Compassion? Friendship? Nettie's head was spinning. She wanted to be alone, to cry alone, and she was angry at Gilda more than she'd ever been. Who the hell did she think she was, inserting herself into Nettie's private life that way? And now suggesting *this*.

"I have to lie down," Nettie said, cutting her off.

Gilda muttered, "Alright." Outside, someone slammed a door. They could hear laughter, from children riding their bikes around the courtyard. Nettie saw Gilda raise her hands in the air in surrender before walking toward the door. She'd never thrown anyone out before, but she'd had enough of this constant intrusion, and she wasn't ready to deal with what she was already trying to put behind her.

"I was just trying to help, you know . . . If you need anything, you come knock. I'm here for you. At least until end of the month. Jim and I are headed to Chicago for the Democratic Convention and we're probably just going to stay there. We just feel like it's where we should be right now."

Chicago. What the hell was it about Chicago that made everyone want to go? She turned and faced the sink, hoping Gilda would understand. She heard the door close behind her, Gilda's footsteps fading away, and her heartache return.

"Shit!" She pressed her body against the sink and gripped it, seized with panic.

Nettie spent the next two days sitting up in the dark, waiting. Mostly, she stared into oblivion until she fell asleep at dawn. When the phone rang, she jumped on it, hoping it was Melvin, but it was always Tante Mado checking up on her. Melvin did not call. She sat alone with herself and began to accept the fact that it was possible, just possible, that Melvin was not going to return. She recognized fear growing in her like a tumor, so palpable she could reach in her chest and touch it. She didn't want to decide on her own.

SHE'D ASKED DR. Johnson to test her, and he'd looked at her with a lack of surprise. "You'll have to wait about two weeks," he said, lowering his voice. "Once the results come in, I can call you."

Sitting in front of a man she respected, who had taken the time to write her letters of recommendation, Nettie hoped he didn't hear her heart pounding. Now he was staring at her as if she was just another patient, but also probably judging her. If she were pregnant, what would she do about it? Continue working? Forget about medical school? The greatest terror was, of course, telling her aunt. Tante Mado would not survive this, she thought.

"I wish you'd come after your first missed period," Dr. Johnson said. "We would have known a lot sooner."

Dr. Johnson sounded like a disappointed father. She imagined all the questions running through his mind that he wasn't asking. Why did she allow herself to get pregnant? Why hadn't she been more careful? As if she could explain to him, if she needed to, that she was in love, that in a wild way, she'd wanted this, in the moment of lovemaking?

"Have you talked to the father yet?" Dr. Johnson asked.

Nettie shook her head, unable to speak. She couldn't look him in the eye, either. Still, she wanted to ask, Do you think I should tell him? But she refrained. She didn't want to seem weak. She'd considered not telling Melvin at all. Why bother? He was so far away, and she didn't even know when he'd return. When he'd last called, he sounded energetic, happy about what was happening in Chicago. He was excited about the new chapter and a young leader there that was already getting his name to spread, a man so charismatic that he'd made a name for himself as an orator, someone as remarkable as Dr. King himself.

"I wish you could be here," Melvin said. "I wish you could hear him yourself."

Nettie knew what he meant. He wanted her to catch that fire, to experience this the same way she'd experienced Brother Stokely. Or Dr. King even. The voice of a man born knowing, born to be exceptional.

But since that last phone call, she hadn't heard from him at all. Maybe all that mattered truly was the revolution. Love was an afterthought. Maybe she was delusional in entertaining the idea of a future with Melvin. Maybe she should go to Gilda and ask her for her doctor's name, get it over with. But she was sure Dr. Johnson would help. He would have to refer her to someone he knew. Still, Dr. Johnson insisted on waiting two weeks for the formal results. She didn't want to wait any longer. She already knew with certainty. Maybe she didn't have a choice. Maybe she should talk to Gilda after all.

In the middle of the night, Nettie lay in bed and let her hand glide toward her belly and held it there. Knowing that this tiny embryo planted and growing in her womb was Melvin's made her shiver. Did she want this? Was she ready for one of those small cubs she'd seen in the Panther meetings, running around the place, climbing on their parents' laps? Could she do this alone, without Melvin? Her eyes embraced the dark, and she could hear her own heart pounding in the silence.

DR. JOHNSON CLOSED the clinic door and looked at Nettie. She held his gaze, determined. They were in the People's Clinic, and they both silently agreed privacy was needed. She didn't want anyone overhearing them.

"I'm just not sure I want you doing this," he said. "I don't believe it's right."

Nettie looked at him, struggling to keep the pieces together inside of her.

"Everybody makes mistakes, Antoinette." Dr. Johnson said. "But you should talk to the father. Give him a chance to support you. Especially if he's a Panther."

"I can't!" She raised her voice to cover his. "I can't tell him. I don't know where he is, or when he's coming back, or *if* he's coming back."

"What about a family member? Can you talk to your aunt?"

Nettie was bewildered. Daylight filtered through the window and bounced off Dr. Johnson's shoulders. He looked like a heavenly being, and it bothered her even more to see him like this, reasoning against her own despair. Men. The problem was men. Clia was right. Maybe this was something she had to decide with other women of the same thinking. Tante Mado was a woman, but she could not go to her. Her aunt would never understand. She'd be too blinded, Nettie felt, by her own resentment over Nettie's commitment to revolution. She should have taken Gilda's offer.

"If you won't help me, I'll just find someone who will," she said.

She wished she didn't have to speak to him this way. She couldn't make him do something he morally opposed, and she held his gaze defiantly, even as someone rapped on the clinic door.

"We're closed!" Dr. Johnson called, his eyes still on Nettie.

The door swung open. "I know, I'm looking for Nettie."

Nettie's heart sank deeper in her chest, and she gripped the folder in her hands to avoid dropping everything. Melvin walked in, the door wide open behind him. She froze, unable to speak. Just like that, as if nothing happened, as if he hadn't been gone for nearly two months, he was strolling back in. He greeted the doctor, shook his hand, and Dr. Johnson looked at the both of them until it was apparent that he understood.

"I'll leave you two to it."

Dr. Johnson shut the door on his way out. Melvin smiled, and she felt everything inside her crumble. She wanted to hold him, and yet she would have to tell him. And yet her tongue weighed a ton in her mouth. When Melvin came toward her, she clenched her jaw and stepped back.

"Don't," she said, shaking her head.

"I know you're mad. I know you wanted me to call."

He was taking her in his arms before she could resist, and her anger melted away when their bodies finally held each other. Inside and out, her walls crumbled, and she wrapped her arms around him and kissed him.

"I found out we were coming back two days ago, and I barely had time to get my shit together," Melvin said, pressing his forehead against hers. "I just got on a plane. I couldn't wait to see you."

He breathed on her face and she welcomed that familiar warmth she'd longed for, the spice of tobacco that perpetually clung to him. Her stomach turned over. "You didn't find yourself another man while I was gone, did you?" he joked, kissing her lips. "Say no."

"Oh, Melvin . . ." She sighed, opening her eyes. "We need to talk."

He looked at her, searching for an explanation in her eyes, and she couldn't say anything else.

"Not here," she said. "Let's go somewhere else. Anywhere else."

THE OCEAN BREEZE blew in a salty mist from the Pacific. Melvin held on to the pier's railing and looked out to where the water licked the flat rocks that bordered the Golden Gate. Ship horns blared in the distance. Nettie watched the surface of the ocean glitter under the late afternoon sun. She kept her composure, took a breath, and looked toward the water, its surface veiled by smog, the horizon broken by distant ships.

"How is it that you've already decided on this, without me?"

There was reproach in his voice. She pretended not to hear it.

They were the only ones there, standing near the rocks. Seagulls cawed. He kept his hand in his pocket and looked toward the horizon. The more she looked at him, the more she could feel herself falling all over again into that precipice of doom.

"I'm trying to do what's best," she said, holding back tears.

"Best for whom?"

His voice was hollow. She heard it bounce against the wind. Her heart was racing. She didn't like the way this conversation was turning into a confrontation.

"I don't have a lot of time, and you left me very little choice," she said, her voice cracking. She didn't want to sound like she was blaming him, but she had to let him know. "I had to decide on my own."

"But Nettie, *this*? You were going to let some honky doctor sterilize you, scrape our child out of your womb like it was nothing? We're trying to get off the plantation, God dammit, not stay in it."

Nettie's heart caught the words *our child,* and it left her breathless.

"What was I supposed to do?" she said. "You have no idea what it's like to be in my shoes, to be waiting for a phone call from you for weeks. I didn't even know when you were coming back."

She could feel something cracking in two inside her chest, and it hurt. This was not quite the scenario that had played out in her mind. Looking at him was hard. He was now placing a burden on her shoulders.

"Melvin . . ." Her eyes burned, so she gazed at the water and saw nothing in the picturesque landscape of the city but isolation, a monstrous, empty machine in which she did not belong. The bridge was a metallic specter suspended over the vastness of water, and the sky a mouth agape.

"I'm not down with that," he said.

"I'm not asking for permission, here."

"Why tell me about it, then? Hmm?" Melvin stepped away from the railing, his head cocked, looking for her eyes. "Why are you telling me if you don't give a rat's ass about my feelings on the subject?"

She could not tear her eyes away. Now they were wet and he was peering into her, so deeply she couldn't bear it. It was okay to cry, she said to herself. She could allow herself to.

"I'll tell you why," he said. "Because this isn't just about you. It's about *us*. You and me. We made this child together. You can't now turn around and butcher my child without involving me, not if I get a damn say about it."

She hated the sound of those words, *scrape* and *butcher*, as if he'd studied the method and its details.

"I can't do this," she shouted. "You go away, and you come back whenever you please. What about me? My job? Medical school?"

"I don't give a damn about these things right now!" Melvin took a deep breath, composed himself. He looked at her. "I go away because I have to. It's a duty. I'm not escaping you, Nettie. I want you to come with me."

"What?" Her heart dropped too quickly. "What do you mean?"

"Come to Chicago with me!"

Nettie shook her head, confused. She felt as if she was, all along, a hot air balloon tied by a stake to the ground. Now, one of the strings was now undone.

"School will always be there, jobs exist everywhere, but you know what we won't always have? This. A fucking chance. A chance at making effective fucking change. I told you I was serious about that shit. I told you, I'm here to burn the world down to the ground and rebuild it. I told you about my dreams. Now, we're having a baby, that's part of that rebuilding. So, move to Chicago with me. Huey wants me to transfer there. Let's go together."

Chicago. All these trips had been a practice run for what was to come next. Nettie felt the world collapse around her, and yet the ocean and sky were still in place. The bridge was still affixed to that backdrop. Melvin was still an inch from her face, demanding she maintain his gaze. But she turned away. She had never been to Illinois and she hated the place with a passion now. She felt Melvin's hand on her arm, squeezing it firmly.

"I'm not leaving you," he said, grabbing her arm, squeezing it. "And I'm not leaving without you either. The very fact that we are here, talking, that we exist and love each other, means this was meant to be. That's radical. That's revolutionary, Nettie. Revolution cannot wait." Melvin's eyes were aglow with a distinct fire. He pulled her close, sealing the space between them. The call of seagulls suddenly flying overhead was now a supplication.

"*This* is revolutionary," he said, his voice dropping even lower. "You dig what I'm saying? To create life in the middle of this chaos? To bring hope into this world of shit, you and me, that's revolution. Anyone who says otherwise has massa mentality. Don't let massa snatch our baby away. I won't allow it."

He lowered his voice.

"We'll be just fine, I can provide just fine. You need to trust that I can do that. You need to trust, period, that you and me, we are unstoppable. When we come together, stick together like the fingers on one hand, like a fist . . ." He raised his fist in the air to show her what it meant, and all she saw was the same fist raised every day, the same Black Power fist. "Nothing comes between us."

Nettie's mind was racing. She was going to have to tell Tante Mado. Change her life. Follow him into the unknown, and it was terrifying. But she knew she had to. If Melvin was in the world with her, going through this with her, then she could do anything.

"You're out of your mind thinking you can fix this with an abortion, because this system has told you that this is some kind of problem. For us, it's not a problem. It is a gift."

Melvin was so sure of himself that he was beginning to wrap a rope around her, drawing her in like the driftwood she was. She let him pull her in, one word at a time. His lips pressed against hers and it felt like a healing balm. When they looked at each other again, the sky had darkened a shade more.

Melvin ran a hand over her hair, a shine in his eyes.

"We good," he whispered. "I know you. I know what you can do. That's why I keep coming to you, every night of my life, I come to you. I climb in your bed.

Make love to you. It's not just because I enjoy good pussy. It's because I love you, Nettie. I trust you. I'd take a bullet for you. That is what I want. To go down with you, fighting for our lives. Alright? So . . . do this with me. Burn this world down and build another one with me."

She rested her hand on his chest, felt his muscles under the fabric, and dug her fingernails deeper in his flesh. She wanted to hurt him because her heart was hurting now. Part of her still clung to what he said, that he came to her every night. How she wished this were true. It wasn't, and yet he had gotten under her skin.

Melvin was undoing everything. Her life, her dreams, were falling out of the sky into the ocean. Clia was right. Once he started rapping like that, it was over.

"Don't take that away from me," he whispered, his hot breath soaking her skin. She welcomed it, much like she welcomed the warmth of the sun on a cold day. "Let me be a father."

He held her closer, and she let the sweetness of his kiss dictate the rest of the story. *Chicago*. That couldn't scare her. They could not be afraid. They would be invincible. Melvin's hands running down her back grounded her. They looked at each other and she ran out of words. She rested her forehead against his. The ground felt firm under her feet. She inhaled the sea salt, sharp in the air, listened to the sound of waves crashing, and felt her trust anchored into the dark folds of his shirt.

BOOK TWO

Chicago, Illinois—1969

We say you don't fight racism with racism. We're gonna fight racism with solidarity. We say you don't fight capitalism with no Black capitalism; you fight capitalism with socialism... Socialism is the people. If you're afraid of socialism, you're afraid of yourself.

—FRED HAMPTON

13

"A LOT OF people get the word 'revolution' mixed up and they think 'revolution' is a bad word. Revolution is like having a sore on your body and then you put something on that sore to cure that infection. And I'm telling you that we're living in an infectious society right now."

The room was warm with body heat, a pleasant change from the crisp autumn air outside. Men and women who'd come to hear Fred Hampton had begun to catch a kind of spirit, a fire that led them to fill the room with responses. *Yes! Right on!* They clapped loudly, and the gravitas of his persona pulled Nettie in, the way Brother Stokely's had. Stokely felt like ages ago. But it was over a year since the death of Martin Luther King Jr. She'd been in Chicago a month now, California still clinging to her body like a shadow, her previous life still choking her in her sleep. Something had to keep her alive. Something had to help her pretend there was light in the darkness. She turned Fred Hampton and the Black Panther Party of Illinois into medicine.

"I'm telling you that we're living in a sick society. And anybody that endorses integrating into this sick society before it's cleaned up is a man who's committing a crime against the people."

This was Fred Hampton. This revolutionary brother, the chair of the Illinois Party, who was already making too much noise for the establishment, was everything Melvin had said and more. The podium on which he stood was surrounded with Panthers, their eyes scanning the crowd for danger. For pigs. Agents crawled in their midst here, too, just as they had in Oakland. The Party had grown too quickly, too big, too important, and Whitey was getting nervous. Police harassment had doubled since the Chicago chapter had launched.

"You see, people get involved in a lot of things that's profitable to them, and we've got to make it less profitable. We've got to make it less beneficial. I'm saying that any program that's brought into our community should be analyzed by the people of that community. It should be analyzed to see that it meets the relevant needs of that community. We don't need no niggas coming into our community to be having no company to open business for the niggas. There's too many niggas in our community that can't get crackers out of the business that they're gonna open."

Fred, or Chairman Fred as they called him, was going to lead this nation one day. Hearing him speak was almost a religious experience. The way he stood now at the lectern of Olivet Church, leaning into his Louisiana drawl and his half-preacher-half-future-lawyer confidence, were too compelling for anyone to look away.

"We got to face some facts. That the masses are poor, that the masses belong to what you call the lower class, and when I talk about the masses, I'm talking about the white masses, I'm talking about the Black masses, and the brown masses, and the yellow masses, too.

"We've got to face the fact that some people say you fight fire best with fire, but we say you put fire out best with water. We say you don't fight racism with racism. We're gonna fight racism with solidarity. We say you don't fight capitalism with no Black capitalism; you fight capitalism with socialism."

Nettie's eyes went to Melvin. He was among the Panthers near the podium, facing the crowd. She knew he was listening. Every now and then he nodded, his fist in the air. Every now and then he leaned in to whisper something to someone next to him, another Panther, and it took a minute for Nettie to register why she was suddenly feeling uneasy, a slow tickle of discomfort in her chest. It wasn't a man Melvin was talking to. It was a woman. A stunning sister, too, short hair under her beret, eyebrows penciled in. Who was she? Nettie had never seen her before, but then again, Nettie was the new face here. She was still learning to find her way home in this city.

The woman smiled and whispered something back to Melvin. She was not part of security. Or was she? Whatever she was, something about her unsettled

Nettie and she fought the urge to stare. Her stomach suddenly felt larger, more present, and she looked down at the swelling still barely showing under her shirt.

"We ain't gonna fight no reactionary pigs who run up and down the street being reactionary; we're gonna organize and dedicate ourselves to revolutionary political power and teach ourselves the specific needs of resisting the power structure, arm ourselves, and we're gonna fight reactionary pigs with *international proletarian revolution*. That's what it has to be. The people have to have the power: it belongs to the people."

Next to Nettie, Simone and Afia were clapping. Afia was even standing now, drinking in his words. A young mother of two working graveyard shifts at Union Station, she'd joined the chapter as soon as it formed. She'd been one of the first women, along with Simone, to approach Nettie after she settled in with Melvin. Afia's man, Tulane, lived in the basement of Nettie and Melvin's house. Nettie wasn't sure whether Afia and Tulane were really together anymore or not, but they both took care of their children and it seemed to be all that mattered. It inspired her how Tulane was with his children. He shared the basement with another brother, Forte, an ex-convict, a brother from the block, who had joined the Panthers but knew Melvin from way back when. Along with Tulane, Forte had become a security officer assigned to Melvin's detail. After the raid of Eldridge Cleaver's house last January, each member of leadership had bodyguards, and Melvin was no exception. This was the life she'd stepped into, and there was no glamour in it. No glory. Not even the promise of a rising sun. To the outside world, men like Melvin might have seemed like dead men walking. To the inside, they were warriors, soldiers, men full of power and capability, and women liked that. Nettie could see the very glint of admiration in this woman's eyes as she stole glances in Melvin's direction. She wasn't even trying to be subtle. Something burned Nettie in the chest, and she would have blamed the baby in her belly for the heartburn but she knew it was something else. Hurt. And it wasn't a new feeling.

She'd felt it as soon as she'd gotten to this city. She'd chalked it up to her own loneliness and homesickness, that feeling that Melvin was slowly drifting from her. Then she thought it was his new role, his assimilation back into Chicago, the meetings he constantly held or attended, the knocking on doors, the need to show out and flex all the muscle to gain the trust of this community. Melvin was committed all the way, he breathed the Party and ate it for breakfast, literally, with the children in the morning. He was starting a local breakfast program from inside a local church a few blocks from the Panther office on Madison, so he was always in dialogue with someone from the church.

A lot of these people however, Nettie noticed, were women. Melvin liked to talk to women. He tried to be subtle about it, but right now, as Nettie watched from afar, he was exchanging words with a sister Nettie didn't know, and for the second time, she noticed how Melvin's gaze lingered a little too long after talking with her. Or how the woman herself would reciprocate with a smile. And Nettie didn't like how she felt about it. She couldn't shake the feeling that they knew each other, the way perhaps he knew Blue and interacted with her back in Vallejo.

"We have to understand very clearly that there's a man in our community called a capitalist. Sometimes he's Black and sometimes he's white. But that man has to be driven out of our community, because anybody who comes into the community to make profit off the people by exploiting them can be defined as a capitalist. And we don't care how many programs they have, how long a dashiki they have. Because political power does not flow from the sleeve of a dashiki; political power flows from the barrel of a gun. It flows from the barrel of a gun!"

What brought her back was this, Fred's voice rising like an invisible cloud of fire between the people gathered there, and the vocal assertion about power: it would never be given to the oppressed. It had to be taken back, and the taking had to be violent. These were the cards dealt to Black people. Shoulder to shoulder, elbow in someone else's rib, she felt alive when he spoke.

Chairman Fred was now running down a list of names: Men who had died in the struggle for the people, men who had their freedom stolen away. Men who did it all for the people rather than maintain the status quo. Huey Newton, Bunchy Carter, Bobby Hutton. Thoughts of Lewis came to Nettie immediately. Helping him, holding his hand, tending to that wound that killed him, this was where her heart needed to be. Helping. Healing. Nettie needed to find schools around here, to take classes so that she could still apply to medical school. She felt the walls of a classroom, the voices of teachers she hadn't met yet, calling to her. She needed to get back to her original purpose, like her father had wanted for her.

"We have decided that although some of us come from what some would call petty-bourgeois families, though some of us could be in a sense on what you call the mountaintop, we could be integrated into the society working with people that we may never have a chance to work with.

"Maybe we could be on the mountaintop and maybe we wouldn't have to be hidin' when we go to speak places like this. Maybe we wouldn't have to worry about court cases and going to jail and being sick. We say that even though all of those luxuries exist on the mountaintop, we understand that you people and your problems are right here in the valley."

Fred was winding down now, she thought. He could go on for what seemed like hours, but every word was worth its weight. Nettie shifted in her seat when she felt a slight flutter inside, the baby moving a little bit more now than last week. She hoped for a boy, for some reason she couldn't explain. Maybe because of Melvin. She bit the inside of her cheek.

"We in the Black Panther Party, because of our dedication and understanding, went into the valley knowing that the people are in the valley, knowing that our plight is the same plight as the people in the valley, knowing that our enemies are on the mountaintop—our friends are in the valley, and even though its nice to be on the mountaintop, we're going back to the valley. Because we understand that there's work to be done in the valley, and when we get through with this work in the valley, then we got to go to the mountaintop."

Yes!!! The pews of the church were nearly crumbling from the weight of excitement in the hips of the women and men in attendance. Nettie applauded.

"We're going to the mountaintop because there's a motherfucker on the mountaintop that's playing king, and he's been bullshitting us. And we've got to go up on the mountaintop not for the purpose of living his lifestyle and living like he lives. We've got to go up on the mountaintop to make this motherfucker understand, Goddamn it, that we are coming from the valley!"

The people had been prepared for this moment, and in unison they raised their fists in the air and yelled out, "Power to all the people!" Even the church leaders, all standing in the background, were stomping their feet and shouting.

Ever since the chapter had launched, they had been more than receptive to the idea of change beyond bearing arms, "survival pending revolution," as the Panthers called it. They'd offered their banquet hall to the local Panthers' Free Breakfast Program, and this was where Melvin could be found most mornings, planning his breakfast program, setting up shop.

Nettie continued to clap for Chairman Fred, but out of the corner of her eye she watched Melvin walk toward the door in the back of the pulpit, down the hallway. He was alone. Nettie's eyes searched the crowd for the other sister who was with him, but she didn't see her. Somehow, she'd disappeared in the crowd, or maybe she was still there hidden in the sea of faces, undetectable from a distance, and Nettie felt a dryness in her mouth before she swallowed her own fear.

NETTIE CLASPED NAÏMA'S wrist and cleaned the injection site with alcohol. She used her gloved hands to gently tickle the young patient's fingers to help her relax.

"Just a little prick on your finger, that's all," Nettie said with a smile. "I'll be done before you know it."

It was clear to Nettie that Naïma had some place else to be. The girl sat in the waiting room, tapping her foot, compulsively looking at the clock, and then out the window. A fine rain had been falling outside all day, dripping against the windows. Nettie could feel the cold teeth of winter even through the glass, feel them sinking deeper in her bones.

"It runs in my family," Naïma said in a sweet, honeyed voice. "I saw Dr. Hernandez last time. He said I should know if I carry the . . . what did he call it?"

"The trait," Nettie said, readying her needle. "A good idea, especially when you have a baby on the way. It's good to know."

"What if I do? Then what?"

Naïma was bundled up in heavy faux fur. Underneath, she was wearing tight sequined pants and high-heeled boots, and a top that still revealed her cleavage despite the cold. She was bearing too much flesh for this brutal weather, Nettie thought, but then again, Naïma was native to Illinois. Nettie wasn't. She hated this cold with a passion.

"If you do carry it, it doesn't mean you'll get symptoms or get sick," Nettie said. "But it's good to know. Then we can help you and your baby if the need arises. If you want kids."

She measured her words carefully. It was one thing Nettie had almost lost the habit of, speaking to patients. Working in the free clinic with Dr. Hernandez allowed her to reimmerse herself in that world, and the more she did, the more she missed home. The clinic was a lifeboat in the sea, a raft she could cling to and stop herself from drowning. Because that's what she was. Drowning. Chicago was the sea, gray and choppy and unfamiliar, and Nettie could not breathe.

Ever since she arrived here with Melvin, she had found herself engulfed in activities and meetings and canvassing and newspaper selling, and it had overtaken her to the point where, for the first two months, she had not stopped to think about her aunt, about California, about her future plans. And then slowly, as the days pushed on, Nettie began to remember. She began to miss that smell of alcohol on cotton balls, the sound of curtains drawing between patient and doctor, the cold feel of metal and glass under her hands when she cleaned and organized supplies. She missed her own self. And more than anything, she missed that relief on a patient's face after a visit, the way a child or an elder beamed when she offered them comfort. The way Lewis had counted on her even in his final moments returned to her, and she remembered what she loved most about this: the comfort she brought, like her father had done for his patients.

She squeezed Naïma's finger and the blood pooled red. She was comfortable here doing this work, maybe even happy, Nettie thought as she collected the blood in the pipette. And yet, guilt clung like a shadow as she thought of Tante Mado, her aunt's eyes closing and not reopening after Nettie had dropped the news on her. The memory was still painful. It was better not to remember.

Above her head hung a large banner with the Puerto Rican flag and an assault rifle and the words EL PARTIDO DE LOS YOUNG LORDS SIRVEN Y PROTEGEN A SU GENTE. On the opposite wall, another banner featured a leaping black panther, mouth wide open to bare the menace of fangs and claws, alongside a photograph of Eldridge Cleaver with a mean stare. Cleaver was now living in Algeria, but he remained the center of admiration for some. Nettie felt unsettled by his excessive, fiery personality, and then there were stories about his past, the violence against women, things she struggled to reconcile.

"Almost done," Nettie said.

Naïma was coming here often for all sorts of screenings. She listed an address shared with her boyfriend and her frequent visits to check herself for venereal diseases had begun to trigger an alarm bell. Nettie had overheard Dr. Hernandez comment on her bruises. But they were unable to offer any assistance if Naïma wasn't asking for it herself. She was no longer a minor, and it was up to her to reach out. It was a shame, Nettie thought as she considered the girl before her. She was so pretty, with deep dimples in her cheeks that formed even when she wasn't smiling, and large doe eyes. She reminded Nettie of a doll.

"How far along are you?" Naïma asked, glancing down at Nettie's stomach.

"Almost five months," Nettie answered. "I took my test, too, just like you."

Nettie was still in disbelief, sometimes startling at the image of herself in the mirror when she undressed or layered her clothes. A baby was definitely growing there, a child, now the size of a fruit or a fist, large enough for Melvin's hand to cradle in the dark when they lay in bed. Her new morning ritual was to rub cocoa butter all over her stomach while singing "Ti Zwazo," a song she'd learned growing up that she'd forgotten about until she'd seen a tall, handsome Harry Belafonte sing it on television. "Yellow Bird," he called it. Nettie had cried that evening. "What's wrong, Nettie? What's the matter?" Melvin had said. He'd thought it was the move, a long haul from the West Coast to the East, hours on trains that left her sore and uncomfortable. He thought it was the climate. It was hormones, she said. Just hormones. I'll be fine.

But it was the song. There was a fault line now running down the middle of her heart. The song had been a call from long ago, a piece of who she was, and she couldn't even remember the words because they were now in English. It made her angry, that it was now repackaged for everyone else as a song from the Caribbean with no known origin, as if it had never belonged to her people in the first place. She had to remember the words. Maybe if she could get her aunt to talk to her again one day.

Tante Mado's face haunted Nettie, how it had been a black moon full of bitterness and disappointment upon learning the news. Pregnant? Nettie?

Impossible. When her eyes finally opened they were like craters, full of tears. "After all I did for you. Look how you ruined your life, your chance at medical school. Look at you running into the fire. You're just like your father after all."

The more she yelled at Nettie, the more Nettie's chest filled with rage and despair.

"Not only are you pregnant, but . . . Chicago? Why so far away from me, with someone you barely know?"

Nettie asked Tante Mado to trust in her. She knew what she was doing. But Tante Mado rolled her eyes. *Trust?* She cried in her handkerchief, as if she was in mourning.

"Melvin is a good man," Nettie repeated. "We are in love. That's worth risking everything for, isn't it? Haven't you ever been in love?"

Tante Mado shook her head and let the tears fall. There was nothing more to say until it was time for Nettie to pack her things and return her key to the landlord. Then Tante Mado had come to see her off and hugged her quietly. She'd slipped Nettie an envelope with cash. For the baby, she said. Maybe a crib, some warm clothes.

"It's cold in Chicago," Tante Mado said, as if Nettie hadn't considered that part.

There was a long silence as she watched Nettie box up the last remaining items in the apartment. Finally, Nettie turned to her and said, "It's going to be fine."

Tante Mado shook her head. "You're going to need help with the baby," she said. "I don't understand why you won't just stay here with me?"

Something else was calling, she explained. She said those words Tante Mado didn't want to hear. *Revolution. Fight. Change.* This baby was going to be part of it all, and she knew it was a difficult thing to ask her aunt to accept. Leaving Tante Mado in Oakland had been more painful than she'd expected. She wanted her aunt to be here with her now, she wanted to feel her presence and hear her voice now that her stomach was growing, now that small baby shoes and blankets had entered the house. A baby was no frivolous thing. How foolish she'd been to think she could do this alone!

Naïma reached inside her purse, pulled out a small compact mirror, and checked her reflection, then patted her hair down and twisted out some lipstick to reapply a coat. Nettie watched her lay it on meticulously, an art she seemed to have perfected.

Before she shut the compact mirror, her eyes met Nettie's briefly in the mirror.

"I don't think a baby would be safe with me right now."

Her words iced Nettie to the core. She was unsure how to answer. Did Nettie know herself? How could she guarantee safety to this child growing inside her? She considered Naïma's eyes, which were going to the clock again.

Naïma bit at her fingernails, once painted a pretty shade of violet. She turned her large eyes toward the window and watched people come and go. Nettie was convinced that Naïma was coming to her and Dr. Hernandez for more than just a screening, likely trapped in an abusive relationship. But Dr. Hernandez was right. They couldn't force her out if she didn't ask for help.

"Why don't we schedule you for your next visit?" Nettie said. "The doctor will chat with you more about your results then. Is there anything else I can do for you? Anything at all?"

She looked at Naïma and paused, hoping the young woman would fill in the silence with her own words. Surely those bruises on her body could be prevented. The girl said no, hopped out of her examination chair as if it were too hot. Nettie grabbed a flyer from one of the drawers, something she'd been stacking for the young women who came in for clinic visits.

"Take this," she said. "It's about our Free Shoe and Clothing program. My friend Simone works there. She helps young women with clothing for babies, food . . . shelter, if they need it."

She hoped Naïma understood. There was no other way to offer help without crossing a line. Dr. Hernandez would agree himself. Naïma took the flier and studied it. Nettie collected her materials slowly, giving her time to ask or volunteer information, time to say something. She might be holding her breath a while, but she didn't want to feel helpless again like she'd felt with Clia. She had to do what she could to help.

Naïma spoke up, softly. "I've already tried." She looked suddenly small in her eyes. "Leaving, I mean. It's not always simple." She batted her eyelashes. "I don't suppose you could understand. You don't know men like Larry."

"You don't know the men I know," Nettie said. She pulled out a pen and some paper and carefully jotted down an address on a piece of paper. "After you see Simone, you go here and talk to him." She wrote Melvin's name down in all capital letters and gave her the note. "I'll come with you if you want."

Melvin, and all the brothers in the Party, were not the kind of men Naïma's boyfriend wanted to cross. She knew the community believed in the Panthers. Their sheer presence at anyone's doorstep alone had been known to frighten the occasional abusive husband or pimp, or landlord.

"Thanks." Naïma looked down at the note and then at Nettie, and for a while she looked like she wanted to say something else, then she slid the note in her pocket. She secured her fur around her slender frame and headed for the door. At least she'd taken the note. That was hopeful. Nettie knew she'd made a bold promise about Melvin helping Naïma. There was no doubt that the Panthers could take care of that, but the Party had a lot on its plate. They had political campaigns to run, as well as breakfast and other free food programs, free clinics, busing programs, too much to do already. They could not go door to door fixing domestic problems all the time.

The young woman was gone, the door opened and shut behind her. She hoped she hadn't pushed too hard, overstepped her bounds. It wasn't her business, after all. Why insert herself in people's lives? Maybe it was to make up for Clia, to atone for her lack of action, for her helplessness. Nettie could not fix her own failure there, but she needed to keep trying.

She remembered how Simone and Afia had come visiting Nettie after their move with a basket of second-hand baby clothes. "I heard our section leader is going to be a father so I wonder if you might need these." Simone and Afia had helped her clean the house without asking. They'd dropped food off without asking. Immediately, they invited her to meetings and they made it a point to introduce her to other mothers. There were always children running around. "When your baby comes," Simone said, "you'll bring it here and let it learn with the other cubs. We watch each other's babies here like our own, we raise them." They had a system that worked. A konbit. Nettie was grateful for it, but part of her was terrified that she might miss seeing her baby grow up. She would have to work, after all, and yet she wanted nothing more than to spend time with her child, a luxury maybe she could not afford. And she did still hope that she could apply to medical school. She fantasized about applying to Roosevelt, perhaps, taking classes there at night.

"There's this clinic on the West Side," Simone had said. "Just opened, and they are in serious need of a medical staff. They got this one doctor volunteering his time, Dr. Hernandez, from the Young Lords Party."

He could really use the help, Simone had said. Finding more volunteers was a challenge ever since the police had started raiding clinics. So there Nettie was, still green from California, unfamiliar with her surroundings and in a new community where she knew no one, meeting Dr. Hernandez on site, telling him about her research and field work for Dr. Johnson.

"We run similar programs for the community here," Dr. Hernandez said. "We go door to door, too, to make visits when they can't come here. It's not easy work. We got pigs breathing down our necks—"

"I'll take it," Nettie said.

She was convinced he'd heard the desperation on the edge of her voice, the need to claw at something of her own. Maybe he heard her thirst for some kind of control. Here in this densely populated windy city of projects and skyscrapers, bridges and mortar and clouds, she felt she was slowly losing her mind, her thoughts detaching from each other and running amok between streets and corridors. Dr. Hernandez was saving her life and he didn't even know it. He shook her hand and squeezed it. "Bueno, welcome Hermanita!"

She had a purpose, no matter how temporary. And she liked working with Dr. Hernandez, because of his energy. He was fast in everything he did, walking around the clinic, stopping here and there to talk to a patient in the waiting room. He even spoke rapidly.

"Simone said you're from Haiti, is that right, Hermanita?"

"Yes. I was born there."

Dr. Hernandez looked in the distance for a while and Nettie was sure he was thinking, or trying to remember something. She was prepared to answer the usual questions. Where was that on the map? Why was she here? And yet nothing of the sort came. Instead, he started to speak, what Nettie first surmised was a memory, and then realized was a speech, something half familiar and half foreign. The words *Saint-Domingue* caused her ears to perk up.

"'I want Liberty and Equality to reign in Saint-Domingue. I work to bring them into existence. . . . Unite yourselves to us, brothers, and fight with us for the same cause.'" Dr. Hernandez paused and smiled. He was younger than she expected, she could see now, but so deeply passionate and committed that he looked wise beyond his years. "You familiar with that speech, aren't you?"

Nettie stood there, perplexed. No, and she wanted to remember, badly, because she immediately understood that she should know. And she smiled, her face burning with shame.

"Toussaint Louverture at Camp Turel," the doctor explained. "No one seems to know it, don't feel bad."

She wanted to say she didn't remember it, didn't even recall learning any of it. But she was rendered speechless. How should she know anything anymore about where she came from? Dr. Hernandez had learned it in school, memorized it, he said, back in Puerto Rico, where his father, a history teacher, had taught him all about revolution.

"We will do great things here, I know it," he said, shaking her hand once more.

He reminded her of home, even if she didn't remember home well anymore, and within days she'd found something familiar in Dr. Hernandez, something she'd lost and could now hold on to, something that called upon her daily to come here and do the work.

As she walked home, her eyes searched for the green buds now sprouting on the bare branches of trees, and near the sidewalk at the border of grass and frozen flowerbeds. Spring was returning and it was about time. She was eager to see green leaves again, feel the air against her skin. She missed sunshine. The wind didn't blow as forcefully today, and perhaps she could get used to this degree of chill, where it wasn't freezing. She listened to her own heels clicking on the sidewalk and to the rhythm of herself wandering a city, alone. Even though she'd memorized the streets home, she often recognized how easy it was for someone like her to get lost, despite Melvin's best arguments. "Chicago's like a grid, everything designed and aligned in a pattern that makes it easy to learn. You see it that way, you can't get lost." Easy for him to say. Melvin knew this place by heart, from the buildings and parks to the different housing projects and homes built here after the great fire.

Garfield Park's vast expanse of trees sprawled under the sky, their limbs like distorted hands held up in worship. The wind blew softly through them, and Nettie wrapped her scarf around her neck a little tighter. She measured her own breath, watched it fog the air in front of her face when she exhaled, and she didn't hear the steps behind her at first. They were almost inaudible, fusing with her own rhythm. But soon, she became aware of them: *step, step, step, step*. Nettie instinctively glanced over her shoulder. There was a man strolling behind her, a white man dressed in a crisp gray suit and a coat, wearing a black fedora. He held her gaze and grinned, his teeth flashing like little warning flags, and Nettie picked up her pace, her heart pounding at the realization that she was being followed.

14

SOMETHING ABOUT THIS man felt wrong. He didn't fit here, and the hair on her body raised when she heard him hurry his step, too, matching hers, and soon she could feel him catching up.

"Miss Boileau? I just want to talk to you."

Fear bit into her and she stopped abruptly, spun on her heels. The man stopped, too. His hands were buried in his coat pockets. He was no one she knew. And yet he knew her name. The tip of his nose and his cheeks were now pink from the cold.

"Do I know you?"

She spoke firmly, meaning to sound as threatening as she could. The man offered a half smile and caught his breath, fogging the air a little.

"No, but I know *you*."

He reached inside his coat and Nettie thought about fleeing. But she didn't, she wasn't sure why. He came closer and produced a wallet and opened it, let it stand in the light long enough for her to read the insignia, and the letters sprawled across the small badge. She could tell he was watching her, carefully, and her blood turned cold.

"My name is Archer," he said, putting his identification away. "I just want a friendly chat. I'll walk with you. You're on your way home, right?"

A shudder crawled up her spine. Her eyes swept the park. She hadn't realized it before, but she understood now. She was being watched. How else did this man know her name, her destination, and her schedule? She briefly considered running, but walking was better than getting in a car with an agent, especially one from the Federal Bureau of Investigation. It was better out here. Besides, she had nothing to hide from him.

"What is it you want?" Nettie asked. "Don't you have criminals to arrest or something?"

He was undeterred. "A shame really," he said. "Weather is much nicer in Oakland, you could have stayed there and graduated, you know? Instead, you chose this life, with Black Panthers."

Nettie kept walking, her pulse racing, her blood cold. She could see, in the distance, the back of the buildings signaling the clinic was not too far, maybe just a few more blocks.

"You chum up to domestic terrorists," Archer said, his voice now icy like the wind. "You get yourself caught up in communist ideals, and that Melvin Mosley character . . . Love sure blinds people, doesn't it?"

"Is that why you're here?" Nettie asked, her heart thumping in her chest.

"You think you know him," Archer said, "but you have no idea what's really going on."

He stopped in his tracks and Nettie knew he was now in control of the conversation. He was forcing her to stop, too. Under his coat, his freshly ironed suit and his collar were stiff, like him. She saw his left eye twitch a little. His nostrils flared as he huffed.

"Did you know he was an explosives expert in his rank back in Vietnam? Did he tell you about that village? The one he blew up with the women and children he killed? He was quite good at his job, until that bomb went off, got him in the process, nearly killed him. . . . You've seen the scars."

She tried to remain calm, to listen to what he was saying, but her ears had hooked two words now, *women and children*, and they were bouncing around in her head. Blaring, like alarms. Impossible. Not the Melvin she knew.

"I don't like radicals," Archer said. "I think the world would be better off if your lot refrained from breeding at all, you see?" His eyes went to her belly and Nettie felt a cold wind rip through her. "You come over here all smug, and you put on a show of benevolence, like you're all saints, so these poor, naïve people out there can find you trustworthy. Breakfast for children? Free clinics? Give me a break."

Nettie tasted metal in her mouth. Contempt pulled the end corners of his mouth into a grimace. He straightened his spine and she could see that it was customary for him to walk, talk, and own the space around him in that way. Telling her she didn't belong in it.

"You came all the way here because your feelings are hurt about a breakfast program?"

Nettie clenched her jaw in defiance. She resisted the urge to flee when he stepped closer, into her space, and looked into her eyes.

"We're feeding children," she said. "Nothing more. Why does this bother you?"

"Don't get cocky," he said. "It doesn't become you. Besides, I'm in a good mood today and I'm feeling generous, and I know you're different from the rest of them. Why don't you shut your smart mouth and listen?"

Nettie could almost smell the frustration oozing from his pores and she hated him instantly.

"You're so confident in that boyfriend of yours, aren't you? You think the world of him. I see how you slither your way through this city, taking over the ghettos like you're some kind of godsend Negro league or something. . . . You think he'll be able to protect you when the war knocks at your door?"

"You don't know anything about me or Melvin."

"I do know. I know when he takes a piss, when he goes to sleep, *where* he slept on those nights he didn't come home to you. Do you know?"

Nettie's eyes narrowed, and the air burned her until they filled with tears. She took a step back. This felt violently intrusive. As if the eyes had been following her even inside the intimacy of her own home.

"I can only imagine how that makes you feel," Archer said. "He brought you here, pregnant and all, and now he puts you in this position. Shame."

"None of this is any of your business," Nettie hissed, clutching her purse until her knuckles burned.

"Listen, Nettie, I'm going to level with you, because you're a smart girl." He took another step. "The Federal Bureau of Investigation wants information. You have information. We could reward you for said information, and if the acquisition of this information runs you into any expenses, we would gladly cover those, too. I could tell you a lot of things. But . . . you'd have to do something for me, in exchange, you see? We could work out a deal, you and me."

His shoulders were rather large, and she noticed for the first time how imposing he was. He seemed heavier than she had first noticed.

"I want to know more about Melvin," he said. "About his detail, about his relationship with Fred Hampton, where they're planning to start their next breakfast program. You don't have to get in trouble. All you need to do is keep your eyes open, tell me when they're meeting, what they're discussing. We just need to know so we make sure no one does anything crazy, keep the city safe. And in exchange, I can tell you who your boyfriend is seeing. I can do more for you, too. Take care of your aunt back in Oakland. Wouldn't that be nice if you could make sure she was well cared for?"

Nettie's tongue was now a sack of stones. She couldn't find the words to speak.

Archer stepped even closer, now breathing in her face.

"You know what? We could take care of that baby of yours on the way. Wouldn't it be beneficial for you if your child was cared for? Medical bills, school . . . College, so he doesn't drop out like you did. The bottom line is, a lot of good could come out of this. We don't come to an understanding, then things will get out of hand. People are going to get hurt."

Nettie felt a sickness crawl in her stomach as he handed her a card from his pocket, urged her to take it. A group of people walked by, chattering, lowering their voices when they came close. She knew they were watching. By now, people had seen them.

"Are we done here?" she asked, stepping away. "I have nothing to say to you. I'm late."

Nettie took off, walking quickly. This time he didn't follow. Nettie picked up her pace. By the time she made it down the block, and reemerged within the busy street block, she was out of breath, and her eyes were wet. But she didn't turn to look over her shoulder.

THE DINNER TABLE was quiet that night. Although they were hungry, the eating was slow. Forte and Tulane had cooked together, and Afia had brought their children over to eat with them. Only the children were unperturbed. The adults were chewing and avoiding each other's gaze, until Forte said he'd heard stories like this before, from other Panthers in New York, and back on the West Side in Los Angeles. For a while now, rumors were swirling of brothers and sisters in the struggle who'd been slipped hallucinogens, whose phones had been tapped, who'd received letters from other Panthers containing divisive information.

"They're sending agents in our midst to infiltrate us," Forte said. "Motherfuckers are on us. Notice how they always seem to know when and where to show up? Notice how the harassment's escalating lately? We can't even go to a meeting without getting stopped and frisked. How do they know the place and time of our meetings?"

No one told him to watch his language around the children. Forte couldn't change if he wanted to. He'd been in and out of the joint enough times, he said, to absorb a certain kind of talk that was difficult to shake.

The greens sat on a plate next to pieces of bread, and today they had the luxury of chicken, and everything smelled good, but Nettie had watched them all shut down around the table as if their souls had been sucked out by her account. Her eyes scanned each face, and she saw the uniformity of unspoken fear.

"Breakfast program hit a nerve," Tulane said. "That's saying something."

"They got another thing coming if they think we'll let them take food out of the babies' mouths," Afia said, ripping a piece of bread with her hands. She had stunning almond-shaped eyes and a head full of dreadlocked hair that framed her face like a giant lion's mane. When she talked, her hair bounced. She was already wearing her uniform for work that night, selling train tickets at Union. "Mothers aren't going to allow that," she said. "Anyway, what is there to do when we have new faces joining the Party every day?"

"It ain't just the new faces you got to worry about." Melvin leaned in with his elbows on the table. "It's us."

A few eyes looked around the table briefly before looking down at their food. Others never looked up, staring fixedly at something on the table, quietly digesting the uncomfortable truth.

"Knowing one of *us* could be talking to the pigs. It's how they know. That and they're listening." Melvin dropped his voice. "Tapping our phones. I suggest we watch what we say."

"So, that's it?" Forte asked.

Melvin looked at him. No one had answers. Melvin turned to Nettie. She forced herself to swallow the chicken, ignoring the knot in her throat.

"What else did he want to know?" Melvin asked. "Besides the next meeting—"

"I told you, he didn't get to ask me much about that," Nettie said. "I told him I had nothing to say."

She had already explained what had happened—the agent, his name, how he'd approached her, and what was offered in exchange for information—leaving out details about what this agent claimed to know—Melvin's infidelities, his stint in Vietnam— and not mentioning his offer for the bureau to fund her and her baby if she agreed to inform. "I told him to go to hell and I came straight here."

She bit her tongue. She wanted to say more to him, though. She knew it wasn't the right time to talk about who he might be screwing behind her back. Was it that woman at the church? But that conversation had to be private. A small voice was whispering to her, in the back of her mind, that she should separate their private problems from the Party problems.

Later that night, the moon glowed yellow outside their window like a cat's eye. There was still an icy wind blowing through the city. Melvin tinkered with the radiator as Nettie shed her first layers of clothes. Her ankles were swollen, and she was desperate to put her feet up, but it had been too long she'd walked around with these questions in her head.

"Did you see Dr. Hernandez?" Melvin asked.

Nettie paused, and gritted her teeth. She knew where this was going.

"Yes, and I'm not going to quit this job after I just started, Melvin," Nettie said.

"I meant did you see him," Melvin said, removing his jacket and throwing it on the chair. "Did he check on the baby?"

He wrapped his arms around Nettie and brought her close in a moment of tenderness they only reserved for their bedroom, with the door closed and no one to peer into their love but themselves. He pressed his lips against her forehead and she sighed, mildly embarrassed.

"I'm not due for another exam until next month," Nettie said. It was nice to feel his warmth. She let herself relax. "Don't worry about it. What's going on with the rent?" she whispered.

She always lowered her voice when discussing money or rent, remembering that Forte and Tulane lived here on and off. Making a socialist model of living had not yet been perfected in their household, so until Forte and Tulane could make the rent steadily and as long as they kept the house clean, Nettie was learning not to mind. She wasn't sure how they made their money, other than odd jobs here and there, but theoretically, the arrangement was a good one. Practically, there were kinks in the road and Nettie didn't like kinks. Not with a child on the way.

"We'll figure rent out, don't worry about that right now."

Melvin removed his sweater. There was a shadow of fatigue on his face. Maybe tonight wasn't the right night, but when would it ever be?

"Why don't you ever want to talk about Vietnam?"

"What?" He glanced at her. "What do you mean?"

"You never told me what really happened."

He slowly turned around and her heart sank. His eyebrows sank into confusion. Nettie felt her heart beat faster.

"That agent said something about a village. About explosives."

Melvin chuckled, but it wasn't really out of amusement. She could almost feel a quiet rage building up in him, his breathing changing. He stiffened. She hadn't rehearsed this conversation enough and now she was nervous because Melvin was just staring her down, but not speaking.

"I didn't think it was appropriate to bring that up out there. But you never tell me anything about the war. You never talk about it."

"What else did he say?" Melvin's voice cut through the warmth in the room.

"He mentioned women and children and explosives and I didn't need to hear it. I know you would never do that. I know you wouldn't hurt women and children. I just . . . I just want to know what happened, and I want to hear it from you."

"Is that all?" Melvin's hands were on his hips. He'd descended into a dark place now. Nettie stared at him and hesitated, but then, Why not? Now or never.

"He said he knew things about you, about where you sleep when you don't come home at night."

"And where is that?"

Did she really need to spell it out? Melvin turned his back, faced the window so he could look out into the street. The radiator hummed, cutting through the unbearable silence.

"And you believed him?" Melvin finally asked.

"Are you?"

"Am I what?"

"Sleeping around, Melvin."

Melvin shook his head, stepped away from the window, and grabbed his coat. He headed for the door.

"Wait. Where are you going? I thought we were talking. Talk to me."

He slammed the door shut behind him. A photo of Nettie and her father fell off the top of the dresser. She picked it up and held it, looked at her small face next to her father's, measured the glow in his eyes, filled with pride, as he looked into the lens. She quickly set the photo back on the dresser as she felt the tears come on. No crying, Nettie told herself. If you cry, that means Tante Mado was right. And she couldn't be. Not when Nettie loved Melvin the way she did, not when she'd let herself be persuaded for the sake of her child that she should be here, with her baby's father. It was going to be alright. Right?

It was nearly four in the morning when she opened her eyes. She'd drifted to sleep, somehow. A door closed in the distance. Then she heard footsteps in the hallway. Her heart sat on her chest like a boulder, heavily, but she didn't move. The bedroom door opened, and she knew he was back, slowly peeling his coat off, moving in and out of the bathroom until finally, he slipped under the covers and stayed there, still. She could almost hear him staring at the ceiling. She turned to look at him so he would know she was awake. She rested her hand on his chest. He didn't look back at her, but then he spoke softly in the dark.

"I don't ever want to talk about that," he whispered. "I need you to accept that. I'm not particularly proud of the things that took place there."

She closed her eyes. He had the right to cling to his darkness if he wanted to. She didn't have to wrestle him out of everything.

"I didn't do anything I wasn't ordered to do. If they tell you otherwise, then they're lying. Everything they say is a lie." He finally turned to look at her and she couldn't see him in the dark. Just an outline of him, of his face blending in the shadows. She felt his breath on her face. "They're putting ideas in your head and you buy into them, and that's how they divide us."

"You really think we matter that much to . . . pigs?"

"It's not . . . about . . . the two of us," Melvin said, suddenly slowing down, thinking this through. "It's about how they can use us to get to who they want. . . . They're playing psychological games! This is the war, all over again, except this time the war is here and anyone who isn't awake, who isn't with us, who isn't in the vanguard, can't see the difference."

Melvin pulled the covers over their heads and suddenly they were drowning in pitch blackness and in heat. He breathed on her forehead. She remained still, wondering whether someone was actually listening in right now. Or perhaps they were all collectively growing paranoid. Not knowing drove her nearly mad.

"You have to hang on to trust," Melvin said. "Don't let them get to you."

Then, before she could ask, Melvin reached out and placed his hand on her stomach, let it rest there so the baby could feel it and stir, softly. Melvin hugged the bump and the weight of his arm made her feel safe.

"Nothing some pig says will change how I feel for this cause. And for you. No pig, no agent, no woman, no one can get between us like that."

Melvin knew how to say things without saying them. She didn't know if there were other women or not, but she knew he was here now. And she knew she wanted that to be enough. They had a home. A bed. A structure to their lives. So, his lips on hers were reassurance, a confirmation of what they had together. Her eyelids drooped and she wallowed in the warmth of his body. The air was thick now, heavy with sleep and the sound of Melvin breathing, snoring. Nettie remained still, afraid to disrupt the peace now fallen unto them.

15

THE VOICES IN the Panther headquarter offices that evening were all talking rapidly, rising and falling.

"I'm not obligated to," a man shouted. "We shouldn't have to. We work hard for what we have, and that's my bottom line, young man."

She approached the room where Melvin and Forte often sat, answering the phone and conducting meetings. She normally stopped by if needed, and there was now a shortage of help in the office. Constant threats and growing reprisal from the police at various Panther locations had frightened off some of the volunteers, and Nettie developed more admiration for the ones who still showed up, who believed in the cause. The task was simple: open envelopes, separate the donations from the phone and light bills.

Both Forte and Tulane were there now, standing at opposite ends of the desk where Melvin was seated. She could see through the half-open door that another man was standing opposite of Melvin, leaning in and shouting. She recognized Mr. Reed, a local grocer who had had it in for Melvin since the chapter launched, ever since the Panthers began their political education classes and rallies about driving out capitalism from their block.

Mr. Reed was in his early seventies, and hadn't retired. No, now that Nettie remembered, she'd been in his store before, and he'd abruptly asked her to leave. He was not allowing Panthers to take over his store and scare away his customers. He was not interested in the Panther movement or vision.

Melvin studied him and gave him a look that would send a man running. "You're telling me you can't share a piece of bread? You can't make that simple contribution for the people? You're that selfish?"

"I work hard to stock my shelves." Mr. Reed buried his hands in his pockets, stubbornly. "I can't give away free food and make a profit. I've lived here too long and I go to the same church my community goes to. I pay my taxes. You can't coerce people into giving away what they worked hard for," he said, vehemently shaking his head. "That ain't right."

Nettie grabbed a stack of envelopes from the desk outside the door. It was where she would sit if she needed to start sorting, but she remained on her feet, listening. Melvin sat still at the desk. Under his leather jacket, all he had on was his shirt, buttoned up to the neck, the collar still raised to protect himself against the bite of winter outside.

"Alright," Melvin said.

Forte smirked. He was about the same height as Melvin, with wavy gray hair at his temples, long enough to pull into a ponytail at the back. He was a handsome man, with lean facial features and a lean frame, and he was just as charming with the women as he was cunning with everyone else.

"Don't you worry, Mr. Reed," Melvin added, searching his pockets for what Nettie knew was a match. He came up empty. "It's cool. Why don't you go on home? No one's going to come and shake you down for donations. You can't give what your heart don't got."

Melvin bent to Forte without a word. In the office light, they looked like shadow men, dressed in their black clothes, the leather of the jackets catching the lamplight like small fires. Forte, as if on cue, pulled out his matches and lit one. Melvin leaned into the flame, lit his cigarette by sucking on it calmly, placidly, the glow illuminating his face until the air was thick with smoke. Then, Melvin blew his smoke up toward the ceiling and turned back to Mr. Reed. "Have it your way."

"See . . ." Mr. Reed raised his eyebrows. "Now that sounds like a threat to me, and I don't like it."

"What you don't seem to understand is that Black Panther Party demands unity. We just want to give the people what they need to survive without reaching to the oppressor for a handout. To move together. Black Power. You hip to Black Power, my brother?"

Mr. Reed didn't answer. Instead, he glanced at Forte and Tulane, then at Melvin.

"Because if you are hip to Black Power, you wouldn't be on board with the greedy, avaricious businessmen actively participating in the robbery of our community without giving back. You should be helping our survival programs."

"What about MY survival?" Mr. Reed roared.

"We all need to survive together. The key, brother, is *together*. Unity, you dig my meaning? If you won't help, then alright then, go on about your business. You won't move with us, then move out of our way so we can get shit done."

Mr. Reed's mouth opened, but no sound came out. Instead, he huffed and puffed a little. Then, she watched him curse under his breath and walk away. The outrage had brought out a big vein on his forehead, bulging.

Nettie finally looked at the mail in her hands, and it was luck that led her to pay close attention and to even be here that day, she decided, when she found an envelope with her name on it. Something addressed to her. Who was writing her here? Not her aunt, Nettie thought, as she inspected the handwriting.

Tante Mado was still too upset to engage with her these days. Whenever they talked on the phone, Tante Mado would often talk about herself, her day, what work was like, and then, eventually, she would drop hints of her own loneliness. "I'm beginning to forget what you look like."

And Nettie would always reassure her that Chicago was only a flight away. "You're coming to see us after the baby is born, aren't you?"

On the last call, after a long silence, Tante Mado had sighed and mumbled something about medical school. "It's a shame you didn't go after all. You're going to become one of those women who missed the opportunity of a lifetime, and before you know it, you'll be pregnant again and again . . . You'll have twelve children by this man and still be cooking his meals, and life will have passed you by."

Nettie wasn't sure if her aunt said these things with malice, but they cut her either way. She swore she'd stop calling. But she missed Tante Mado, the only family she had left, and so she'd hoped the envelope was from her. But it hadn't been mailed to the house. It had been sent to the Black Panther Illinois Chapter Headquarters, and from there it had been forwarded to Melvin's office in Lawndale.

Nettie tore the envelope open.

Dear Nettie,

I hope you kept me in your thoughts, my dear, even though I know you are busy now. I'm in Chicago with Jim, and our political organization met with your Deputy Chairman Fred Hampton. What a strong and charismatic leader, he is! He is going to grow larger than life. You know what I mean, don't you? The way they talk about him, it's like he's the messiah and this revolution is the second coming. And we are all ready for it.

Anyway, we met them at headquarters on Madison, and then I looked at the photographs on the wall, and there you were. You and Melvin, is it? Your boyfriend? What a small world! They said they could forward my letter to you. We're attending the SDS Convention of June 18th. Jim, me, a whole bunch of us. We're going to bring this war home, once and for all. Will you be there? We are eager allies, and one of our leaders has new radical ideas on change. I'd like you to meet her, too, if you can. Please come out and see us. We have a lot to discuss. The winds of change are blowing.

Love,
Gilda

"THERE'S NO MORE SDS to speak of," Melvin said, solemnly. "Those left standing want to be called Weathermen. She needs to be straight with us on that."

Melvin's car had just parked by the curb, in downtown Chicago, right at the address Gilda had given her.

"I guess," Nettie said, glancing out the window. "Like I said, it's not like we were best friends. Are you sure about this, Melvin?"

The meeting place Gilda had invited her to was on a canal that fed the Chicago river, an old fishing distribution company with bars on the windows. Everything in the vicinity seemed to be either a storage facility or a defunct factory. She thought perhaps this was a mistake, that they were in the wrong place, until she noticed lights at the windows. A voice within her told her to exercise caution.

"I know what you said," Melvin said. "She was a neighbor. Nosy. Still, she knew how to get in your business. . . . Let's hear what they have to say," Melvin said.

Forte was in the back seat, still, looking at the building, studying it, waiting for someone or something to move. He looked around for a bit, assessing the area, and then sat up in his seat as if waiting for the green light.

"We're just going in to talk, right?"

"I just want you to listen," Melvin said. "I need to know we can trust them before we get down to talking."

Forte exited the vehicle first to go scope out the place further, leaving Melvin and Nettie alone.

Nettie shook her head. Whether she liked it or not, she had to accept that her "friendship" with Gilda put her in an odd position. She had to leverage that in order to get the Party what they needed. And right now, they needed more weapons. Two weeks ago, their office on Madison had been raided by the FBI. The agents had confiscated weapons and cash donations, and in their frenzy, they'd uncovered a storage of cereal to feed the children, piled it up, and set it on fire. Nettie remembered how that agent in the park had told her that things could get ugly.

"Keep our needs in the back of your mind," Melvin said as he stepped out of the car. "Don't get lost reminiscing."

"About the good old days," Nettie said sarcastically.

The Weathermen had been zealously moving for an allyship with them. Perhaps a little too zealously. Their goal, as far as Nettie could tell, was also to topple imperialism and capitalism in ways more radical than SDS. And although allyship had become a formidable strategy initiated by Fred Hampton—who'd managed to rally the Puerto Rican Young Lords, the predominantly white Young Patriots, and even local gangs against the power structure—the Weathermen's tactics were questionable. When they made their their alliance with the Black Panthers public in their manifesto, touting that now people would know "which way the wind blows," Nettie found something in the slogan ominous. It was an odd threat, one that sounded not only vague but also terrifying, because it denoted unpredictability.

A young man with long hair down to his shoulders opened the door before they even knocked. He had warm brown eyes and seemed to recognize Nettie, Melvin, and Forte immediately.

"Welcome."

"Is Gilda here?" Nettie asked.

The young man disappeared, leaving the door slightly ajar. Someone coughed inside. Through the opening, Nettie could see someone's legs splayed on an old, faded couch. The interior and the entryway were illuminated with a red bulb. How anyone lived in such lighting was beyond her. The building still reeked of salt, and mildly of codfish, she thought. There was a table at the entrance, and a small warehouse room in the back with cases and crates that seemed empty and were poorly stacked in piles, nearly up to the ceiling.

The door opened wider and Nettie was greeted by a tall, bony woman with straightened red hair and a sickly grin baring all her teeth, her eyes barely visible behind pink-colored glasses under long bangs.

"Howdy, neighbor! Hey! Look who's here!"

Gilda threw her arms around Nettie, pulling her in, greeting Melvin and Forte, and soon they were stepping inside the house where new faces gathered, all of them white, all of them eagerly shaking hands and introducing themselves. Gilda was her bubbly self, gushing over Nettie's belly and petting it.

"You look so adorable," she said. "How are you feeling?"

"Fine," Nettie nodded. "Just fine. How have you been?"

"Busy!"

Gilda glanced over at Jim, who still looked athletic, except he seemed to have lost a bit of that deep California tan. They were offering Melvin and Forte something to drink.

Some of the women ogled them with a kind of hunger, Nettie noticed. One of them had struck up a conversation with Forte, and he gladly obliged, plopping down in one of the small couches in the entryway. "Why don't we go out back?" Gilda suggested. "We can get some air, catch up a bit."

They headed through the back of the building, and Nettie saw the quantity of aisles and stacks of boxes and crates the warehouse could hold. The boxes were not labeled, the tarp used to contain them was torn here and there.

"What is this place?" she said, following Gilda to a side door marked EXIT.

"It's safe here," Gilda said. "One of our friends owns this, or his family does, I think. We come here from time to time. Meetings and such. They own this and a couple of other small factories Southside."

They stepped through the door and Nettie inhaled, grateful to be outside. The air was cool and smelled of brine. They walked down the side of the building to an open lot with a few containers, and old tires and fishnets strewn about the place. Nettie could also see the canal, gray and menacing. She crossed the lot and followed Gilda, who was still talking. They were staying here, Gilda said, until the storm had passed. Recent anti-war protests had pitted them against the Chicago PD and then against each other.

"Watch your step, there's a lot of junk back here."

Nettie followed her, hands in her pockets, eyes sweeping the area, stepping over fishing netting, pieces of rebar, and buoys left haphazardly here and there. They stopped at the retaining wall, and Nettie leaned over it. The edge pressed against her stomach as she took in the scene. On the other side of the water, she imagined there were more warehouses and buildings, and inlets. She looked down and noticed the drop down to the bank. Without that wall, she'd take a good tumble five or six feet down before rolling into the water, if the trees and bushes on the bank didn't stop her first. Beyond that impenetrable tree line, the water was dark, and as the wind blew, it wrinkled and its surface chopped.

"You can actually walk from here all the way down that way, three blocks down," Gilda said, pointing down to the left. "And you'll find a small paper recycling factory, also one of our meeting places. We scout out those places when we meet, see where to move if trouble comes up."

Nettie felt her initial tension melt away as Gilda paused for a smoke. She was wearing a pink sweater and equestrian boots, always elegant, even in her efforts to topple her oppressive, imperialistic war-mongering government. She spoke like that now. It was her revolutionary vocabulary, largely improved, she said, because of Jim.

"Oh, did I mention we're married now?" Gilda said, beaming. She lit a cigarette. "What about you and Melvin? You guys ever getting married?"

"We don't talk about that," Nettie said. "Black Panthers don't really worry about marriage. It's a bit of a . . . *bourgeois* notion." It was funny hearing herself regurgitate these sentences. She'd become full Panther, without even noticing.

"When you find your lover and he turns out to also be your comrade, I suppose you are bound for life and you go down together," Gilda said. "Wouldn't you say? Like, you have a common sense of purpose. . . . It makes you stronger than any other couple out there, don't you think?"

Nettie lowered her eyes. Melvin had said this to her, long ago, and she could remember how she had accepted that at the time, because it was so good to be in his arms, to be vulnerable with him. It was good to love him. But now that she constantly worried about losing him, there was a crack in that love, a fissure made worse by growing paranoia and scrutiny. That was the unspoken truth about revolutionary love. Nettie looked at Gilda and wanted to say so much to her: Just you wait, for agents to follow you, interrogate you, intimidate you, for your trust in your comrades to waver.

"What about the baby?" Gilda asked. "How far along are you, now? Do you know what you want it to be?"

"Doesn't really matter. Although I'd be happy with a boy," Nettie admitted. "I'd like to see a small Melvin running around."

She'd often imagined what he would look like, this baby inside her. She had become convinced it was a boy, convinced she could tell. He would have eyes and eyebrows like Melvin, and she would watch Melvin cradle him in his arms and parade him around during rallies like he was another limb, another part of him, born out of her but made for his strong arms to carry. She couldn't wait to be a parent, but she was even more excited for Melvin to have that. He'd pleaded and argued for this well enough, she thought, back in Oakland, when she came so close to ending this pregnancy. This was her child, yes, but it was really Melvin's baby.

Gilda offered an amused smile. Her cigarette smoke thickened the air. She let the ashes fall onto the ground and pressed the bone of her hip against the edge of the wall. Nettie worried about her falling, too, she didn't trust anything in their environment to hold their weight. But Gilda seemed trusting, as always, secure that it would be fine. Perhaps it was because she knew the place.

"I'm never having children," Gilda said. "Not in this world. Not as long as the government keeps drafting young men to go die in that bullshit war."

Nettie felt a slight sting. What an odd thing to say to a pregnant woman, she thought. Did this mean she was manufacturing children for the war? Gilda seemed to realize her faux pas and quickly apologized for it.

"I'm sorry, I wasn't trying to offend you. I know you're happy to be having a baby."

"It's okay," Nettie said, feigning a smile. "You're just being honest."

Gilda studied her for a moment, watched her with eyes full of questions.

"Do you like it here? Do you like Chicago?"

Nettie shrugged, surprised at the question. She wasn't sure how to answer, and she wanted to default to a yes, but she thought about it. Carefully. She missed Oakland, the weather, the familiarity of the place, her aunt.

"I didn't think I would," she said. "It's certainly not Oakland. It's different."

It was harsh, cold, and the work they did felt harder at times. But she loved the people here, she thought. The women of the Party here worked and organized in a way that made her love differently. And she wanted to articulate all of that, but Gilda was already cutting her off.

"Is it Melvin you love? Or is it Chicago?"

There was the Gilda she remembered, with the impertinent questions. She shot her a look and Gilda smiled.

"Here I go again," she said, "I can't be helped. Don't be mad at me, Nettie. I'm just . . . always trying to figure you out, aren't I?"

"Yeah," Nettie said.

Gilda dropped her half-finished cigarette and crushed it under the sole of her boot, laughing off her own indiscretion. She finally looked at Nettie with a sparkle in her eye.

"I like you." Gilda giggled. "That's why I pry, I guess. I do that. I ask things because I want to know people. It's how I am. I can't—"

"Can't be helped?" Nettie nodded. "I know . . . How long are you in Chicago?"

"As long as it takes." Gilda said. "We have a lot to do here. The Days of Rage are upon us. We have to stick around for that, for the Chicago Eight, and besides, we are rallying behind the Black Panthers as you are the vanguard of the revolution . . . There's too much happening here right now."

"Being the vanguard means being directly in the line of fire," Nettie said. "You know they've launched a full-blown war against us."

"We know."

Gilda motioned for Nettie to follow her back into the building, and Nettie felt grateful for that. Melvin was on the couch next to Forte, and they were talking to a group of Weathermen sitting opposite them. The floor was littered with empty bottles of pop and whiskey, and ashtrays. Melvin was smoking, but he wasn't drinking. He rarely trusted food or drinks offered to him outside of his home. There were rumors about Panthers having been drugged to make them talk. No one could confirm whether it was true or false, but Melvin wasn't taking any chances.

"We see this as an opportunity to awaken the white masses that haven't gotten the full picture of this revolution yet."

The man who was talking, Gilda whispered to Nettie, was named Philip. He was a University of Michigan student who'd been appointed as one of the Weathermen's lieutenants.

"We want the white kids to overthrow imperialism," Philip said. "They've so far done nothing but protest, or sit in, positions too pacifist in the face of the death and destruction the American government is inflicting upon other nations. We're dead serious about revolutionary action, and we want to provide our full support to the Black Panthers in any way we can."

Melvin was listening, nodding, but not talking. He glanced at Nettie and signaled for her to come sit with him. She didn't see much room there, but she went over to him, and Forte scooted over so she could sit. As soon as she sank into the couch, Melvin tapped the ashes from his cigarette and blew the smoke up overhead smoothly.

"Right on," Melvin said. "That's nice. Power to you and your people for doing what you feel is right. We're over here doing what's right for our people, and the pigs decided to retaliate against us for taking care of our community."

"We know that," Philip said, nodding. "We are fully aware of their tactics."

"I don't think you are *fully* aware," Melvin said, cutting him off. "See, Black Panthers are the number one threat to security. It's what the FBI said. Terrorists. Meaning, the pigs will do anything that they can to rid themselves of us. Anything. That motherfucker Hoover said it himself, in so many words. We know what it is, we've seen this before. We've been seeing this for hundreds of years. But now, we fight. It's one thing to attack us, but now they're attacking our survival programs. Our breakfast programs. Where we feed children."

An eerie silence fell onto the room and sank in like dispersed stones into a pond. Nettie watched the faces across from her take in Melvin's words.

"These fascists burned down the food storage up in Madison," Melvin said. "That's a new level of treachery, downright inhumane. I take that very personally. They confiscated our donations. They confiscated our guns." Melvin took another drag from his cigarette and then motioned toward Nettie. "My woman here is the reason why we're even here. She and Gilda go back to Oakland. I'll let her take over this meeting from here, say what she has to say."

Nettie's heart skipped at least two beats. She did not expect Melvin to put her in this position, on the spot, like this. She looked at him, but he wasn't returning her glance. Instead, he was looking straight ahead, unimpressed and unbothered, as Panthers did in the face of scrutiny. Nettie scanned the room. Everyone was now looking at her.

"We could use serious resources for our programs," she said. "Food, medicine, donations, and we need to tighten up our security." She took out a list from her pocket, one Melvin had asked her to pass on to Gilda. She opened it and laid it out on the small table between them. Philip looked at her, and next to him, Jim leaned in with interest.

"Here is what we need," Nettie said. "Each time our offices get raided, they confiscate our best weapons. They make up some story about illegal possession, even when we have permits for those. Can you help with that?"

Melvin was still silent, but he was observing. Forte cleared his throat next to her, waiting for them to answer. The men and women in the room glanced at each other, and then they all looked at Philip.

"We can get you more than that," Philip said.

Nettie raised an eyebrow. She saw Gilda smile, Jim running a hand through his hair. Next to her, she could feel a fire in Melvin as he contained himself. He was burning. But somehow, he was letting her conduct the meeting. With his eyes, he pressed her to keep going.

"What does that mean?" Nettie said.

"We are still organizing," Philip said. "But if you give us a few weeks, we can get you some of the arsenal we're acquiring. Stuff you've probably never seen before. I'm talking big things. Big, big things that go, you know ... *kaboom!*"

Philip used his hands to mimic explosions. Some of the men giggled, their eyes glowing with dangerous delight. Nettie looked at Gilda and saw there was a kind of childish delight in how she laughed along with Jim, the way she looked at him as if she herself no longer existed. As if someone else had taken over her body as a host. She watched Gilda use her thumbnail to scrape dirt from under her other nails, painted a deadly shade of grapefruit pink. Then, she finally cleared her throat.

"Look, you say you are serious about change," Gilda said. "Weathermen is dead serious about it."

Nettie tightened her grip on the edge of the couch. There was a fervor coursing through these white bodies across from her that forced her to question herself. Gilda had always been different from Nettie, but today, with those colored lenses on her glasses, it was clear that they all had come to a conclusion that the real world, out there, was neither pretty nor simple. Gilda now saw her own government as a deceptive machine. But only now. Nettie herself had always been the same person: Black and constantly exposed, vulnerable. They had lived different realities until now, when they wanted to fight the same system. But something about this particular conversation felt unsettling to Nettie. It was what Philip said. *Kaboom.* It was the length to which they seemed prepared to go.

"With explosives?" Nettie asked, shifting uncomfortably in her seat.

"With anything you want," Philip said. "This is war. Just give us some time. We promise. You won't be disappointed. You're about to witness so much of what we're capable of."

"What kind of explosives?" Forte leaned in with interest. "We talking dynamite or something more homemade?" He wanted specifics. How many could they spare for their location alone? And how much would that cost? "Could that blow up, say, a police station full of pigs if we wanted to make a point? Because the only good pig is a dead pig."

In Nettie's head, there was now a growing feeling of danger, and the more Forte asked questions, the more the feeling became amplified. She could feel the walls around them close in and she tried to catch her breath.

"We have built sophisticated kinds, enhanced, if you know what I mean." Philip was still talking, grinning as he detailed various recipes and maneuvers, to "ensure efficiency." He grabbed one of the bottles on the table between them, raised it in the light and tilted it so everyone could see what was in it. A single nail, about four inches long, rolled inside the brown glass. Nails, Philip said, could be embedded in the material and they could spread out with the detonation, fly. "Like little birdies set loose," he said.

Nettie was afraid to move, but her eyes went to Melvin instinctively. Like birdies? Melvin looked at her and extinguished his cigarette.

"Let's just stick with guns for now?"

Forte picked up on Melvin's tone and the conversation went back to the weapons, but sitting around the room with Philip and Jim and Gilda, all these kids talking bombs, was starting to drive Nettie out of her mind. An internal voice was screaming in her head.

She turned to Melvin and whispered in his ear. "We should go, talk about it first."

The room was quiet, and for half a minute Nettie thought Melvin was going to push back. Then he nodded, and she saw his Adam's apple dance as he swallowed.

"Right, let's roll."

On the drive home, Forte did most of the talking, skeptical that these kids had any of the firepower they talked about. "I'll believe it when I see it," he said. But, also, that would be far out. If they could get their hands on these weapons, they would definitely be sending a clearer message. They could do real damage.

"Just imagining the look on pigs' faces when we pull out that kind of heavy artillery," he said.

Nettie and Melvin were silent during the drive. They let him rave on like a child who'd just returned from seeing an action film. It wasn't until they were alone that night in their room that they talked, Melvin standing in the door-way of their bathroom, watching her sort through their laundry. She turned one of Melvin's shirts inside out. She needed to make sure the inside collar and armpits were washed clean, and she always turned everything inside out to get those tough corners.

"So," Melvin finally said. His arms were folded on his chest. "What did you think of all that?"

"What do I think?" She laughed nervously. "I think we need stay focused on our own thing. Do things our own way."

"I think they can help us," Melvin said. "They have what we need. Guns."

"They're completely irrational," Nettie said, snatching the pockets inside out. "You heard them, didn't you? Bombs with nails?"

"I'm not interested in those, but I'm interested in what else they can offer. I think we have grounds for an alliance."

Nettie stopped, the shirt still dangling from her hands, her fingers caught in one of the pockets. How could he even entertain such an idea? What she heard and saw tonight was enough to make her throw up.

"Are you going to bring this to the Chairman?" she finally said. "Because I know what he'll say. He'll say NO, and you know it."

"You don't know what I'm gonna do."

Even as Melvin walked away, she could still hear the word *kaboom*. She had no doubt that Gilda and these Weathermen were sincere in their zeal. And she didn't know what frightened her the most: that passion for disaster, or the deaf-ening sound of Melvin's wheels spinning as he decided what to do. She almost missed it, the piece of paper at the bottom of Melvin's down coat that was going to be washed in soap suds and disintegrate. She pulled it out. The paper was pink and soft when she opened it. Handwritten in cursive.

"Melvin, I have a donation for pick up. Can you come over Saturday—9 p.m.? We have a lot of catching up to do. I've missed you. I hope you still like black-eyed peas. O."

Nettie's hands went cold, and for a while, she stood there, mouth open. O? Black-eyed peas? Nettie felt the air thinning, and she tried to catch her breath. There. Jealousy. There was no room for it in what they did, and yet here she was, eyes stinging with tears of rage. He didn't even try to hide this note. Or did he forget to destroy it? What if it didn't mean much to him? Nettie sat on the edge of the bed, clinging to reason. A donation, maybe nothing more.

Nettie inhaled and found the courage, deep inside a hidden well in her chest, to fold the piece of paper up. Saturday night. That was tomorrow. She slipped the note back inside her own pocket quickly and kept folding mechanically, silently, her eyes already spying the time on the clock, counting the hours.

My dearest sister,

Ever since I came here, I've thought of you and your orange grove. How are you adjusting now? There are days where I wish I'd taken you up on your offer to get away. I didn't have a reason to run then, and now . . . Now I just worry. I am afraid.

Melvin and I are alive and still engaged in the daily activities of our struggle, but this place frightens me. I am alone and lost without you and your friendship, and your love. Chicago is not Oakland. It is cold and brutal, and merciless. There is so much that I want to tell you, but I worry even about writing you because Melvin's paranoia has convinced us that we are being watched and monitored. Surveilled. He wouldn't like me writing, especially to someone who isn't in the Party.

Winters here are merciless, and while I love the people around me, the danger that comes with our work is palpable. Every day, someone gets beaten, arrested, harassed by the police who stop at nothing to undermine our progress. Sometimes I think Chicago P.D. is worse. But we will win! We must win if we are to achieve freedom. Maybe not one like you have found, in that orange grove of yours, but a freedom for all of us here where we can feel joy without the constant fear of reprisal. I miss you. I wish you were still fighting that fight with us. But most of all, I wish you were here. Please write back. My last letter to you has gone unanswered and I've received no postcards. You know where I live.

In love and sisterhood always,

Nettie.

She paused before dropping the letter off in the mailbox. No one was waiting behind her, so she didn't feel rushed, but she felt eyes on her as she struggled with her own emotions. People whisked by with packages and envelopes, and even behind the wall of the mail slot she could feel movement, see shadows walk past, men and women pulling bins filled with envelopes. Was it worth writing these days when Clia hadn't replied at all? Maybe this would be the decisive letter, the one to indicate whether Clia had moved on and just didn't want to write anymore. Or maybe not that often anymore, because she was busy. . . . Nettie dropped the letter in the slot anyway and now, it was gone. She couldn't take it back. She left the post office hopeful, but also resigned to that strange, unpleasant feeling that inside her, everything was crumbling.

16

FORTE POINTED OUT Mr. Reed's grocery store on their way to the new bakery on the South Side.

"Check this out!" He slowed as they drove by the building that still sported Reed & Sons Groceries in large cursive letters on the glass windows. "Didn't we tell him? Look, barely anybody shopping in that store right now."

Nettie repressed a shudder as she pictured him actually emptying out his shelves, returning to his family penniless. Forte continued to drive before he could create any more traffic behind him.

"We can only hope he'll come to his senses before it's too late." Forte shook his head. "It's the price you pay when you're unwilling to live as one with the people. He knew what was up."

"I don't want to scare everyone away with those tactics," Nettie said. "We want donations to pour in."

"I don't scare people," Forte said, glancing at her. "What do you mean? I'm always cool. We're cool. You cool?"

Nettie had watched Forte intimidate his share of people, including police officers who drove past the office on occasion, by staring them down. Sometimes, Forte would stand on the front porch and use his fingers as a pretend revolver, aiming at them and pulling an imaginary trigger.

"You know what I mean," Nettie said. "All I need is for you to help us load the car."

"Don't worry, I'll keep my mouth shut," Forte said. "You're the boss, yes, ma'am."

She shot him a look, trying to decide whether he was joking, or whether he was one of those macho males in the Party whose ego cracked like an eggshell every time a woman opened her mouth. She could never tell.

"New Horizon," Nettie said, pointing at the sign in front of the warehouse they were looking for. "This is it."

Forte pulled over by the curb to let her out. "You go on ahead," he said. "I'll go around through the back and wait there."

She stared at him. Was she supposed to lift up boxes on her own? With a visibly pregnant belly?

Forte grabbed the loosie tucked behind his ear and pinched it. "I'm just gonna smoke this real quick."

Nettie got out of the car and slammed the door.

The warehouse was quiet, dimly lit. But Mrs. James welcomed her with a nod. She already had a few boxes ready in the back room, lined up for her to fill. The room smelled of cleaning product, ammonia, and something fragrant to cover the smell. She beamed at Nettie, and her cheeks puffed beautifully like full-ripened peaches. Nettie had met her only once before, when she came to the clinic with her granddaughter. She wanted to help support the Party, she said. She and her husband ran a medical supply business, and maybe there were donations they could make.

"I'm giving you all what I can, because what you're doing is good," she says. "We have a surplus of medical gloves, all medium and small sizes, but that should do the job I hope? We have a few stethoscopes here, and a couple of thermometers. Not a lot, but better than nothing."

Nettie watched her fill the boxes with with bandages, syringes, cotton, anything she had kept for the Party. She felt a rush of excitement.

Mrs. James looked up at her. "If y'all have a fridge, I could get you insulin."

"Oh! Mrs. James. Really?"

Mrs. James had a small batch of it in her refrigerator. She'd worked with a lot of doctors who had leftover insulin and knew it had to be kept in a temperature-controlled environment.

"I'll sign you a receipt, too, so you keep it as record of donation," Mrs. James said. "Just in case."

Nettie nodded and thanked her. She liked that Mrs. James knew and understood things. She swallowed her tears of joy. So many of their patients were diabetic.

"The police come by here all the time," Mrs. James whispered. "Wouldn't be surprised if they showed up again. Telling us we shouldn't participate in no communist program, and all that. I say I give to whoever I want to." Her hair was held in place under a fine mesh net and she wiped her brow as she wrote out a receipt. "I know who feeds my babies. Don't really care if they're communists."

Nettie helped Mrs. James close the boxes, one by one, a total of ten boxes. It was almost unbelievable, the goodness that stirred someone to give just to support others. She couldn't wait to see the look on the staff's faces when those came in.

"Thank you," Nettie said. "I'll go get my comrade to help me."

Nettie looked down the dark hallway and followed the path between shelves stocked with supplies. The smell of ammonia was even stronger back here. Mrs. James disappeared into the back office, where Nettie could see a desk, a typewriter, lots of filing cabinets. Nettie opened the back door and stepped out into the fresh air. It smelled stale, like all the alleys she'd ever walked through, like decomposed trash and gutter water, but still, it was air. She didn't smell reefer or cigarettes. She looked left and right, on both sides of the alley. Forte's car sat there, trunk open, back doors unlocked, but he wasn't in it.

She went down the steps, called out his name, but still no sign. How far did someone need to go to smoke? Nettie walked to the end of the alley under the sun, sidestepping puddles and trash. Some spots on the wall were darker than others and reeked of urine. Maybe he went out to take a piss, she thought. Given the odors surrounding her, it was highly probable. Maybe she should leave him alone, go back to the store and wait. She heard the rumble of an engine in the alley perpendicular to where she was.

She approached the corner, the cold winter air biting at her face, and pulling her scarf up to protect her cheeks and nose, she followed the sound. A car was at the curb, and a man was at the wheel. She saw his face behind the window, and then someone approached the car. Forte. He leaned into the passenger window, talking to the driver. Nettie recognized Forte's pants, boots and jacket, even with his head in the car. But she couldn't see the driver. Why was he talking to

Forte? Not really your business, she tried telling herself. Turn around. Go wait inside.

But her body was grounded by the cold and by curiosity until a good two minutes elapsed, during which she tried to hear what they were saying, and she couldn't. Forte nodded. She saw him dig into his pockets and pull something out, small, a flash of white, folded in a square, and she saw Forte hand it to the driver. Then he backed away from the vehicle. The voice in her head was clear now, distinct. Leave.

When she stepped back, she brushed against the trash cans. The metal lid fell on the ground with a clatter, the car took off, and Forte spun around on his heels to find her there. He registered her presence and immediately grinned, but it was odd how in her own aggravation and embarrassment, she thought she saw some color drain from his face.

"Hey! What are you doing over there, Sister? Spying on me?"

He was handsome, especially when he smiled, but something about that grin chilled her. Nettie watched him immediately take out a joint and light it, and she shook her head, her mouth quickly shaping an answer.

"I got worried. I was waiting for you. I called for you but you weren't there. Who was that?"

"Nobody." He walked back in her direction, and she felt the cold suddenly penetrate her skin. She realized how alone they were out there, and suddenly she wanted to be back in the store. But she didn't want to look any more suspicious. Forte stopped inches away from her, looked down at his joint, and then at Nettie. She could smell the distinct fragrance of cannabis, even more potent than what Gilda used to smoke.

"And don't you be telling Melvin neither," he said. "I mean, it's one thing for me to smoke a little weed, here and there, and another to be making a little money off of it, you dig? I don't need him to know I'm dealing."

"Thought you said it was nobody."

Forte looked at her and she hoped he couldn't see through her nervousness. He shrugged.

"It's against code, I don't need to tell you that," she said.

"They *say* it's against code, but is it against code?" He sucked his teeth and pursed his lips a little, like he found the whole thing amusing. "I mean, I could tell you stories. But look, don't be like that. Not you. You and me, we're cool. You gotta understand, some of us got it hard out here. A brother's gotta eat. Just . . . keep it to yourself, and there won't be nothing to talk about."

Nettie felt the protest accumulate in her throat. Melvin should know, but she also didn't want to be the kind of person who ran to rat others out. She had other things to do.

"Can you just help me load the car, please?" Nettie said.

"I'm coming, I'm coming."

"And . . ." She looked at him. "Don't put me in that position again. I don't like it."

She walked away from Forte and could hear him steps behind, and the sound of her own heartbeat, pounding.

17

"I'M PICKING UP a donation tonight," Melvin said. "I'm going to be late."

They'd just finished collecting donations for the Sickle Cell Fund at an education meeting, which included a little speech Nettie found herself giving. She didn't mind talking about it, she knew this territory well. Symptoms, testing, treatments, all an overview. She even pictured Clia in the audience, nodding along, and it made her heart hurt a little less. Melvin stood there, watched her for a while, too, and she tried not to look directly at him. That made her heart hurt more. And now he began to pull the table back.

"Are you okay?" he asked.

"Yeah." Nettie forced a smile. She wanted to yell at him but she held her composure and took a breath. "I'm doing fine."

Melvin stopped, watched her grab her bags. He offered to take her home first but she said she was riding with Afia. He looked like he wanted to say something and she hoped he would. She could see him in the light the way she'd seen him before, in that gun range a year before, correcting her posture and her grip on her weapon. She missed those days. He did still make her feel that way. But now, since that note, she felt wounded.

"Do you want me to come with you?" Nettie heard herself ask. "Used to be, you'd take me along with you. Down the coast line to Vallejo. Remember?"

Melvin nodded, offered a hint of a smile. He was full beard and mustache these days, allowing facial hair to take over his jawline and age him a lot more. It was attractive to Nettie, and she gathered it pleased other women, too. She thought of this mysterious woman, O., grazing his lips and mustache, kissing him, taking him in her bed and inside her. Her cheeks stung.

"I remember," Melvin said, stepping closer. He dropped his voice so he could only be audible to her, and leaned into her ear. "But things are different now. Go home and rest."

He didn't kiss her. Melvin wouldn't, in public like that, but something in the way he looked at her before walking away almost made her change her mind.

Was Melvin still in love with her? In the car, Afia turned to her and waited patiently for her to settle in.

"Are you really sure you want this?" Afia said.

Nettie stared straight ahead. Outside, the evening wind shifted toward the lakes and Nettie felt alone inside, like all the doors that were thus far open were now beginning to close. She saw people walk out of the building, and soon, she caught sight of Melvin. He was alone. Nettie's heart sank. Why was he moving without his bodyguards? She watched him get inside his car, a dark blue Plymouth that seemed to growl and purr at the same time when he started it.

"Yes. I'm sure."

It was just about nine thirty. In just a few minutes, it would be ten on Saturday night. She knew he was headed to meet this person who wrote the note, O. And she wondered if he would handle himself the same way he did in Vallejo, with Blue, or if he would stray and betray her. She needed to see it for herself

"SO WHAT'S YOUR plan if . . ." Afia glanced at her before turning the corner. She was doing her best to stay one car behind Melvin. "If you don't like what you see, what are you going to do?"

Nettie didn't answer. But she knew she would have to leave Melvin. And that was why she needed confirmation. They were now driving into a residential working-class neighborhood, and Nettie saw him park his car near the curb facing a row of townhouses. He got out, and Afia pulled up to the curb a few steps away under a tree. As soon as she put the car in park, Nettie hopped out.

"Nettie! Wait! Shit . . ."

Her legs were moving. Nettie was barely in control, but she needed to stay with Melvin. She was terrified of losing him, of not knowing where he went, and terrified of not knowing anything at all. She had to be sure. She saw him clearly as he adjusted his coat and checked himself in the window of his Plymouth. Tall. Handsome. Sharp. He didn't even need his beret. He barely wore it anymore so as not to catch unwanted attention from the pigs. She saw him go up the steps toward a door and knock. He waited. And she saw the woman emerge from the dark, smiling, and wrap her arms around Melvin.

They were talking. Whispering. This felt as it had with Blue. Except this one was leaning in, clasping Melvin's arm in an attempt to draw him in a little closer, raising herself on her toes to join her lips to his. She was kissing Melvin. Nettie's heart pounded in her throat.

"Melvin!"

She heard herself say his name. Everything was automatic, even the way Melvin glanced at her, startled, and pulled away from the woman who suddenly stood straight, stiffening her back. Nettie stepped closer to the porch, closer to them both until she could see them, see her.

The woman patted her hair a little, as if to fix whatever she felt was out of place. She was beautiful. The way Blue was beautiful. The way every woman Melvin had ever looked at too long was beautiful.

"What are you doing here?" he asked.

She marveled at his level of calm. It was unsettling, and she would have run out of words and breath if her anger weren't boiling at the base of her throat.

"What am *I* doing here?" Nettie said, suddenly furious. "What are *you* doing?"

"Is this . . ." The woman looked at Melvin and then at Nettie, and Nettie hated her instantly. How dare she even open her mouth and speak right now? Nettie's head began to spin. Lack of oxygen, emotions, something snapping in two inside her. She shifted her eyes toward the woman, who stepped back and slowly closed her door.

"You followed me here?" Melvin said, staring at Nettie.

"I followed you here, yes." Nettie's eyes welled and she tried to hold it in, but it was useless. "I won't apologize for it. Don't say I'm at fault either because . . . oh Melvin. Why?"

It hurt so badly, to know that everything was crumbling. It hurt.

"This isn't what you think," he said softly. "You're reading this wrong."

"What do I think it is, Melvin?"

Her belly cramped a little from the rage. She felt like a fool. As if Melvin could read her thoughts, he stepped in closer and shook his head.

"No, you're way off. I told you what it was."

"Work? Picking up a donation?" She narrowed her eyes. "That's what you said."

Melvin paused. With a flicker of his tongue, he licked his teeth and waited for a beat. Something to calm himself? Something to wriggle his way out of a lie with? Except there was no lying his way of this.

"You're acting crazy right now," he said finally. "What's gotten into you?"

"I found her note in your pocket, Melvin!" She shook her head. "That's how I followed you here."

"Note?" Melvin looked puzzled, his face scrunching as he looked at her. "What note? What are you talking about?"

She dug it out of her pocket and threw it at him. She didn't crumple it, which caused the note to fly and sway slowly before falling against his chest. Melvin caught it, opened it. He read it. She saw him shake his head, grappling for an answer. He looked at her and shrugged, still puzzled.

"Where did you get this?" He held out the note. "This is bullshit, Nettie, I don't know what this is."

"Really?" She was suddenly exhausted. Tired. They stared at each other and she knew in that moment that she'd lost her mind. "You're going to deny it now, even with that note in your hand?"

"I've never seen this before."

"Shall we talk to your girlfriend, then? Should we ask her?"

"You've got to stop this!"

Something was very wrong, and it was percolating inside her now, a jumble of words, of thoughts, things suggested by that agent, lines on a piece of paper, the lingering look of women when they talked to him, their hands grazing him on purpose. She didn't know what was true anymore, or what was not, and she hated this feeling of confusion. She nodded, stupidly, and heard herself breathe deeply as if an entire building was sitting on her chest.

Without saying another word, she turned and walked back toward the car.

"Nettie!" Melvin ran after her, and she kept walking, unwilling to respond, trusting her feet would know what to do against the pavement. But he caught up and gripped her arm.

"Don't touch me!" She yanked her arm away.

"Listen, Nettie—"

The wind was leaving her lungs too quickly, or maybe she wasn't taking enough deep breaths. Everything around her was out of order, even though the buildings were still. The sound of traffic rushing past from the street, the voices and sounds of the world, blended into one and it was all too much. She didn't belong here.

"I need you to listen. Be cool. I don't know what you think is going on, but this has to stop. This note is phony! This . . ." He pointed to the door behind him. "This has nothing to do with you! It's nothing."

"But it's EVERYTHING!" Nettie was screaming now, falling over the edge of a bottomless precipice. "It's everything to *me*. All of me is invested in this. Do I not matter Melvin?" Her voice was breaking now, her throat too knotted to finish a sentence. Melvin's eyes narrowed. He bit his lip and she could tell he was exercising restraint.

"I gave you everything . . . I sacrificed everything. I'm carrying your child."

Melvin's eyes were somber as he dropped his voice. They'd started to garner too much attention. A face appeared in a window behind him, two doors down.

Melvin tried to say something, but nothing made sense anymore. His voice came out distorted, like a damaged track on an old record. Nettie wiped a tear away with the palm of her hand. The cold bit hard against the skin of her wet cheek. It was time to let go, of everything. She needed to admit it and she needed sweet relief.

"I have to go," she said. "I'm tired. You're right. I shouldn't have followed you here. This . . . this isn't worth it."

She didn't look back, even as he called her name. "Nettie! Hey, Nettie!" She couldn't hear him anymore.

Inside the car, Afia was still at the wheel, clutching the wheel and tucking her shoulders in, in an effort to disappear.

"Shit. Are you okay?" she asked.

"Drive. Just drive, please."

She could see Melvin striding toward the car, his face looking for hers behind the windshield. She could hear his voice shouting her name. But Afia didn't wait for another order. They drove past Melvin, who was gesturing, trying to reach the hood of the car and bang on it for her to stop. But she couldn't bear to look at him. She kept her eyes fixed on the townhouses, the windows with the lights on, the doors closed, the gray walls of an ocean of a city that persisted in drowning her, and then she closed her eyes, trying to remember where it was in this world that she belonged, where she could breathe.

SHE WANTED TO run to the airport and fly back to Oakland, beg her aunt to let her in, and at least be with her only living relative. But the more she thought about it, as Afia drove, traffic rushing past them, the more Nettie thought about what that meant. The very idea of Tante Mado gloating about having been right, how Nettie didn't know about love, how this child was going to hold her back, the more she started to despise her aunt. A bitterness crawled up her throat. She took a deep breath and clutched her stomach. The baby fluttered in her womb.

"You alright?" Afia glanced at her. They were almost home. "I shouldn't have taken you there. You shouldn't put yourself through this."

Where would she go now? Should she go to a shelter? They'd driven in silence and now, Nettie turned to look at Afia. Instead of her face, Nettie wished to see Clia. It was as if she could see her eyes, her mouth, her stunning brown face beaming back, glowing with a love much fairer. It was Clia that broke her, the memory of her friend's embrace came back along with a flood of sadness. Nettie burst into tears.

"I'm sorry," she stammered. "I'm so sorry."

"Sorry for what? Sister, I know you're not apologizing to me. You haven't done anything wrong."

Afia pulled over in front of Nettie and Melvin's house. The lights were on inside. Tulane was probably there, or Forte, cooking a meal Nettie wanted no part of. She wanted to lie down, but not here. She couldn't stand to look any of these men in the eye. She was convinced now that everyone knew, and she was the only one naïve enough to believe Melvin would be faithful. She was swimming in darkness, not being able to see around her or underwater. Not knowing what was true or not was torture. Maybe she was naïve, clueless about love. Maybe Tante Mado was right all along. And if that were the case, maybe the writing was on the wall. There was no happiness or joy to be found.

Afia leaned in and took her by the arms, let her weep against her. Nettie sobbed like a child, for her child, and when she finally felt the initial wave pass, she sat still. If this had been Clia, she would have kissed her.

"I don't know where to go," Nettie whispered. "I have no one here. I know no one."

"Yes, you do," Afia said. "You have sisters all around you. You're going to be just fine, even if you have to come to my parents' house tonight. I'll take the couch, you can sleep in my bed. That's what we'll do. And then we'll go from there."

She pulled away from Afia. "I don't want to kick you out of bed," she said. "I just . . . I should go back home to Oakland. That's what I should do."

"You belong here, Nettie," Afia said, pulling her key out of the ignition. "I'm not letting you leave. We got work here, a new breakfast program starting in two days, a clinic to run. Chairman wants all of us there."

Afia leaned under her seat and pulled out a folded pamphlet. She held it up in the light of the lamppost. Nettie could see now that it was a coloring book, a four-page book with drawings made by amateur artists. "I want you to see this"

The cartoons depicted the police seizing and confiscating boxes of cereal.

"The pigs are going around distributing these lies about the Party, telling people the Panthers are poisoning their kids, feeding them dope, pressuring supermarkets not to participate in food donations. They're getting people out there to think we're racist against white people and teaching children racism, wanting to sabotage our program. We need to stop that propaganda, or a whole lot of kids are gonna go hungry, with no food and no education. My kids. You understand? Your kid, too, in just a few months when he's born. . . . So . . ."

Afia caught her breath. She knew those words had tolled like a bell between them. She could feel the vibrations in the words. *My kids. Your kid. Hungry.*

"We got to do something. *We.* That means you, too, and you running off to Oakland, running because of your broken heart, that isn't change. That isn't revolution. Stay with us, Nettie. Stay. Don't let emotions run you off your own sickle cell testing. You are a revolutionary!"

Nettie stared at Afia, stunned. Afia's locks danced when she talked. How come they all sounded the same? How come every time she tried to pull away, this organization found a way to make her stay?

"You're about to have a child with a Panther," Afia said. "You can't run off. You got to stay and assume power over things. This is your life, this is your destiny, and you can't let dick and pussy problems disrupt your commitment to this revolution. I'm seeing too many people come and go in this organization, like they think this is a game. It's not a game. You are either in or you're out."

Nettie didn't know what to say. She needed to think, but there was no time, and she was running out of air. She couldn't go in the house. If Melvin wasn't there, he would be soon enough. She had to get out of here. So she nodded. She was going to stay and fight. Her child needed a father, after all, and maybe by the time she gave birth she could stomach speaking to Melvin again. How could she say no to staying and helping?

Nettie got out of the car, numb from head to toe. She went in, with Afia behind her. Forte was inside, stirring up something that smelled salty. Ham. He turned to look at her and said something she did not respond to. She went in her room. She didn't have a lot of clothes, but she took the warmest ones, her jewelry, her passport, and most important, she took the framed photograph of herself with her father. That one especially would carry her through. That was her heart. Herself. In the bottom of the drawer was an object wrapped in a silk scarf. Her gun. She tried to decide, quickly, whether it was worth taking it along.

Nettie closed the drawer, her hands clammy and cold. No. She needed to leave Melvin behind for now, and this gun was a piece of him. She stuffed her father's picture inside her bag and quickly left.

THE CLINIC PHONES were ringing off the hook as Nettie started her shift. Her body, still sore and heavy with sleep, dragged to the examination room while the receptionist rushed to pick up.

"It's going to be one of those days," she said, groaning.

Still, Nettie smiled. It was a good problem to have, a busy day where all ten of their examination rooms were filling up.

Dr. Hernandez nearly bumped into her, coming out of his exam room.

"Hey, Hermanita, there you are! I've been waiting to ask you: that insulin in the pharmacy, is that you?"

"Hi Doctor, yes, it's from Mrs. James. A donation."

"Mrs. James?"

Nettie tried to recap for him, her throat and mouth still pasty. He was thanking her profusely, his eyes shining with gratitude as he pulled out his pen and wrote a prescription. The patients he'd just seen walked out of the room and Nettie let them talk. She needed a second to put her things down, to collect herself.

In the back office, she took off her coat, put her bag down and sat down, dismayed. Night and day had blurred into one. She hadn't slept properly since she'd spent the night at Afia's parents' house, and then the next night at Simone's. Simone's house was empty. She had a couch where Nettie could sleep, and this way Nettie wouldn't be a burden on Afia's parents, which was a relief. "I'm sorry," Nettie had said. "I don't mean to get you all involved in my mess."

Eventually, she'd be forced to face Melvin again. Just not now. She couldn't bear to look at him without aching. She needed peace, and the second night at Simone's, she realized she wouldn't find it there, either, when Melvin came knocking, looking for her.

"She's not up for your rap right now, Brother, you're just gonna have to leave her be," Simone said. She was firm on it. This was her house, she said, and he couldn't come in unless Nettie wanted to talk.

She almost felt bad for Melvin, but not bad enough to get up. She covered her entire head with the blankets and closed her eyes, and fell into herself, warm and unafraid, curled up with Clia in her mind. The memory of Clia's breath against her face hurt, too. Clia had always been right, about everything. She'd seen through Melvin in a way Nettie was too blinded to see. Nettie hooked on to this truth and stayed like this all night, awake, ashamed, and empty.

And she still felt tired from it all. She patted her cheeks with both hands, hoping to jolt herself awake. She could feel the bags under her eyes.

"Un poquito de café? Just a drop. I made it myself con leche, mira. You look like you need it!" Dr. Hernandez said, walking in with two cups in his hands as the fragrance of hot coffee filled the room.

When she sipped it, she felt somewhat revived. Not only was it good, but it was coffee like she used to have. It reminded her of her childhood. Dr. Hernandez had a tendency to do that, to remind her of who she was before all this.

"What's going on with you, Hermanita? Are you even sleeping?"

Nettie put the empty cup down and thought about the question, about how to answer it. It was one of those rare instances where someone genuinely was asking, out of concern and out of friendship, and she wanted to say no, she wasn't sleeping at all. She was tired. She felt she'd aged since moving to Chicago, rattled by betrayal and fear, so much fear all the time—that something horrible would happen to her, her baby, or to Melvin, even when she was angry with him, and to all of them. All of those Panthers working tirelessly, constantly facing danger. It was all so overwhelming. And she wanted to say it, but when she looked at Dr. Hernandez, she saw he, too, was tired. He was also part of the people, also tired and in danger, and what good would it do to bring it all up again?

"I've just been thinking about home visits," she said. "Could you help at all this week? We already have a couple of doctors on board, it's not a transportation issue. It's . . . those who don't trust clinics, doctors, hospitals. They don't want to come in. But maybe we can go to them? Offer help, friendly house calls?"

Dr. Hernandez didn't answer. She realized he was staring down at her feet. He set down his coffee and reached for her ankles. Nettie held her breath.

"May I?" he asked.

She allowed him to touch her ankle and squeeze where the flesh was swollen, held his fingers into the skin and then let go. The impression of his index and thumb remained. He looked at her and she looked away.

"It's fine," she said.

"You're not putting your feet up," he said sternly. "You *need* to put your feet up. This is not acceptable. Let me take your blood pressure."

He looked at her as if she was one of those patients that didn't follow instructions. She bit her lip, containing her anger.

"That's not necessary," she protested.

"It's a precaution, preventive care is the best care and I'm doing this for the baby," he said. "Did you even eat this morning?"

Nettie's face was hot. Dr. Hernandez, always so good and courteous with patients, was now showing impatience with her. He was opening drawers, one after another. She knew he was looking for equipment, and she wasn't going to tell him where it was.

"Did you?" Dr. Hernandez shifted his gaze toward her. "What did you have for breakfast? Por favor, dime. And if you say nothing, you're getting examined right now."

Nettie set her cup down and pushed away from the table. Before she could open her mouth, he cut her off.

"You can't come here and offer wellness to people, to young pregnant mothers, and not take care of yourself. I can't allow that. Do you even know the mortality rate for pregnant Black mothers in this country? Yolanda!" He called out for one of the medical assistants. "Yolanda!"

"Oh, now I'm dying from swollen feet?"

This almost felt familiar, as if she was arguing with Melvin all over again, over something happening to her.

"I'm talking about preeclampsia, Antoinette, we're just trying to avoid complications. Why are you giving me a hard time over this? Yolanda!"

He opened Nettie's drawer but found nothing, and Nettie let him search because now something else was troubling her. There was a sudden, heavy silence throughout the clinic. No phones ringing, no voices, no sick patients coughing, and Nettie felt a peculiar sense of dread as the hair on her neck stood. Yolanda was not responding. Nettie walked over to the door and saw nothing, no one.

"Hey, where are you going?" Dr. Hernandez called after her.

She walked down the hall to the reception area. The people in the waiting room all had their hands up in the air, the receptionists and the medical assistants were all on the ground. What Nettie saw, then, was a quick flash of men in uniform, and a blur, and she felt a sudden painful tug as someone grabbed her by the hair.

"Chicago PD! On the ground! Nobody move!"

Nettie was pulled and then shoved against the desk, and a sharp pain flashed through her as she landed brutally against the edge. She fell to the ground and registered the hard vinyl against her belly. She tried not to cry out but the pain was too sharp to be ignored. Police officers began to swarm in and ransack the

office. The children were screaming and crying, huddling in corners as the officers turned over desks, emptied medical cabinets. They disappeared down the
hall.

Nettie wanted to speak, but she couldn't, the pain radiating through her. In
the corner of her eye, she saw Yolanda and the other volunteers on the ground,
flat on their stomachs, with their hands up. Then, she was staring into the barrel
of a gun. A man's face came into focus at the end of the weapon, and she could
nearly smell the hostility on his breath as he huffed.

"She's pregnant!" a voice shouted. It was Dr. Hernandez, now also on the
ground. He looked in Nettie's direction. "Please don't hurt her!"

Nettie's mouth moved, but suddenly she was missing the words, or they
were stuck in the back of her throat. The clinic was now filled with a cacophony
of voices shouting, policemen yelling, and the cries of children that could not be
silenced. Nettie's ears buzzed. The fridge! They were dragging the small fridge
from the pharmacy now.

"No, please don't!" she managed. "It's our diabetes medicine."

She felt something ramming into her back. The officer's foot, or knee,
pressed too hard, and Nettie felt her belly nearly rip. She couldn't see, but it was
a move intended to keep her from squirming.

Black shoes rushed past her. Nettie watched in horror as the officers tilted
the fridge open, pouring all contents out, and vials shattered on the floor, the
clear liquid splashing in the crushed glass. She tightened her jaw to stop herself
from screaming. Her mouth filled with spit and she swallowed her rage. What
was it that agent had said? Things were going to get ugly. People were going to
get hurt.

NETTIE DUG HER fingers into the mattress and clenched her teeth. The pain
was debilitating, sharp, like a chainsaw ripping through her belly.

"Hold on, Sister, be strong! The doctor's coming soon."

The light was too bright overhead. Afia meant to be soothing but Nettie
found her voice alarming. Nettie had tried hard to ignore the cramps the last
two days. She could still feel the sharp pain in the small of her back, where the
officer had stepped to keep her against the floor. She had done her best to pretend that she was all right, but the blood that had dripped down her leg from

the bedroom to the bathroom, in the middle of the night, could not be ignored. It came in a gush, something uncomfortable, as if she was dipping in a hot bath, and by the time Simone saw it, Nettie was in tears. "I'm sorry. I'm sorry."

Nettie opened her eyes. For a brief instant, the throbbing subsided and she could see the bright light overhead. Afia's kind face was beaming back, but it was a forced smile. Her lips were painted a dark brown, almost black.

"We're just waiting to hear back from the doctor," she said. "He's just outside, talking to Dr. Hernandez."

Nettie wrapped her fingers around Afia's and held them. She wanted Tante Mado. Or Clia. Someone who she wouldn't feel ashamed of holding. She was embarrassed that Afia and Simone had to see her like this.

"And Melvin is outside, too. I know you don't want him to—"

"No, no!" Nettie's pulse raced. "Not Melvin, please."

"It's going to be fine, Nettie, I won't let him in if you don't want to." Afia lowered her voice. "I'll do whatever you want. But . . . he's the father."

"No!"

She was surprised Melvin was even there. She knew how much he distrusted hospitals, particularly this one. He always said it was where people went to die. He always took issue with what he saw as not just cases of malpractice, but medical racism. But Dr. Hernandez insisted they were equipped with a trauma center and they could provide what she needed.

"Can't you give her something for the pain?" Afia called out.

Nettie couldn't hear them outside, but then suddenly, she knew the doctor was in the room. When she opened her eyes, still writhing, he was there on one side of the bed with Dr. Hernandez right behind, and now Melvin was on the other. She knew, immediately, that things were just as terrible as she'd imagined. She knew when she saw Melvin's face that protesting his presence would be pointless. He looked very serious, but there was something in his eyes that filled her with dread. His hand reached for hers and clutched it. Everything within her collapsed.

"Miss Boileau, Dr. Hernandez and I both agree on the next course of action," the doctor said. She couldn't even remember his name, but he spoke directly to her, looking in her eyes. "I'm not getting a fetal heartbeat, so the best thing to do is for us to go in and surgically remove the baby."

Nettie froze, eyes shifting from the doctor to Dr. Hernandez, and then to Melvin, who was not speaking. He was calm, stoic, but the look in his eyes made her want to weep.

"It's the best course of action," Dr. Hernandez said. "And we need to do it now."

"No!" Nettie's hands went ice cold. Numb. "What do you mean? I don't want to lose my baby. Please!"

"Nettie, if we don't do this, you might die. You understand me?" Dr. Hernandez squeezed her hand. "Tell me you understand. I need you to consent to this operation."

She looked at Melvin, tried to plead with him, but she could see in his eyes there was nothing he could do. Nothing anyone could do. There was paperwork for her to sign, and once she did it, the ceiling began to move and a wind rushed past her face. They were wheeling her out to the OR. A nurse was running ahead, but Nettie's eyes searched for Melvin's face. He was gone. It was happening too quickly. She wanted to grasp time and freeze it. Everything blurred. Where was Tante Mado? Why couldn't see her aunt and hold her? Why didn't she listen to her the first time? Questions bumped and collided inside her. The hallways of the hospital were glacial, white, dissolving. She was alone, drowning in her own fear.

18

RAIN. SHE COULD hear it falling somewhere, but she was dry and warm. She used to love the rain. She used to remember what it smelled like, when the wind blew in that mineral fragrance. She used to know it was going to rain just from breathing. The last rain she remembered was the storm outside when she made love with Melvin, their first time. Nettie opened her eyes.

She blinked, reached for her bedside table, and grabbed her pills. She swallowed the pentazocine without water, those contractions inside her uterus still biting like fangs. She was low on pills. They'd given her just enough for two or three days after leaving the hospital. Now that there was no baby, she had had to find a way to stay pain-free and numb.

Nettie sat up on the bed and took a breath. She was at Simone's. Sometimes she opened her eyes and couldn't remember where she was or how she'd gotten there, but today she could recognize her surroundings. Ever since the hospital, Nettie couldn't find the words, or the strength, to even look at Melvin in the eyes when he came to see her. She could tell he was angry in the way he chained-smoked outside Simone's house, detached from the world, in the way he would argue with Simone in muffled voices, in the way he slammed his car door and sped off. But there was too much emptiness inside her to care.

She'd returned to work, but it wasn't really her there, walking down the street to the clinic, screening patients. It was a shell of a woman, what was left of her after violence had chewed her up and spat her bones out. Dr. Hernandez tried to argue against her returning so quickly. "Oye, cabezota, why don't you stay home? You should rest longer." She didn't want to hear it.

"I'm okay," she managed, injecting as much confidence as she could into her response.

"It's not about whether you physically can work," Dr. Hernandez said. "It's about grief. What you went through isn't easy, Nettie."

"I'm fine."

She wanted to keep going, to force herself into a readjustment. And yet she knew, and Simone knew, that things were not fine. When she wasn't at the clinic, or at a meeting, or at a rally, Nettie locked herself in her room.

There was a knock at the door. "Nettie? Are you awake?"

She couldn't find the strength to answer. All she wanted was silence, a way to travel back home from within. She couldn't do that with people around. When they saw her now, what did they think? Did they all look at her with pity? Did they talk about her?

"You still haven't eaten today."

She recognized Afia's familiar voice and sighed, wishing her away. Maybe if she ignored her, she'd go away. Nettie started to get dressed. The door swung open and she saw Afia come in, her locks pinned atop her head in a majestic bun, messy. Dreadlocks framed her face beautifully. Simone came in behind her.

"You can't do this to yourself, you know." Afia said. "I won't let you." She placed a tray next to Nettie on the bedside table, and Nettie could smell sweet, warm corn bread.

"You need to eat something today," Simone said, clearing her throat. "Can you make that effort?"

Nettie looked away and slowly pulled a sweater over her head. There was a certain comfort in hiding her face, even if briefly, behind the knitted wool.

"Don't turn away from us, Nettie, this is important. We need you to eat. Get better. All this medicine you're taking . . . You have to eat."

Nettie willed herself out of the reality of the room again, although she could hear Afia talking about *needing* her. But what she was saying had nothing to do with her own needs. Rather, it was the needs of others. The Party needed her. The clinic, for crying out loud, needed her more than the day or two she now worked.

Serve others, please others, do for others.

She didn't belong here anymore. Not just here, in the apartment. Here in this city. Here in this world. She wanted to run, but there was nowhere else except Oakland, and she didn't know now how she would face Tante Mado. She imagined herself returning, stomach flat, childless, loveless. She had to swallow her pride and go back to Oakland, didn't she? Endure Tante Mado's told-you-so's for the rest of her life? Leave all she'd started doing here behind?

"I am sorry for all this trouble. I'm just so tired."

Nettie pulled herself up into a sitting position. Surely, there was a place where she could go. Surely, she could feel again someday soon. Yet every morning, as much as she tried to do for the people, she felt a pull toward darkness.

Since the beating, the loss of her baby, Nettie felt she was caught in a familiar nightmare. A memory all too real, of swaying blades of sugarcane leaves in the evening breeze, the call of parrots cleaving a blood orange sky and her father's eyes wide open as he lay dead. Now when she sat on the edge of the bed, she knew death would always live on the edge of her, baring its teeth. Loss of a baby. Loss of her father. Loss of her aunt. Loss of her mother, of herself, all of it clung like a second skin.

"You're tired because you've been through a lot," Simone said, sitting on the edge of the bed. She looked at Nettie. "Food is important. Without it, you can't be strong. And we need you to be strong. Honestly, you need to talk to Melvin."

Simone's eyes softened, but her voice was deep, her tone serious.

"I can't keep holding the brother off forever," she said. "You and him need to talk."

Afia got up and walked to the window. Nettie wondered if this was a lack of gratitude on her part, giving up on life this way. The days after the miscarriage, these women had lassoed Nettie back into the fold. It was as if they were afraid to lose her to the darkness. They were always there. Simone would come see her at the clinic and accompany her to meetings where they collected donations for the party. She forced Nettie to rest. The women would read Nettie articles from the *Black Panther*, messages from Huey P. Newton, articles about the war in Vietnam and imperialism's evil, all beautifully illustrated: black and brown hands strangling a pig out of the ghetto, a panther preying on a rat wearing an Uncle Sam outfit. Everything that was in the paper was like scripture to Simone. The poems, the songs, the letters from leaders, kept her alive, kept her informed of what was happening and, more than anything, kept her alert to what pigs were doing, but also to the fact that what the party was doing was instrumental to the survival of their community.

Since the miscarriage, Simone's company had become a crutch. And it wasn't just Simone. It was all of them. Even Naïma, who'd been a patient of Dr. Hernandez, had heard the news and was coming to visit her at the clinic. All of these women, Nettie realized, had developed a support system of their own. The more she thought about it, the more her eyes peeled wide open onto a reckoning: that unification, that nurturing, held a magnificent kind of power. In a matter of weeks, they had gathered around and tried to stitch her back up as best they could, and Nettie felt very much like a patchwork quilt. Like the ones in Simone's living room, colorful, warm, and heavy with history. This kind of presence, this perpetual concern, that was love. And that was all she'd been seeking. So why couldn't she enjoy it right now? Why couldn't she accept it?

Simone inched closer to her now.

"I don't know what it's like, losing a baby," Simone said. "But we are concerned for you, rightfully so, Afia is worried. I'm worried . . . Melvin comes here every other day asking to see you and I have to kick the brother out like he's some kind of bum I'm evicting. I don't like it. Your mess is our mess now and we want to help you. We are legitimately worried. Take a helping hand when you are offered the chance, why don't you?"

"I don't mean to be a burden," Nettie said.

The words came out distorted, she could hear them in her ear as if delayed by a warping in time.

"Are you alright?"

Simone leaned in and grabbed the bottle of pills from the table next to her, examined the label.

"Yes, I'm fine."

"How many of these are you taking? Wasn't this just meant to last you two or three days?"

Nettie clenched her jaw. She hadn't expected so much scrutiny. It wasn't anyone's business. The pain was supposed to go away, wasn't it? And it hadn't. And she'd asked Dr. Hernandez, but he wouldn't prescribe anything more than an over-the-counter paracetamol. Was there something stronger? Sure, just not one he was willing to prescribe to her. What other option had she been left than to ask the one person she knew could provide pain relief?

Forte had been hesitant, she could see it in his demeanor, the way he studied his shoes for a moment before answering.

"Does Melvin know about this?"

"What does Melvin have to do with it?" she shot back, flustered. "This is my body. Can you help me or not? I can ask around and find somebody else—"

"Yeah, you should have instead of asking me, you should know better. You know what'll happen if they find out?"

"*Now* you worry about them finding out? Just forget it, then," Nettie said. She should never have asked, but she needed the pills; there was a way she felt when she was on those pills that numbed everything inside. It was better in that space, that peaceful high where there was no anger, no rage, no sadness or loneliness.

She'd started to walk away, wondering if maybe Dr. Hernandez would notice if she took some from his cabinet. It would be theft, and it wasn't right at all, but she wasn't thinking about others' feelings anymore. Not right now.

Forte had caught up to her. "Alright Nettie, wait. Don't . . . It's cool. Okay?" He nodded. "I got you. Just don't tell anyone about this. Not one fucking soul. Is that clear? I don't want things to get *ugly*."

He'd gotten her pills that same afternoon, in a little plastic bag. He called them blues. They made everything better and all she needed was one, no more than two a day, and she didn't ask questions. She'd paid him what he asked with the cash she'd saved to buy her baby winter clothes, and swallowed a pill right after that. Then the next day, another, and the next day, two. It was what carried her through the motions of the day, the work, and the feeling that she could take care of herself at least.

"Where did you get these?" Simone asked now, handing the bottle to Afia, who held it up to the light.

Nettie shrugged. She could see the disappointment in Simone's eyes. Both her and Afia got up and walked to the other side of the room. Nettie couldn't hear what they were saying, and she wanted to protest, she was sitting right here after all, wasn't it rude of them? And yet she was losing interest in speaking, her tongue wouldn't articulate for her.

"Nettie?" Afia turned to her. "Why don't we go for a ride together tomorrow?"

Nettie finally felt something in her chest, something breaking again, cracking. A ride to where? Right now, she would give anything to ride back to Oakland. Or maybe Florida, to see Clia. Clia would be taking care of her now if she were here. She'd be wrapping her hair, putting on her lipstick for her, ushering her out the door every day. Clia knew how to shoulder burdens, how to carry the world until she couldn't anymore. Why couldn't she have been there for Clia? The more she thought of her friend, the more she missed her strength, and the worse she felt about her own failures.

Simone and Afia stepped closer and leaned in, and their faces were almost like globes of light, enlarged and maternal in a way that made her feel uncomfortable.

"I know a place in Wilmette." Afia looked at her with a kindness that Nettie felt she didn't deserve. "It's in Milwaukee, three hours away. I've been there myself. A place where you can be helped. It'll be good for you to get away from here, be with other women."

Nettie stared at them, bewildered. Where was she going now? All her life she'd been pushed from one place to another.

"You won't be a burden, trust me," Afia said, smiling. "They won't let you be. Let's go. Together. You and me."

"We'll write a letter to Central Committee on your behalf," Simone said. "We'll petition for you to go take a leave from the party for medical reasons and . . . I'll talk to Dr. Hernandez."

"Milwaukee?" Nettie eyed the women, frightened. She didn't know anybody there! That would take her even further away from everything.

Afia squeezed her hand this time and Nettie let her, her insides cold and unyielding. There was nothing else to lose.

NETTIE STOOD IN Simone's kitchen and dialed a number and leaned against the wall. There was a ring, and her heart beat faster. She considered hanging up, considered that maybe she was making a mistake calling, but she waited through five long rings anyway until finally, Tante Mado picked up.

"Hello?"

She wasn't asleep yet. Nettie could tell by her voice that she was still very much awake, probably up cleaning or organizing her house as she often did. Nettie's tried to say hi back, but her voice cracked and the sound she made was incomprehensible.

"Hello? . . . Hello? Who is this?"

"Bonsoir Tantante." She sank into a chair and squeezed the fabric of her skirt in her hands. She shouldn't have called. Tante Mado waited for an answer, but none came.

"Nettie? Is that you?"

Nettie couldn't see anymore. There were tears, veils of tears obstructing her view.

"Tantante . . ." She felt like a child again. Auntie. It was all she could say, before the dam broke and she let herself bend over, and weep.

"Nettie? What is it? What's wrong? Are you hurt?"

Yes. She was. She was hurting somewhere so deep, deeper than the scars in her womb, deeper even than the wound in her heart. There was something broken inside her and she couldn't fix it. She cried, and blubbered, and tried to pull herself together, but it took a while before she could clear her throat.

"What happened?" Tante Mado sounded alarmed, panicked. "Are you alright? Is the baby . . . Is the baby okay?"

"No . . . There's no baby. There isn't a baby anymore."

"What?"

Nettie blurted out what she thought made sense. There was an accident, and the baby didn't survive. Nettie said she was sad, constantly sad all the time, as if she was grieving her own death. Even losing her father didn't hurt that way. She had been physically cleared for discharge from the hospital and had returned to Simone's, but emotionally and mentally she couldn't function anymore.

And for a while, Tante Mado said nothing.

"I . . . I just want to come home," Nettie finally blurted out. "I want to be home."

"Oh . . . my darling. I am so sorry. I wish . . . I wish you could. But . . ." Tante Mado hesitated a bit and then cleared her throat. "I don't know that it would be wise of you to return."

Nettie sat there, cold. Of course. What was she thinking, asking to come home? She'd left her aunt's house out of conflict in the first place. How could she trust that the space was once again ripe for her return?

"It wouldn't be safe," Tante Mado said. "Two men came over here, asking about you and Melvin. Said they were FBI."

"What?" Nettie's heart leapt in her chest and started racing.

"I can't say too much over the phone," Tante Mado said. "I probably already said plenty. . . . Listen, Nettie, are you alright? What the hell is going on? The FBI? This Melvin, he's not hurting you, is he?"

Nettie was reeling. Agents harassing her aunt, too?

"No. . . . No, it's nothing like that," Nettie said. Not exactly.

"I'll get on a flight and come see you."

"No!" Nettie shook her head. "I'm not home. I mean . . . I'm staying with a friend."

"A friend? What friend?"

Nettie said it was a woman, someone who wanted her to stay a few days and get away. She said it was safe. "I do wish you could meet her," Nettie said. "You would like her. She's kind, in a way that reminds me of . . . home. Something about the way she likes to care of others, feed them . . . She reminds me of the people in Haiti."

It was so long ago, so far away, that Nettie almost felt like Haiti was a mythical place. Had she really lived there?

Tante Mado sighed deeply. "Haiti . . . After all these years, isn't it time to admit that this is where your heart is?"

Nettie's eyebrow twitched.

"I plucked you from there to get you away from all that bloodshed," Tante Mado said. "And still, you keep running to it head first. Like a little bull. You are your father's child, no matter how hard I try. At this point, why should I keep trying to stop you? Maybe Haiti is what you need."

Nettie pressed the receiver against her ear. Maybe she'd heard wrong. "What did you—"

"It's been years," Tante Mado said. "Years of me trying to change you into something you are not. You are a fighter. A rebel. You keep running right into the fire, and perhaps this is too much for me. Bigger than me. Perhaps it's even too much for you, Nettie, I don't want to see you destroyed. I don't want to see you arrested, or in prison. Not here, not in this country. . . . Maybe it's just time to go back and let yourself rest, truly rest, before you apply yourself to help your people, the way your father did."

Nettie raised an eyebrow, her heart racing mildly at the words she was hearing.

"What? You want me to go back there? After what happened?"

"It's been years, no one will really know who you were anyway, or what you are now. Maybe it's time. Maybe you'll be successful in fighting a revolution, in changing the things that need to be changed. You can . . . reopen your father's house and—"

Nettie's head was swimming. Her father's house? How could it be? She thought it had been sold by now. After all these years, there was still a house there?

"You never asked about it," Tante Mado said. "I was perfectly fine with you forgetting. The house is empty, but someone watches over it."

"Who?" Nettie's palms were sweaty now.

"Augustine, the same neighbor who took you in after . . . She was the one who called me to tell me about your father. About you. I came as fast as I could but you know, the neighbor's kept an eye all this time. So, you do have a place to go. You have a homeland."

There was a buzzing in Nettie's ear now, as if she'd been dropped into a large, windy tunnel. Her father's house. Her house. A place she only saw in distant dreams, shutters opening in the morning over a dewy garden full of secret herbs. Her father pouring out that first sip of coffee for the ancestors, the spirits living around them. Pieces of a home, that's what she remembered now. Her father's body falling onto that same ground. Her father's bones were still there, where he had drawn his last breath and spilled his blood. He lived there, feeding the mango trees and the sugarcane.

"You would let me?" Nettie asked in shock. "You . . . You're always so afraid of what might happen if I do."

There was a pause, and then her aunt chuckled softly.

"You're not like me," Tante Mado said. "You're not afraid to do things. You are never afraid of anything and I hate to hear you so afraid, and so alone. Do you have money? I can send you some, for yourself. Not for you to share with

Melvin. You hear me? Not for Melvin. I know how crazy love can be. Women rarely stay away from the men who wrong them, it seems . . ."

Nettie listened, her heart pounding. Her aunt meant something else, this wasn't just about her and Melvin. Her aunt said she should go to the nearest Western Union, and that she would transfer her some cash. "A woman should always have cash. You never know."

Nettie gripped the telephone cord. On the wall, a photograph of Simone was staring back at her, wide-eyed and solemn, next to a familiar woman in a tailored suit and glasses. Shirley Chisholm.

"You don't have to do that, Tantante," Nettie said, a tear rolling down the inner corner of her eye. "I'm okay."

But Nettie was lying in saying so. After all, she was on the phone crying to her aunt, wasn't she? She wrapped the telephone cord around her finger. There was a brief silence on the other line, then a chuckle.

"Don't be stupid," Tante Mado said, sighing. Nettie imagined her falling into her seat, sour-faced. "Of course, I do."

NETTIE SANK INTO the mattress that night, her eyelids heavy, everything in her body too liquid. When she woke up tomorrow, she'd be on her way to Milwaukee. She would get better, she thought, and when she came back she would fix all the broken things. She would return to the clinic, put in work and take classes if she could, and she would go from there. Maybe go to Haiti if she was bold enough, to the place where her roots were still planted, a place where her father's blood still irrigated the land.

She slept a dreamless sleep, something warm washing over her. She heard voices at first, but saw nothing. She wasn't sure how long she slept, but when she awoke, it was to the sound of the phone ringing incessantly. She opened her eyes, gazed outside the window and saw nothing but darkness. What time was it? She stirred, her limbs still heavy with sleep.

The phone rang and rang, and she thought maybe she should get up to answer, but suddenly it stopped. Nettie closed her eyes and hoped sleep would come again, and it almost did, until the knock at her door startled her.

"Nettie? Nettie, are you awake?" The bedroom door opened and she saw a silhouette enter her room.

"Simone?"

The light at her bedside came on and Simone was standing there stunned, as if she'd seen a ghost. Nettie sat up in bed, alarmed.

"What's wrong?"

Simone tried to speak but her eyes welled and rain fell out of them, large drops washing down her cheeks. Nettie's hands gripped the edges of her blanket.

"Fred . . . They killed Fred. They killed the Chairman."

BOOK THREE

———————————

Love does not begin and end the way we seem to think it does.
Love is a battle, love is a war; love is a growing up.

—JAMES BALDWIN

19

ON THE DAY of Fred's funeral, snow and silence danced together, cloaking the city in darkness. The way the flakes fell out of the sky and landed on the ground filled Nettie with a new kind of terror, compounded by the glare in everybody's eyes. Nettie found a seat in the pews, where hundreds had assembled, staring straight ahead. Whispering. She stared instead at her shoes, at her knees, at her hands on the black dress she wore, anything to avoid looking at the open casket ahead.

Around her, members of the Party spoke in hushed tones if they spoke at all. Others relied on their communal code and shut down. You never knew. *There could be agents everywhere.*

She looked around for Melvin, but there were too many people and Melvin remained elusive. Maybe he wasn't here. Maybe he was with that woman, maybe they were both here in the church pews, come to pay respects to Fred Hampton, and if he was with her, what would Nettie do about it? She tried not to panic. If this was the case, if he was with someone else, then so be it.

People were lining up, quietly, to go up close and see Fred, but Nettie remained seated. She kept scanning and then spotted Melvin beneath a new layer of overgrown beard and mustache. He looked old. She could see him slipping into someone else's skin. Melvin leaned in to take his final look at the Chairman and bid him goodbye, and he seemed so tired, avoiding conversations and handshakes as he walked away.

Afia had warned her that Melvin wasn't the same. In the nights that followed Fred's death, he'd descended into a place of darkness, and it was noticeable. "I hear they went out raiding drug dens and seizing weapons, him and Forte," she had said. "And Tulane. And I don't think Fred would want that." The women had abandoned their Milwaukee plans, although the pills had seemingly lost their sway over Nettie in the aftermath of the news.

Nettie waited until Melvin returned from the casket, and then walked up front to look at Fred's lifeless body. She shut her eyes, but even then, Nettie could see all the other men who had made the newspapers, Denzil Dowell and Bobby Hutton, and little Lewis himself. She could see all of them and more. She could see Melvin. She wondered whether Melvin could see this, too, his potential future.

It was so simple to kill a man, she thought. She watched Melvin nod as Forte leaned in to whisper something in his ear. So simple to kill a man, and yet impossible to kill his legacy, his words, his ideas. On December 4, 1969, two Panthers slain. The newspaper spelled their names under their photos. "Fred Hampton, 21 years old. Mark Clark, 22." Both gunned down inside Fred Hampton's home in what the Chicago police department referred to as a "shootout," a loss for the entire world. Fred was only older than Nettie by a year. We are barely adults, Nettie thought. And yet we are dying. Melvin could have died that night, too. It would have been that easy. The story the pigs were sharing was simple, so simple that everyone was starting to see through it. There were more questions left unanswered, and the more the police press conferences tried to revise the story with their own accounts, the more they looked suspicious. They'd shot so many bullets through Fred's apartment door, it looked like the metallic surface of a cheese grater. Nettie had gone to see it, like everyone else who had come from all over to see the aftermath of the massacre for themselves. The blood was still there on the steps, in the hallway where they'd dragged his body. Nettie's stomach clenched when she saw it. The nausea crept up when she put herself in the shoes of Fred's pregnant fiancée, who had miraculously survived that night along with a few survivors. She thought of how she'd lost her own, about the lack of regard and concern for a woman with a baby in her belly, about the callousness of the pigs.

People had traveled to the funeral from the West Coast, and from the Southern states, Panthers from other chapters, in Louisiana and Tennessee. The East Coast had sent their members from Detroit, Michigan, New York, and New Jersey. There were Young Patriots in the crowd, and members of the Young Lords. All had come to bid Fred goodbye, all in black, all having studied and learned their common language, saluting the chairman with a fist up in the air. *I am a revolutionary! I am a revolutionary!* But in the sea of men and women and children, Nettie felt she was drowning in aloneness. It wasn't right, to be witnessing such a difficult rite of passage with no one to support her, but there she was, wishing she'd never left Melvin's side. Now she was where she was, sitting in the pews of an overcrowded church, fighting off the urge to run. And there Melvin was, over there by the casket, stoic. She followed Melvin's gaze as he turned to look over his shoulder. She didn't know what Forte was talking to him about, but Melvin looked suddenly slightly more alert.

She could almost hear Fred's chant, a rallying cry through the thin veil between life and death. Fred Hampton made her feel alive and made her feel possible. Made her feel like she, and so many other people out there like her, had found the instrument or the voice needed to fine-tune their lives and get into action mode. He had given her hope, and the establishment had snatched that feeling away. If she felt that way, then she was certain Melvin did, too.

She saw other familiar faces in the crowd. Gilda was with Jim, and they lined up to pay their respects. Nettie remained still to avoid catching her attention. She didn't want to talk to her or anyone else for that matter, and explain the loss of her baby. They walked past the casket and stopped, and Gilda put her hand to her heart. Nettie watched them talk to Melvin and then leave the church, and then Forte walked out right after them with Melvin right behind. Nettie got up from her seat and followed.

She stood on the steps of the church and scanned the crowd. They were on the other side of the street, huddled in conversation. Gilda was nodding, and Jim was saying something that got Forte to nod fervently before muttering to Melvin. All of it made Nettie uneasy. She couldn't hear what they were saying and it was almost too much to bear, knowing that she had been excluded from the conversation. She watched Gilda and Jim walk away, arm in arm. Melvin and Forte were left standing there, talking as they watched the couple walk away.

"We're going for coffee over at Brother Willis's house, you want to come with us?" Afia said, grabbing Nettie by the arm. Her eyes were hidden behind dark sunglasses. "There's a meeting there. Come with me."

Nettie nodded and followed.

Brother Willis had known the deputy chairman personally. Everyone was exchanging memories of the Chairman and the breakfast program's beginnings while they poured coffee into their cups. She couldn't find much appetite to eat, but she could listen to some of those anecdotes and memorize them in order to think of Fred Hampton the right way, the way he ought to be memorialized. Then, someone in the room asked the question.

"What do y'all think happened?"

Was it drugs? Fred didn't smoke, or drink, so it wasn't likely. No, they'd thought about it and turned the question about in their minds, and the only conclusion was that someone slipped him something.

"Drugged him?" The words fell out of Nettie's mouth, and there were shrugs and more conjectures, and her ears buzzed with the sound of her own heart pumping fast. She thought of her own deception. Those pills.

"With Fred's death, people are leaving the Party," someone said. "They're scared, and we are going to be left short-staffed in our survival programs. We can't have that happen."

The local leaders were in agreement: the breakfast program, the medical centers, the free food and clothing programs were going to continue no matter what. Nettie listened to them talk and wondered what this meant for her. She could continue to stay with Simone if she needed to, but she'd started to feel uneasy. Simone had been kind, patient, and glad to have company in her house, or so she said. But Nettie was beginning to feel too mothered, as if she'd moved in with a parent who expected her to always be in need of advice, or direction.

She needed to talk to Melvin, but she didn't know how to face him. She was terrified, even paralyzed, at the thought. What could she say? Would he even want to talk to her? She was going to run into him at meetings and activities at some point, and it was going to get worse. She hadn't rehearsed her lines yet, hadn't decided how to talk to him and tell him she was leaving Chicago. That was what she'd considered doing, until today. Until she laid eyes on him and saw him like this, and it pained her.

She looked around now for Melvin. Maybe they could talk now, she thought. She needed to know that he was alright, but she knew he wasn't.

"Have you seen Melvin?" Nettie found Forte on the back porch, smoking. "I need to talk to him."

"He already took off," Forte said, scratching his throat. He spit over the railing and into the snow. "Asked me to stay behind. Must be an important date or something . . ."

Forte trailed off, and she swore she saw his eyes dart toward her, as if this was a deliberate dig. He kept smoking. "I'm sorry, I shouldn't talk like that."

"Some bodyguard you are," she said. "You let him run off like that?"

"I don't know what I am anymore . . ." His tone was harsh. "It's a little hard these days to get Melvin to . . ." He stopped himself. "What are you? My captain? As far as I'm concerned, you're not even around. Last I heard you were off somewhere *on leave*. Doesn't fall in line with what I'd consider to be revolutionary, to take off like that, but hey, it's not my business to know what you do."

Someone opened the door, and people came out on the porch, went down the steps. Others were going in the house, cutting through Forte and Nettie and all that smoke he was emitting, just sucking on his cigarette. The air smelled sweet, a fragrance of herb rolled into his joint.

"You're right about that, it's not." Nettie kept her eyes glued on Forte, and she made sure he could read the coldness in them.

"I'm just making observations. I assumed it had to do with all the *blues* you'd been having. You know?" He smiled grimly as he emphasized the word *blues*. "Melvin never learned about that, did he? You didn't go and tell him anything, did you?"

"You'd know if I did," Nettie said. "Anyway, I don't take those anymore. I'm good."

"Oh, good for you then. So . . . what, now you're back and you want Melvin back, too?"

"Also none of your business."

"Right," he nodded, returning to his cigarette. He leaned on the railing, peering over the back neighborhood, the alleys and fences of other houses where snow blanketed the grass and the road. He drew on the cigarette and blew the smoke between them. "I know, more speculations on my part. I just figured you took time off because of what happened, you losing that baby and all . . ."

She could see that he was glancing at her when he said it, as if to test her reaction.

"See you around," Nettie said.

Nettie went back inside the house and left him on the porch. She was beginning to feel smothered by him. Talking to him brought back nasty memories, fuzzy ones, about pills, about him in an alley right before she caught him talking to a stranger, dealing. About him giving her those blues and demanding her silence. Forte was no angel. She knew that. But if he wasn't, then what was he?

20

GILDA WAS WAITING for Nettie outside of the library, sitting on a bench. Nettie thought she looked like something out of a postcard, something truly American, maybe something she would have sent a boyfriend fighting the war in Vietnam. She was wearing a pink fedora, and a coat, and beneath the pink lenses of her glasses, she looked like a nymph. She looked at Nettie above her glasses and waved.

"Hi." Gilda stood up slowly. There was a moment of silence. "What . . . Are you . . ."

"I'm fine," Nettie said, looking around. They could talk and not necessarily worry about being heard. "I had an accident. It's fine now, it was a few months ago."

"I'm sorry."

They ordered a coffee from a small café. She'd called Gilda a week after Fred Hampton's funeral. Nettie wanted to talk privately, and the two women walked through the park's maze of untrimmed bushes.

"I'm glad you asked me to come," Gilda said. "It's nice to have friends. Even back in Oakland, we never talked much."

"I'm sorry," Nettie said. "I think I always felt overwhelmed."

"I understand, there was always a lot going on, especially when Steve came into the picture," Gilda said. Then, she caught herself. "So, what's going on?"

Nettie kept walking, sighting a bench in the distance where they could sit. She took one end and left room for Gilda to sit on the other. They sipped their coffee and Nettie thought about how to say what she wanted to say, without seeming inappropriate.

"I heard some of you were in New York recently? I just want to warn you to be careful."

Gilda stared, stoic. Nettie realized she was going to have to work harder for information. "You're throwing Molotovs at a federal judge's house?"

"Revolutionary violence is the only way," Gilda said. "That's how we get them to listen. What happened to Fred, that was wrong. What's happening with the Panther Twenty-one, that's wrong. There must be consequences."

"We're not asking you to do any of this," Nettie said.

"Maybe you should!"

Nettie looked at Gilda. There was something in her eyes that could not be named, something Nettie could not change or touch if she tried. She'd had that same look at the house on the canal, when they all met up.

"All my life I wanted to feel alive," Gilda said, now searching through her purse. She was looking frantically for something that wouldn't turn up. "All my life, I wanted to wake up from this big, easy, deadly fucking dream. Everyone around me is just asleep. I finally get a chance to wake up and do things I feel are right, things that could change this country and that starts with the proletarian struggle. I am in it. Now you're here to judge me? We want the same things you want."

Nettie felt she was back at square one. She'd had this talk before with Gilda, alongside Forte and Melvin. Nothing had changed.

"You keep saying that," Nettie snapped. "But this isn't the way. It's not what Fred wanted. Which is why he denounced Weathermen, and frankly you should, too. You're going to get innocent people murdered."

"When I found out you were with the Panthers back in the Bay Area, did I come to preach to you about it? Did I ask you to leave the organization? Did I tell you it was *dangerous*? Members of your organization are dying at the hands of the same institution we want to fight. We're all up against the same evil."

Gilda was a lioness, posed like one, shoulders back, her neck long. "You saw what they did," she said. "You think they can commit such a grave injustice, such a great crime, and just walk away with a slap on the wrist? Look at what they did, and what they keep doing everywhere they go, a great imperialistic machine grinding up everything in its path, and yet we're the violent ones?"

"I just keep thinking something horrible is bound to happen. I'm afraid people will die. I heard what you all did to that judge's house up in in New York? Arson?"

"No one died!" Gilda rolled her eyes. "We were sending a message, to free the Panther Twenty-One!"

"You could have killed somebody! If you can prevent a catastrophe, I'm asking you to do just that. Can't you talk to your people? Tell them to back off?"

"You really think I can just waltz in and make demands like that?" Gilda said, her hands still digging inside her purse, overturning a pack of cigarettes and a small wallet of green velvet until she produced a set of keys. "What's with you anyway? What happened to the revolution?" She stood up with her coffee and looked around, flustered. "You can't stop this. This is way bigger than you can imagine. They're called Days of Rage for a reason, you know. This is over my head, over yours. It's not something I can stop."

Nettie felt a wave of panic rising in her but she tried to will it away.

"Thanks for the chat," Gilda said.

Nettie watched her walk away, devastated by her own sudden aloneness. She was going to be tormented by this guilt, she knew it already, going behind Melvin's back. She'd just wanted to talk sense into someone, but Gilda was too far gone to help bring an end to the madness. Maybe she could go up the line of leadership, talk to a deputy minister or someone else who could listen, but what could she say? That she had a bad feeling about a secret alliance between Weathermen and Melvin, in defiance of the Party's shunning of the group? She had no concrete information and she would look foolish.

Nettie walked down the main street to the beat of traffic, cars rushing by, honking. She ached for peace, for something quieter than this. In the distance, she saw the arches and lights of Union Station. She could get on a train and leave, she thought. She had the money order her aunt had sent now. She was beginning to feel a great fear building inside her, that something awful was going to happen to them all. Something that was going to cost them everything. She could feel it when she turned the street corner, as if a clock built inside her very bones was measuring her pace and also, there was another sensation, as if warning her that someone was watching her, following her, maybe. She froze and turned around, her eyes sweeping the landscape of gray and brown stone and concrete, and trees, and people, but saw no one.

21

"YOU LOOK BETTER," Dr. Hernandez said, unstrapping Nettie's arm from the blood pressure monitor. "Much better. How are you feeling? Are you eating well?"

"I'm fine." Nettie took a breath, eyed the clock behind him on the wall. If she could get out of there fast enough, she could still catch Melvin in the office.

"That's not what I asked," Dr. Hernandez said.

"Yes, I'm eating again," she said. "I feel stronger. I'm not in pain. I think I'm better."

Dr. Hernandez wrote down some notes she couldn't see. Nettie put her coat back on and walked out of the clinic as fast as she could, but Melvin had already left, so she headed toward the house. If he wasn't there, she would wait for him. Talk to him. She still had a key, and she could let herself in.

She hesitated at the door, not knowing whether to knock first. But she did anyway, and then she turned the key in the lock. Breathe, Nettie, she thought as she stepped inside. You can do this. Just talk to him.

The familiar scent of the place smacked her first, a mixture of the incense stored in boxes that she liked to burn in the house underneath a layer of cedarwood, pine, tobacco, and the sweat and dust trapped in the fabric of their only sofa, the fabric worn and dark where bodies usually landed. She had always sat close to Melvin when they had time to crash on the couch, but she remembered, as she closed the door behind her, that those times had been rare. Their living room had transformed into a place for meetings, a place for other comrades to crash.

Nettie heard voices. She couldn't hear them clearly but they were male voices, weaving through Taj Mahal singing on the radio, "Everybody's Got to Change Sometime."

"Melvin?"

She got no answer. They must not have heard her coming in. She stepped toward the kitchen and recognized Melvin's voice. She could tell it apart from anyone's; it had touched her somewhere no one else had and had imprinted itself in her body. The other she strained a minute to identify. The singer crooning on the radio was singing something about being born by the river, about running ever since.

"Lower West Side, off of Ashland. Checked it out myself. It's cool."

Forte. She could recognize his voice now. She could form a mental picture. They were talking in what they thought were hushed voices, but she could still hear them.

"There's nothing there," Melvin said. "It doesn't feel right. We're too exposed."

Nettie paused, felt the wood creak under her foot, but they didn't hear. She inched toward the opening, the door left ajar just enough that she could see Melvin's back. The back of his head. He was sitting at the table with Forte facing him.

"Exposed? In a deserted place? Won't be nobody there. I mean, everything else is boarded up. The only thing living out there is rats."

She couldn't see what was on the table, between them, but she could her a rustle of paper. Forte's eyelids drooped lower as he stared Melvin down, the whites of his eyes shining.

"You scared now? We've met in worse spots before, Melvin. We got this. We bring the money, we swap and then we split."

"We got no cover for this," Melvin said. "No backup. Central's not informed. It's just us. Something goes wrong, we go down. Penitentiary. You willing to go back?"

Nettie saw a slight hesitation in his eyes, but Forte kept on.

"Why you buggin', brother?" Forte said. He looked to be busy writing something, or doodling on a legal pad. "Shit is different now. Central can disapprove, but they'll see we did what needed to be done."

There was a slight pause. She heard Forte's voice again, resolute. "This deal can't wait, it's now or never."

Then Forte looked up and his eyes stopped on her. He rose quickly from his chair. "Didn't know you were here, Sister."

Nettie's heart jumped and she quickly stiffened. She felt her face grow hot with embarrassment. What an elementary mistake! She shouldn't have eavesdropped, and now she was caught. She stepped into the kitchen and made her way to Melvin, her heart beating faster. Melvin looked up, startled by her presence. He sat up in his chair.

Her voice came out more faintly than she wanted. "I didn't know you were having a meeting," she said. She glanced at Melvin, then at Forte again. "Is this about the Weathermen?"

Forte lowered his eyes and quickly started to collect the papers on the table. There was a map, something drawn by hand, and some pages typed up that she couldn't read.

"Didn't know you were expecting company," Forte said.

She looked over at Melvin, who was staring at her. Her hands suddenly felt clammy. She wiped them against her coat.

"I wasn't," Melvin said. "What are you doing here? Don't you know better than to walk in on people like that?"

"I knocked," Nettie said. "I have a key. I called out for you."

The silence that ensued was nearly piercing to the ear. Melvin shot a look at Forte. "I'll see you later," he said.

Forte tucked his papers under his arm. On the cover page, she noticed the tail end of a doodle, what looked like arches of a rainbow and an arrow. Or a lightning bolt? He walked past her, so close she could smell the Dax on him, hair pristine and catching the light.

They said nothing, her and Melvin, waiting to hear the door shutting behind Forte, and it surprised Nettie that she and him were on the same wavelength like that.

Melvin got up and walked to the kitchen counter. He opened a cabinet and pulled out a bottle of amber colored liquid Nettie thought was vermouth. She raised an eyebrow as he grabbed himself a glass.

"Are you drinking now?"

He didn't respond, but he paused as he twisted the cap off the bottle. She expected this, the cold shoulder, this aggressive, angry silence. She wanted to protest but it was too soon, she thought. She didn't want to come off swinging like that.

"I went to see you at the office but you'd already left," Nettie said. "Was this what I think it was?"

Melvin nodded as he capped the bottle. She searched for answers in his gaze but he drank, swishing it about in his mouth before swallowing, and the grimace told her he didn't like it.

"You sure ask a lot of questions for someone who's been gone a long-ass time."

"I saw you talking to Gilda and Jim," she said. "This is serious, Melvin, you know we're no longer in alliance with them. You know Fred denounced them. Whatever you're planning, it's reckless. It's counterrevolutionary."

"I know what I'm doing," Melvin said. "No one will know. Unless you feel the need to snitch. Do I have to worry about you snitching?"

"You're gonna let people talk you into these situations? You? I don't understand it."

"I can't make you understand it." Melvin slammed the glass on the counter and his drink splashed onto the Formica. "I guess you have to reach a place where . . . where you just can't forget. Or forgive. You just have to set things right. Why am I even explaining this shit to you?"

"This isn't the way." She whispered this, afraid he would fly into a temper, but it needed to be said. She couldn't believe the man she knew, the one who moved through the world unafraid, who effected change, this man she loved, was breaking, falling, crumbling from his very center. "You're better than this. What happened to you?"

"What happened to me? What happened to *you*?" Melvin's face was stone, now, but his eyes were alit with a dangerous fire. "Where's that woman who went in deep with me when we decided to ride together, who was working in service of the people? For the people? Where did she go when I needed her? You allowed yourself to be tricked and manipulated. You left. You bailed on me instead of staying the course and I fucking resent you for that. Where were you?"

"I lost our child." Nettie found a way to say this calmly and she could tell Melvin was disconcerted. He took a breath and she could nearly feel the searing heat of his anger from a few feet away.

"I was beaten and I lost the baby I was carrying for months, your baby, and I'm the one in the wrong? Doesn't that mean anything to you?"

"Don't! Don't say that. How could you suggest that? . . . I'm not the same man I was last year, or last month. You don't know that, you don't know how I feel about it because you just up and left. You never called," he said. "You just took off."

This was much harder than she'd anticipated. Now Melvin was making her out to be the culprit.

"We have lost the voice of an entire movement," Melvin said through gritted teeth. "Fred died. You know I was supposed to be there that night? In his apartment, on watch?

"He made me leave because it was too crowded, so I went home. And that very night, this happened. They just wiped him out, just to send a fucking message, just to terrorize us. And you know what? I feel it's working. I feel it . . . I feel . . ."

Nettie heard Melvin's voice crack for the first time. He looked out the kitchen window at the trees, the cars driving past. A very quiet snowfall was now coming down. Nettie could see the snowflakes floating, like the powdered sugar fallen off clouds, a speck landing on the window sill.

"You feel what, Melvin?" Nettie asked, her heart breaking. She had to have compassion for that, for a soldier in crisis. Melvin the lover was breaking off in her mind. She was speaking to the revolutionary. His eyelashes were wet, but he did not shed a tear. Instead, he looked right at her.

"I feel empty. I should feel pissed and I am, but mostly I feel empty and I've never felt like that before. I don't want this to be the end of the road. I can't let that be. There's too much at stake. All the things we owe each other, all the things we want to do as a people, all the things we've lost in the fight?"

He frowned as if to ask if she didn't feel empty either. How could she not?

"We were finally making a change. I don't want to stop now. We will never have this opportunity again, to seize this time."

"I know." Nettie could almost reach and touch that sadness in him. "It doesn't have to. We can go on. If we say it does, then it does."

She realized her words were suddenly mystifying. She surprised herself. She was thinking of a collective *we*, the people, together. And yet Melvin was looking at her quizzically. "We? Who's we? You turned your back on me and now it's *we*?"

"I felt betrayed by you."

"I told you, that woman meant nothing. I do what I do to get what I want and I'm out. I wasn't going there to betray you."

"I don't care. I was hurting. I needed to take time away from you, handle the pain. I was high."

The words fell out of her mouth and the tears pooled in her eyes, but she held those back. She was determined to say what needed to be said.

"I was strung out on pills." She had to make him see. "I was in pain, and I asked Forte to help me. He gave me those pills. They made me feel good for a while but then . . . things got dark."

Melvin faced Nettie and they stared at each other like hawks, watching prey.

"You did what?" Melvin's face turned to stone.

Forte was always there, wasn't he? Nettie thought about him whispering in Melvin's ear, about him giving her those pills, about him in the back alley of Mrs. James's medical supply house, and how he always was so good at drawing her into his problems. At making her sympathize. And Forte, wasn't he the one pushing for extreme violence? Always going on about the pig?

"I needed painkillers," Nettie said. "He provided them."

"What are you saying? Forte got you high? He was pushing that shit on you?"

"He pushes that shit on anyone," Nettie said. "I'm not the only one. I asked him because I know about him, his habits. I know he deals, I've seen him with my own eyes. Or at least that's what he said he was doing."

Melvin held on to the kitchen counter, dismayed. He stared into the empty sink.

Her brain hurt from a sudden revelation. What if the man they knew as Forte wasn't Forte? What if he wasn't dealing but was a rat? What if he was still here, listening? She couldn't be sure anymore, of anything. Melvin took her arm, pulled her close. There was a slight squeeze on her elbow as she was made to stand before him. He looked closely at her eyes.

"I'm fine," she said. "I'm sober. I just saw the doctor. I'm good."

She could feel herself softening. She hadn't been this close to him in so long, she could feel her body catch fire, slowly, even when the images of this other woman crept back, a distant memory now, trying to cloud her judgement. She lowered her voice.

"I'm worried about you," she said. "What if you get hurt? What if he betrays you?"

"Watch your mouth," he said quietly, squeezing her arm again. She could tell he was unhappy at her suggestion. "It's Forte we're talking about."

"I'm only thinking of you," she said. She felt him soften. "What if I'm right?"

"Then I'll deal with it!" Melvin looked up toward the hallway leading to the front door. He looked at Nettie again, and this time, he let go of her arm. He went back to his drink. "I can handle it. Anyway, is that why you came here?"

She looked at his glass and the liquid swirling in it. It did smell sweet and tempting, and she could use the courage. But Melvin had never found courage in a bottle before. She knew he was not much of a drinker.

"Can I have one of those?" she asked.

She thought he would refuse, but to her surprise, Melvin didn't ask questions. He poured her a drink as well. After all they'd gone through, perhaps he felt she was entitled to it.

She took the glass, dipped her lips in the alcohol, and let the warmth and sweetness burn her throat, her tongue, her chest. She felt a tingle at the tip of her fingers. Nettie took another sip from her drink and rested the cup on the table. Once the vermouth burned, she knew she could draw from a deeper place with a little more courage.

Melvin poured another splash of vermouth in his glass and tightened the cap back on the bottle. He kept his eyes on her the whole time. "How did I not see it?" he asked.

"We both had our work and everything was so new. There was so much I had to juggle. This place . . ." She hesitated and then, she said it. "I think I was scared of everything, of this decision to see it through with you, and I was furious with you about that woman, that note, the baby . . ."

Outside the window, night was unrolling a twilight-blue tapestry across the sky. Framed in that darkness, outlined by the kitchen light, Melvin was the perfect photograph of a man fighting to keep control. He looked tired and she could almost see Melvin in the future, the way he would look someday if he lived long enough to see more children in his life. More joy.

She felt tired, too. She leaned against the counter, her back to the window. For a while, they said nothing. The radio switched to another song, and Nettie's eyes turned to Melvin. He shook his head and she could tell by how his jaw was clenched that he was stuck on something.

"You know what Chairman Fred said that one time, Melvin, that we can't forget? That the Party produces leaders. That if they took him out, there would be others. Others like you. You know how many people are walking in his steps right now?"

"And when they take me out, who will be left to walk in my steps?" Melvin hardened his gaze. "My unborn son?"

Nettie shuddered. He stepped closer, close enough that she could feel his body heat now. He reached and took her hand in his. She heard an unexpected tenderness in his voice, forcing her eyes back to his. His thigh was now right next to hers and she could detect his familiar scent, that second skin. His hand felt rough and she liked that roughness. She missed it. He squeezed her fingers a little.

"Please stop drinking," she pleaded, her eyes in his. "It's not you."

His father had taken up drinking and he didn't want to be like his father. She remembered him saying this to her, moons ago over a dish of fried chicken, after a ride to Vallejo. Now, Melvin tilted the bottle and poured it into the sink, and the golden vermouth disappeared. Something warm tingled in her chest as they watched it wash down the drain. He dropped the empty bottle in the sink.

"There," he said. "I don't even like that shit anyway."

It was so good to know there was humor in him, still. Her heart felt like it was bursting.

"I should never have pressured you." Melvin was leaning in now, pressing his lips on her forehead. "I wish I could take it all back and I wish I'd listened to you. When you said you didn't want to do this, I should have let you do what you wanted. You didn't even want a child."

"I did," Nettie said, cutting him off. "You talked a good game and you did convince me, and I was scared to death about the future, for us. But the truth is I did want to have your child. I got excited about it."

"I was so angry when you left," he said softly. "All I wanted was for us to be happy. And we lost that. I wanted you to ride with me knowing damn well we may not have a tomorrow. Having a baby with you was a promise that there could be a tomorrow, you know?"

Her eyes stung. She took a deep breath. "It was good though, for a short while it was . . . I'm glad I got to experience this with you."

Melvin stared at her and she saw him flinch. A twitch in his eyelid. His hand ran along her face, and she let him, her heart swelling like a balloon. She tried not to cry but her eyes were wet now.

"That's why I worry about you," she said. "I want you to stay alive. Finish what you started here, so that you can help the people take back their power. It's what you were meant to do. It's what you wanted."

Melvin's thumb caressed the shape of her mouth, following the contour before stopping in its center. "What I wanted was to do all of that with my woman by my side."

She looked at him, dismayed. "I don't want to spend my life worrying about being betrayed."

"I will never make you feel that way again," he said softly. "I swear it."

Damn. Melvin was so good, she could feel herself slipping through the cracks of the trap he'd lain with words. Smooth. She tried to hold her smile back but she failed.

"Now what? You running off to Simone's again?"

She tried to look away but Melvin cupped her chin and redirected her gaze. He wanted to see her eyes. "Or are you gonna stay?"

Nettie's eyes were locked in on his and she knew she was falling in them, dangerously fast. She let her eyes study his nose, and the space above his upper lip where dark, coarse facial hair was growing. She shook her head and part of her felt sad in that moment at the realization that once again, Tante Mado had been right about so many things.

He leaned in and let his mouth cover hers as if to whisper directly into it. She waited for his kiss and it felt brutal when it came, when he filled her mouth with his hunger, biting her lip. Her entire body shivered with new wanting. When he embraced her, he nearly crushed her, taking control of her entire small being, lifting her up off the floor and sitting her on the kitchen counter. He wrapped his arms around her waist and squeezed her, his breath hot against her face. She kissed him in the dark and stayed with him, forehead to forehead, mouth to mouth, heartbeat to heartbeat as the wind whistled a homecoming song outside.

22

NETTIE HADN'T COOKED a meal in a long time. Her new living arrangements had forced her to rely on Forte to do most of the cooking, and even when she was at Simone's, she had stayed out of the kitchen, as it gave her friend great pleasure to cook. Simone couldn't help her need to mother. But since she'd been back, three days now, she felt the need to assert herself a lot more. It was Friday. There was always something to do, but she wanted some peace and quiet.

At the table behind her, Afia was breaking off pieces of bread for the kids. They all gathered around the table and did what Nettie did: dip their bread into the stewed okra on their plate, picking up the slimy sauce with bits of seeds, and if they were lucky, some meat. This was one of Nettie's favorite dishes from home, one she'd practiced with Tante Mado on those days when the homesickness and heartbreak of being fatherless had left her catatonic with sadness.

"This is good," Afia said.

Her son, the eldest of the two, grimaced when he swallowed. He didn't enjoy okra but he didn't complain. Nettie winked at him.

"You can eat around, Amari, I won't take it personally." She laughed. Okra was a misunderstood vegetable. Here, people always seemed to reject it, and for a while, she'd forgotten about it, too, when she'd moved out of her aunt's and had to live on sandwiches to pay her rent. Now, it was hard to find. Only certain markets would carry it.

Nettie sat at the table and watched them eat. She was waiting a few more minutes for Melvin to come home. If he wasn't here in the next ten minutes or so, she would eat and shower, and wait up for him. She was hoping they would have some time tonight, to themselves. She wanted to suggest again that he step back from these plans he had, unapproved by his local leadership, although she wasn't sure who would step in to intervene now. There were cracks and disagreements starting now, a split beginning between those who were clinging to Eldridge Cleaver and those who remained with the original leadership of Huey. The Party was slowly being pulled apart like that great piece of bread Afia had broken, into chunks and bits.

There was a silence as the children ate. Afia was watching them, and there was no mistaking the look on her face. There was a shadow there that even an untrained eye would see.

"Did you hear about Mrs. James?" Afia finally asked.

"What about her?" Nettie said. "Our medical supplier?"

"Pigs shut her down, said they found some violations, phony . . . Anyway, she's closed. Temporarily. But closed."

Not Mrs. James! She didn't deserve that, but more important, Nettie could not figure out how this happened.

"They weren't supposed to know she was donating to us," Nettie said. She could still recall Mrs. James's conversation with her about what the police had said and how she told them she wasn't giving goods to the Party anymore. Nettie lowered her voice. "How did they find out?"

"I don't know but . . . they know. These pigs got eyes and ears everywhere."

Nettie bit down on a corner of her fingernail. Her mind raced. Eyes and ears everywhere, that's what Melvin believed, too. Afia cleared her plate. Tonight was her night shift at the train station, and she still had to drop the children off at her parents' house.

The front door opened and Melvin walked in with Forte. Damn. She knew Forte might come, but it was Friday. She'd wanted Melvin to be away from his influence at least for a night. Nettie readjusted her shoulders to dissolve the tension she felt building in her muscles. Forte was her brother. She had to accept it, it was the way of the Panther, and she tried to remember she didn't own this house, this space, this person named Melvin.

The men ate without even exchanging a word. But Nettie saw their eyes, the looks they exchanged once or twice, the glances they cast at the clock on the kitchen wall. Eight o'clock. Outside the window, darkness had settled. Forte offered to wash the dishes. There was a charge in the air that she couldn't ignore.

She was removing her earrings when the bedroom door opened and Melvin walked in. He shut the door behind him quietly and went to their radio on the chest of drawers and turned it on. Static filled the air, voices coming in and out, until finally he settled on some music. He turned the volume up. Nettie spun around and waited, the dresser now pressing hard against her back.

"It's tonight," he said.

He leaned in closer and whispered what she already knew. "I'm riding out with Forte at ten thirty," he said, pulling out a set of keys from his pocket and placing them in her palm. Nettie blinked when she recognized his car keys.

"That's . . . a couple hours from now."

"Take my car, and meet me out by the place and wait. Can you do that?"

"But Melvin—"

"Simple yes or no, don't argue!" Melvin's face was a hair away from hers. "I'm deciding this last-minute. I don't want you involved, but I don't like not having a cover. Is that cool with you or not?"

Nettie nodded quickly. She didn't want to go but she had to because Melvin was asking her, directly. This could be dangerous, she thought. But she'd planted a seed when she'd started talking about Forte, and now he couldn't shake those thoughts away, that perhaps something would go wrong. He'd been thinking about what she said.

"Make sure no one sees you," Melvin said. "Turn off your beams. Wait for me to come out and if I'm alone, be ready to haul on out. Can you do that, Nettie?"

"Yes, I got it." Her voice sounded strangled. "But . . . why not call it off?" She whispered, too, hoping her voice would not travel past Melvin under the cover of music. "Just cancel the meeting."

"I can't," he said. "We need shit, Nettie. We lost our defense. I'm not going to pass that up. It's just a precaution I'm taking, you dig? You don't want to do this, you can stay home."

"I'll be there."

Melvin watched her, took a breath and dug into his other pocket. He pulled out a piece of paper and gave it to Nettie. She could see an address on it, and a familiar drawing or tracing. Nettie held it up more in the light and recognized it right away as Forte's doodle. She looked up at Melvin, eyes full of disapproval. Melvin pressed his lips on hers and left them there. For a moment, she didn't want the spell to break, the sweetness of his lips attaching to hers with conviction. Then he walked out of the room and left her there. Nettie caught her reflection in the mirror and she stared at this young woman staring back, questioning everything.

NETTIE CLUTCHED THE wheel, the leather seat now warm under her, her heart thumping in her throat. Something about this, about the silence of the place, made her want to dash out of there. The only people who went to the riverside of the city's deep lots, she'd heard, were people looking to be beamed up. Even Forte had said it once. Folks who don't wanna come back, final frontier and shit. And she could feel it as she'd entered neighborhoods she remembered from driving to meet Gilda and Jim that first time. She remembered the dark bushes and vines that clung to the abandoned structures, a couple of them burned down, most of them boarded up. A few stragglers hobbled around or loitered at the corners, quietly watching her glide down the road in Melvin's car. Nettie's eyes scanned every one she saw, but it was dark, and they all began to blend into the same dark shapes, hard to define under hoodies and jackets.

As she turned onto Ashland Avenue, the streets became completely deserted. She passed a row of old, gated-off piers, some barely standing in the icy dark waters of the canal. The piers resembled skeleton bones, dark and ominous. At the end of the narrow street, Nettie recognized Forte's car, its dark green chassis refracting back the yellow tint of a rising moon as it came to a full stop and hugged the curb. Nettie tightened her grip on the steering wheel as she turned in and parked at a distance. She watched Forte and Melvin get out of their car. Forte's step was assured as he led the way toward the fishing distribution house, and Nettie recognized it. It was where they'd met up with the Weathermen.

Melvin hesitated, his eyes sweeping the area. He looked in Nettie's direction and her heart raced faster. He then followed Forte and the two men walked in through the front entrance, Nettie noticed, after three knocks.

She lowered the window and waited. Melvin had told her to stay in the car, but she was itching to get out and follow them. She looked toward the fishing house and thought she saw a glow, something light up in the back. A yellow light. Which made her realize now that perhaps it hadn't been on before. Her heart skipped a beat. What if something was wrong? She thought she heard a voice, a sound from the distance. In her rearview mirror, she saw nothing. But she was now convinced she'd heard something.

When she stepped out into the frigid night, she questioned herself. *Are you sure?* She wasn't. It could be dangerous, she knew it. But she wasn't going to let that stop her. The wind blew, biting against her face, carrying with it the strong odor of brine and old rotten wood. And again, voices. She needed to know what was happening without announcing herself. She went around the back using the side alley, stepping cautiously, afraid to make any noise, to step over something or lose her footing, allowing her eyes time to adjust to the darkness. She could see the light shining through a window, and she went toward it. For a while, the voices died down, and all she heard was the wind picking up like static in her ears. Her bones ached in the cold. Then, she heard voices again. Melvin and Forte!

She stopped near the window. The voices were now more distinct. She inched closer, hoping to see more. Through the grime on the window, she distinguished a corner of the warehouse, shelves and aisles half empty except for a few set of boxes and crates, quite different from the first time she visited. The two voices grew increasingly loud. She could hear someone pacing the room.

"I don't like this. Ain't nobody here. Nobody outside either."

Nettie leaned in to look, taking a risk she knew she might regret. But it was dark out there and the light was inside. Chances are, they wouldn't see her.

"They must be around here somewhere, it's probably . . . nothing."

She recognized Forte, his hair pulled back in that familiar ponytail, his temples gray. She could see his profile, and when she inched even closer, nearly pressing her face against the window, she saw Melvin pacing, shaking his head, eyes sweeping around. "What do you mean, it's nothing? They left this unattended so they could go take a piss?"

Melvin gestured toward something she hadn't noticed before. A dark satchel on the floor, wide open. Nettie saw what looked like bundles upon bundles, tightly packed. In the corner of her eye, something moved. Forte was pacing, looking at his watch, and suddenly turned to the window. Nettie dropped to the ground, flattened herself against the wall. How foolish it would be of her to be uncovered! She waited, heart pounding. She had to get out of this spot. The window wasn't safe. She heard them talking again.

"Something ain't right, that's for sure."

Nettie slowly rose back up on her feet, flat against the wall. She glanced through the corner of the window, holding her breath. Her eyes went to Melvin and she saw his face harden in a way she'd never seen before.

"Let's just be cool," Forte said. "Let me get to a payphone—"

Melvin's voice cracked like lightning as his hand went into his pocket.

"Ain't no payphone out there man! "

Nettie's throat was dry. Melvin raised his arm and Nettie could see he was holding his gun! Panic began to set in.

"You don't think I know? You think you can set me up, walk out on me like that?" He emphasized the last word and spat it out as if he could taste it.

"Melvin, what are you doing? Put that shit down!"

Nettie thought she'd collapse in the wind. It was too cold, but she couldn't leave now. She had to get in that room. Her legs carried her closer to the side door and when she pulled it open and stepped inside the warehouse, her heart was in her throat. Melvin aiming at Forte.

"Melvin!" she shouted. She knew instantly it was a mistake to reveal her presence but everything was unfurling too quickly. Forte reached inside his coat.

"What the fuck are *you* doing here?" he roared.

Nettie thought about her own gun, the one tucked in her pants that she had brought all the way here and never withdrawn. How foolish she was!

That sound, that horrible sound that made her cover her ears. The light overhead flooded everything, and even in the midst of such brightness, she couldn't see anything over the detonation of the gunshots. She watched in horror as Melvin grunted. He looked down, his gun landed on the ground, and then he fell to his knees, his face contorted into a grimace. "Shit!"

Nettie couldn't have stopped herself if she wanted to, couldn't stop herself from screaming. By the time she covered her mouth, it was too late. Her scream was barely muffled. Her ears rang. Forte spun around and Nettie instinctively leaped out of the line of fire. Another gunshot went off, this time in her direction, as she ducked behind a row of crates. She heard him curse, hissing through his teeth. "Shit!" She couldn't hear, still deafened by the shots. But she ran. Forte was shooting again, and this time the sound was louder. He was on her tail.

Nettie ran into the night. She was outside in the cold, and her first instinct was to run back to the street where the car was parked. But she immediately froze. There were flashing lights coming up the road. Pigs! How? How? No time to think. Nettie's mind raced as she turned around and ran toward the back of the building. She had to get out, now, before Forte caught up with her. She headed toward the wall and she could hear him exiting through the door now, behind her, and she ran even faster.

There was a drumming in her chest, so intense Nettie thought her heart would stop. Her entire body was lit from within, and it propelled her into the chill of nightfall. She couldn't turn around now, but where else could she go? Ahead of her, the wideness of the canal stretched out like an invisible sea, blending with the shadows. An occasional light winked against its surface, and Nettie could see that the water was iced over. That was it. The end of the road. She wasn't going to go out like this, was she? Nettie went for her own gun, went to withdraw it when another shot ran, past her right ear. She couldn't hear anything else but her breath, and it fogged the air. Help! She needed help, she knew she was doomed. Dread squeezed the air out of her until her lungs burned. No one was coming to help. She cocked her small revolver. There was no other way out of this. He was not going to let her live. She shouldn't have come, she shouldn't have been a witness. Now she knew too much.

Nettie's mind raced. What were her choices? She could jump in and two things might happen. She could fall through the ice and drown in the unbearable coldness of the canal. Was she ready to die like this? And what good had she served at all, before she crossed over? What about Melvin? Or if the ice was solid enough, she could run. Figure out how to get out. But there was no way she would escape without leaving Melvin. Then suddenly, she remembered. The drop! There was a drop that sloped down into the bank, so perhaps she wouldn't fall into the ice. Not the way she remembered it.

She heard Forte's footsteps pause a few steps away from her. She turned and kept her arm tucked gently behind her, so he wouldn't see. One of them was going to die. If it was going to be her, she had to die fighting back.

"Please don't shoot!"

Forte stepped closer. In the black night, only the pale yellow moon cast a faint light upon his face. Nettie felt an entire empire of trust crumble inside her, collapsing onto itself. She saw his eyes burn with something she'd never seen before, a kind of devastation and rage. His lip quivered, but he kept his gun on his target.

His voice snapped the silence in two. "Why are you even here? You weren't supposed to be part of this. Why do you always have to get in the goddamn way?"

Nettie felt she was swallowing needles. She had no answer, but could feel the tears stinging her eyes, and she prayed the cold would freeze them. Her hand trembled slightly behind her hip as he lowered his gun slightly, let it point away briefly.

"Why can't you ever mind your own damn business, Sister?" Forte said.

She felt a short-circuit somewhere in her brain. Nettie shook her head, her face softening. His face was so smooth, if the darkness could just dissipate, she swore the sky itself would envy the evenness of his brown skin. How many times had this face laughed with her? Teased her? Called her "sister" like that? How could she now be at his mercy, in his sight, her life hanging by a thin thread?

"You don't have to do this," she said. "Please."

Forte looked at her. She didn't need to see his eyes to know they were filled with darkness. "You just don't understand a goddamn thing, do you?" He didn't blink. "You've left me no choice. I'm not going back to jail."

Before he could pull the trigger, Melvin's voice came back to her now. Don't question. Don't hesitate. She aimed fast, bringing the small piece out into the moonlight. Right between the ribcage. The gunfire popped and a flash of light ignited the darkness.

23

FORTE'S GUN FELL on the ground, and he dropped. She kept her gun on him, afraid he would move, or try to deceive her by feigning death. But he did not budge.

Nettie took a step forward, then another. The wind whistled cruelly in her ears as she inched closer, both of her hands holding the gun to stabilize the tremor in her hands. Forte's face was turned toward the distant lights of the pier, his eyes wide open, unblinking. Dead.

Nettie kept her weapon aimed, took a few steps closer to make sure she was seeing correctly. Forte's silhouette still lay there, immobile.

She started to head back toward the building. She wanted to call Melvin's name but she heard a crackle, or a voice, and another. Police radio? She couldn't hear what was being said. She couldn't wait.

She thought she heard a door shutting. Or was it the wind? Then, she saw a flash of light, a car, maybe? And another? She looked into the darkness and she heard the rumbling of engines. Pigs, lots of them. Nettie thought one more time about Melvin, laying there, in his own blood. She couldn't get to him without running into the police. Melvin himself would have told her to run, and she heard him, heard her father's voice, too, shouting in her ears. Run! She bolted back the other way, toward the wall, because now she could hear footsteps approaching. They would hear her, she thought, and they would give chase and track her down like an animal. She kept running, out into the sugarcane brush again, slipping through death's fingers. Forte's body was still lying there and she ran past it. She held her breath and leaped off the edge of the wall and into the mouth of the dark.

She hit the slope hard, and for a moment, she panicked as she rolled down the bank of the canal, smashing into dirt and rocks. Her ankles hurt from the impact and Nettie gritted her teeth to avoid screaming, until she abruptly stopped. The ground beneath her was frozen, and for a while she stayed still, unable to move, hurting all over, and terrified by the realization that she'd rolled all the way onto the edge of the iced canal.

After a while, her eyes opened, as she listened for sounds, for the crackling terror that would indicate a shattering. She could fall in and drown. Die of the frigid cold. It would be a stupid way to go. That's what Melvin would say, and she nearly laughed when she realized the ice was still firm under her. Slowly, she inched over to the bank. Where would she go? If she were lucky, she'd make it to another warehouse, and get out that way, but there was ice everywhere and she couldn't take the risk of running on it. It would be foolish. She needed to crawl back up the bank somehow, and make it back to firm ground. She needed to run. The icy winds alone would kill her. Then, Nettie realized to her horror, she heard a commotion in the distance. They were going to come and look down there, and terror seized her. They were going to see her. Surely, they'd come looking for the shooter who took Forte out in the back of that building. Where to go?

Nettie moved quickly, climbing up the bank, but then sliding down as she couldn't grip anything on her way up. She began to panic. She couldn't go back to the river. She had to get out. The trees. If she could head to the trees and the bushes, she could remain unseen there. She let herself slide down the bank again, jagged rocks cutting into the palm of her hands, and she hit the ice again, this time convinced it would crack. But it held. And Nettie hobbled quickly toward the clump of trees. She entered the thicket and clung to tree trunks. Here, in the bushes, she was surprisingly sheltered against the gale.

There was commotion overhead, footsteps, then shouting that got lost in the wind. Nettie closed her eyes. Melvin. She'd left him behind and she wasn't sure she could forgive herself for it. But she couldn't go back. Not now. She pressed her forehead against the bark of a tree. Her bones felt like they would snap. She was going to stay here and freeze, only to be found one or two days later, or maybe never, wrapped around a tree on the canal, on foreign soil.

Just as Nettie's bones felt like they would snap, she remembered. The paper recycling factory. Gilda had mentioned it, and if she could find it, she could hide there. Or maybe get out of here completely. Home. She thought of home, of how warm it was, and instead of thinking of her bed, of Melvin's body against hers, or his radiator humming in the night, all she could think of was the sun on her skin. Not a California sun, not Oakland in the summer, not even driving down the Pacific with Melvin, but of where she was born. Where she was cradled, in the fields of sugarcane and the green valleys of her home, of her father standing with her knee-deep in the river.

She had to get out of this place. Go away, far away, where she could never suffer from these winds, where the sun knew her name.

She thought of Melvin, of what might have happened up there, but soon, there was a silence fallen onto the water, broken only by the howl of the wind. They were gone. She knew it by how still it was, and how dark. No lights sweeping from flashlights. No sirens flashing in the distance. They were all gone. And Nettie fearlessly let go of the tree.

She moved carefully among the thicket, grabbing limbs and branches to find her way to more solid ground. Her gloves clung to the bark a little too long at times, sticking to a thin layer of ice that had formed over the trees. Keep pushing, Nettie, she thought. Don't stop. She was determined. She was going to get to the bank, one way or another. She couldn't stay here. She had to move and keep moving.

When she finally emerged from the woods, the ground was firmer and she could see a path ahead. Nettie was nearly breathless. She needed heat, quickly, especially for her feet and her hands, which felt increasingly numb. She shoved her hands inside her pockets, hoping to warm them up, praying this wasn't frostbite setting in. Her mind raced. Where could she go? She wanted to find her way back to Melvin's car, which she'd driven up here, but this would mean going back out to the street, through the thicket of police vehicles, dogs and officers that no doubt now crawled all over the scene. It wasn't safe, and surely, she thought, the police had seized Melvin's car as well as Forte's by now. She couldn't risk that.

Quickly, she ran along the bank toward the paper factory. She nearly missed it, running wildly past the sign on the fence that begged trespassers to keep out. She squeezed through a tear in the chain-link fencing, ran a little and then faster and faster, until she thought she'd collapse. She went around the factory, looking for another exit onto the main road, and found another opening in the fence. She squeezed through again, her muscles trembling from the cold.

The streets were dark, but soon she could see light, and a bridge not too far away. She wasn't going to make it far. Then, the voice in her mind awakened her again. *You know how to survive, Nettie. You've done this before.* The more she ran, the more this moment was returning, sensations familiar to her in her legs. Pain. Images and sounds and horror flooding her brain all at once, the sharp edge of sugarcane leaves cutting into her skin. She remembered suddenly how she didn't stop, didn't even dwell on the pain, how the air burned her lungs and the only thing she could think about was her father. She could almost hear the neighbor's voice when she arrived at his house, trembling. *Nettie? What happened?*

She had no words right now but she could do this.

Nettie ran. She felt alive again, a little. If she could only find a car. A taxi. A main thoroughfare, even a phone . . . She could make it. And make it where? She thought of this, suddenly panicked. Back home, to their house? It dawned on her that this would be a mistake.

Something caught her eye in the distance. A gas station. She ran down the dark alley across the street, keeping her gaze fixed on the station. She was almost there. She leaned against the dumpster to catch her breath. The cold air hurt her lungs when she inhaled, her throat burned when she exhaled. She reached inside her pocket and felt the shape of the revolver, still there. She took it out and held it in her gloved hand, and her heart broke at the thought of what she was going to do. She could remember their reflection in the mirror when she pointed it, his breath against her ear as he taught her how to hold it. It had served its purpose. She lifted the lid of the dumpster and stood on the tip of her toes. There were bags of trash inside, too many. The container was brimming with bags, and she couldn't imagine dumping the gun in there. It was too risky, she thought. Someone could see it. Nettie checked her surroundings, breathless. She couldn't just throw it in a bush. Think. Think, Nettie. The answer was right there in front of her, at her feet. A storm water inlet, right against the curb, its black mouth open.

She tossed the weapon in, she heard a faint splash, like a rock thrown into the ocean and sinking. She didn't hear it hit a bottom but she imagined it did, and somehow nothing in her lifted. Instead she wanted to weep, to mourn the loss of the one material gift Melvin had ever given her. It wasn't that she loved the gun. It was what the gun symbolized for her, a bond between her and him, and it was now gone.

By the time she arrived at the gas station, there was an ache in her chest like a knife plunged deep in the muscle. A clerk stood behind the glass, but there wasn't a single car in sight. Quickly, she shut the door behind her.

"We're closing, there's no gas."

Nettie walked toward him and stopped at the counter. She looked at him and heard herself speak. "I need help," Nettie said, finding her voice. "I need a cab. A phone. Can you help me?"

In the light, the man looked older than she first thought, Middle Eastern perhaps, with a thick beard and dark eyes. He stared at Nettie, taking in her appearance.

"What happened to you?"

Nettie hadn't rehearsed what she should say. She was too cold anyway, and she shook her head. It was warmer inside the store, and her eye finally adjusted to the burst of colors around her, the bright packaging of candies and sweets, the treats and the convenient bottles and cans, and the smell of diesel in the air.

"I just . . . I'm lost. I need a car. Can you call for me? A taxi?"

The man stared at her, long and hard. He was probably wondering how she'd ended up here in the first place without a car. Did she walk? No bags, no purse, just her with that look on her face, like someone who'd seen the devil in the flesh and ran away. She could see herself in the glass, reflected back. He looked hesitant and Nettie was too numb to say more.

Then, behind the glass window of his office, she saw him pick up a phone and dial. She waited, to hear what he was saying. If he was calling the police, she wouldn't stay. She'd keep running. But then she heard him speak, even though he was doing so in a low voice. He was requesting a cab.

THE TAXI DROVE her to Union Station. She had just enough in her pocket to pay him, and maybe a few dollars for a candy bar or a drink if she needed it. The driver had tried to ask her questions, but she said nothing. She needed to think but it was difficult. All she could see when she closed her eyes was Melvin, his blood soaking his shirt. Melvin's kiss that morning. Her love. And then, there was Forte. Dead. Killed in self-defense, she thought. But still, why did it feel this way? You killed a man, Nettie thought. You killed him and spilled his blood. How did everything go wrong so quickly? And what was she going to do now?

She was out of money now, she thought as she went inside the train station. But she was praying her timing was right. Union Station was buzzing with activity, the distant rumble of incoming trains that sounded like the end of the world. People rushed past, looking for cabs or help with their bags. Nettie ran toward the ticket stands, one by one, scanning the faces behind the windows. And then she spotted Afia.

"Hey! Get in line, Miss! Get in line!"

Nettie didn't care about the irked voices yelling after her. She quickly went to the window and knocked. Afia was wearing her uniform, returning change to a traveler, when she suddenly looked up. At first, she had a scowl on her face. Nettie imagined she looked ghastly. Perhaps many people came to her window that way. But then Afia's face morphed immediately from annoyance to surprise, and then concern. She quickly approached her microphone.

"Nettie? What . . . What are you doing here?"

Nettie stared at her. How to explain? She hadn't thought of that, of saying all that needed to be said behind a window. She knew people were watching now, listening. Voices were now making announcements on the microphone, and in the distance, she could see the silhouettes of trains pulling into the station, and out. Slowly, she saw Afia's face change, finally understanding that something was wrong. She quickly got up, whispered something to the clerk sitting next to her selling tickets, and hopped out of the booth. Nettie stepped away from the line.

Afia took Nettie by the arm and quickly guided her away. They ran toward the restroom area, past the benches and lamp posts, past the shoe shiners and the newsstand brimming with newspapers. A strong smell of cleaning solution emanated from the bathroom when they walked in. Nettie could smell a staleness underneath, body odor and urine still lingering. A few women carrying bags rushed out of their stalls, shouting orders at their kids to hurry, and the children followed, drowsy with sleep. Outside, a rumble of engines rose in the air, and a mother shouted the train was coming. Nettie stood there, in front of the mirror, while Afia inspected her. Nettie finally noticed it now, what Afia had reacted to: there was a nasty cut along her face, and she was covered in dirt. On the wall by the sink, someone had scrawled words barely legible about Mayor Daley. Her stomach was churning. Something wasn't right and it had to do with that pain in her chest, a sourness, a complete sense of dread.

"What happened to you? Are you hurt? Answer me, Nettie!"

Nettie just stared back, trying to process all of what had happened and how she could explain it. She must have cut herself rolling down the slope or maybe when she went through the fence? She didn't know anymore. But all she saw in her mind was Melvin's blood. She wanted to say it, but the words were stuck in her throat. Afia's long dreadlocks swayed as she shook her head in dismay.

Their eyes met in the mirror and, suddenly, Afia went quiet. Nettie could feel her shudder. Afia squeezed her hand. "Melvin?"

Nettie wanted to cry but couldn't. The tears were not coming, even though she felt them on the inside. Terrible things had happened, but she didn't want to say anything right now. Afia would have to gather the pieces herself. Nettie glanced at the grimy mirror and saw more than her own reflection. She saw fear. This was what Melvin felt. Paranoia. She looked around, her eyes checking under each bathroom stall. What if people were listening? What if the police showed up? What if they knew she was at the scene today and were looking for her, and followed her here? Or, what if Afia was also one of them?

"Oh Nettie . . . What happened?"

Nettie quickly shook her head. She had to trust Afia right now. She had no choice.

"I don't know if . . . Forte shot him. I shot Forte. I need to get out of town. Can you help me?"

The words spilled out of her mouth. Was she even believable? She wondered if Afia would suspect or accuse her, but all she could do was throw a wild, pleading look in her direction, and Afia nodded. She held Nettie's hand against her chest, and Nettie could hear her heart begin to race. They stood there, both silent, staring at each other's reflections in the mirror, knowing what getting out of town meant. Leaving everything behind and going underground, a scenario Nettie hadn't even imagined. This was not living, she thought. It was hiding, forever, and she wasn't sure this was viable. Yet she couldn't take chances, either. She had to go away.

She waited in the bathroom while Afia left to make a phone call. Nettie sat on a toilet, numb, listening to footsteps and voices outside her stall. Handwritten slogans and shapes were carved or etched on the walls of the stall around her, names of lovers inside hearts, people pleading to be heard. Some of those drawings had been partially rubbed off. Slowly, Nettie felt those words lift off the surface of the walls and begin to buzz in her ear. She swore she could hear them whisper, or hiss, or maybe it was just the women outside by the mirror.

Nettie pressed her head against the stall wall, and behind her eyelids, all she saw was Melvin's face. Melvin, whom she never wanted to lose. Slowly, she felt half of her heart turn to rock. She was angry. At Melvin himself, for his stubbornness, but angry mostly at a world that did not care about the lives of others in this struggle, about the body of a man on a fishing wharf, about the life of a man murdered in his sleep. The world kept spinning, and she was angry for it.

Most of all, she thought as she waited, she remembered that those men who called the shots and decided on everyone else's lives, the pigs, the establishment, the powers that be, that decided on everyone's health and survival, were all to blame. Why did they get to live and decide who got to die?

Nettie felt something swell in her throat. She covered her mouth with her gloved hands. She wasn't even getting a chance to say goodbye to Melvin—didn't even know if he had survived—and it hurt, to lose everything in so little time, and to have no clear vision of tomorrow. Something hurt deep in her belly, a pain that felt familiar. No . . . She pressed her hands harder against her mouth and screamed a voiceless, soundless scream into the leather. She bit down on her fingers, hard, and felt her body break down, crumble into separate pieces and parts, as she finally gave in and wept.

24

THE MAILBOX OUTSIDE by the main road and the address on the postcard were the same. This had to be in the right place. And yet, Nettie felt paralyzed.

Nettie had ridden in terror from Chicago all the way to Knoxville, Tennessee, then switched to a Greyhound, and since the bus had crossed into the South, she'd felt slightly less terrified. Three days she'd been on the road, and riding into Florida had filled her with anxiety. She still didn't know if Melvin was dead or alive, but she knew she couldn't call yet to find out, as they might be tapping any Party member's phone in Chicago. She didn't even want to reach out to her aunt. She had to get away, far away. Perhaps this was where Tante Mado was right. Perhaps it was time. She let Afia put her on the train to Knoxville, and after a couple of bus transfers, she had made it down to St. Petersburg. The bus had felt safe once she acclimated to the faces riding in it, once she trusted that each and every passenger was focused on reaching their own destination. She'd looked over her shoulder at every stop, but then after a while she relaxed into her seat. No one was looking for her unless they knew she was there at the scene. No one but Melvin.

There was a commune there in St. Petersburg where she could stay, full of sistas who could help her figure a way out of the country if she needed. They could take her as far as Cuba if she wanted. But what Nettie wanted, at least for now before she put miles and oceans between her and her past, was to make it to Clearwater. She took a bus from St. Petersburg, gazed outside her window at the wide-open fields of sunflowers and foliage. For miles, there was nothing but that, and the occasional house, until the bus finally stopped to let her out. She had to walk the rest of the way, down a narrow stretch of road surrounded with wilderness in the direction where they'd told her to go. Her heart pounded with each step. It was her, alone, and no one else for a long while under the cloudless, spotless blue sky, until she reached farmland and groves where workers roamed, knee-deep in tomatoes and peppers, and watermelon. There was a sweet fragrance floating in the air as she approached her destination. All around her, Nettie saw nothing but green citrus trees, leaves green as jewels in the sun. Finally, she was there, staring at this small house sitting on what seemed to be acres of farmland.

Based on the address, yes, this was it. Her tired feet had combed long stretches of road and landed her here, and what if she'd come all this way for nothing? She didn't have a phone number for Clia, just an address. She couldn't even call ahead. It was three in the afternoon, the sun blazing down on the house right after fresh rainfall, a scent of rain still clinging to the air. There was a truck parked under the carport. On the front porch, Nettie distinguished potted plants and herbs, and a mat where someone had left a pair of boots. Nettie felt the gravel crunch under her feet. Yes, Clia lived here, she said to herself. She needed to believe it. There was no time to waste. She had to return to the commune by sundown. It was the rule.

The wooden planks creaked under her feet as she stepped onto the front porch and knocked. In the window, something moved. A curtain. She thought someone had peeked out. She saw an orange cat sitting on the windowsill, staring straight at her. Nettie knocked again. Nothing. She waited and knocked again, louder this time. No one came.

Nettie fought the sadness that now overwhelmed her. Should she wait? Maybe she should go back. She stepped down from the porch, turning over the disappointment in her heart when suddenly she heard a voice behind her.

"Yes? Can I help you?"

A woman had come from the back and now stood in the carport. She was in overalls and drops of sweat slid down her forehead and neck. She was stunning, with long, thin dreadlocks falling down her back and held by a scarf. The woman raised a hand over her eyes to shield her face from the afternoon sun.

Nettie saw her cheekbones and the slant in her dark eyes as she tried to study her. This was not Clia.

"Hi," Nettie stammered. "My name is Nettie. I'm looking for Clia Brown?"

The woman stared at her blankly, no smile. In fact, she looked mildly suspicious. Her eyes shifted, surveilling their surroundings.

"I'm a friend," Nettie said. "From Chicago."

The woman continued to stare, unimpressed. She waited for Nettie to elaborate, and Nettie began to explain, everything coming out in a stammer. They were old friends. From Oakland, actually. Clia had written her, that was how she knew where she was, and she was hoping to catch her friend one more time before leaving. The woman did not seem moved. So this trip had been pointless after all.

Another voice interrupted them, right behind her. "Antoinette?"

The sun blinded her for a moment, but when she could focus her gaze, Nettie recognized the familiar face coming toward her from the other side of the house. A woman, also in overalls, dripping wet with sweat. That beautiful, regal face, and that hair, that wild, untamed, sunburnt hair that trapped daylight in its curls.

"Clia..."

They looked at each other for a moment, speechless, and Nettie tried to explain how she'd made it here, or maybe she tried to say hello and I missed you, or maybe tried to say that she was running, too, running away, but it was all too much because the words were caught in her throat. The cat stretched at the window, arched her back, and meowed silently before sitting down again. Clia stepped closer, the gravel now resounding under her feet, and before Nettie could find her words, Clia was reading everything in her, her own eyes filled with tears. When her friend embraced her, she closed her eyes and inhaled. That sweet fragrance of Clia's oiled hair, the sweat, the long-lost scent, overwhelmed Nettie, and she broke inside.

THERE WAS A surreal sense of wonder in walking down the rows of citrus trees in this orchard that Nettie couldn't deny. Yet this was real. The grass and dirt were real as she took each step, and Clia was here next to her. They walked arm in arm in complete silence, just listening to the birds. When they left the house, for the first few minutes, they could feel Harriett's hard glare on their back as Clia strolled away with her. Clia had to reassure her without turning. "Don't mind Harri, she's . . . overprotective."

Harriett hadn't said much when they all entered the house. She'd put on the coffee and offered them something to eat, but Nettie couldn't put anything in her stomach right now. Her nerves were shot, and the smell of hot maple syrup and butter made her feel ill. Still, she was too grateful for Clia's touch to feel guilty or polite. She knew she was intruding. She hadn't sent word she was coming, and now she was infringing on their space. And it was hard to explain to Harriett, she supposed, that they went way back, they were friends, more than friends, even. Nettie wondered how much Harriett knew. She wanted to ask Clia if they had talked about Oakland at all, about the two of them, but what was there to talk about? They hadn't been lovers but once. None of that was important right now.

"She has the right," Nettie said. "Does . . . she know about us?"

"Us?" Clia looked at Nettie, shook her head. "No . . ."

She took a deep breath and felt the air restore the chaos in the pit of her stomach. She nearly wanted to cry. Nettie considered the fruits on the trees as if they were gems, just like in her dream. The trees were mostly giving, bright oranges dangling wherever the eye could see, and where there were blossoms, there were bees, buzzing happily from limb to limb. Some of the branches were covered in netting to protect the fruits from the cold snap. Winter wasn't as harsh as Chicago down here, Clia said, but sometimes it was too much for the oranges. Any sudden drop in temperature could kill the crops.

"She knows I left my old life behind, she didn't expect anyone to come here looking for me is all. It's quiet here."

"Picking oranges?" Nettie said. "That's definitely not nursing school."

"No," Clia said. "It's not. But nursing school can wait. I needed to be here. Do something different. Be away from my old . . . demons, if you will. I needed to know I could be free, without Clayton's help, you dig?"

"Of course."

They turned where the row bifurcated. The house was no longer in sight. Nettie looked over her shoulder, hoping Harriett was now completely out of sight, hoping they could be fully free from anyone's gaze. Clia stopped, finally, and held Nettie's hand under the sun. Her hand felt rough, but Nettie let her squeeze hers and looked in her eyes.

"What happened, Nettie? Why are you here? You didn't tell anyone about me, did you? Clayton?"

"NO!" Nettie shook her head. "No, of course not!"

"What about Melvin? Is he here, too?"

Nettie swallowed. She wanted to say so much to Clia, and there was so little time left since she was leaving in just a couple of days. She couldn't bring herself to tell what had happened. Where to begin?

"No," she said.

Clia frowned. "Oh . . . Are you running?"

"I'm going back home," Nettie said.

"Home? And you came here?" It took Clia a moment before understanding what this meant. She looked in Nettie's eyes. "Oh. Home. I see . . . Did something happen?"

Nettie nodded. A lot happened. Clia's facial expression began to change, making room for confusion. Nettie told her about Chicago. About the baby. And then, the blood, so much of it from so many people, and then that night on the canal, how she'd had to run in the cold and not turn around since.

"Shit," Clia muttered as she listened. "I knew it. I always knew it. And you lost your baby? Nettie . . . How are you even still standing?"

Nettie didn't know how to answer that. She was just now realizing it herself, having laid out the past two years of her life. She could see it now, seasons of loss. How was she still standing? When the silence became deafening, Clia began walking again. Birds glided overhead, a flock of white winged ibises heading south. Nettie followed.

"Do you think Melvin . . . Is he dead?"

Nettie couldn't answer for a while. She thought of Melvin, gone. Yet, she let her hand wander to her stomach, and her eyes welled with tears. "No."

Clia looked at her, and her eyes followed her hand, lingered there on her womb. Then, her face brightened as if a light had turned on. "Nettie? Oh . . ."

Nettie smiled, and continued walking. She didn't need to elaborate. She just knew. Even if there was no doctor to test her, no way of confirming, she knew. She'd recognized the sickness in her stomach in the mornings, the pain so familiar to her that night. She'd been there before. No, Melvin was very much alive somewhere in her. And that knowledge was both comforting and terrifying.

She walked side by side with Clia, listening to their footsteps. Melvin was a good brother, Clia said. He was so good. And Nettie hated hearing it. Each time she said it, it was like plunging a knife deeper into a wound Nettie hadn't yet cauterized.

"You could have died." Clia bumped against her gently. "You really did all this? You fought back against that man? Just you and a gun? I mean, damn. And now you're running home with a baby? Into the unknown? Alone? Shit, Nettie..."

Nettie felt her face grow hot. She kept walking, eyes glued to the ground where lizards crossed, losing themselves in the green grasses. Maybe that was bad. Nettie suddenly stole a glance toward her friend, suddenly frightened that she'd told her too much.

"I don't know what or who they're looking for," Nettie managed. "I just don't want to stick around and find out. Is that crazy?"

"Of course not, I'd be running, too. They'll never let us win," Clia said, shaking her head. "This war won't stop until they have us all in the ground. We always knew there were agents among us. But turning our own against us? Surveillance? This is fucking low."

Nettie glanced at Clia, her profile ever regal in the sunlight. She noticed Clia still said *we* when she spoke. *Us*, as if she had never left the organization. "One day, we'll be old and we'll tell the next generation about all this. We'll tell them what we did. We'll have to, because the pig is going to lie about everything. Make us into the enemy. You'll tell your baby, won't you?"

Nettie looked ahead, her eyes stinging.

"Yes. I'll tell him, or her, or whatever it is." She chuckled. In Haitian Creole, she would have no need to rely on a male or female pronoun. There would only be *li*. "This child will be born in it. There'll be no confusion about who their father is ... was." She tripped over those words before adding, "They'll know who these men and women are, who we are. Revolutionaries. That's forever."

There was a tinge of admiration in Clia's eyes. Nettie saw it but didn't think twice about it. She believed this, wholeheartedly now that she was being asked. Now that she'd gone through the fire and survived it.

"And I don't want to believe for one second," Nettie said, her voice slightly trembling, "that they won't have to fight it themselves. The struggle, that's also forever. They will never give us what we ask for, unless we take it. My ancestors knew this, that's how my people won freedom. We take it. And as long as they won't give us what we want, we'll have to fight for it. I'll teach my children that."

She would teach this child everything. How to pick up a gun in self-defense, or in defense of others, how to love the people wholeheartedly, how to be a leader, how to bring the community together to make things happen, and how to fight for the right to live out loud and outright, for the right to *be*.

"Damn!" Clia nodded. "Right on."

Nettie wanted to laugh but what came out was a sigh. So much had happened in between Clia's leaving and now. Change was more than a given. She was a new person, and yet constantly in flux.

Clia looked at Nettie for a moment.

"So, why did you come here?"

Clia gestured back in direction of the house. "You could have stayed back there, in that commune, and gone home. Why come here?"

"I just needed to see you. I just wanted to."

"Why?" Clia stopped again, her eyes in hers. "What for?"

"What do you mean?" Nettie shook her head, dismayed. "You've always been there for me, and I just felt like I should have been there for you, shown up . . . Done better by you."

"It wasn't your responsibility to fight for me," Clia said and sighed. "I don't understand why you think you can stand up to Clayton or any motherfucker out there better than I can."

"I missed you," Nettie said.

Nettie felt tired. She didn't come here to fight. Now that she was staring at Clia, all she wanted was comfort.

"I'm trying to forget you, too, you know?" Clia said. She looked back over her shoulder, ensuring they were truly alone. When she turned to look at Nettie, her eyes were wet. "I had just decided to stop writing you letters and here you are now, at my door. You can't do that."

"Is that true?" Nettie felt her heart crack. "You don't want to see me?"

"I wanted you to come down with me," Clia said. "You remember? I said, maybe you should come down here and pick oranges with me and you thought I was crazy. I told you what was up. You should have listened to me, and you should have come with me."

"Leave a job in a doctor's office to come pick oranges with you is not crazy?" Nettie laughed nervously. "Besides, how would that have made a difference?" Nettie nodded toward the house. "You have Harriett."

"I would have made anything work for you," Clia said, seriously. "We could have been somewhere else, for all I care, but we would have been together, you and me. But you were already infatuated with Melvin. You should have chosen me."

"I chose the Party," Nettie said.

"You chose *him*. Stop lying to yourself."

"I love him!" Nettie cleared her throat. "I love Melvin. I truly do, and I can't apologize for that, even if it makes me foolish. . . . But it doesn't make me stupid. And it doesn't mean I don't love you."

Her cheeks felt warm. Clia looked at her with something that resembled pity at first, and she didn't like it.

Nettie wanted to turn around and run again, but she didn't. She turned her back to Clia and wiped her tears with her sleeves. Her dress blew into the cold breeze, and she tightened her jacket around her. There was a soft sound of gravel as Clia approached. Then, Nettie's heart soared when her friend wrapped her arms around her, tightly. They stood there, baking in the sun against the wind, eyes shut, listening to the commentary of parrots in the distance. Then, Clia's voice whispered in her hair close to her ear, her breath warming her a bit.

"It's alright," she said.

They stayed in this embrace until the sun began to burn more, singing the skin on the back of Nettie's neck. She clasped her hands around Clia's arms and held her there, grateful for the contact, for Clia's body nestling against hers.

"Tell me you can smell that."

Nettie paused, tilted her head back a little to inhale the crisp air, hoping to catch what it was that Clia was referring to. And she did. A sweet, saccharine fragrance in the breeze. She opened her eyes, and the sunshine washed over her like a rainbow. She tightened her grip on Clia's arms, dug her fingernails in her flesh, and smiled.

"Yes," she whispered, eyes wet with tears. "I can."

They held each other in silence, the afternoon light dimming in the sky. The orange-blossom essence clung to the air. Nettie absorbed it into her skin, reveling in the rush it gave her, a thrill over a new kind of freedom.

ACKNOWLEDGMENTS

THIS BOOK WAS a work of labor that could not have been produced without the valuable input of such an amazing community. I cannot thank the following people enough:

To my agent, Charlotte Gusay, thanks for believing in the work I do and always being so patient with me and with it

To my editor, Kathy Pories, such a wonderful eye! Thank you for letting this work breathe and helping me get it into the shape it deserved, and allowing it to be.

To the people who first put me on the right path and directed me to the true story of the Party, including valuable readings and key figures: Baba Kwame Kalimara and his wife, Iya Eniola, who both continuously mentor me and guide me with education.

A sincere, heartfelt, and eternal gratitude to the former members and volunteers of the Black Panther Party for Self Defense, and especially these two: Mr. Billy Che Brooks, Deputy Minister of Education for the Illinois Chapter of the BPP, who has been carrying me through this project from the beginning, providing me with education, insight, readings, and interviews, and helping me understand the larger context and force that is the Black Panther Party; and Les Wood, former member of the Boston Chapter of the Black Panther Party, for the various phone interviews and anecdotes provided, and the point of view of a former foot soldier.

And to journalist Stan West, for his insight and his amazing articles about the Party, notably in his *Essence* magazine piece on the Party and its fiftieth anniversary

Thank you to Dr. Emma Leila Streissane Jerome Clay for her valuable insight in helping me understand the research behind sickle cell anemia.

To my parents-in-law, Debbi Claxton and Gordon Merritt Sr., for their invaluable insight on Black history, Black power, the Vietnam War, the Great Migration, and their firsthand perspective on America before, during, and after the Black Panthers.

To my friends and readers Corey Ginsberg, Kathy Curtin, and Marina Pruna; to my readers Marva Hinton Gibson, Michelle Swinea, and Dr. Donna Aza Weir-Soley; and to dear loves Michele Jessica Logan, Marly Louis Jeune, and Lourdes Stephane Alix.

THE RESEARCH FOR this book was extensive, and in addition to interviews and lectures, I was also fortunate to get my hands on some reading materials. I salute Dr. Keisha N. Blain's incredible Introduction to the Black Panther Party syllabus, which pointed me to various sources on Black Power and the Black Panther Party itself. I'd also like to acknowledge the following readings: *Black Against Empire: The History and Politics of the Black Panther Party*, by Joshua Bloom and Waldo E. Martin; *The COINTELPRO Papers: Documents from the FBI's Secret Wars Against Dissent in the United States*, by Ward Churchill and Jim Vander Wall; *The Black Panther Party: Service to the People Programs*, by the Huey P. Newton Foundation, edited by David Hilliard with a foreword by Cornel West; *From the Bullet to the Ballot: The Illinois Chapter of the Black Panther Party and Racial Coalition Politics in Chicago*, by Jakobi Williams; *The Black Panther Party [Reconsidered]*, edited by Charles E. Jones; *Revolutionary Suicide*, by Huey P. Newton with an introduction by Fredrika Newton; *A Taste of Power: A Black Woman's Story*, by Elaine Brown; *The Black Panthers Speak*, edited by Philip S. Foner; and *Waiting 'Til the Midnight Hour*, by Peniel E. Joseph. Also instrumental were Ashley D. Farmer's *Remaking Black Power: How Black Women Transformed an Era (Justice, Power and Politics)* and Donna Murch's *Living for the City: Migration, Education, and the Rise of the Black Panther Party in Oakland, California*.

I've always been fascinated by the minds of radicals, but this particular history was of interest to me for years, ever since the death of Trayvon Martin. I had heard of the Black Panther Party, of course, but the constant killings of Black people at the hands of the police had catapulted me into a very deep introspection about history, about power, and about how Black people around the world engaged in struggle to be seen and respected on equal footing.

It was the Stanley Nelson Jr. documentary *The Black Panthers: Vanguard of the Revolution* that pushed me down the rabbit hole of research. But moreover, it woke me up to a vivid memory of having seen these figures of the Black Power movement and revolution before. Where? I sat on the edge of my seat when the answer came: on my father's bookshelves. I remembered his books that I had grown up around. He was an avid reader of anything that spoke of the Black experience, from the African continent, through Europe, and the Americas, and it was there that I first saw, as a little girl, the covers of Angela Davis and Eldridge Cleaver's memoirs, and those of Malcom X, Muhammad Ali, and Frantz Fanon. I realized then that I had known these people before, and when I heard their speeches and read their words, it was an awakening to what I felt I always knew, almost as if I knew what they were about to say before they said it. It takes a real revolutionary to go the distance the way they did.

The recorded date for the first Free Breakfast Program in Oakland was January 1969. But this program did not occur overnight. It took work and planning by incredible minds, from the imagination of Huey P. Newton and Bobby Seale to the management skill of the women who organized and ran this program. It took planning, consulting, finding the right locations, ensuring that the sites and appliances were up to code with government standards. The novel starts in 1968, and later that year, my character finds herself in the early stages of this program through these communal activities. Similarly, given the fact that the Panthers clinics started in 1969, Nettie is already offering some healthcare services at home and through a doctor's office before they start to offer these services from their local BPP office. Sickle-cell-focused healthcare from the Panthers is officially recorded to have begun around 1970–71, but I imagined a doctor who was already volunteering his time and efforts with the Party and already looking at this disease and seeking answers with the help of assistants.

The character of Dr. Johnson is inspired by the amazing icons of the Party who provided healthcare to the people, but he and Dr. Hernandez are entirely fictitious. Also fictional are the satellite offices in California and in Chicago, as well as the clinics and churches, and faith workers and churches that made these programs possible in the novel.

I'd like to express the gratitude I feel for the people who lived through that incredible time period, who were empowered to help their brothers and sisters, and who today make me feel empowered in the knowledge that revolution is for all of us, and that we are capable of anything through solidarity.

And I'll wrap up by thanking my husband, for standing by during this whole process with encouragement and for suffering through my roller coaster of emotions while I worked on this book and used him as a sounding board. Props!